leslie's curl & dye

dl white

books by dl white.com

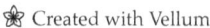 Created with Vellum

dedication

one

. . .

LESLIE

My favorite time of day was three o'clock. Especially in the summer. Especially on a hot summer Friday.

The salon's front door was propped open in a futile effort to let hot air and the scent of singed hair escape. Heavy bass from the boom box on the counter, accented by the cackle of laughter drifted out into the heated atmosphere, where the air was so still, the power lines sang. I glanced down the row of salon chairs, each occupant receiving the best hair care that money could buy. At least on this side of Potter Lake.

"I'm just sayin'," Earline, the town gossip, offered in not-so-hushed tones. "I heard that she wasn't living in the marital home anymore."

"Well, where's she living then?" asked Dorothy Rae, seated in the chair next to her. In one arm, she cradled a plastic case full of grey rods, from which she fed her stylist when she received a tap on the shoulder.

"Wait... she's living with him?" Earline pursed her lips and hummed, glancing away. Not answering, but answering.

"Ooh, she didn't wait long, did she? Went right from one

house to the other. No stop in between to even get her bearings."

"Well, why should she? She got a man willing to take her from her husband's house," said Earline. "And a husband willing to let her get taken."

Dorothy's thin lips twisted into a conspiratorial smirk. "That's how young women do these days," said Angela Evans, mid-press and curl. Her legs were crossed, a pair of pink sneakers peeking out from under the flowing smock with the peeling Curl&Dye logo imprinted across the front. "They try marriage on for size and if it doesn't work right away, they leave."

"Carl and Macey have been married for over ten years, though," I pointed out. "And we all know Carl is a flirt. If he's faithful, I'm a pink unicorn."

The entire shop laughed at my half-serious comment on the situation. If the barber shop was where men gathered to bond with other men, chat about man things and dap each other up, then the beauty shop was the same for women. It was where we found solace and camaraderie, and a bit of gossip on a hot day in a full salon.

The conversation moved from the affair between Macey Raymond, wife of Potter Lake's most successful attorney and Thomas Cayhill, owner of Cayhill Building Supply, to the annual all-church fish fry to be held the following day. For a town that only boasted 6,900 residents, Potter Lake had a church on every corner. A person could visit a different church every Sunday and not run out of churches for a few months. The fish fry wasn't just a fish fry. All manner of food —chicken, fish, pork chops, all the sides and famous desserts would be for sale. The annual event was a fund raiser for the town's recreation center and an unofficial competition between churches. Mount Pleasant Baptist had "won" every year for the last three years, bringing in more funds than any other church, but there'd been grumbling that it wasn't fair because they had three times the congregation of every other church in town.

"Cheryl Ann's peach cobbler ain't better than mine, but folks show up to buy her out every year. I think Pastor Bell is bribing folks to come out and buy up all the food from Mount Pleasant tables." Earline was getting all worked up again. Her stylist, Tamera, chuckled while pulling rollers from her freshly washed and dried hair.

"You think so?" My client asked, her gentle voice riding just above the sound of the blow dryer. "They never have any food left at the end of the day."

"Pearl," I chided, leveling a strong side eye via the mirror at the woman in my chair. "Do not encourage her. She doesn't have any proof for anything she's said today. Make that anything she's said in the last twenty years."

"Oh hush. You just mad ain't nobody hangin' on to what you say." I chuckled while running my fingers through Pearl's mane, coating it with moisturizer.

"I am not in competition with you, old lady. People buy up your cobbler too, and if I remember, Solid Rock sold clean out of food last year. Now, stay still so Tamera can finish your hair. I heard you have a date tonight. Who's taking you out?"

I heard something about big mouth young people, and then the room darkened. I turned to find a tall figure blocking the sunlight.

"Zeke standing in the doorway like he's expecting an invitation," said Earline, twisting around to stick her nose in some more business. Tamera tapped her shoulder and she righted herself, giving a slight smile in the mirror. Earline never missed her bi-weekly appointment. Though her hair may have turned a brilliant white, it was still thick and lustrous and she was vain about its upkeep. Truth be told, Earline was vain about everything.

"Zeke, come in, if you're coming," I said, waving him inside before returning my hands to Pearl's hair. "We're trying to get some air circulating through here and you're blocking the flow."

I waved him inside and, since he was so tall, he had to duck to enter the salon. Ezekiel Simmons was our resident "salesman". Anything you needed, from electronics to music and movies, Zeke probably had it in his trunk. I'd scolded him about selling bootleg media and boosted merchandise in my shop, so I gave him the "single eyebrow lift" to let him know I hadn't forgotten about the warning.

Zeke gave me a slight head nod while a forest green back-pack slipped from his shoulders. From inside he pulled various Ziplock bags, some stuffed with cords and cables, some holding devices still in packaging.

"Afternoon, ladies. Any of y'all in need of—" Zeke made a point of glancing at me before he finished his sentence, "—legit electronics, accessories, movies, new tunes? I got some of those sticks you put in your TV for extra channels." He moved through the shop, handing out bags and giving the usual spiel. "I got Amazon fire sticks, charge cords for your cell phones and your tablets. I got cell phones and tablets too! Talk to ya grandbabies from wherever you are."

"There you go talking about grandbabies, Zeke," Angela chided, reaching for one of the bags. "Not all of us are old and tired."

"Who you callin' old and tired?" Earline primped in the mirror and smiled at her reflection. She'd even had her eyebrows shaped. "I'm going dancing at the senior center. What are you doing tonight? Warming up the left side of your couch?"

"Zeke, let me see one of those chargers," said Pearl. "Is this one where I can charge my phone in the car?"

"Yes, ma'am," he answered, stepping right to her and squatting so he was eye level with her.

The clatter of voices and commotion in the shop was one of my favorite sounds. I inherited Curl&Dye from my mother, who'd inherited it from her mother. The salon once consisted of a kitchen chair set on a hastily built sunporch on the side of a little country house. When it was cold or it rained, Grandy couldn't do hair because the porch didn't have walls. Eventually, Pop enclosed the space and Grandy operated out of the house until the lines got too long.

Mama took over and moved the shop into town. Since she was the only beauty salon outside Healy and ladies had to get their hair done for Sunday church service, she always had a full shop. Women would wait for hours to get their hair done by Lee Baker.

I never intended to be third in a line of Baker women at the helm of the Curl & Dye. Running a salon was never going to be my livelihood, but three years ago, I had to leave my job at a Chicago investment firm... in a hurry. When you're dating one of the managing partners and he's about to be investigated for fraud, a small town is a great place to hide from the men in black suits and wingtips.

Potter Lake wasn't the kind of place where my business degree would matter, so I went to Healy School of Beauty, twenty miles west of Potter Lake. I learned the mechanics of hair care and was eager to bring new techniques and brands to a shop that was still using Dark & Lovely, Blue Magic Hair Grease and Pink Oil—products that had long since become taboo in the Chicago shop where I'd been a regular.

After Grandy's stroke, Mama wanted to dedicate more time to taking care of her. Not only that, but the shop just wasn't as busy as it used to be. The Curl&Dye was a Potter Lake institution, almost as old as the little town itself, but once the textile mill closed and townspeople lost their jobs, clientele started to drop off. If I didn't take over the shop, she would have closed its doors.

I took the bait. I plowed what I could into renovations, breathing life into dark, plain rooms. Bright paint went on the wall, Mama's old salon chairs got a good clean and polish, and I started recruiting stylists from Healy School of Beauty. The shop pulsed with new life for a while, but it's been slowly declining again. Noise, while a sign of good business, doesn't pay the light bill or the rent.

A shrill ring added to the sounds in the air. Since she was the closest, Tamera reached over the partition separating the front desk from the rest of the salon.

"Curl & Dye, Tamera speakin'... hey there, Ms. Paulette." She winced, reaching for the appointment book. "I can fit you in around five. Five thirty works fine. You want a full set?" She scratched details across the block marked 5PM, then paused. "A pedicure, too? We're goin' all out tonight. I got you."

Tamera dropped the phone back into its cradle and shot me a withering look. "She's bringing her ugly feet in here around five thirty."

I tried to hold in my snicker, but it didn't work. The rule was that if you caught it, you took it, unless someone wanted to take it for you. Hardly anyone wanted to take Ms. Paulette.

"Got to stop being so eager to answer the phone."

"Got to stop putting me at this station right next to the phone. If I don't answer, I get the ugly eye like I'm the receptionist." She finished fluffing Earline's hair and handed her a small mirror. "Ms. Earline, make a young stylist happy and tell me how you like your hair and these eyebrows."

"Well, I think I look right nice," she declared after a few moments of close inspection. "My date is going to like looking at me."

The entire shop erupted in laughter, to which Earline paid no attention. Tamera whipped the smock away with a flourish and Earline rose from the chair, little black purse in hand.

"You never told us who you're going dancing with, Earline." I removed the smock from Pearl's shoulders and offered her a hand to help her stand.

"And I'm not going to, because it's none of your business."

"She's going out with that handsome Colonel Davis, the one that just moved here from Healy. He's in one of those new townhomes they built over on the other side of the lake."

Earline frowned. "Pearl, I swear, your mouth is big as I don't know what. If only your brain was as big."

"It's not like it's a secret. Y'all been having lunch every week for a month!"

I hid my amusement at Earline being bested while she and Pearl paid their bill. "Have a nice day ladies. Earline, I'll expect an update on tonight's date."

"You can expect all you want. Don't mean you'll get it."

"Come on here, old lady," said Pearl, pulling her friend out of the door and into the sunshine.

"She sure don't like being gossiped about, but she'll tell you everything about everyone else," grumbled Tamera. "Sometimes she'll get carried away and talk about you to your face."

I laughed, uncapped a bottle of water and took a healthy swig.

"Now that Earline is gone, we can talk about her boss," said Angela. "Did you hear that one of those big box stores is supposed to break ground later this year?"

"Wait a minute," said Tamera, pausing while cleaning up her station and waiting for Ms. Paulette to come in for her appointment. "Every time I turn around, something new is going up over there. I thought we were supposed to be voting on which businesses were coming to Potter Lake."

"Well," Angela continued, leaning forward. "You know my husband, Eugene, sits on the city council. Apparently, the Mayor wasn't even going to show them the bids for construction. The contract went to some Healy Company that bid it out for less than it'll cost to build, so you know they're going to be taking shortcuts, using cheap material. Anyway, Eugene said it looks like it's going to be one of those one stop shop kind of places. You know, where you can get gas and groceries and some flip flops and a microwave all in one place."

I grabbed the broom from Tamera since she was just leaning against it. "Mayor Adams is not doing what he said he was going to do. He said he wanted to prop up the economy by helping people open businesses on that land that's just sitting over there. He didn't say anything about selling it all off and putting Pinkney's Grocery and Gitty Up Gas and Ella's Boutique out of business. He didn't say anything about putting money in some pockets over in Healy and not hiring able-bodied folks right here in Potter Lake to do the building. The Curl & Dye is already suffering with that new co-ed salon over there—"

"Guys N' Dolls, you mean?" Angela asked.

I suppressed a shiver at the mere mention of the name of that shop. "Nobody asked Kade Cavanaugh to bring his NBA money back to Potter Lake and throw it around. Let alone to open a salon, knowing good and well Curl & Dye is over here."

Angela chuckled. "Well, I'm sure the Mayor was a little starstruck to know Kade was back in town. And then to know he wanted to invest some money?" She shook her head, eyebrows lifted. "He fell for Mayor Adams' scam hook, line and sinker."

"I don't know how much of a scam it is. He's got a full salon and we don't."

"Eugene went in there and got his hair cut last week on his way home from work. He said it was cheap; I said it looked cheap, like the barber took a weed wacker to his head. I told him not to go back in there, looking like who did it and why."

My head wagged slowly, side to side as I handed the broom back to Tamera. "People like new and cheap, and unfortunately, that shop fits the bill."

We closed at 8 o'clock on Fridays, but unless I had

appointments, I started cleaning up my station around seven. Tamera and I ended up tag teaming Paulette and her hammer toes. Gisela and Evonne, recent Healy Beauty graduates fulfilling their apprenticeship requirements, began their end-of-day routines as well.

"It was a good day, ladies," I called out as I began to pull the day's receipts.

"I wish it was like this every day," said Tamera, gliding a dust mop down the center of the room. She made a pass, then turned and made another one. Flyaway hair that sometimes missed the broom began to gather in a pile, ready to be scooped up and tossed away.

"I know," I mused, adding up the day's take, my calculator making a loud clicking sound as my fingers flew over the keys. "I've been trying to advertise on Facebook and Twitter, but hell if I know what I'm doing on there."

Evonne snorted, turning away from her station where she was untangling curling iron cords. "Healy Beauty said this was the only shop in Potter Lake. If that's so, where are the younger people getting their hair done? I'm so tired of doing press and curls, I could cry."

"Curl & Dye used to be the only shop in town," explained Tamera. "Until Guys N' Dolls opened up. Like Leslie said, people like cheap. I guess they don't care how it looks."

"Guys N' Dolls is a flash in the pan. You walk in there and take a number and sit. And wait. Guys get an ugly, cheap ass haircut, and Lord knows what's happening on the Dolls side of that shop. Ladies around here can't afford to look like just anything. You wait—" I said, shaking my finger at them all. "Somebody from Guys N' Dolls will give someone orange hair, or mess up a cut, or leave a texturizer in too long and their hair will fall out. They'll be back to Curl & Dye, pretending they never left."

"I hope you're right," mused Tamera.

"I don't," muttered Gisela, sucking her teeth and tucking

away her mobile phone. "Once my apprenticeship is up, I'm going over there to get a job. This place blows."

I glared at Gisela, willing myself to keep my response civil. She'd been riding my last nerve since her first day. She had a few weeks until her apprenticeship was over and I was counting down the days.

"Oh really?" Tamera, who often said what I was thinking, sauntered toward Gisela's station. "If this place blows so much, why not pack up your shit and head over there right now?"

"Because... I...have to finish here first."

Tamera shrugged, stepping closer. Gisela took a minuscule step backward, but it was a step nonetheless. Her face had reddened and her eyes widened.

"You seem like you're a girl with a lot of options. You got so much shit to say about where you're getting a job after you leave here. Just go now, since you're going."

"I... can't..." She stepped backward again, bumping into the cart where she stored her materials.

"That's right. You can't. So if I was depending on a favorable review from the owner of this place to get my license, I would shut my trap about how I'm going right to our competition when I'm finished here."

"I'm not obligated to love it here," Gisela shot back.

"And we're not obligated to keep you here," said Tamera, speaking slowly, enunciating each word. "I don't care that you've finished your coursework. You get no signature on your final papers, you get no license. And if it was up to me, you would be walking out of this shop for good tonight."

Gisela shot a desperate glance in my direction. I shrugged, then went back to my bank deposit slip. Tamera wasn't being completely truthful, but like I said, that girl had been getting on my nerves for months.

"So, once again, if you just do your job, you'll finish out here just fine. But if you've got more to say on the subject, we can discuss throwing your shit into the street and you going along your merry way."

"Tam." My tone told her everything I didn't need to verbalize. She backed away from Gisela, her eyes still shooting daggers.

"I'm tired of her, Leslie. Tired as hell."

"Take five. Go get some air. Okay?"

She slammed the salon door open so hard, it bounced against the brick wall behind it and stormed out. I watched her pace the parking lot for a few moments before my gaze returned to Evonne and Gisela. Both were quiet and busy at their stations.

I finished the deposit, then rolled the chair away from the desk, grabbed two bottles of water and stepped outside. Tamera sat on the curb in front of the shop, squinting into the waning sunlight. In the distance, the lake sparkled as the sun sank below its banks, throwing shadows off of the half-constructed buildings on the other side. I shook my head, as I almost always did. A perfectly wonderful view, ruined by greed and commerce.

"You know that was out of line, right?" I plopped down next to her with my bottle of water and handed her one. She took it and screwed the cap off. Her mouth was still set in a terse line.

"She's got a lot of nerve. We're in there talking about how the Curl & Dye is losing business and she opens her mouth about where she's going when she's done with her apprenticeship."

"She's not obligated to stay, Tam. Neither of them are. It's a short term gig and after she and Evonne leave, we'll get two more."

"It's not just that. I don't even want her to stay. She wants to leave, good riddance. But I hate how she rolls up here every day in her new car and new clothes, complaining about every blessed thing, as spoiled as week old milk sitting out on the counter. Some of us have more than clothes to pay for. My photography business isn't anywhere near off the ground. If we close..."

She shook her head, unwilling to finish her sentence.

I wasn't willing to finish it either, out loud or in my head. "I'm doing what I can, but no amount of specials and discounts is bringing our walk-in rate to where it used to be and people are starting to not show up for standing appointments."

"Got to be something we can do," she muttered, her head dropping to rest on her knees.

"Grandy would be devastated if she knew this place was closing."

"I'm a little happy she can't know." Since her stroke, Grandy's health had been declining. Recently, Mama had to put her in a home so she could get better care.

"For that matter, Mama won't be too pleased, either."

"Oh Lord," she groaned. "I can see Auntie Lee's big lips forming the words I told you so from a mile away."

I laughed, even though Tamera was talking about my mama. Our mothers were best friends and Tamera and I grew up as close as sisters. Gina always had a pot of something on the stove and a pitcher of something to fix what ailed you. That's what I loved about Potter Lake—the small town mentality. How we cared for each other. All of that would be lost if we let Mayor Adams turn Potter Lake into the next Healy. We liked Healy right where it was. Twenty miles away.

I stretched and yawned, then pushed myself up from the sidewalk. "I say we call it an early night. How about you?"

"Hear, hear. You wanna get a drink? I'm in a mood and I need something to set it right."

two

. . .

KC

"Hey, KC. What's good, man?"

"Yo, KC! Good to see you."

I strolled through my shop, a co-ed salon in a growing area of this little place called Potter Lake. I liked the view from the center aisle between two rows of red leather chairs with sterling silver pumps. Every seat was taken, every barber standing behind a client, the buzz of clippers joining the strains of hip hop streaming via satellite radio. On three different flat screen TVs, Sports Center was tuned in, but on mute. We only turned the sound on when we watched a game.

"KC! You up for a lil' hoop action tonight?"

I'd almost reached my office at the back of the shop when Kendrick, my head barber, hit me with an offer I couldn't refuse. I was a fiend for basketball and played every chance I got, especially on the league we'd set up last year. I couldn't play pro ball anymore, but that didn't mean I didn't still love the game. And it didn't mean I couldn't wipe the court with a few of my employees from time to time.

"Who's playing?" I stopped at Kendrick's chair to talk and to inspect the cut he was giving. It looked to be the standard $8 deal. No frills, no gimmicks, no extra time. In the chair... out of the chair. I was trying to get it through the thick heads of the other barbers that we made less money when they agreed to do specialty cuts. They took more time and time was money. And since I'd been without that pro ball paycheck for a while, I was eager to be in the money.

Kendrick named off a few players, fellas I'd played with before. Some from the league, some we knew from around town.

"Are we playing street ball or rec center ball?"

"The only kind of ball there is, man. Street. They're holding that fish fry fundraiser at the park across the street from the house, so we figured a lot of guys will be around and we can get a good game going. Unless that knee has you tapping out."

I gave him my get outta here look, the twisted lip and the side eye, before I held out my palm and waited for him to smack, then grip it.

"I have my brace in my gym bag. See y'all at the court around seven?"

"Bet. Come hungry. Monica is making chicken wings."

My eyes narrowed as I sucked in a deep breath. "The honey barbecue ones?"

"The honey barbecue, the Sriracha, the Thai curry lime—"

My mouth watered at the mention of Thai curry lime. Sometimes Kendrick's wife got in a mood and made a batch of different flavored wings. After a sweaty game of basketball at the park courts, I'd cross the street and eat myself sick.

"I need to go wherever you met her. Monica puts a hurtin' on some chicken wings."

Kendrick chuckled, flipping off the clippers and brushing

wayward hairs from his client's neck before whipping the apron away. "College, dear brother. That's where I met that sister."

I stepped away from Kendrick's chair and resumed the trek to my office. "Oh, yeah. That's right." Kendrick had been my college roommate the year I dropped out and went pro. He met Monica the next year. "No thanks. I left the classroom behind years ago, man."

"I'm just saying... sometimes you gain more than knowledge when you sit in a classroom."

I heard Kendrick, but I wasn't really hearing him. It wasn't like I was against college. I stayed on the Dean's List at Healy University but I was there to play ball, so when it came down to a choice of being the star player on a small town University team and vying for a coveted internship at IBM and entering the NBA draft... I chose ball. Much to the disappointment of a few people in my life, but the money helped my family and being in the NBA gave me a life I could have only dreamed of.

I made it to my office and unlocked the door, dumping the handful of mail I'd picked up from the front desk on top of the stack that seemed to be growing by the day. I knew what they all said without even opening them: DELINQUENT. THIRD NOTICE. IMPORTANT. I was ignoring them for the moment. I dropped into the chair behind my desk and pushed the stack of unopened mail further away.

Kendrick had run the register receipts a little while ago, and my lips pursed as I stared at them. We were running customers through Guys N' Dolls as fast as possible and still not hitting the numbers I wanted to hit. I'd sunk a chunk of my savings into the business and they weren't being replenished to my liking.

A soft knock sounded at the office door before it swung open and my twin sister, Teresa, walked in. TC got all of the personality. I got all of the height. I tended to withdraw unless I was on the court. Teresa was vivacious and outgoing, which made her role as Manager fitting for her. I belonged back in the office, crunching numbers.

"'Sup, TC."

"Not too much," she chirped, eyeing the stack of mail and then sliding the gold-flecked brown eyes that were identical to mine in my direction. "I was over at the fundraiser; brought back some plates for the guys." She gestured toward the stack of mail on the desk. "So you're building the Leaning Tower of Late Notices?"

I slouched in the chair. It squeaked its argument as I tipped it back and glared in her direction. "Man, T... don't start."

"Guys N' Dolls is going to finish before it even gets started if you don't open up some of these bills and pay them. Some of them say final notice, KC." She rifled through the stack, which got on my nerves, so I smacked her hand away. She popped me upside my head.

"Ow!" I grimaced, rubbing the tender spot where she'd hit me. "Bully."

"I didn't hurt that big head."

"I'm not in the mood, TC. What do you want?"

"The utilities man was here today. He was about to shut us down, but I talked him into waiting a day. I said I could talk to you tonight and get him a payment. You owe a grip and you've got twenty-four hours to pay it. You're being ridiculous, KC. I know the money is in the bank."

"Yeah, it's in the bank. I want it to stay in the bank."

TC rolled her eyes and folded her arms over the vibrant Guys N' Dolls logo on her chest. "It's real dumb to not pay bills. You're still waiting on money from Mayor Adams?"

"He said it was coming—"

The scowl TC gave me could scare a criminal. "And in the meantime, your shop is going to shit. Don't lose this place because you're trying to depend on some man's word."

I exhaled, puffing my cheeks out and blowing paper across the desk. "I'll pay the bill tonight. Alright?" I stared at her until she shrugged.

"On your word?"

"On my word. And I'll open up the rest of these and see what we're looking at."

"Have you talked to Mayor Adams about the money?"

"Every chance I get."

"And what does he say?"

"Same thing he always says," I answered, scrubbing my face with the palm of one hand. I smoothed down my goatee by habit, then slipped my hand behind my neck and squeezed the base of my skull. I felt a headache coming on. That wouldn't stop me from playing ball but it would make for a miserable game. "I'll try him again. What are you about to get into?"

"Heading over to the park to watch your fine ass friends play ball and eat some of Monica's wings. See you later?" She held out her fist and I bumped it, after which she turned to leave, grabbing the knob to pull the door closed. Before she left, though, she stuck her head back in. "Utilities, KC. I'm serious."

I grabbed a pad of post-it notes, threatening to throw it at her. "I said, on my word. I got this."

———

THE GAME WAS ROUGH, but it was just what I needed to round out a long week. Two teams of four guys playing basketball in the haze of the setting sun on faded blacktop was like therapy to me. I pushed myself from one end of the court to the other, as hard as I could push without putting my knee out. Dripping with sweat and breathing like I'd run a marathon, I gracefully accepted the game ending handshake from Kendrick, captain of the opposing team.

"And now," Kendrick announced, both fists raised in the air. "Wings! My house! Bring your girl, bring a friend, and do me the courtesy of bringing the beer."

I sat down on the bench alongside the court and released the adhesive straps to my knee brace. I stuffed it inside my gym bag and stood, swinging my arms and arching my neck from side to side to stretch out. My shoulders were tight, but it wasn't from the game.

I'd logged into the utilities company website before leaving for the game and made an electronic payment. TC was right. The money was there, right in the bank and plenty of it. But I wasn't supposed to have to pay the bills that were piling up. At least not with my own money, and the fact that I was laying out much more than Mayor Adams had told me I'd have to put up was about to give me an ulcer.

I dropped my gym bag in the truck and slipped my keys into my pocket, then wound through thinning park crowd toward Kendrick's house. The porch was littered with people, from the vintage swing to the kitchen chairs dragged out to the front steps. Others leaned against the railing that lined the porch, cold beers in hand and trash talking already in full force.

"What up, KC?"

"Brought your A-game tonight, man."

I stopped to slap at a few palms before pulling the screen door open and stepping inside the house. Kendrick and Monica's place was comfortable and familiar, an upgrade from the cramped apartment they'd lived in since they graduated from Healy U. It felt lived-in even though they'd only moved in a year ago. I spent a lot of time at their house, sat at their kitchen table plenty of Sundays. And I never missed wing night.

I stepped through the living room and waved at Jeremy, their six year old, and his friends who were more interested in video games than they were in me. There was a time when a room full of kids would swarm, asking for autographs and tickets to ball games. Sometimes I really missed those days.

The smells in the house reminded me that I hadn't eaten since the hard, dry chicken sandwich I'd grabbed from Chicken Hut, one of the new restaurants in the strip mall near the shop.

"KC!" Monica's face brightened like it always did when I stepped into her kitchen. I bent to hug her, wrapping my arms around her expanding waist.

"How much longer do you have to let little girl cook in there?"

She laughed, her hands roving her round belly. "I can tell you've never known anyone who's been pregnant before. We've got some time yet."

I shrugged. "My experience with the ladies pretty much ends at practicing making babies."

She gave me a pat on the arm before returning to tossing chicken wings in her famous chili lime sauce. Once the wings were glossy, she poured them into a foil lined pan and slid the pan under the broiler.

"A few minutes and those will be done. I know they're the ones you're waiting on." She tucked a hand into the crook of my arm and led me toward the bar stools lined up at the island at the edge of the kitchen. "Kendrick says the shop is doing really well. Getting more business every day, especially women."

I nodded, clasping my hands together, trying to keep the expression on my face blank and nonchalant. From Kendrick's point of view, the shop was doing well. From mine... I needed to have another conversation with Mayor Adams.

"Yeah, the shop is doing okay. I need some more female stylists, though. People get restless and start leaving if they have to wait too long. I only have two girls that can work with chemicals."

"You should talk to my neighbor's daughter. She works at a little salon on the other side of the lake."

"There's still places open over there?" A sizzle from the broiler caught Monica's attention. She slid off of the stool and headed toward the oven.

"Every week I run my granny over to that old grocery store. It's like the senior center reunion up in there. What's the name of it? Pinky's? Pinkney's? Whatever. May as well be the Piggly Wiggly."

"Mayor Adams said he was selling off the land and putting new businesses over there, too. He didn't say anything about shops still being open."

A few years ago I'd been languishing in Kendrick's guest bedroom, trying to decide what I was going to do with the rest of my life. I'd been a member of a professional basketball team, a well-known player. It wasn't like I could go out and "just get a job" like my parents kept advising me. What kind of job did they think I could get with a busted knee and no degree?

I let Kendrick and a few others drag me to a seminar about opening up a business in a nearby town even smaller than the college town of Healy, Georgia. Mayor Adams gave a pretty speech about land that was available for development in Potter Lake, promising incentives to those willing to invest. I was lured in by the temptation of not having to pay operating expenses for at least the first year.

After Guys N' Dolls opened, the excuses began to roll in and the promises from his wide, stark white smile were broken. More than a year later, the money I was promised was still "coming".

"If that's true, then that little salon is probably in its last days," said Monica. "You should talk to her, see if she's found a spot to jump to."

"There's a beauty school over in Healy. I could grab some graduates from there."

Monica grimaced over her shoulder as she opened the broiler drawer. "I don't know about a beauty school graduate putting chemicals on my hair. The ink won't even be dry on the license."

"Let me get that," I said, sliding off the chair. I grabbed a couple of oven mitts and bumped her out of the way. She let me pull the pan out of the oven and set it on top of the stove. I basked in the pungent mix of sweet and heat as I pulled the mitts off.

"I know you're gunning to be first, so..." She reached toward a stack of thick paper plates, perfect for wing nights. "Go for it."

An hour later, I tossed the last drumstick bone onto the pile on my plate and sighed into the night air. I was fat and happy, very content and a little drunk. Behind me, the screen door squeaked open.

I turned my head to see Monica sauntering out of the house, followed by two women, with a Cheshire cat grin spread across her lips. I inwardly groaned, knowing at first glance that this would be the last time I'd be happy for a while.

She eased herself down onto the step next to me. The two women that had followed her out of the house chose to stand. Both were short from where I sat, but then again, when you stood 6' 4", everyone was short. One wore her hair in long locs that spilled down her back; the other had a short cut like TC.

"This is my neighbor's daughter and her friend. I happened to look up while I was washing the dishes and I saw them walking over from the park. This is Tamera and Leslie. Ladies, this is KC."

"I uh..." I cleared my throat, nodding at both ladies. "We ... uh—"

"What KC is trying to say is that we're old friends," snapped Leslie, flinging her locs over one shoulder. She always did that hair flip thing when she was good and mad. "And I use the word friend very loosely."

I swallowed hard.

Then swallowed again.

I hadn't expected to see Leslie again. Not here in this town, and not in this lifetime. It had been at least fifteen years since she stormed out of my dorm room after I'd broken the news that I was dropping out of Healy and going for the NBA draft. I'd tried to talk to her before I left school and I sent her a few letters while I was on the road. My calls went unanswered and all my letters were returned, unopened. I took the hint and stopped reaching out and I was pretty sure that I'd never seen her again.

Leslie had changed, but in a lot of ways, she was the same girl I remembered—iconic long hair, except in locs now; creamy brown skin, big doe eyes, full juicy lips. I remembered those lips. With her hand on the generous curve of one hip and one leg kicked out, I had full view of her open toed sandals and fiery red pedicure. She wore a pair of leggings and a fitted tee shirt. Cute and casual, like she wasn't dressed to impress anyone but herself. She was always so casually sexy. I liked that back then. Actually, I liked it a lot now.

"What's up Les?" I gestured at her, showing my sauce covered hands. "I'd give you a hug, but I dug in and I'm a mess." I pointed to the other girl, the short-haired one with the matching frown. "Tam... it's been awhile. Good to see you."

"Cut the shit, KC," Tam spit at me. She propped a hand on one hip and gave me the up-and-down with an evil eye.

"Whatever, Tamera." Tam and I were never good friends. The few times I hung out with her and Leslie, we butted heads all night long. She didn't think Leslie should be spending so much time with me and made her opinion known often. Her attitude toward me wasn't surprising. It was just... old.

"So... what are y'all doing here?"

"Your neighbor was kind enough to tell us about how our shop was closing down and asked if we'd like to meet the owner of Guys N' Dolls and see if we could get jobs there." Leslie's lips pursed into a tight little bow.

"Oh. Okay. Yeah, the Mayor said everything was pretty much dried up on that side of the lake. I didn't know...that uh...." I coughed, trying to give myself a minute to breathe. "So you took over your mom's shop?" I asked Leslie, then directed my attention to Tamera, who was still shooting daggers at me. I kind of wanted her to back up a little bit. "And you work there, I guess? How long do y'all think you'll be open? I mean, I guess I'm asking if y'all will be looking for salon positions soon. I need more female—"

"Leslie's Curl & Dye is not closing any time soon, KC. Your shop is already stealing my clientele. There's no way you're taking my stylists too."

The realization that I was staring at competition I didn't even know I had hit me like a ton of bricks. I offered the ladies a wide, friendly grin. "Look, I'm not really trying to put Curls and... whatever out of business—"

"Leslie's! Curl! And Dye!" Tamera shouted the words out at me, with foot stomps to match. "Memorize the name. Wait a minute, you won't have to, because we are going to be all. up. in. your. business."

The two ladies gave me a dirty look as they left, taking the path around the side of the house instead of walking back through the front door. Monica hid an amused smile behind a faux innocent expression. I handed her my plate and playfully cut my eyes at her.

"You couldn't warn me?"

"How was I supposed to know you knew them? Besides, it was fun to watch you flop around like a fish out of water."

Kendrick joined us on the step and tossed an arm over his wife's shoulder. "Who were those girls?"

"Those women run a beauty salon on the old side of Potter Lake that Guys N' Dolls is apparently putting out of business," Monica offered.

"I'm not putting anybody out of business. I mean, not on purpose."

I shook my head, my brain a complete mess of words, my body vibrating with shock at seeing Leslie again after so long. She meant a lot to me, back in the day. We were close and I knew how hard her mom, Lee, had worked to keep her shop open. I had no idea that opening my shop put hers in jeopardy. But I was already open... what was I supposed to do?

"We get you, man," said Kendrick, laying a heavy hand on my shoulder. "You're just trying to have a shop open. But now that you know about your competition, you have to step up your game."

"What? Why?"

"Because they know about you. And if they think you want their business they'll do anything to keep it. This might mean war, man."

I heaved a long, heavy sigh. I wasn't in the mood for war.

three

. . .

LESLIE

"What was that about?" I hissed at Tamera as we made our way through freshly cut grass. She reached the gate separating her mother's house from the neighbor's house and lifted the lever to swing it open. After I walked through, she followed and dropped the lever in place, locking the gate behind us.

"What was what about?"

"All of that all up in your business noise. You made it sound like we were going to send the mob through there or something."

"Humph," she huffed, leading me to a glass topped wrought iron patio table and pulling out two chairs. "Maybe we should. Would serve him right."

"Like we even know anybody like that. Closest thing Potter Lake has to a mob is Zeke Simmons and his friends. We could send him over there to sell some bad bootleg movies."

Tamera sucked her teeth and folded her arms across her chest. "He pissed me off. *Uh, when y'all think y'all shop will close and y'all can come work for me?*" She mocked, imitating his very slight Texas drawl. "Smiling all wide and friendly like there's not a shop that could use the business he's taking away."

"He said he wasn't trying to take our business. He was just open."

"Leslie..." Tamera rolled her head in my direction and leveled a glare at me. "Last night you were boohooing with me about Guys N' Dolls and now you're defending him?"

"I'm not defending him. I'm just saying—"

"Oh, girl don't even start lying. You've been avoiding KC since we heard he moved back here and now we see why. One look at that big hunk of man, one listen to that... that fake humble southern drawl and you folded. Like you always used to do around him."

"Folded? How did I fold? I told him my shop wasn't going anywhere."

"Which should have been said to him a long time ago. Like when he first opened, but nope. You refused to go over there and set him straight. All I'm saying is, don't let all that dust and those cobwebs—"

"Tamera Louise, do not go there. We can talk about your cobwebs too."

That made her laugh, which made me laugh. Of the two of us, she was always more emotional and I always had to calm her down. It wasn't like she was wrong, though.

The NBA had been good to KC. I was trying hard not to be affected by it but I wasn't blind. He was always muscular, even back in college. Now he seemed taller, if it were possible. Solid and stocky, thick arms and legs, wide shoulders, smooth skin like whipped chocolate, soulful brown eyes with gold flecks... and I never pictured myself as the kind of girl who was drawn to a tattooed man but when I wasn't yelling at him about taking my business, I was admiring the artwork that was his sleeve tats. He'd grown a goatee that framed his full lips nicely and had a nice head of jet black hair that needed a line-up.

Handsome wasn't even the word for it, if I was being honest. A big, chocolate, sexy motherfucker built like a loco-motive fit the bill much better. But no matter how dusty my situation, I wasn't on the market. Especially not for KC.

"I'm not letting cobwebs make my decisions," I said, picking up my end of the argument. "I'm stating facts and trying to keep a level head between us. You can't go around threatening people, Tam."

She mumbled something that sounded a lot like I know, but she never liked to admit that I was right so I didn't want to take my chances in asking her to repeat it.

"Well, what are we going to do? He seems to think Curl & Dye is closing and if I have anything to say about it, he's dead wrong."

I reached across the few inches of space between us and rubbed her forearm. "I know you're worried, but we're not down and out yet. We'll think of something."

"You girls want some lemonade?"

Gina stepped out of the house onto the patio with a pitcher and three glasses, wearing what we called her Weekend Frock. It was an old weathered house dress, dark blue and covered in bold flower print. Tam and I hated that thing but she pulled it out every week. She said it was her relaxing dress and after a long week at Primrose, she needed to relax.

"Is it regular lemonade or *good* lemonade?"

She set the pitcher down on the table, then began to fill a glass to the rim. "All my lemonade is good lemonade. But it's Saturday night, it's cool enough to sit outside and I've got my relaxing dress on. What y'all think?"

"Sounds like the good stuff." Gratefully, I took a glass from her and sipped a bit off the top. Her vodka lemonade would definitely take the edge off. She poured another glass and handed it to Tamera before pouring one for herself and taking the seat next to me.

The evening air was full of the sounds of a southern summer—crickets chirping, cicadas singing, leaves rustling in the rare breeze that blew through the spacious backyard. We sat in silence, admiring the nice atmosphere, sipping our drinks.

Gina and Tam used to live a few houses down from us, but she had taken advantage of a builder's incentive to buy a home on the "new" side of Potter Lake. I hated to admit it but her townhouse was nice. Brand new build, appliances included, front and back yard and two car garage. If I wasn't so vehemently opposed to how Mayor Adams was systematically shutting down old Potter Lake, I would have moved over a long time ago.

"I thought you two got invited next door? I saw that nice young lady come out and say something over the fence, then the next time I looked through the kitchen window, y'all was gone."

"We did," I volunteered before Tamera could get started. "Turns out her husband works for the guy that owns the family salon in the new strip mall. Potter Lake Commons, they're calling it."

"Oh, how fancy," she quipped, her eyes rolling skyward while sipping her lemonade. "Used to be a field of overgrown weeds."

"Anyway, he claims he wasn't aware that we were still open. He tried to give us jobs in his salon."

Gina laughed. "I can only imagine how that went."

"I told him where he could stick his job," said Tamera. She glared at the house next door through the bushes and formed devil horns with her fingers, pointing them at the house like she was putting a hex on it.

I rolled my eyes and sipped my lemonade. "How was Grandy today, G?"

"No change. I still read the front page of the newspaper to her every morning. You know how she likes her news stories."

Grandy was a news junkie. She would read the Potter Lake Times front to back every day and the Lake Chatter, a little rag that was mostly gossip and came out every Saturday. When the internet became a big thing, you could find her at the desk early in the morning reading the newspapers that she didn't have delivered—Atlanta Journal Constitution, New York Post, and the Business Chronicle. When she wasn't reading the news, she was watching it. She watched CNN like it was a soap opera. She had her favorite newscasters and everything.

"Have you been to see her lately?"

"Last weekend," I answered with a nod. "I'll be by there tomorrow. Mama usually goes on Saturdays."

"Good. Good." Gina sighed, staring into her glass. "Get your time in. She knows you're there."

"We will." I paused a beat to let the somber moment pass, and then asked, "So we worked all day and missed most of the good stuff at the fundraiser. Did you make anything for dinner?"

four

. . .

KC

I limped down the center aisle of the shop, smiling and nodding as best I could as I made my way. I'd tried to rest my knee all day, but I'd played that game like I was back on the Herons and all of that effort had taken its toll. Usually I could get away with only wearing the brace when I played, but since I could just barely get out of bed, I was wearing it all day.

"Ay, KC. I didn't mess you up or nothin', did I?" Erik was in the middle of a cut but flipped his clippers to the 'off' position as I passed his chair. "You're favoring kinda heavy on your other leg."

"Man, you wish your weak skills did this to me."

"I'm just trying to check in on you, seeing as how you're my boss, but if we're going there—"

"Watch it, E," piped up Kendrick from behind his chair. "First off, I'm your boss. KC is my boss. And secondly, my boss, Mr. NBA, doesn't like for folks to make notes on his game. Even that weak free throw about halfway through."

"The one that was all air? I know which one you're talking about."

I laughed off the usual ribbing I took when my team won. Kendrick's team was full of sore losers. The swollen and painful knee was well worth the hash mark in the win column.

"I've got a busted knee and my team still beat y'all. How does that happen?" I shook my head and continued my trek to my office.

"Yeah, it was a good game or whatever, but the real show was after the game."

I stopped and turned, giving Erik a mental message to shut up, but he didn't catch it.

"After the game? What happened?" Asked another nosy ass barber.

"Two women showed up and had some words with KC. Did you see that one girl, the fine one with short hair? She put her hand on her hip and she was like... what she say? Something..."

"She said she'd be all up in his business," volunteered somebody at the front of the shop.

"Yeah, that's the one." Erik smiled. Gripping his clippers and a comb, he returned to edging the back of his client's head. "I'd like to be all up in her business."

"Hey, watch your mouth," I said, pointing at Erik. "Don't worry about those women. It's just a thing with another shop. Y'all get back to work. We've got customers to serve."

I heard the gossip continue, just in more hushed tones behind my back as I approached my office. I needed to sit down, give my knee a break. And get away from this talk about Leslie from Curl & Dye.

I'd looked them up when I got home, trying to get a feel for what was going on over there, how close they might be to closing up shop. By the looks of their online presence, they were already dead in the water. There was nothing to the Facebook profile. The cover photo was a snap of the front of the shop, a plain looking store front with peeling lettering on single pane glass windows that spelled out CURL & DYE. From time to time, a coupon deal on a cut or a service was posted, but for the most part, the page looked empty. Unused.

Guys N' Dolls, by contrast, was all over the web and social media. When Kendrick wasn't cutting hair, he and Monica ran a Marketing and New Media firm. He hooked us up with a dynamic website and we were everywhere from Instagram to Facebook to Twitter to Snapchat. Any time a new platform popped up, Kendrick made sure we had a presence there and we kept our accounts populated with current photos and a weekly flyer. People came from all over the place to get a cut at Guys N' Dolls.

"See," I said to myself, groaning with relief as I lowered into my chair and propped my knee up on the chair I'd dragged around the desk. "It's not my fault that shop is going under."

"Who are you in here talking to?" TC popped into the office, the familiar blue zippered pouch in the crook of her arm. "You know talking to yourself is a sign that you're a little..." She twirled her finger around her head and whistled.

"I'm not crazy. Not yet, anyway. What's the day looking like so far?"

"See for yourself." She handed me the envelope and dropped into the other chair. She kicked up her feet and propped them on the desk, something I hated, but she ignored my protests so I stopped making a big deal out of it. "Whew, it's good to get off my feet."

I unzipped the bag and pulled out the wad of bills and the credit card slips. "Feels like a good day so far. You count it?"

"Nah. Didn't want to be up front thumbing through a bunch of cash."

I nodded, moderately pleased. This morning's receipts would replace the money I'd spent paying the utilities. Which reminded me that I needed to make another call to Mayor

Adams. I stuffed the bills and slips back in the pouch and zipped it up.

"You want me to do the bank deposit? You look locked up right now."

I glanced at my knee, snug in its brace. It was throbbing, but starting to feel better now that I was resting it. "I'd appreciate it. Having a bad day today."

"Have you been back to that doctor? Now that you've been off the court for a while, another surgery might—"

"I'm not going back under the knife, T. It's inflammation. Nothing to feeling better but rest and some Advil." I reached for the mega-sized bottle of pain reliever that I kept on the desk and unscrewed the top, shook out a few of the brown pills and swallowed them dry.

TC sighed, pulling her feet off my desk and pushing herself up out of the chair. "You're so stubborn."

"Am not," I retorted, with a grin.

She grimaced and sucked her teeth, then snatched the pouch from my desk, inadvertently bumping my knee with the bag.

"Ouch, you bully!"

"It was an accident."

"You did that shit on purpose! You know my knee hurts and you smacked me right there with the bag."

"I said it was an accident. You'll know when I do something on purpose. Gimme a deposit slip and stop being a big baby."

"Excuse me?"

I looked up to find Leslie standing in the door of my office, a cautious half smile on her lips.

"Oh. Hey. Uh..." I tried to stand, but she stepped in, her hand raised.

"Don't get up. I heard about the knee." She turned to TC and offered a hand to shake. "I recognize you from KC's old pictures. You must be TC. I'm Leslie; I own a salon on the—"

"Other side of the lake, yeah." TC shook her hand and gave her a wide, friendly grin. "You're all anyone is talking about today."

She swiped a hand across her forehead and blushed. "Listen, I wanted to apologize for that ambush. Monica told us to come over. She wanted Tamera to talk to KC about a job since that little shop she worked at was closing. And as the owner of said little shop, I saw red and... we went rogue."

"I understand that," I told her. Because I did. "Now that you know where we are, you see what we're doing here. There's more than enough room for you and your staff to come over. It'd be nice to work together after all this time."

A shadow crossed Leslie's face, taking it from friendly and apologetic to a rock hard sneer. "I told you...the Curl & Dye isn't going anywhere. I'm not coming to work for you. Not when I own a shop."

"Oh. Okay," I answered, with what I knew was a snide snicker but I couldn't help it. "That's why you and your little pit bull was up in my face about me taking your customers. 'Cause Curl & Dye isn't going anywhere. Listen..."

I paused, for just a moment, to let the sounds of the busy shop filter back to the office. "Does your salon sound like that today? You're here, so I'm guessing no."

She huffed, blowing an errant loc of hair out of her face. "Of all the places you could have ended up, why are you back here? Why didn't you go home?"

"This is home. I would think you would be happy to see me back here, starting up a business, establishing some roots—"

"When your roots pull mine out, we have a problem. You honestly never thought to check if my mom's shop was still open?"

"Being honest...." I sighed, wagging my head. "I got caught up in opening this place. I wasn't going to drive across the lake looking for a beauty salon to make sure I wouldn't be someone's competition. Besides, last I heard, you were shacked up with some square in Chicago. I didn't know your mom's shop still existed, let alone that you run it now. But now that I do, all I can say is..." I shrugged my shoulders, leaning back in my chair. "May the best man win. And by the sounds of my shop, today at least? I'm the best man."

Red-faced, Leslie sucked in a loud breath and her lips curled inward. I braced for an onslaught, the kind I knew she was capable of. But she didn't scream or curse or even cry. Leslie turned on a heel and stormed out of my office.

"Well." TC leaned against the desk and folded her arms. "That was... interesting."

"*Pffft*." I blew a short breath and shrugged a shoulder. "That's nothing, T. Really, it's... nothing."

"Didn't sound like nothing. I remember you talking about her, about how she dropped you. You went in on her just now. You don't think you're still a little hurt about that?"

"Ancient history, T. I haven't seen or thought about her in a long time, in a lot of years. I know what she's doing, and it's not going to work."

"And what is it that you think she's doing?"

"Trying to give me the guilt trip to get me to back off of building this business. If people want to come here I can't stop them."

"True. True." TC nodded, one of those slow nods that said she had more to say. "But—"

"But nothing, T. I wasn't trying to shut her down before and I'm not trying to now. That shop has problems that didn't start with me." I forced myself up from the chair and snatched the zippered pouch from TC, then limped out of my office.

five

. . .

LESLIE

I was still fuming, trembling as I pulled into the parking lot outside the salon. I sat in my car, sucking in dry air and trying to relax. It wasn't working.

"*Hunh!*" I shot out into the quiet interior of the car, pounding a fist on the steering wheel. "May the best man win? Like he has a chance at winning."

Big talk, but a glance around told a different story. The lot used to be so full that I couldn't sit down all day. Today, I could count the number of cars in the parking lot on one hand and have fingers left over. Truth be told, the whole block looked like a deserted island.

I checked my watch and popped the latch to open the door. I had an appointment coming in and we needed all the business we could get.

The front door to the shop was propped open, the sounds of Kendrick Lamar wafting through the opening. The air inside was noticeably warmer, stuffier. And even though there were two dryers running and music playing, the place seemed... dead.

Tamera and Evonne had clients. Gisela was reorganizing her supplies. Again. It was something she did to look busy so she didn't have to do anything else.

I reached across the counter and flipped the switch to turn the music off. All hands stilled; all heads turned in my direction.

"I have a headache," I offered in explanation. "I can't take that noise right now. Gisela, could you fold some towels, please? I can see the basket overflowing from here."

I watched her roll her eyes, then push her cart away and stomp to the back room to grab the basket. I caught Tamera's eye, but she wasn't watching Gisela. She was watching me.

"What's your problem? And where've you been? Don't you have Mrs. Isaacs at one o'clock?"

I busied myself with organizing my station and tying on my apron. I filled the pockets with my usual tools—comb, brush, a small mirror and a couple of clips and bobby pins.

"I don't have a problem. And yes, I have a one o'clock. That's why I'm here."

I felt her stare, even though I refused to lift my eyes from the appointment book to meet her gaze.

"You didn't answer my other question, but never mind. I already know you've been at KC's shop."

My head shot up and I instantly regretted doing so. The smug I knew it expression was all over her face. "Did you get what you wanted?"

"What is it you think I wanted?"

"For him to be nice and say something in that lil southern accent he thinks is sexy. Why, sure Leslie. I'd be happy to start sending clients back over to you, for no other reason than you asked me to."

I sucked my teeth and rolled my eyes, flipping the page in

my appointment book loudly. "That is not why I went over there."

"Then what did you go over there for? To look at him? Talk about old times? Maybe talk about how he dumped you and rolled up out of here the second a better life came calling?"

"He didn't dump—"

"Look at who?" Evonne butted in, pulling a round brush through her client's hair.

"Nobody," I answered. I dropped the appointment book and headed for the kitchen to get ready for Mrs. Isaacs. She would want to refresh the silver rinse on her hair but she liked a specific recipe and I needed to mix it up.

"The owner at Guys N' Dolls," Tamera answered, at the same time. "He used to be an NBA baller—Kade Cavanaugh? He and Leslie... let's just say they go way back."

"What?" I heard Evonne screech. "I used to love me some Kade Cavanaugh. He went to Healy. Then he left to go pro and—ohhhh."

"Didn't I say nobody? I distinctly remember saying nobody," I yelled from the back room, which housed the mixing sink, a shelf built into the wall, a small card table and four chairs and the oldest washer and dryer set in the entire county. How it was still running, I didn't even know. Jessup Plumbing had had to make plenty of emergency calls to deal with that washing machine and the old pipes that fed it.

"So, what did he say about trying to shut us down?"

"Okay, guys..." I sighed, coming around the corner and standing in the middle of the room. "I can't believe we're having this conversation in front of clients, first of all. Second of all, he's not trying to shut us down."

"He doesn't have to try, Les. He just is," Tamera finished.

"And third... yes, KC and I go back, way back to his pre-NBA days, before he was a big damn deal. I guess I thought I could remind him that we used to be friends and see if he could understand the situation from my point of view. He claims to have not known we were over here."

"Don't mean it's true, just 'cause he says it. And I mean... he knows we're here now. What's he going to do?"

"Just like you said, what can we expect him to do? He's got that big, shiny shop with red leather chairs and fancy floors and huge flat screens everywhere. He's rolling at least ten deep with barbers. That shop was so full today I could barely walk down the center aisle. And he's in a brand new shopping center where he might have a chance to catch walk in customers. We're..."

I turned in a slow circle, my arm extended to demonstrate the extent to which we were not Guys N' Dolls. "We're photos so old the corners are curling, taped to dingy walls. We're plain white linoleum floor tile. We're old black salon chairs and only half of them even work. We're the same people, day in and day out, week in and week out."

I grunted, my lips pressed together in a tight line. I was all caught up in the emotion of losing my shop, of seeing KC again, of trying not to remember the time we had together, when we were on the cusp of something that could have been amazing. And then the moment it all fell apart. And that was the problem; I was caught up in emotion and not using any of the business sense I'd learned in my courses at Healy.

"The Curl & Dye doesn't have the luxury of being the only game in town anymore. If this shop means anything to any of us," I said, catching glimpses from Gisela, Evonne and Tamera, "We have to do more than sit here moaning and waiting for people to come in."

Ironically, the door swung open and Mrs. Isaacs came in, her hair covered in an indigo blue scarf. Cara Isaacs had only been coming to Curl & Dye for a few months. Her husband, who worked for the postal service in Healy, passed away last year. She'd moved to Potter Lake in hopes of a slower, calmer life. Cara always had a ready smile and a funny story. I was in the mood for both.

"Afternoon, Mrs. Isaacs," I greeted her, grabbing one of her hands and leading her to the shampoo bowl. "It's good to see you. Go ahead and get comfortable. I'll be right back with your rinse."

I emerged from the back room, stirring the rinse mixture in a plastic bowl to the sounds of laughter. Mrs. Isaacs was mid-story.

"You should have seen Garth's face," Mrs. Isaacs was saying, between chuckles. "Raspberry red! He was fair skinned, about Leslie's tone. I bet when you get angry or embarrassed, it shows."

"Every emotion shows on Leslie," quipped Tamera.

"That's not true," I argued, pulling a cape tight around Mrs. Isaacs' neck and reclining the seat so that her hair hung in the shampoo bowl. "And I'm not light skinned."

"The hell you're not," she argued back, continuing our life-long argument about the honey-beige skin I inherited from my mother and Grandy. Tamera was a sun kissed, dark bronze but that did not make her the resident expert on skin tone. Besides, black was black and I was black. At least that's what my mama told me when the girls used to pick on me for being so light.

"Well, anyway," she continued, raising her voice above the sound of running water. I pumped shampoo into my hands from the industrial sized bottle we kept at the sink and began working it through her hair, creating a thick, rich lather. "Garth hadn't realized that he'd misdialed the phone number and called some kind of sex line. That man was almost blind and half-deaf, so by the time he figured it out, they'd already billed for the first two minutes. At $4.99 a minute!"

She was cackling, laughing so hard she had to stop.

"When we got the bill," she continued, after she'd caught her breath, "—and 966-HOTLOVE showed up, he turned so red I thought the top of his head might blow off. I told him he'd best stop acting like he was young with good eyesight and wear his bifocals."

"And did he, Ms. Cara?"

"Every day, child. Sun up to sundown, Mr. Garth Isaacs had his specs on. He was never paying ten dollars to be vain ever again."

The shop erupted in that sound I liked—laughter. I chuckled along with everyone else while I rinsed Mrs. Isaacs' hair and wrapped it in a towel, then led her to my station. I towel dried her hair and pulled out the blow dryer to finish the job. Once it was dry, I began to brush the silver rinse into her hair and let it set.

The topic of conversation bounced from who was sleeping with whom and thought nobody knew; to who brought lunch to her husband at work, only to find out he'd been fired two weeks ago; to what Mr. Torrence was caught doing in the back of his taxicab on Saturday night. A few walk-ins filtered in and between Tamera, Evonne and Gisela, the shop was busy. Every seat was occupied and the sounds of good hair-stylists doing good hair filled the air.

"Excuse me?"

I'd been lounging in my salon chair, enjoying a few minutes off of my feet, when a heavy set older woman entered the shop, a scowl sitting on thick red lips. Behind her, a girl cowered with her shoulders hunched, a Potter Lake Tigers ball cap on her head.

"Y'all do natural hair?"

I shot up from the chair to greet her, but she seemed in no mood for pleasantries, so I got right to the point. "Yes, we do natural hair here. What can I help you with?"

The woman reached for the girl, pulling her around in front of her. She yanked the cap from her head, which garnered a collective gasp from the entire shop. The poor girl looked mortified.

"Mmmhmm," hummed the woman, those red lips pressed together. "She had asked me if she could dye her hair gray, like all the kids are doing. I told her no, that she would look ridiculous. She decided to defy me and do it herself. She didn't like it, because like I had said, she looked ridiculous. She tried to wash it with a whole bottle of my dish detergent, but I keeps a mixture of bleach and detergent in that bottle." She thrust a finger at the child's head. "Look at this mess!"

My jaw had been hanging open since I saw the fragile pile of... something atop that poor child's head. I quickly recovered and led the girl to my salon chair, never taking an eye off of the orange and grey rat's nest. It was so dry it was brittle and standing on end. I was afraid to touch it, but then I figured... how much worse could it get?

I waived Tamera over, since her client was leaving. She approached my chair with wide eyes and her eyebrows near her hairline.

"So...?" I lowered my voice while I draped a cape over the girl's shoulders and fastened it at her neck. "Shave it off?"

The girl whimpered and I smacked Tam on the arm. "Stop it. How about a color lifter?"

"Nuh uh. You gotta strip that color out." Tamera bent down so that she was eye level with the girl. "What's your name, honey?"

"Patrice," she whispered.

"Speak up!" yelled the woman that brought her. "Bold enough to do what I told you not to do. Bold enough to try and hide it. Should be bold enough to help these ladies fix this mess you've got on your head."

"Why don't you..." I paused, and began again. "If you'd like to have a seat, Ms..."

"Mrs. Mrs. Joyce Black. This here is my granddaughter Patrice."

"Mrs. Black, would you like a bottle of water?" I guided her to the three empty chairs that served as a waiting room and got her settled with a bottle of water from the cooler. I glanced over my shoulder and saw Evonne approaching my station to consult with Tamera. I turned back around and asked, "So you take care of your granddaughter?"

She nodded, after gulping a few swallows of water. "I got her while my daughter is deployed. Army. She's over in Afghanistan through the end of the year."

"And... she wanted to dye her hair gray because..."

"Oh, it's the new thing; I don't understand it," she said, pawing at her silver streaked hair. "While most of us are coloring our grey out, all the young-uns at her school have silver hair. I thought it was silly, and I knew she'd look terrible, but she thinks she can get over on old Joyce. So I don't care what you do to her hair, so long as she doesn't look like a freak show when we leave here. She'll be working off what it costs to fix it, so throw everything at it. She'll learn that when I say no, I mean it."

With that, she emitted a loud grunt and opened her large purse, pulling out a magazine and flipping open the cover. I stood and patted her on the shoulder. "We'll do our best to fix it."

"Mmhmm," she hummed, flipping through her magazine.

I returned to my station and joined Tamera and Evonne. "What's the plan?"

Tam nodded at Evonne. "You're the student. How would you fix a dye job gone bad?"

Evonne circled the chair, brushing the dry tresses with her fingertips. I loved when I could see the wheels turning, the mind rolling through options to correct a problem.

"I'd start with a clarifying shampoo to strip the color out."

Tamera nodded, waving at her to continue.

"Then... I'd do a hot oil treatment. Leave it on for a good while. Then apply a nice chestnut brown to get it somewhere back to its natural shade. She shouldn't do a thing to it except a weekly condition, and keep it moisturized."

I nodded, proud. So did Tamera. "I'm in full agreement with your diagnosis and plan of action. So... hop to it."

I stepped aside and pulled Evonne behind the chair. "You can use my station since she's already here."

"Oh...." Evonne's large brown eyes seemed even bigger in that moment, full of fear but also, if I wasn't mistaken, some anticipation. "You mean you want me to..."

"Go for it," I encouraged. "Tam and I are here if you need us."

"You're going to let a student work on my hair?" Patrice suddenly found her voice. It was shrill and whiny.

"Patrice, honey..." I bent so I could whisper in her ear. "Right now, Evonne is your only hope. I suggest you pray that we don't have to shave your head."

I felt her shoulders sag and watched her eyes slide closed in resignation. I chuckled and walked away. Evonne couldn't do any worse than Patrice already had. She wouldn't be playing in hair color again any time soon.

Patrice and her grandmother didn't leave the shop until late, but she had a manageable head of dark brown hair, an armful of olive oil infused products and strict instructions from Evonne on how to baby her hair for the next few weeks. Mrs. Black was so impressed that she made an appointment for Patrice to return in four weeks.

"Great job, Evonne. You saved her hair, because I'm sure Grandma was about to grab the clippers herself." I gave her a pat on the back and grinned at her proud expression.

"Thanks. I appreciate the chance to do something besides a press and curl." She reached for the broom that I had in my hands and headed toward the stations. "I'm going to sweep up and get out of here."

I sensed movement at the door and opened my mouth to let the customer know that we were just about to close. To my surprise, Kade Cavanaugh stood in the doorway. Earlier in the day he'd worn a pair of shorts that looked like he'd pulled them straight from the dryer and a misshapen t-shirt. Tonight, he wore khaki carpenter shorts and a form fitting black t-shirt that spread over his pecs and hugged his biceps and...*whew*.

I reached out to grip my chair since I was a little light headed. A lightning bolt of attraction punched me in my chest and rushed through my body so quickly, so fiercely, it took me by surprise. I inhaled deeply, sucking in a steadying breath before I addressed him.

"Evening, KC. I'd have thought your shop would be too busy for you to be over here, checking out your competition."

He smiled, quietly laughing while his eyes surveyed the salon, starting at the reception desk, a plain old desk from Caine Brothers Wood Works. Then he took in the mismatched leather chairs that comprised the waiting area; the salon chairs with peeling vinyl patched with black tape and the shampoo bowl that was a refurbished and redesigned laundry sink. To the naked, and maybe the more upscale eye, the Curl & Dye wasn't much to look at. But people came to the Curl & Dye for the atmosphere.

"I mean, with all due respect, Leslie..." KC shrugged and gestured toward the small salon. "You're not my competition."

That lofty, lightheaded feeling was zapped as quickly as it came on. I felt like I landed face first on the pavement. There went my moment of attraction.

Tamera stood beside me, her arms crossed. "Look who decided to slum it over on the old side of Potter Lake."

"I'm not... slumming. I hadn't been over here since I moved back and—"

"And you decided to pop in and start some shit with us?"

KC's eyes narrowed and his brows formed "V" of irritation. The glare he gave Tamera gave me an uneasy feeling.

"Tam, why don't you close out the day for me? Pull the receipts and get the deposit ready." I led her to the front desk and pulled out the chair for her to sit. As soon as she was settled, I grabbed KC's arm and guided him back out of the shop into the warm evening. I heard Tamera grumbling, not even under her breath, as she sat at the desk and began the daily closing ritual.

"What do you want?" I asked him, noticing the enormous black Escalade parked in front of the window. "We're about to close up."

He shrugged a shoulder, tossing his keys from one hand to the other. Back in college he used to do the same with a basketball. "I just... was around and—"

"Bullshit. You have no reason to be on this side of the lake except to be snooping around this shop. So... what? You wanted to gloat? To say some more shit about stealing my clients?"

"I'm not steal—" He heaved a deep sigh and shoved both hands into his pockets. "I felt bad. About earlier. You surprised me by showing up at the shop. I felt cornered and I get mouthy when I feel like that. Listen, I think we got off on the wrong foot—"

"No, I think the foot we got off on was right. You came out here and opened a business in direct competition with mine—"

"That was not my intent, Leslie. I keep telling you, I didn't know this shop was here."

"Well, now you do." I paused, giving a wide-eyed stare at ruggedly bushy eyebrows, at long, undeservedly lush lashes, at almond shaped eyes, at full lips and well-edged goatee. Damn, he was fine. Had always been fine but... damn, he was fine.

"Now I do," he acknowledged, with a head nod. "All I'm saying is that we should be able to co-exist."

"Co-exist? Seriously?" I gestured toward the building that was The Curl & Dye, catching a glimpse of Evonne and Tamera standing in the middle of the shop watching us talk. I pulled him away from the window, toward the driver side door of his truck.

"It would be one thing if you were just a barbershop. Most of the men in this town do their own hair; they only come to me if they want something real nice. That cheap cut you offer is perfect for them."

He scoffed, but I ignored it.

"We can't co-exist because women are going to your shop instead of mine, for services I offer, my mother offered, my Grandy offered for years. Your shop could lose a customer or three and it wouldn't hit your bottom line. I need every client I can get. Your shop is some kind of..."

I shrugged, shaking my head. "Get rich quick scheme, it seems. Except you're already rich, so now you're just being greedy. The Curl & Dye is my bread and butter. It keeps me and my parents in food and electricity and Grandy in good care at Primose Gardens. It's about more than a cheap haircut."

I began to back away from him and his truck and his intoxicatingly sexy smelling cologne. It was making me heady and I was feeling all kinds of really familiar feelings from being too close to him.

"I just want to run my shop, KC."

"And I want to run mine," he responded, a hand splayed across his chest. "What do you want me to do, Leslie? Close up, give up my business 'cause you got first dibs?"

I sighed, lifting my face to the starry sky. "No," I finally answered, making my way toward the front door. "I want you to stay out of my way. You do your thing over on that side of the lake and I'll—"

"Leslieeeeee!" Gisela's high pitched wail made me whip around, my eyes wide in expectation. She tore through the shop from the back room out to the parking lot. "The pipe busted again! Hurry!"

"Shit!" I hissed, rushing back inside where water was gushing from the back room and quickly spreading through the shop and toward the front door.

"Where's your shut off valve?" I heard KC yell, hot on my heels.

"Behind the washer!" I yelled back. Tamera was already pulling the washer away from the wall. KC helped, easing the old monstrous machine out of its spot and reaching his long arms behind it to shut off the water at the valve. The busted pipe stopped gushing, now just trickling out what was left inside.

Gisela and Evonne grabbed the towels stacked on the shelf and began sopping up water. Tamera grabbed the mop and bucket and began swiping waves toward the drain under the sink. KC was squatting in front of the pipe, inspecting it.

"Looks like it's been soldered a couple of times. Not very well, though. This pipe needed to be replaced a long time ago, Leslie. It's not to code."

"I know," I said, leaning against the doorjamb. "The last time Jessup was here, they said it was a temporary fix until I replace them." I waved a hand at the mess that was our plumbing system. "The whole place needs to be redone. I just haven't... yet."

"I could probably give you a better fix. At least replace this pipe. It'll buy you some time."

KC looked up at me from his squatting position. His eyes were earnest, his expression neutral. It was as if time had never passed and we'd never had that conversation where I gave him an ultimatum. And he didn't take it.

I chuckled, grabbing his arm, then laughed at the thought that I could pull him up. He was well over a hundred pounds heavier than me. "I don't need you to fix my pipes, KC." Not those pipes, anyway.

Once he'd slowly made his way up, I urged him out of the shop and toward the front door. "I have a daddy and a grand-daddy, and believe it or not, there's still a plumber or two over here. They'll come out and take care of it."

KC stood next to his truck and glanced back at the other

girls working hard to clean up the mess, like he didn't want to leave.

"Go on, get back to your shop. They must be helpless without you telling them exactly how to give that cheap ass haircut y'all do."

"You got jokes." KC chuckled, the sound of it a light rumble from his chest that hit me directly in mine. My feelings were all out of control and I needed this man and his eyes and his laughter and his chest and his cologne to get the hell off of my side of Potter Lake.

He opened the driver side door and climbed up into his truck, slamming the door shut. The truck roared to life a moment later, then I heard the quiet whirr of the window sliding down.

"Not for nothin, but you know my dad is a General Contractor. I learned the business inside and out, growing up. I know my way around a busted pipe and some plumbing, too. Let me know if you need some help. Aight?"

I rolled my eyes and turned to go back inside. I would have to be bleeding and on fire to ask that man for help.

six

. . .

KC

"Excuse me, grump ass? What crawled up your butt? And where have you been all day?"

I almost snapped at TC to mind her own business before I realized that my business was her business. And I was grumpy. After spending most of the day alone, sulking, I'd finally responded to Kendrick and TC's texts to meet them at Thai Bistro, a quick serve Asian fusion restaurant a few blocks away from Guys N' Dolls. We had tried most of the new restaurants that had opened up lately. Thai Bistro was one of our favorites.

I showed up an hour late and slid into a booth next to TC, looking like I'd just rolled out of bed. Because I had.

"Don't start, T. I'm just..." I grabbed a menu from the table, flipping it over to peruse the drinks. "My whole day was a waste of gas and a clean suit."

"Your meeting with the Mayor was today, right?" Kendrick asked. When I nodded, he responded with a slow, single bob of his head.

TC didn't quite catch my drift. "And?" She demanded, her lips twisted in a scowl.

"And what? Does it look like it went well?"

"Lay it out, man. What happened?" Kendrick waved down the waitress so I could order a drink. When she stepped away, I started talking about how my day began with hope and determination and ended with me wondering if I should just set my business on fire and collect an insurance check.

Potter Lake City Government conducted business out of a two story brick building that was once a factory. The first time I'd met with the Mayor, he'd proudly given me a tour of the gutted and renovated space that held no resemblance to the carpet manufacturer that used to be housed there. Carney Carpets had been one of the first casualties of the downturn of the Potter Lake economy after a nearby textile mill closed.

I'd dressed to impress, pulling out one of my old "post-game press conference" suits. I wore a new tie and pocket square, shined my shoes, and slid the agreement that had been drawn up between the Mayor and I into a thin folio. When I walked into that office, I was ready to talk, man to man. Businessman to businessman. Face to face. No more voicemail tag or unanswered email or dodging me in public.

I greeted his receptionist, an older woman with a shock of brilliant white hair, deep cocoa skin and a racy shade of red lipstick on her lips. Her desk plate read Earline and though she was pleasant, her overall attitude told me she didn't put up with mess. I hadn't planned on giving her any trouble.

"Have a seat, Mr. Cavanaugh," she said, after I had checked in. "I'll let you know when the Mayor is ready."

I sat in one of the guest chairs to the right of the reception desk, which was a long plane of wood rumored to be salvaged from the former factory. It looked cheap and slapped together to me, but the Mayor had been so proud of himself for reusing materials that I just smiled and nodded while he gushed.

While I waited, I reviewed my paperwork. The agreement that I'd signed with Mayor Adams and the City of Potter Lake stipulated that I'd receive a cash incentive and a break on city taxes once the business I'd promised to set up had been in successful operation for six months. Guys N' Dolls had been open three times that, but I hadn't seen a check, nor had I heard a firm date as to when I would receive it. He'd always said it was 'coming' or 'tied up in city council' or simply ignored my inquiries. We'd both signed the agreement nearly two years ago.

A low warble sounded at Earline's desk and after a hushed exchange via the headset, she lifted her head and smiled. "Mayor Adams will see you now. Just down the hall, the first door on your left."

Every step I took rang throughout the whisper-quiet office. The floors were hardwood, also original from the factory, stripped, stained and buffed to a shine. At the first door on the left, I stopped and stood in the doorway.

"Sir," I called out, interrupting what seemed to be a riveting game of Solitaire.

Mayor Quincy Adams stood, extending a hand to me as he crossed the room. The overhead light reflected in the shiny dome that was the crown of his head. He still held onto a few tufts of grey hair around the back and sides. I stepped into his office to meet him halfway, grasping his hand and giving it a few courteous pumps.

"Young man!" He boomed. "So nice to see you. Thank you for coming in."

I nodded, gracious as though he had invited me to his office when I was the one to request the meeting. Pleasantries exchanged, we each took our seats and got comfortable, eyeing one another, each waiting for the other to begin the meeting.

"I stopped into the shop the other day," he finally said, pointing upward, to his head. "Got a nice edge-up from uh...

Kendrick, I think it was. Gave me a good shine, too. Only eight dollars... helluva deal!"

I nodded. "It looks great, sir. Glad we could be of service. The shop is exactly why I'm here, Mr. Adams—Mayor Adams. I was hoping to discuss this agreement we signed, about me opening up a business in Potter Lake in exchange for certain monetary promises—" I pulled the agreement from the folio and read from a highlighted page. "A tax abatement for the first year of operation and a cash incentive in the amount—"

"Well, son..." He cleared his throat, bringing his hands together in steeple formation, tips touching. "Let me go ahead and stop you there. I realize it's been awhile since we talked." Mayor Adams paused to stare at his hands, heavily ringed. His fingernails had dirt underneath them. "Let's just say that the situation has changed."

An eyebrow lifted, more out of curiosity than anger, but anger was quickly catching up. "Changed? How so?"

"Ah...well..." He stalled, rising from his chair and beginning a slow pace across his expansive office. "Son, I'm afraid I let my tongue wag a little more than I should have. The City Council didn't actually approve the funds I had promised to incentivize business owners to open up shop in Potter Lake. They had earmarked those dollars toward a special project, which is already underway and—"

"I have a contract that we both signed, right here in my hands—"

"That isn't worth the paper it's printed on. The money isn't there. Simply put, I promised money that doesn't exist and there's nothing I can do about it." He paced one way and then another, refusing to catch my eye and the stare of death that I was leveling in his direction. "Now, I'm sorry. I know you were counting on it, but from what I hear, the shop is doing pretty well. You shouldn't even need the incentive. Every time I pass by, all the chairs are full and there's a line out the door. Guys N' Dolls must be raking it in, hand over fist."

I was trying—and failing—to keep my temper in check. "Yes, sir. Guys N' Dolls is doing alright. Today. But the first year was a struggle. I plugged a lot of money into the shop because I knew I'd be getting it back from the city. Now a big chunk of my savings is invested in this business and I was hoping to have replenished those savings by now."

"I don't see any reason why you can't do that from current sales. What are you doing with the money, son? Eating it?" He chuckled, his jowls jiggling in time with the sounds coming from his mouth.

"I'm paying bills, Mayor Adams. I'm keeping the shop running. I'm making payroll and stocking product. I could really use those funds, if only so we can get ahead. We need a computer scheduling system, and I've noticed a few areas that need attention—"

"Yes, yes. Well... that's hardly the business or responsibility of the Mayor's office, is it? That's all in the cost of running your business."

"But sir—"

"What language do I have to speak to get you to understand, Mr. Cavanaugh?" The mayor's face had turned dark, a scowl making already unseemly, pug-like features appear even more so. "You aren't getting any money. You can wipe your ass with that agreement. That's about what it's worth. That or throw it in a fire as kindling."

He lumbered toward the door and pulled it open wider, as if ushering me out. "If you paid for parking, Earline will see to it that you're validated. I have a meeting in a few minutes, so..." He waved a pudgy hand toward the open doorway.

I slowly stood, heavy realization coming to me. I'd been scammed, basically. The Mayor never had any intention on paying out that money. It was a ruse to get people to open businesses in Potter Lake, to pay business and property and city tax, to line his pockets.

"So... just like I figured," said TC, "and just like I've been telling you, there's no money coming."

"Yeah, T... just like you said, there's no money coming. You want a cookie for being right?"

"You want to get off my back, just because you're embarrassed about believing the words that came out of that man's mouth?"

"T... KC... chill." Monica piped up from the corner of the table, shushing us like we were squabbling children.

For most of our lives, TC and I bickered like cats and dogs. Our parents never understood why we didn't have that bond, that sibling understanding, that best-friendship that twins are supposed to have. They didn't get it. We did have that bond. We just had a funny way of showing it.

TC and I were best friends from the moment we were born. TC knew me better than anyone, which was aggravating, because she was always telling me about myself. She was always my right hand, always right next to me. If I got in trouble for something, it was likely that TC was there too, getting the same punishment.

We kept each other on the honor roll. She ran drills with me for practice and came to all my games. But when it came time for us to choose colleges, I wanted TC to go and do something on her own. I wouldn't let her lose her spot at SMU just to follow me to Healy; nor would I let her drop out of college to follow me around the country playing basketball.

But TC couldn't stay away and as soon as she'd graduated, she started traveling with me. She helped me with my schedule, getting me on a bus or a plane or to a doctor's appointment. She managed my life. I never asked her to move to Healy after I left the NBA—she just showed up one day. She knew something was going down and that she needed to be here. And she was here, managing my shop, being my right hand. Getting on my damn nerves.

"Look, y'all. I'm just not in the mood to rehash how much I've messed this up. That's rolling on repeat in my head right now."

"You haven't messed anything up," Kendrick argued. The waitress stopped to drop off the beer I'd ordered. He slid it across the table to me. "You own a co-ed salon—a successful co-ed salon, I might add. Said salon is full of people every day, at least on the men's side. With the women's side, we have some goals to meet, but we're already under our competition's skin, so we must be doing something right."

The mention of Leslie sent my mind down a path I'd been trying not to let it wander to. I'd been tempted to ride by the Curl & Dye to check out that busted pipe, but that would be the most thinly veiled reason imaginable just to see her again. She so obviously wanted nothing to do with me and I didn't want to suffer the wrath of Tamera so soon again either.

"Think about it, KC," said Monica. "You used your savings, not a loan, so you're not in debt. The area the shop is in is growing like a field of weeds. I heard there's a convenience store going up around the corner. You're in a great place to grow. And don't worry about that little old beauty shop on the other side of the lake. There's a reason the Mayor said all those places were already closed."

"All those old school, yesteryear types of places?" TC sucked her teeth, then reached for a glass of ice water, gulping down a few swallows. "Why would I drive across the lake to go to some old timey hardware store when we have a brand new Landry's down the street? I guess I understand being sentimental, and I'm sure Leslie's nice... but I don't see how they think they're going to stay afloat, not with this side of the lake booming like it is."

"I just thought of something." I sat up, angling myself so I could see Kendrick, Monica and TC. "The same deal that the

Mayor struck with me is the same deal he must have struck with everybody. So all of us new business owners are sitting around, waiting for money that isn't coming. He told me today that I could wipe my ass with the agreement he signed; it wasn't worth the paper it was printed on. He's getting away with a crooked deal and killing half of this town to do it. And that's really getting under my skin."

Kendrick chuckled, shaking his head. "He's walking around town like 'who gon' check me'? But really, who's gonna check him, though? He's an elected official. How do you remove someone this town elected to office?"

"By... not re-electing him?" TC offered, lifting a shoulder in a shrug.

"Quincy Adams has been Mayor of Potter Lake for..." Monica shook her head, her eyes wide as she tried to calculate the years. "A long time. No one has ever opposed him. And I don't think anyone will."

"Got to be something we can do. Can the City Council reprimand him?"

"They haven't so far. Don't know if they'd be willing to. They meet every other Tuesday over at the recreation center. Maybe you should drop into a meeting."

I stroked my goatee, pulling at the softly graying hairs. In my early thirties, I was already dying my grays. "Might be the move. Either they don't know what he's doing or they haven't been made aware of how widespread his scam has run."

"Or they don't care," Monica added.

"We all need to band together and go to that meeting and demand some kind of change or justice or..." TC shook her head and tossed her hands up in a helpless gesture. "Some-thing. Let's do something instead of sulking and mumbling about it."

"Yeah," I agreed with a nod and a tug of my goatee. "But I'm thinking. There's us new kids on the block. But what about the other side of the lake—"

"Why are you so obsessed with those old people?" asked Monica, laughing. Her dessert had arrived and she was happily spooning ice cream into her mouth.

"Because it's not just old people. I drove around for a few minutes over there last weekend. Outside of Leslie's shop, there's plenty of doors still open, lights still on, businesses hanging in there. There's a seedy little bar over there— parking lot was full. The bowling alley was poppin'. An ice cream shop had a line out to the street. But let Mayor Adams tell it, there's nobody over there and everything's closed. Like I said... he's killing half of this town. On purpose."

"So you think those people, the old ones and the young ones are going to step up to the city council and complain about him?"

"Why not? They see what's going on, don't they? They feel their livelihoods, their businesses slipping through their fingers with every new foundation that gets poured. With every new business that goes up over here, another one over there fails."

"Okay, but Mayor Adams is an institution. And they probably hate everyone over on this side of the lake. How are you going to get their attention? How are we going to bring everyone together?"

An idea was rolling around in my mind, taking form and snowballing, the more I thought about it. "We have a common enemy. And I have an idea."

seven

· · ·

LESLIE

My car rolled to a stop in my usual spot in the gravel driveway next to Daddy's work truck, Mama's sedan and Pop's pickup. We'd had a good day, but business fell off early and I made the executive decision to close up. It was rare that I got to sit at the kitchen table with my family on a weeknight and eat dinner while it was hot.

I crunched my way across the driveway to the screened-in front porch. Back when Grandy and Pops first moved into the house, the porch was where you could find them both, rain or shine, side by side in their respective chairs. Now it was just Pops in his chair, still dressed in his motor-oil stained overalls, an unlit cigar hanging out of his mouth and staring into the air. He had the newspaper open in his lap but he wasn't reading it.

"Pops? You alright? Is your sugar low?"

He grunted, startled, his shoulders bouncing with the mild jerk. The newspaper slipped from his lap to the worn wooden boards. He bent to pick up the pages, then pulled the cigar from the corner of his mouth.

"I swear my hearing is goin' out. Didn't even hear you pull up. I'm aight." He tapped the chair next to him, gesturing me to sit. "You home early today."

"No sense in four of us standing around waiting for someone to come in."

His head bobbed in a nod of understanding. He and my father ran Hill Automotive, an auto towing and repair shop that had seen a sharp downturn in the last year, just like me. A chain auto repair shop had opened across the lake and since then, business was still limping along, but nowhere near where it had been.

"I heard you and that young man with the new salon had words. 'Bout time somebody said something to him."

I reared back, eyeing my grandfather, though I shouldn't have been surprised. If I sneezed on Main Street, people in the furthermost corner of Potter Lake heard about it an hour later. It was my least favorite part of living in a small town and why I had avoided talking to KC for so long. I knew it would get around and I didn't have a single desire to explain my actions.

"Who you hear that from?"

He shrugged and popped the cigar back into his mouth, bringing the pages of the newspaper close to his face so he could see the small typeset. "I hear things, 'round town and such. Care to unload on an old man? I fancy myself a... whatchacallit? Armchair podiatrist?"

I giggled, dropping my bag between my feet. I wasn't entirely sure that Pops knew that KC and I had history. He wasn't a secret, but I didn't talk about him much. At first because I didn't think the feelings I had for him were mutual. And later because I was embarrassed that they weren't. I didn't know if Pops was asking if we had talked or if we had... talked. There was a difference.

"You know I knew him in college, right?"

Pops nodded.

"Well, we didn't part on good terms, so I had been avoiding seeing him. I was forced into it the other night, and it wasn't a friendly conversation. I told him what I thought of him moving back here to open up a business that was killing mine. I don't know what I expected him to say to that, but it felt good, finally saying it."

"What did he say to that?"

I snorted. "He said I wasn't competition. That he didn't open his shop to kill mine so if it happened, it wasn't his fault."

"Mmmhmmm." Pops mused, chewing on his cigar. Then said, "Sound like you want him to make things right, apologize for all of this you goin' through right now."

"That's not what I wanted at all, Pops."

"You sure?" He leaned over toward me, his eyebrows raised practically to his hairline, those beady browns trained on me.

"I just want him to play fair, you know? Because it's me... not just some random out there, but... me."

"I guess that's a sign of the new times in Potter Lake. Personal relationship means less and less."

"And there's less personal relationship. I know everybody over here. Over there?" I angled my head in the direction of the lake that separated the two sides of town. "I don't know those people. Might as well be a whole another city. And I don't care about them either."

"Still, the boy sounds awful cocky, like his business can't fall in a hot second."

"He kind of has a right to be, though. He does a lot of business."

"Bet he don't do it as well as you do."

"He doesn't. But he's shiny and new and cheap. People like cheap."

Pops grunted, shaking his head. "People think they like cheap. Cheap don't last. Thinking about that pipe we fixed in the shop. Cheap was good, right nice until the pipe busted again. You hang in there. People don't really like cheap as much as they think they do. They'll be back to quality soon enough."

I wanted to grab onto those words and hang on to dear life. I just didn't know if I could afford to attach myself to such an idealistic life raft.

"I need to put this business degree to work, though; think of ways I can keep my shop open. Not just for me, but for this town. It's the principle of the thing, you know? You can't erase history with a coat of paint and big ol' sign out front."

"That's true. Same for Hill Automotive. Been around for damn near thirty years. Hate to see it fall to some franchise Midas over there. That nursing home bill is going to keep coming." Pops paused, staring into the air, again. "At least for a little while. Got to be able to keep paying it."

"Pops, you know we can all help to pay that bill."

"I already told you, that bill is my responsibility—"

"And I already told you that we are family and we help each other out. You been over to see Grandy today?"

He gave me a nod, his lips pursed. A few days a week, he carted his brown bag to Primrose and had lunch with her. More like eat lunch and talk while her eyes stayed fixed to the TV or some object in the distance. Occasionally her eyes would move, especially if it was early morning and she was fresh enough to recognize your face or the sound of your voice.

"She's comfortable. That's what I'm concerned with. Long as she stays that way."

The one welcome change that Mayor Adams had made to Potter Lake was the Primose Assisted Living facility that had opened two years ago. With the residents of the town getting older or sicker, it was a small comfort to have a local facility

to care for them without having to move them to some imper-
sonal old folk's home in Healy.

"What's for dinner?" I asked, changing the subject. Pops
didn't like to talk too much about Grandy. If she was comfortable, he was content. And as long as Pops was content, the
rest of us followed suit.

"I don't know what Lee got cookin' in there. Probably
something it's too hot to be eating."

As if her ears were burning, the front door swung open
and Mama tipped her head out. "Oh, Leslie, I didn't know
you was here. I had to come out here and see who your
grandfather was talking to. Thought he'd started talking to
himself and we'd have to get a double room at the home."

"I ain't gone crazy yet."

"Yet being the important word. Anyway, come on in here.
It's never too hot for my meatloaf. Acting like you're not
gonna scarf down two servings."

I grabbed my bag, then offered a hand to help Pops stand.
His knees weren't what they used to be. I followed the rich,
heavy scent of meatloaf, mashed potatoes and gravy and
green beans to the kitchen, where my dad was already seated
at the head of the table, punching into his phone with the tip
of his thumb.

"Hi, Daddy," I greeted him, bending to drop a kiss on his
cheek. He was a hardy man, with dark walnut skin, callouses
on his hands and dark deposits of oil under his nails. He, too
still wore stained overalls. The sleeves were rolled above the
elbow and the first three buttons were undone, revealing a
grimy t-shirt underneath.

He glanced up and flashed his signature, ready smile at
me. "You're home for dinner. Now your Mama doesn't have to
remind me leave enough for you to eat." He winked, then
went back to his phone. "Pops, look here. We're gonna have to
eat and run. Somebody's looking for a tow over near the
Junction."

The Junction was the railroad tracks on the very edge of town. Way back in Potter Lake's history, the town had been a stop for the railroad, delivering goods and passengers about once a month or so. Since Healy had FedEx, UPS and the like and could just drive a truck to town, the Junction didn't see much action. But what with all the building on the other side of the lake, the railroad had been making more stops lately, bringing lumber and supplies.

"Who needs a tow from over there?" He asked, watching my mother load up a plate with a thick slice of meatloaf, an extra dollop of mashed potatoes and gravy and two spoonfuls of green beans with onions. Pops had always been tall and lanky but ate like a horse. Two horses, some days.

"Probably one of those workers building something over there that don't know about that patch of mud alongside the tracks. I pull somebody out of there once a week at least."

"Shouldn't y'all head over there now?" Mama asked. "Dinner will keep."

"Where they goin'? They can wait until I've had my wife's famous meatloaf."

I made a plate for myself and ate while listening to my father and grandfather chat about the ins and outs of towing and auto repair like they didn't work together all day and live in the same house.

"Leslie, you're awful quiet tonight," said Mama. "I forgot you was even here for dinner."

"She been letting that other salon get under her skin," Pops interjected, his fork full of his next bite. "I told her to hold on. Things will be right again."

I pushed my half eaten plate away. "I don't know, Pops. I really want to believe that. I can't help but think some of the blame sits on the Mayor's shoulders for this. He's pitting competition directly against us—"

"Well, I don't see how this is Quincy's fault. With a rise in population, there should be a rise in businesses to serve them."

My eyes rolled at how hard Mama stanned for Mayor Adams. She voted for him at every election—like she had a choice, since he often ran unopposed. But even if he had been opposed, she'd never vote for anyone but Quincy Adams. Even if he was putting her daughter's livelihood at stake.

"Mama, the only reason there is a rise in population is because there is a rise in businesses. People didn't just up and decide to relocate to Potter Lake. It's not a response to anything but the Mayor and this city wanting more money. I don't know how they expect me to pay the tax bill with no business."

"Maybe somebody should say something to him," Daddy suggested. "Or maybe y'all should get your heads together and put some work behind wanting to stay open."

"Says the woman who would rather close her doors than go against the Mayor."

Mama spooned up another dollop of mashed potatoes, then tossed the spoon back into the pot, splashing the table with potatoes. "Excuse me for being loyal to the man. Mayor Adams has led this city through leaner times than these and he's been good to us. Yes, we're uncomfortable, but it'll pass."

"I'm just—"

A knock at the front door cut off my growing tirade, and just in time. When mother turned red and started gripping her fork in her fist, she was gunning for an argument and didn't like to lose. I scooted my chair back from the table and rose to escape the tension filled room.

"I'll get that. It's probably Tam. We're supposed to hang out tonight."

"Oh, tell her to come have some dinner. I think Gina is working late tonight."

I ducked out of the kitchen, glancing at the driveway through the living room window. I expected to see the sporty two-seater Tamera had been driving for a few years. But it wasn't Tam's car in the driveway. And it wasn't her at the door.

"Uh... hey." I pulled the door open and stepped back so KC could step inside. A wave of cologne that smelled more delicious than dinner followed in his wake. He pulled a fitted cap off of his head and ran a palm over his waves.

"I didn't realize you knew where I lived."

"Yeah," he said. "My mind isn't everything it used to be, but it's not that bad."

"Ah huh. You've been back, at least in this general area, for over a year. You know where I live but I hadn't seen you until the other night."

KC grinned. "Aight, my bad for not coming to say hello. I didn't think you wanted to see me. And it looks like you still don't, but I was hoping to talk to you about something. About the Mayor."

My eyebrows rose and my lips curled into a scowl. "We were just talking about him at dinner. He's not my favorite subject."

"Mine either, right now. I'm hoping that since we both have an axe to grind that you could help me out with something."

I laughed. Actually guffawed. Out loud. Kade Cavanaugh, owner and proprietor of the business that was burying me alive, wanted me to help him with something.

"I've never heard anything more hilarious, KC."

"I know, it's a big ask. And you don't have to say yes. But maybe after I explain what's going on, you can see past... everything and we can work together."

I was still chuckling, but I led him back outside to the porch. The sun was setting and the breeze blowing through was nice. I dropped into Pops' chair and let him sit in Grandy's old chair. Maybe her spirit would come through and smack him upside his gorgeous head.

"You have five minutes. And then I'm kicking you off my porch and going back to my Mama's meatloaf."

He glanced back at the house and smiled. "Is that what smells so good?"

"Four minutes, fifty nine seconds. Fifty eight. Talk."

"Alright, alright." He leaned forward, his elbows on his knees, his sleeveless shirt showing off miles of rippling muscle. He wore basketball shorts that put his powerful thighs and legs on display. And on his feet were Aris athletic shoes, the brand he repped.

"So, I'm sure you know that the Mayor told us that we'd get money and all kinds of deals for coming out here, living out here, opening up a spot." He glanced at me, the question written all over his face.

I was well aware, and salty because none of the existing businesses were being offered anything of the sort—not a discount, not a penny off.

"My spot has been open for over a year. And for the last six months at least, I've been on the Mayor to make good on his promise. It hasn't happened. And it won't—at least for me, and I suspect every person that picked up sticks and moved to Potter Lake based on his promises."

"Mkay. So this affects me how? Are y'all throwing a tantrum, packing up and moving away? You want me to take my clientele back without attitude? That can be arranged."

He chuckled, shaking his head. "Not exactly. Because at the same time that he's building up over there, he's telling all of us that there's nothing here on this side of the lake. Last weekend when I was over here, I saw for myself that that's not true. He's purposely keeping people off of this side of the lake."

"Mmmhmm. Essentially killing us. That's old news, KC. Three minutes; my dinner's getting cold."

"This is important. Can we be real? And serious?"

"I'm being real serious. You have a problem and you want

me to acknowledge it. When I had a problem, you said, uh, I ain't mean to shut y'all down, my bad, but listen to how busy my shop is." I sucked my teeth and angled myself away from him. "If you think a bone in my body feels sorry for you, think again."

"I don't want you to feel sorry for me. I want you to see the underhanded games this man is playing. I want to bring this up to the city council next week. I called today and put myself on the agenda. I'm going to try to get a bunch of people from my side together to sit in on the meeting. I was hoping you would do the same for your side."

I shook my head. "You don't know these folks over here. Mayor Adams could set fire to their homes himself and they'd still think he was the greatest thing since sliced bread. Only a few of us see through his smiling and baby kissing and glad handing."

"That's what I heard. He's run unopposed for years. But that could change."

"Wait...wha—" I cackled, almost screamed in laughter. One of those gut level laughs you couldn't even breathe through. "You... you think you could go against the Mayor in the next election?"

"Depending on how this meeting goes, I might think about it. Somebody has to do something, Leslie."

"Interesting how somebody has to do something, now that your business is in jeopardy. Fuck mine, though huh?"

KC's head dipped, his chin in his chest, shoulders slumped. "I don't know how to go back in time and fix... everything. If I could, I would. But I'm doing something now and believe it or not, I want both sides of this town to thrive."

The front door squeaked, announcing Mama hanging out of it. "Leslie, I told you to tell Tamera to come and get something to..." Her eyes grew wide with surprise and she came out onto the porch. "Well. Hello, young man. Why is Leslie hiding you out on the porch?."

KC stood, removing his cap again. He offered a hand to my mother, which she shook vigorously. About as vigorously as my eyes rolled at how she was fawning over him.

"Ms. Lee," he drawled, the southern gentleman coming out in him. "I don't know if you remember me–"

"Oh, of course I remember you. Leslie's friend from over there at the University." She pointed off to the left somewhere, as if that was even in the direction of Healy U. "And then, of course everyone knew who you were after you started playing for the NBA. I'm not a basketball fan but I sure loved hearing the talk around town. It's good to have you back. You all done on the courts, then?"

"Yes, ma'am. I had a bad knee injury that hit at the wrong time. I cut out while I was still young and could do something else with my life."

Mama nodded, just grinning up into his face, halfway in love with the man. I was ready for this day—and this visit to end.

"KC was just leaving. Came to deliver some news and he has to go. Right, KC?"

"Oh, well are you hungry? I could make you a real good meatloaf sandwich to go, with some potatoes on the side."

The grin KC gave her could light up the night sky. Never ask a single man if you can feed him. It was like feeding strays.

"That sounds amazing, Ms. Lee. I would appreciate it."

She nodded, grinning wider on the way back into the house. "I'll pack it up for you right quick. Leslie, maybe he would like some tea?"

I glared at KC, arms folded across my chest, hoping all of my annoyance was evident on my face. "Do you want some tea?"

KC glanced over at me, then almost jumped back at my expression. "I guess not."

"So, what is it that you want me to do?"

He resumed his seat next to me and slid the cap back over his head. Every moment was driving parts of my body absolutely nuts. The sooner he could get off our porch, the better for us both.

"I need some support. I need to know that folks over here feel the same way I feel. The same way some of the folks over on the other side will feel, as soon as they find out there's no money coming. I need the city council to see who they have leading the charge and if they don't know, they should know. And if they know and are doing nothing, they need to be replaced. And so does the Mayor."

"And if he doesn't step down? And he runs for re-election in October?"

"Then he might have some competition."

"From you? Need I remind you how loudly I laughed at that idea a few minutes ago?"

"Why couldn't I? The leader of this country has no idea what he's doing."

I stopped laughing, the smile falling from my face. "That's not even funny, KC."

"Where is the lie, though? If he can do it, I can."

"I don't think it'll be that easy."

"I'm not saying it'll be easy. It'll be better than being swindled by a crook."

The front door swung open again. We both stood and KC accepted the well-packed sandwich and sides in a brown paper bag.

"I had some sweet potato pie left over from the fundraiser last weekend. I cut you a big slice and put it in there, too."

"Mama, you're feeding him like he ain't ate food in a year. You see how big this man is?"

"It's okay, Ms. Lee," he said, cutting his eyes at me. "It'll get eaten, every bite. And I'll send your containers back, too."

"You do that. You headin' out?"

"Yes ma'am," he answered, one hand on the handle to the screen door. "Leslie, I hope we'll talk soon."

"We'll see," I answered, then went into the house and back to my dinner plate, leaving my mother to send him off. A few moments later, I heard the faint rumble of the Escalade start up and pull out of the driveway. I was suddenly ravenous, with a need to keep my mouth full so I couldn't answer any questions about that nice, handsome young man.

eight

· · ·

LESLIE

"What could we offer, that would make people come in?" Tamera tapped a shellacked nail tip on the side of an aluminum can. She'd cleaned the dinner plate Mama made for her and was relaxing on my couch with a Lime-a-Rita. I thought they were nasty, but she'd brought them and I didn't want to insult her choice of drink.

The living space above the garage that could barely be called an apartment had always been meant for my grandparents, but Pops' knees and Grandy's stroke meant that they needed to be in a bedroom on the ground floor. They took my old room when I moved away to Chicago.

When I came back to Potter Lake, I moved into the apartment. I had my own living room, bathroom and bedroom and a few nooks and crannies for storage. I used a small refrigerator for odds and ends I liked to keep cold. A two burner stove, a tiny sink and a microwave for the occasional bag of popcorn made up the kitchen. I ate most of my meals in the house with the family.

"Like, they know we do hair, but we do other stuff too. I do nails and eyebrows all the time. And Evonne and Gisela learned a bunch of stuff at the beauty school. Surely they have skills we can offer."

"But they're leaving soon. I don't want to start counting on them and then they pull out."

"And then take their talents to Guys N' Dolls." She pursed her lips and scrunched up her nose. "What about spa services? We could offer a discount on something with a cut or a color."

"Threading? Massage? What's that hot rock thing?"

"Hot stone massage. We don't have the room for that."

"Hmmm..." I shoved a well-chewed nail into my mouth and chewed on it some more. "Body waxing is still popular. I saw some sugar waxes in the catalog. I could order some."

She groaned, slouching lower on the couch. "I already don't want to look at Ms. Paulette's feet. Don't make me look at anything else on her."

I laughed just as I took a sip. I choked on half a swallow of a too-sweet tasting beer and margarita concoction. "Okay, I didn't want to say anything but let's never get these again. It was bad going down and bad stuck halfway down my throat."

"Agreed," said Tamera, handing me her can so I could pour it out along with mine. I opened the living room window and dumped the cans into the yard down below. When they were empty, I dropped them into a bin I used to collect my recycling.

"I'll take the unopened ones to work. Maybe those two drink that crap."

"What services does KC's crew offer? If they can do it we can do it. Maybe cheaper."

"Men get a cheap haircut, women get the bare basics. No spa services. Wash, cut, press and curl. Don't even think about a color that's not on a box of L'Oréal or Dark & Lovely. Remember he said he needed stylists who could work with chemicals? I told y'all—somebody's hair is gonna fall out."

I opened a cabinet and pulled out a bottle of wine. Tamera grinned and clapped, then hopped up to open another cabinet where I kept clear plastic glasses. She pulled out two and set them on the counter so I could pour.

"So, he's not even offering anything unique and people would rather go over there because he's new?" She picked up both cups and walked them over to the couch and coffee table. "I don't understand it."

"Well, there's also the added benefit of him being a hometown hero of sorts...a small town celebrity. People feel like they're supporting his new career by giving him business."

"A lot of women with stars in their eyes, hoping to be the next girl on his arm. I don't understand that." Tamera took a long, indulgent swallow of wine and tipped her head back with a sigh. "I wonder if he's tapping into that, at all. You know... groupies?"

I wrinkled my nose and sipped my wine. "What brought that to mind?"

She lifted a shoulder in a casual shrug, like she didn't bring it up just to watch me squirm when I thought about it. "Just thinking out loud. But I guess we would have heard it, if he was."

I nodded. The Curl & Dye was still the hub of the rumor mill. That and the Kit Kat Lounge, a bar over on the edge of town. Don't ever let anyone tell you that men don't gossip. Pops comes home with new juice every time he goes in there.

I hadn't planned on talking about it, because KC wasn't Tamera's favorite subject, nor was he her favorite person. But I had to get it off my chest. Talk it out. Make a decision. Help him? Or fight him? Besides, she brought him up.

"So, KC came by here tonight."

I wasn't even looking at her and I sensed the wrinkle appear in her forehead. "He wanted to talk about Mayor Adams."

"He came by here? To your house? To talk to you?"

"Yes, yes and yes. About the Mayor. You know how we always suspected the Mayor promised those folks a bunch of money if they'd move to Potter Lake? Well, KC confirmed that; except he got told today that there's no money. So he and however many people that have relocated their lives to this town on some kind of promise are up Shit Creek."

"And this affects us how?"

"That's exactly what I asked. He's going to bring up the subject at the next city council meeting. He said he was working on rounding up people on his side of the lake and he wanted me to work on rounding up people over here."

"Round us up? What do we need rounding up for? We going to a rodeo?"

"He said he's demanding to speak to the city council about the Mayor's underhanded dealings. And, he says that if the council doesn't respond, he's thinking about running in the next election."

It was Tamara's turn to choke and cough. When she could breathe, she nearly screeched, "He's going to go against the man that's been Mayor of this town for as long as I can remember?"

"He might be out of his mind but he's doing it anyway. Compared himself to the President. Said if he could do it, it could be done."

"We don't need Potter Lake to become a dumpster fire. That's scary."

"It is. I can imagine everything that could go wrong. But..." I eyed Tamera, knowing she wasn't going to like what I was about to say. "I'm thinking of doing it. Not so much to help him. But to at least get our thoughts and feelings out there in front of the city council. Maybe they'll listen to us."

"And if they don't?"

I smiled. "Then life is about to get real interesting, here in Potter Lake."

By 10 o'clock, Tamera was happy and loose but not drunk.

We'd snacked on popcorn while we watched the latest episode of The Suitor, a long running dating competition show. It was old and tired, after ten seasons on the air, but that had never stopped us from watching it.

"If she doesn't kick Anthony off next week, I'm going to throw something," she'd said, grabbing the handles of her small satchel and threading it over her arm. It settled in the crook of her elbow.

"I know he thinks he looks like Boris Kodjoe but he doesn't. And his attitude isn't winning him any favors."

We'd been watching The Suitor since it premiered and even when I lived in Chicago, we had a phone date to watch the show together. Dexter, my ex, thought we were crazy, but getting that call every week and cackling on the phone with my best friend made some of the homesickness go away.

On the weeks the show didn't air, or Tamera had something going on, I was more melancholy and there was nothing he could do to bring me out of it. In some ways, moving back to Potter Lake improved my quality of life greatly. I got to see Tamera every day.

"We can watch next week's episode at your house if you're going to be throwing things. You know the producers are going to keep him. They want to drag this out so we hang on just to see how long he stays on the show. They do it every season."

"I know," she grumbled. "I was hoping they'd use a different tactic this season, but it looks like the same old shit."

"Because the same two old biddies are in front of the TV watching it."

"Ugh... call me when Oprah or Ava produce a dating show."

I laughed, holding out my arms to give Tamera a hug, then watched from the stairs as she walked out to her car. I didn't step back into my apartment until I saw her tail lights go down the street and turn the corner.

I closed and double locked the door, then started picking up. Tamera was a messy guest—popcorn was everywhere, she'd left her wine glass on the table and a nearly empty bottle of water on the floor next to the couch. Once the living room was back in good shape, I shuffled to my bedroom, stifling a yawn behind one hand.

I crawled onto the bed—a full because the room wasn't big enough for a queen sized mattress—and laid on my back, staring at the ceiling. And thinking. About KC.

I probably wouldn't have been, had he not come over that night. I hadn't seen him since he stopped by the shop the week before and I had almost convinced myself that I could forget he existed. But then he brought his tall, muscular, handsomely bearded and tattooed self over to my house and... well, now I couldn't stop thinking about him.

I met KC my first day at Healy University. Potter Lake was only twenty miles west, but Healy was so different, you would have thought it was a hundred miles and light years away. Instead of Woolworth's and the Kwik-E-Mart, they had Kroger and department stores like JC Penney. It was rare that Mama would drive to Healy for something. We made do with what we had in Potter Lake and that was that.

I'd worked hard for two years, saving money so I could live in the dorms at Healy, so when I had unpacked my things and was bored lounging in my room, I skipped down to the Quad, the social center on campus. There was a cafeteria and a little sundry shop to buy candy and soda and newspaper, a frozen dinner if you were desperate.

I rounded the corner, on my way to a party for the freshmen and walked right into a man. A big man. Like... tall, big. Pretty smile. Gorgeous eyes. A dimple in one cheek and an earring in one ear. He wore basketball shorts, socks, athletic shoes and a white t-shirt.

Looking lickable while doing so.

"Ooh! Hey! Uhm... you're tall," I sputtered, cocking my head back at a ridiculous angle to look up at him.

"I am pretty tall, yeah," he said, his voice so smooth it almost slid down my back. "Do you know where the uhm..." He consulted a flyer that looked like it had seen better days. "The Franklin Center? I was looking for the Freshman Welcome Mixer."

"I'm going there. I think it's the next building over. I'll walk with you."

"Cool, okay. I'm KC."

My hand slipped into his easily. They were soft, but had little callouses along the meaty part of the palm. "I'm Leslie. Nice to meet you."

We walked over to the party together, chit chatting along the way. We were in the same dorm, Morrison; and we were on the same floor but different sides. I'd been nervous about living in a co-ed dorm but at that moment I was a huge proponent of it.

As soon as we walked into the Franklin Center, KC saw some guys from his floor. He thanked me for walking with him and said he was going to see what was up with them and he'd catch me later. I was disappointed, but had no intention of showing it. I nodded my head and uttered a brief, "K", and headed to the other side of the room where a buffet table was loaded down with sandwiches, chips, fruit and desserts.

I met a few people that night, though I couldn't tell you their names or what dorm they lived in or what they planned to major in, because I was busy watching KC out of the corner of my eye. I was always across the room, but he was never out of my sight.

After about an hour, I made my way across the room and... accidentally on purpose backed myself into him.

"Girl, that's the second time you've bumped into me," he said, laughing. "Don't even play like you didn't see me this time. I'm 6'4". Nobody misses me."

I laughed, bringing a cup of punch to my mouth for a sip. "I didn't say all that. Maybe I wanted to get your attention."

"Oh you did, huh? That's what I was thinking you was doing." He eyed the room for a few moments, then pulled his t-shirt away from his body, fanning himself. "It's muggy in here. I thought Austin was hot but Georgia is on another level. You want to step outside?"

"Sure. It stinks like ass and feet in here. It's like there's no ventilation."

We headed for the door, fresh drinks in hand. The air was beginning to cool off and a sweet breeze wound through the trees planted around campus. The leaves rustled, creating nice ambience.

"So that was a nice little thing they threw in there. Pretty cool. I think I'm going to like this college."

"Yeah. It was the only choice I had. My parents couldn't pay for me to go to college out of state, so..." I shrugged, lowering myself to a seat on a bench we'd walked over to. KC sat next to me, spreading his long, muscular arms across the back of the bench.

"You look like you play some kind of sport. I'm guessing basketball. Are you on an athletic scholarship?"

"Nope," he said, shaking his head. "Academic. I had a few choices, but Healy gave me a good offer. It was just far enough away from home and they sweetened the pot when they said I could walk onto the basketball team. If this knee holds up, I'll be alright." He palmed his knee, then rubbed it in gentle circles. "I think it's gonna be okay. Good so far, in practices anyway."

He paused, then chuckled. "Man I'm talking to you like I've known you forever."

"I don't mind," I assured him. "I don't want to dominate the conversation. You say something. What are you going to school for?"

I snorted. "Anything but doing hair. I'm not going to be the third in line to be doing some lady's hair for a living."

"I heard that. My dad was hoping I'd be a General Contractor like him. No, sir. Cavanaugh GC will be fine without me."

"Exactly. I mean, the Curl & Dye —that's my Grandy's shop, she and my mama run it— it's okay, if you like small town living. You get to see a lot of people you know on a weekly basis. But I'm setting my sights a little higher. Maybe a business degree. My dad says I have a good head for numbers."

"Me too. I think some people are born for that kind of thing. Where others are more creative, you know what I'm saying?"

I nodded, smiling. "Yeah. I do."

"So what classes are you taking? Maybe we're in some of the same ones."

I named off my classes, and was happy to find that we'd chosen the same English Lit class.

"Cool. Lemme copy off of you sometimes."

"Nawl. I don't get into that cheating mess. But we can study together. I'm great at writing papers."

"How are you at stretching a thousand words into five thousand words, though? That was my trick in high school."

I laughed. "Pretty good at it."

We talked some more, then decided to walk back to the dorm together since the party was breaking up.

"So, what are you doing the rest of the night?" I asked him.

"Hanging out with you. What we doin'?"

His answer fell out just as easy as if he'd said the sky was blue.

"I thought I might go get a movie from Blockbuster. I have a TV and a DVD player."

"Cool. That sounds like a plan. You mind if I roll with you to Blockbuster?"

"Uhm... sure."

I waited for him downstairs in the lobby of Morrison Hall while he ran upstairs to grab his keys and wallet. When he came back down, he had changed into a different t-shirt, shorts and sneakers. He'd also brushed his hair, and, I noticed when he came close, had even spritzed on a bit of cologne. I felt like a schmuck walking next to him. I wasn't dressed badly, a pair of white jeans and a form-fitting t-shirt, but I wished I had thought to run upstairs and change like he did.

We walked to Blockbuster, since it was just a few streets away and the roads around the University were well-lit. We grabbed a couple of movies and added some snacks to the bag, then hiked back to the dorm. He followed me to my room; I keyed the lock and let us in.

I had a double, but my roommate hadn't arrived yet. He spread out on her bed and kicked off his shoes. His feet hung over the edge of the bed, which made me laugh.

"Did they order an extra-long bed for you?"

"Nope," he answered, laughing along with me. "I look like the Jolly Black Giant in these beds. I'm getting used to it though. Gotta curl up in the fetal position, practically." He demonstrated, rolling to his side and curling up. There was a nice little spot that a girl could fit herself into, if she tried.

I shook my head, trying to clear it of those kinds of thoughts. I couldn't tell if KC was being nice or if he was flirting. Either way, I had a man in my room for the first time ever, and I was going to do my best to keep him in there.

I pulled out the two movies we'd rented. "Hitch or Man on Fire?"

"Uh...Hitch," he said, pointing to the one I'd picked out. "That way if it sucks we at least have something to fall back on."

"It's not gonna suck." I popped open the case and slid the movie into the slot. The screen lit up with the movie studio's logo and music, and then the previews began.

"That's where you're watching? Can you see from over there?"

"I have excellent vision," he quipped, sitting up, then moving to dominate my bed. "It's that tiny ass TV I can't see."

I climbed up on the bed and settled into the little space that was leftover. Just what I was aiming for. I was comfortable and almost wrapped up in him.

"Not everything is tiny just because you're the Jolly Black Giant, okay?"

"Okay. But this TV is tiny."

"Look, just watch the movie on the tiny ass TV."

We watched both movies that night. KC ate all of the Jujubes and the Mike & Ike's. I ate most of the Red Vines but he finished them off. By the time the movies were over and he was standing in the doorway, yawning and stretching and popping his limbs, we were almost the best of friends.

"See you tomorrow," he mumbled. I leaned against the doorjamb, watching him drag his feet down the hall toward the other end of the floor. He didn't even try to kiss me... so I figured he wasn't interested. But he was cool, so... maybe I'd just made a friend.

That was our whole freshman year. Movies. Meals. Studying. Classes. Coffee. Snacks. Campus parties. Games. Friends. Close friends. Really close friends. But not boyfriend and girlfriend. I wanted that. I was too chicken to open my mouth and say it. KC was oblivious to my crush on him, and by the time I was ready to say something, he started dating some sorority girl that got on my damn nerves.

That summer was hard. I didn't want to say goodbye to KC but at least it wouldn't be for long. He had basketball camp, so after only six weeks he was back. I drove to Healy a few times a week to hang out with him until classes started, and then we were back on campus. And he'd broken it off with that annoying sorority girl.

We'd decided to register for a business course that fall. We had to get approval to register and at the end of the course, we were basically vying for a highly coveted internship at IBM. KC and I were front runners and it was hard to tell, from day to day, who was doing better.

The day KC told me I could have the internship, because he was dropping out, was one of the worst days of my life. Not just dropping the class, but leaving Healy. He had different, better plans, apparently, than hanging out at a small town college with me.

Maybe I overreacted... but I felt like I had good reason to. I never expected him to call my bluff.

nine

. . .

KC

"So... you went to her house, man? Her house? Like... where she lives?"

Kendrick sat in his barber chair, sipping on a cup of coffee. We didn't open for another half hour, but like me, he liked to get in while the shop was quiet, before the lines started forming and the low murmur of voices and the buzz of clippers filled the air.

I sat in the chair next to him, Erik's spot. I'd been talking to Kendrick and TC about getting after the guys to clean up better. Erik's spot was filthy, with hair gathered in the corners around his station and dried up drops of sanitation liquid all over the countertop. His combs were shoved in haphazard places, his mirrors were just sitting out. Our reputation was everything and I didn't think we could afford anyone talking rough about how we didn't keep the place looking nice.

Our conversation had meandered to Kendrick asking what had been keeping me so busy. And so quiet. I'd been at home or at Rooster's coffee shop, working on what I wanted to say to the city council. I'd made visits to each of the owners of the businesses in the strip mall where Guys N' Dolls rented space, and then spread out to the shops down one side of the newly formed street and up the other side.

We all heard the same party line from Mayor Adams, that there was money, incentives, tax breaks for bringing our dreams and our checkbooks to Potter Lake. Few had heard anything from the Mayor since opening. A few of them, like me, had been running him down for their money. All were surprised, angry even to hear that there was actually no money. All were ready to join me at the city council meeting the following evening to confront the Mayor on the issue.

I'd told Kendrick about going out to see Leslie to ask for her help in getting the other side of Potter Lake involved in the protest. He lowered the cup of coffee he'd been drinking and stared at me as if I'd grown horns.

"I heard she was living back at home so I stopped by. Ms. Lee made me the most amazing meatloaf sandwich—"

"Yo, wait. Her mom made you a sandwich? Like, you were at the house long enough to get a meal? She didn't kick you out?"

I wagged my head. "Nah. She didn't invite me inside or anything. We sat on the porch and talked. Her mom came out to say hey. She remembered me from when Leslie and I were at Healy together."

Kendrick and I had been friends since my sophomore year at Healy. He was my roommate, so he'd met Leslie but didn't know her very well. Like me, he'd heard that she'd packed up and followed some guy to Chicago after graduation. That she was back here was as much news to him as it was to me.

"So what did Leslie have to say about the Mayor? Did she defend his shady ass?"

"Nope. The opposite. She's not a fan. I haven't heard from her but I think I've got her on my side."

"Surprising, considering she hates you."

"Hates me?" I waived Kendrick off as if the very thought was ridiculous. "She doesn't hate me. She's just..."

"Still mad?"

"She'll get over it."

"She hasn't yet. It's been damn near fifteen years."

"I don't think she's been mad for all those years. I think she's mad again, now that we've seen each other. Had some words—"

"And now that your shop being open means hers is in trouble."

"And... yeah, there's that."

I propped my elbows onto the armrests of the chair, clasped my hands and rested my chin on my knuckles. "I'm not sure what to expect tomorrow night. I think that's what's bothering me the most right now."

"You mean you might shoot your shot and then have to come back here and still have to deal with the Mayor?"

"Exactly."

"Welp..." Kendrick turned up his cup, downing the rest of his coffee, then tossed it into the garbage can next to the front desk. "How serious are you about running against him? The next election is in October. That's not a lot of time. That's a lot of money and work. And what if you win? What about the shop? What about—"

"Ay!" I held up a hand against the onslaught of questions, trying not to let the nervousness bubble up through my laughter. "Are you trying to stress me into doing nothing? Let's handle one problem at a time. First, I need to know who's going to stand with me at that meeting tomorrow. I gotta talk to Leslie and see if she's going to help me out."

"Yeah, good luck with that, man. You'll need it."

I slid out of the chair and raised a fist to Kendrick. He bumped it and I turned toward my office. TC would be arriving in a few minutes to open the registers and begin the business day. I had a long list of things I needed to take care of around the shop, things I'd been neglecting in the past week, like burnt out light bulbs and having the front windows cleaned, fixing one of the dryers on the Dolls side of the shop.

My list kept me busy for a few hours. I took my time, watched traffic flow in and out, joked with a few customers and even signed a couple of autographs. By early afternoon, I had wasted enough time and put it off long enough. I grabbed my keys and tipped out of the shop, throwing up a peace sign behind me.

"I'll be back," I told them as I walked out of the front door and stepped to the jet black Escalade I'd bought when I retired from basketball. I paid cash for it, because I wasn't sure how long the money I had saved would stretch and the last thing I wanted was to have a vehicle repossessed. Who knew if I'd have to live in it someday?

I pressed the unlock button and heard the alarm and the locks disengage. I climbed into the seat and started her up, then backed out of my reserved space in the strip mall parking lot.

I was being dramatic, of course, about living in my truck. My parents had raised TC and me with a healthy respect for and a good understanding of money. That knowledge turned out to be useful. There were so many things I could spend my money on. And so many more free things thrown at me, left and right. Everybody wanted me to be seen wearing their gear, their clothing, using their equipment, their electronics. In my prime, my endorsement deals were out of control.

It felt funny, at first, having a lot of money. Our family was comfortable but never well off. Even with the rookie cap and paying an accountant and an agent, I was making more than I'd ever dreamt I could, doing something that I loved to do. Certainly making more money than I would have made sitting in classes at Healy, being the star player on a college basketball team and trying to land a moderately paid summer internship.

The chance to go pro came at just the right time. My mom

had just been diagnosed with Multiple Sclerosis and the insurance policy dad carried didn't cover the entire cost of recommended medication and treatments and doctor visits. I was desperate to find a way to help care for her.

I never told Leslie about my mom. She was my best friend, somebody I knew I could confide in, but I didn't want to dump my problems on her. It wasn't up to her to solve them. When the answer came like Manna from heaven, I did what I had to do. Even if what I had to do was hurt someone that had come to mean a lot to me.

I mean... what was she supposed to do, while I was in practice, on the road, playing games? I couldn't ask her to sit at Healy and wait for me to find time to talk to her, or to sneak back to town to see her. Nah. It was better if I just let her go. I thought she'd get over it. She didn't.

It only took about fifteen minutes to cross the lake to the other side of town and arrive at The Curl & Dye. Leslie was running brisk business—the lot outside her shop, with its faded lines and weeds growing up through the cracks, was dotted with cars. I could hear music and female voices and laughter wafting through the front doors, which were propped open with a box fan circulating air.

My mind immediately went to my shop, which was cooled by central air. I dipped my head to step inside, nodding at a few people who were waiting in chairs next to the front desk, reading magazines and sipping on bottles of water.

Tamera and two other girls were at their stations, with customers in chairs. The air was full of the scent of hot curling irons and blow dryers. Leslie was washing hair at the worst makeshift shampoo bowl I had ever seen. It was functional, but the laundry sink cut down with a dip in one side was ugly as hell.

I wasn't trying to down Leslie's shop... it was just so old school, from the photos of 90's hairstyles on the wall to the low-rent air conditioning system to the busted down chairs and the dull, cracked linoleum tiles. Why she wanted to keep the place open was a puzzle to me.

"KC," Leslie called out, loudly to be heard over the music, the dryer and the spray of water. "Come on back." She angled her head, gesturing me over to her.

I walked through to the back of the small shop, feeling like a giant, until I made it to the shampoo bowl.

"Grab me a towel from around the corner over there?"

I turned, dipping my head around the corner to find a stack of folded towels. I grabbed one and handed it to her. She smiled her thanks and lifted the customer's head out of the bowl and wrapped the towel around her sopping wet hair. When it was secure, she helped the woman stand, and then pointed toward her station.

"Have a seat at my chair. I'll be right there."

The woman shuffled away, taking more than a few moments to reach Leslie's station.

"So, what brings you to this side of town?" Leslie sprayed the remaining shampoo suds down the sink as she asked. "And don't even try that 'in the neighborhood' business. You are never in this neighborhood."

"Nah, I came over here on purpose this time. I wanted to know if you'd thought about what we talked about the other night."

She pulled me around the corner, in front of the tall stack of towels. She pulled one off the top and began drying her hands.

"Yeah, I thought about it. Thought about it a lot."

"Okay." I straightened, standing with my feet apart and folded my arms across my torso. "Are you coming to the meeting tomorrow? Are you bringing anyone with you?"

"I'm coming to the meeting tomorrow. Tamera will be there and I'll be bringing a few people, my dad and grandpa for starters. But it won't be to support you or the other side of town."

"Oh?" My brows shot up in surprise. "So what's the purpose of—"

"The purpose would be to show the Mayor that this side of town isn't dead yet, so stop trying to kill us by bringing in modern replacements. Quincy Adams is shady as hell, and has been for a while. I think the city council is afraid of him, but if we can get any reaction on either side of our issue, it'll mean he'll be out of the picture, which will be good for my business and yours. But don't for a minute think we're marching over to that meeting tomorrow to support you. Far from it."

"Les? You okay back here?" Tamera poked around the corner, sticking her nose in where it didn't belong.

"I'm fine Tam. We're just talking about the meeting tomorrow."

"And how we're not going up there to beg Mayor Adams to give him some money?" She gave me the up-and-down glare, pursing her lips into a scowl.

"Your face is gonna get stuck like that," I told her.

She sucked her teeth and uttered, "Boy, shut up," before dipping her head back around the corner.

I chuckled, hiding it behind a hand. "I like getting on her nerves."

"I see that. But please stop it, because after you're gone I have to hear her bitching about you all day and I'm not in the mood."

"I'm surprised you don't join in with her. Y'all been singing in the 'Fuck KC Cavanaugh Chorus' since college."

"Don't get it twisted. I haven't spent all this time thinking about you, if that's what you're getting at. After you left Healy, life went on."

"Ah huh. Okay, well..." I stepped back, putting some space between her and I. I sensed something stirring up and I wasn't sure I wanted to deal with it quite yet. "I appreciate that you want to approach the city council with me."

"Alongside you. With a completely different issue. Related but not the same."

"Alongside me, then."

"So, if things don't go the way you want them to..."

I raised my hands in a sign of surrender. "I'm just trying to think about one step at a time right now. Let's see what happens tomorrow and go from there."

Leslie shrugged, which made her off-the-shoulder blouse shift. One side fell lower than the other, showing off the strap to her tank top and her light brown skin. The ring in her nose, a small gold hoop, was new but it fit her like she'd always had it. Like any respectable hair dresser, her locs were on point, as was... everything about her.

I'd always thought she was the perfect match, a thick snack that was whip smart and funny as hell. I realized, standing in her shop and trying hard to get along with her, that I'd missed her. Some nights I would lay up in a hotel room in some city, or on the bus with the team, or on an overnight flight wishing I could talk to her. Wishing I'd taken the steps to turn us from best friends into something more, but I was... I don't know if scared was the word.

I thought it would ruin everything, make things awkward between us if I leaned over and kissed her. She didn't make a move either, so I was paralyzed.

This cutie from a campus sorority started hanging around and everything I wanted to do with Leslie, I did with her instead. I have few regrets in life, and that was one of them. Because when it came to actually being with Leslie, I wished I hadn't wasted so much time with that other girl. I could have been with Leslie the whole time.

"Anything else you need to talk about? I need to get back to my chair."

She had dumped the towel she used in a basket next to the

washer, then started emptying the basket into the machine. My gaze traveled to her small waist and generously round ass. When she turned around and realized what had my attention, she shot me a glare that wasn't as vicious as she thought it was. She adjusted the shirt to cover her skin again, then propped her hands on her hips. Which was intended to make her seem more hostile, but the pose perked her breasts up perfectly. And I was having a reaction.

"Nah. Just... I'll see you. Tomorrow. At the meeting."

I turned, rushing back through the shop, knowing I didn't make it out of there before parts of my body made it obvious that Leslie still had an effect on me.

ten

. . .

LESLIE

"What are you giggling at over there?" Tamera asked me, finally. I had finished rolling my customer's hair and had set her under the dryer, then returned to my chair and started straightening up. I was still laughing, long after KC had high-tailed it out of the front door. It had been a long time since I could play with someone; that it was KC I was messing with brought me a kind of evil satisfaction.

"Oh, nothing. Just thinking about stuff."

"Funny stuff? Must be, the way you've been laughing."

"She's laughing at that man running outta here with a raging semi," said Evonne.

"A what?" Angela asked, twisting around in Tamera's chair to ask Evonne to repeat herself.

"A semi. You know..."

Angela shook her head, her brows knit in concentration.

"A semi-erection. Leslie gave the man a stiffie."

My skin flashed hot; I was sure I was crimson. "Evonne."

"What? Excuse me for paying attention. I've always paid

attention to Kade Cavanaugh." She pumped a few dollops of moisturizer into the palm of one hand and rubbed her hands together, then smoothed it through her customer's hair while she talked. "My older brother played college ball with him. Everyone at Healy was so proud; we had a watch party so we could see him make his first TV appearance."

I saw the same game, though I'd never admit to watching his NBA debut.

"So, did you ever sleep with him Leslie?"

I wasn't expecting that question. Not at all, and not from Evonne. I was so shocked and caught off guard, I choked on my own saliva. I coughed so hard and turned so red that Tamera had to pull me out of the chair and lead me to the front door of the shop. She grabbed a bottle of water and unscrewed the cap, then handed it to me.

"Here. Drink."

I coughed, hard, then sucked in a lungful of air. "So I can choke on that, too? What's water supposed to do?"

"Girl, I don't know. Folks just always offer water. Drink it, damn."

I gulped down water and paced the sidewalk, intermittently coughing and drinking. I glanced at Tam and she gave me the same look back. We burst into laughter, holding onto each other for support.

"So was that a yes or a no?" I heard from inside the shop.

"Mind your own business, Evonne," I shouted from the sidewalk.

The first time I got drunk, it was at a frat party with KC. I couldn't even look at fruit punch anymore without thinking about that night—bass thumping from cheap bookshelf speakers, the house crawling with people packed wall to wall, too few snacks and too much of what KC told me was "Trashcan Punch". I found out, when I was bent over a trash can puking up my ever loving guts, why they called it that.

Hours later, I woke up with a swollen tongue, a sour

stomach and what felt like a boulder on top of me. It took a few minutes to realize it was KC out cold, lying on half of my body. I wiggled my way out from underneath him and he didn't move, even though he must have been uncomfortable with his feet hanging over the edge of the bed. I grabbed a clean nightshirt and my shower caddy and tiptoed out of the room. The taste in my mouth was making me sick and I wanted to wash off the smell of that party.

When I got back to my room, the desk lamp was on and KC was sitting up, yawning, leaning back on his hands.

"I figured that was you in the shower. I was hoping you didn't drown."

"I'm okay. I don't actually feel... drunk. Just worn out. You?"

He shrugged. "Same. Tomorrow is gonna suck, though."

"We should drink some water. I heard it helps."

I grabbed two water bottles from the dorm fridge my roommate and I kept stocked and handed him one, then climbed up onto the bed next to him. He sucked his down so fast that I handed him mine and he sucked that one down too.

"I never want to drink ever again," I moaned, leaning against him.

He laughed giving me a playful tap with his fist on my shoulder. "Aw come on Les. You held your own for like... an hour."

I wagged my head, wincing. "That stuff was rank. What was in that shit?"

KC laughed and I groaned as he named off what seemed like every kind of alcohol that ever existed, plus Kool-Aid and fruit juice.

"But seriously, you had a real good time. Until you didn't."

"I don't want to hear about what I did or said. I'm sure I acted a fool."

"So you don't want to hear about offering to have my baby?"

"Shut up, KC."

"Aight. But you was saying some nasty stuff. Downright ignorant."

I blanched, wracking my brain. I didn't feel like I was that drunk. I remembered everything—including getting sick, stumbling back to campus with KC, getting to my room and collapsing on the bed. I did not remember asking KC to impregnate me. Though, I wasn't against us practicing. I'd had a crush on KC since the previous year and maybe my subconscious wanted me to make a move.

"I don't know or remember what I said or anything, but what if... I mean, what if I was serious about that?"

His gaze slid over to me and our eyes met. One eyebrow cocked up as he asked, "About having my baby?"

"No. About me and you. You know, me... and you. Together."

"Together," he repeated. "Like... together."

"Yeah. Like... together."

"Like... together, together."

"You can say it five more times and it will still mean the same thing."

He sat up, his back ramrod straight. The air and the mood in the room changed, just like that.

"Uh... so, you feel okay, now?" He crumpled both plastic bottles in his fist. It was something he did all the time but the mere show of strength on top of being the tiniest bit inebriated was a one-two punch that hit me harder than the trash can punch.

"I feel fine. Why?"

He climbed over me, heaving his body off of the bed and slid his feet into his shoes. "So you can have your bed to yourself. But call me if you need me, aight?"

Before I could respond, he had reached the door and pulled it open.

"Night," he whispered, then pulled it shut.

I sucked my teeth and scowled at the closed door. "I don't want my bed to myself," I muttered aloud.

I turned out the desk lamp and laid back in the bed, where KC had laid. Faint strains of his cologne reminded me that he had been there. Right there. I tossed and turned for a while, making a huge show of pretending to try to sleep. Then I sat up, tossing the covers back and crawling out of bed. I grabbed my key and swung open my door, then stomped down the hall to the other side of the floor.

Even if I didn't know him, it was obvious which one was KC's door. It was the one covered with contact paper with a dry erase marker stuck to it. Girls had left messages for him and his roommate, Kendrick. I glared at the names, written in bubbly cursive with hearts over the i's and shit.

I tapped the door, very lightly. Then, figuring that KC was likely dead to the world, knocked louder. I heard a grunt and a thump inside, then fumbling and the door cracked open.

"Leslie? What's up?"

"Nothing. I..." I played with the lanyard hanging around my neck, the one that held my key. The one that hung between my bra-less breasts that I made sure KC was looking at. "I can't sleep."

"So you woke me up?" I heard the laughter in his voice as the door opened and he let me in. I glanced at the other side of the room, making sure Kendrick wasn't in the other bed.

"He's gone for the weekend. You want to sleep in his bed?"

I scrunched up my nose and groaned. KC laughed.

"Just asking. I mean, there's not much room in my bed for sleeping."

"Well, I... I was hoping we could stay up for a minute."

"You really woke me up because you couldn't sleep?" He shook his head, then grabbed his shower kit from the closet. "Be right back. My breath is kicking my ass."

While he was gone, I pulled up the sheets and blankets that he'd been sleeping in and made myself at home on his bed. By the time he came back, I was curled up, my legs folded up under me, leaning up against the headboard.

"So what's up?" He asked, lowering himself to the bed and scooting up so he was sitting next to me.

I shrugged a shoulder and rolled my eyes up to meet his. "I don't know," I mumbled. "I kind of thought... maybe we could talk."

"About?" He asked, his tone low.

"About what happened in my room, earlier. I came on to you and you ran away like I was a hag you wouldn't be caught dead with."

He was quiet, the room full of the sounds of him inhaling and then exhaling. The scent of mint wafted to my nostrils. I never wanted to taste mint so bad in my life.

"It wasn't like that. It's not that I wouldn't want to, Leslie. But..."

I shifted, moving to my knees, then climbed over his lap and sat on his thighs. By instinct, KC's hands moved to grip my waist through the thin cotton nightshirt.

"But... what? You don't think I'm pretty? I'm not sexy, to you? You fucked that sorority girl—she never shuts up about it. I never get more than a hug or a back rub."

"Leslie, it's not that at all. You're... I mean, you're beautiful. You know I think so; I tell you all the time how fine you are. I keep trying to introduce you to my friends, but you turned them all down."

"Maybe I don't want to date your friends, KC." I scooted up on his lap, closer and closer until our bodies made intimate contact. He wore boxers and a sleeveless t-shirt. I felt his heat—and growing hardness through the very thin pair of panties I'd pulled on. I reached out to touch him, to run my hands across his chest and down his arms and back up again. Then I cupped his face and ran my thumbs over his thick, soft lips.

"Maybe I want to date you."

KC's eyes closed and he swallowed audibly. A couple of times.

"I... Leslie, you had a lot to drink and I don't want to take advantage—"

"I'm not drunk," I assured him, tapping his cheek so he would open his eyes. "Look at me. I'm telling you. I'm not drunk. Are you?"

"N-no. But—"

"So I consent. To... whatever."

KC didn't respond. Just sat there like a bump on a log, staring at me. Which made me feel like shit. If he wanted me, he would have been all over me. Right?

I sighed, suddenly sad and embarrassed and feeling utterly stupid. "I can take a hint. Yes to airhead sorority girls. No to smart girls. Got it."

"Whoa, whoa there," he drawled, the Austin, Texas coming out in his voice. He grabbed my hips, pulling me closer. "Where uh..." KC licked his lips and let his eyes wander to the hard nubs of my nipples standing at attention and poking through my nightshirt. "Where you going?"

"Back to my room," I mumbled, making moves like I was really leaving, but hoping he wouldn't let me.

"You woke me up to go back to your room five minutes later? We're talking. See? My lips are moving, your lips are moving. Sometimes my lips might say stupid things. How about your lips?"

"My lips don't say... or do stupid things."

"They don't? So if my lips and your lips met up, that wouldn't be a stupid thing?"

I shrugged, drawing my lips in to hide the smile that wanted to creep across them. But then I realized he wouldn't be able to kiss me that way, so I released them.

"I was thinking," he mumbled, his eyes on my lips. "When you and me were talking, in your room. I was thinking about kissing you. Would that have been stupid?"

I shook my head. And lifted my face to his. "It would be stupid if you didn't kiss me now, though."

"Like... this?" Soft lips fluttered from my shoulder to my neck, up one side, down the other, and then around again.

I shuddered, my temperature rising. "Yeah..." I was barely breathing, my eyelids at half mast.

KC sat up, moving his legs underneath him and pushing me on my back. He stretched out on top of me and settled into the space between my legs, pressing his long rigid hardness into my core. And then his mouth devoured mine.

It took everything in me to suppress a moan and to not buck my hips into his. He knew what he was doing and, truthfully, I was in the mood to lay back and let him do it. Let his hands rub my skin so gently and softly, with such care and tenderness it almost tickled. Let his lips dust me with kisses wherever he pleased, feather soft.

"That good?" He whispered.

I opened my eyes and brought myself out of the pleasurable trance he'd just coaxed me into. "Mmmmmm..."

He smiled down at me, then pulled back to pull his t-shirt over his head. He laid half on, half off of me, his warmth and weight like a heavy, familiar blanket.

"You want to do this, right?"

"Yeah. You do too, right?"

He nodded, dropping a trail of kisses along the side of my neck. "Been wanting to. I didn't think—well, we can talk about that later, but I have some time to make up for."

"You really, really do. You can start by taking these clothes off of me."

"Mmm... tired," he whined, closing his eyes. "You woke me up out of some good sleep. You do it. I'll watch."

I giggled. "I was looking forward to you doing it. I dare you."

He groaned. "Double dare you."

"Now you're getting wild. I haven't turned down a lot of double dares in my life."

"Triple. Dog. Dare you."

"Man... a triple dog dare? You're not playing around Leslie. You wanna be stripped, huh?"

"That was the point of me asking you to take my clothes off, yes."

"Guess I gotta do it then." He sat up and reached toward the head of the bed and pulled down the bedspread and sheets again. He climbed inside, kicking the sheets down, piling up pillows under his head. "Come on, girl. Whatcha waitin' for?"

I'd be stupid not to move. I sat up and crawled across the bed on all fours, closer and closer until my lips met his, until our tongues swirled together and we were, as quietly as possible, moaning in harmony.

I moved up until I was straddling him again. KC's hands spanned my waist, rubbing up and down, the calluses he'd developed on his finger tips and palms wreaking havoc on my nerve endings. Like an expert, he gathered the hem of my nightshirt and pulled it up.

My arms lifted so the shirt came off and landed next to the bed. My nipples stood at attention, puffing up in the cool air of the room. He pulled me toward him so he could take one and then the other into his warm mouth. I struggled to stay quiet, biting down on my lip while his tongue flicked the sensitive tips back and forth. I writhed on top of him, working myself into a heated, trembling frenzy. I wanted KC so very, very badly.

I rose up onto my knees and hooked my thumbs into the waistband of my panties.

"Pull," I whispered.

He obeyed, pulling the thin material down my hips. I kicked out of one side and then the other. They went flying, landing on the other side of the room.

"I have to find those when we're done."

"Okay," he said, laughing.

"I'm serious! What if Kendrick comes home to find some chick's underwear on his side of the room?"

He shook his head, still laughing. "Then he'll know I got some."

"Oh, he'll know anyway. Men don't believe in not kissing and telling."

"You saying I have a big mouth?"

"I'm saying you'll probably tell Kendrick before he even makes it back to campus. Am I wrong?"

KC paused, pondering for a moment, then shrugged and sucked his teeth.

"I'll probably wait at least until he parks the car."

I laughed, out loud. KC covered my mouth with his. Very quickly, as his the tip of his tongue swirled and teased mine, I was lost again in the space between reality and a dream.

"Here," he said, pulling us out of the kiss and bucking up his hips. "Let's give us something else to find." He lifted his hips and pulled his briefs down, then fished them out from between the sheets and tossed them to the other side of the room. "There. Now we both have some skin in the game."

Now there was, blissfully, nothing between us. I felt him, pulsing and red-hot. I knew he was a guy and a particularly strong wind could do the same thing, but I loved imagining that I was doing that to him. Me. Nerdy black girl Leslie Baker made sexy basketball player Kade Cavanaugh throb with sexual desire.

"KC... do you have uhm..."

"Oh," he whispered, snapping his fingers and hopping off of the bed. He opened a cabinet in the set above the desk and pulled out a box, then a few small squares from the box and put it back. Then he picked up one of the squares and ripped it open, pulling out the latex ring and rolling it on.

Sheathed, KC was... impressive. I swallowed hard. A few times. I... I can take that.

KC got back into the bed and laid down next to me, pulling the sheets and blanket over us.

"So, uh. Not that I'm giving advice or anything, but I think you might find it easier if you uh... ride. Just for a few minutes until you're... used to me."

"I'm not a virgin," I protested, like I wasn't nervous about that very thing a few minutes ago.

"I didn't say you were. I just...I'm not trying to brag or anything but I'm a lot. I want you to have control."

"Oh." That made sense. I guessed. "Okay. So I should..."

"Come on over here, girl," he said in an almost growl, the gold flecks in his eyes glowing bright.

Well, since he put it that way... "Yes, sir." I sat up and straddled him, centering myself above him. And, with a moan that was much louder than I intended it to be, sank onto him slowly, feeling my walls stretch to accommodate him.

"Shit, KC..." I whispered with a giggle. He was grinning while biting down on his bottom lip to keep from moaning too loudly.

"Lemme know when you're good," he whispered.

"Oh, I'm good. I'm real..." I shuddered. "I'm real fucking good right now."

KC began to buck his hips in rhythm and time with my movements. Slow, steady. Deeper, deeper. Nothing strenuous. Or loud. At first.

He fit me like a glove, like he was made for me, filling every void oh-so-well. It was like he knew me, knew my body, how to hit a spot to make me squirm or squeal or bite my lip or roll my eyes; how to make my hips twitch and convulse, how to hold out and when to let go. He was showing off, at that moment.

Intensity and the pure joy of being with him won out

over trying to remember that we were in a twin bed on the men's side of a University dorm. The headboard tapped against the wall in rhythm with our movements, but I'd stopped hearing it. My body moved against his, sweat beading up and dripping and mixing and pooling between us.

KC's breaths came in heavy grunts and short, stuttered gasps. He was shaking, he was so close, and then he was there, tossing his head back, arching up and into me, gripping my hips and squeezing hard, letting out a long, hissing breath.

That was all I needed. "Uhhh…*fuck*... I'm coming!"

"Good for you," came a male voice from the other side of the wall. "Some of us want to sleep, so wrap it up!"

I collapsed onto KC's chest in a fit of giggles. It just slipped out, and kind of loud, the declaration that I had reached the climax of all climaxes with KC, who I'd wanted to give me a climax since I'd met him. But I didn't care. I would just have to deal with the inevitable teasing. Or rather KC would have to deal with it, and something told me he wouldn't mind.

He laughed, rubbing my back, muttering in my ear over my moans and deep sighs. "Now this whole side of the floor knows I got some."

"If it wasn't so damn good, I wouldn't have been loud."

"I got bragging rights, though."

I groaned again, rolling off of him and snuggling up next to him, a leg between his, his arm behind me and curling over my waist.

"I didn't ever picture having sex with you, Leslie."

"Sure, you didn't."

"I didn't. I mean, I wasn't planning on making a move. I didn't want to like... mess things up with us. But I'm glad you made a move."

I rolled my head up, putting my lips in perfect position for a kiss. I imagined a wide, post-sex, hazy grin plastered across my face. "Me too."

"And I won the dare, too. Clearly I won all night long."

"Congratulations. Are you kicking me out, or can I go to sleep?"

One arm tightened around me, the other stretched to flip the switch on the light above the desk. "You can't leave. We don't know where your panties are."

What I thought was the beginning of something wonderful between me and my best friend didn't turn out to be so wonderful.

KC was... different. Distant. I couldn't get him on the phone for anything. He was never in his room, wouldn't meet me for lunch, didn't want to hang out at all. He didn't do anything but sit at the library and go to the gym. When we managed to be in the same room, the air was stilted and stiff, like we weren't close anymore, like we hadn't shared something intimate that was meaningful.

I was embarrassed. I had ruined what we had and he wanted nothing to do with me.

A few weeks later, KC asked me to come to his room. I was relieved, thinking that whatever had crawled up his ass since we'd had sex had finally crawled out. He was sitting at a small side table that separated his side from Kendrick's side. I'd brought a box of Mike & Ike's, and sat down across from him, hoping that if I acted normal he would, too.

He started talking, but he wasn't saying anything sweet.

"I wanted to say I'm sorry for not being around. I know I've been off the grid for a minute."

"Yeah, you have. Is... everything okay with you?"

He opened his mouth to answer but hesitated. Then he shook his head.

"No, actually. I uh... I have some news. And I wanted to make sure to tell you in person before it got around."

"Okay." I poured some candy from the box and popped a

few into my mouth. I was disappointed that we weren't talking about the sex we'd had or how we were going to hang out together a lot now. KC didn't look like a teenager halfway in love with the girl sitting across from him. But he did look like he needed to talk. I gestured for him to go ahead and tell me whatever it was he had to tell me.

"Uh, so. I'm... not going to be around much anymore. Well... anymore. I'm packing up and leaving Healy this weekend."

"You're... what? Packing up and.... what?"

"I'm dropping out, Leslie. I have to go home. I have a chance to enter the NBA draft in June. I need to work out, relax my knee, get ready."

"But... if the draft is in June, why do you have to leave now? What about your scholarship? What about this internship we've been working for all year?"

He sucked his teeth. "Girl, you can have that internship. You're winning anyway. I have other things I need to concentrate on. And I want to save my folks some money. My tuition is taken care of but they're paying my dorm fees and my food plan."

"I mean... I don't understand why you have to do this now? While you're in college. The draft is every year, right? It's not like this is the last NBA draft ever, KC."

"Might not be the last draft ever, but in three years, who knows what my knee is gonna be doing? I want the chance to play now, while I have a chance, before it gets worse. I'd rather play awhile and retire from NBA than never get the chance to go because my knee went out."

I was stunned into utter silence. He talked and talked about his dreams and goals and plans of playing for a pro basketball team. I just stared at him, not believing the words I was hearing.

"But Les... I want us to stay in touch, you know what I'm saying? I want us to be friends."

Friends. After we'd given in to (what I had thought was) a mutual longing and mixed our sweat and joined our bodies and had that... intense experience together... he wanted to be friends. All I heard, of course, was *'being with you was cool and all but it wasn't enough to make me want to stay here. I don't want to date you and I'm about to be rich and famous with lots of girls around me but make sure you sit by the phone and wait for me to call.'*

Yeah, no. Fuck all of that and fuck you, Kade Cavanaugh.

"If you leave Healy, drop out of fucking college where you have a scholarship to do this draft bullshit because you're too impatient to wait until you graduate...." I sighed, picking up the box of candy I'd been sharing with him and pulling the strap of my backpack over my shoulder. "Don't bother trying to talk to me. I'm not interested in being your groupie sitting back here at Healy while you're off being an NBA superstar."

His face fell. His expression was so... helpless, almost desperate. He shrugged those big shoulders and quietly said, "Les, I don't know what you want me to say. I have to do this. I thought you would support me on this."

"Well, you thought wrong. Have a nice life, baller."

And unless it was on TV, I never saw him again until I showed up at Kendrick's house that night. It's crazy how life sometimes brings you full circle. Or maybe it was just that in this stupidly small town, you couldn't just avoid a person for the rest of your life.

eleven

. . .

LESLIE

The recreation center was packed, swarming with people from end to end for the city council meeting. The meeting had been moved, at the last minute, to the gymnasium, much to the chagrin of the youth basketball team. Their regular practice was being pushed back an hour, so they were standing around in gym clothes, shooting death glares at everyone milling about, drinking coffee, slowly moving toward a seat.

I spotted KC across the room and kept an eye on him, exactly as I had so many years before at the mixer where I had met him. He looked nice in a sport coat, Guys N' Dolls polo shirt and a pair of well-fitting slacks. A few people from his staff were there too, including TC, all wearing Guys N' Dolls logo shirts and nice pants or jeans. Tam and I had come in whatever we'd thrown on to wear to work. Lucky jeans, a fitted blouse and sandals was going to have to work for the Curl & Dye team.

Daddy and Pops had, thankfully, changed out of their overalls into short sleeved shirts and jeans. The Jessup brothers were sitting behind us, as were Frank Crawford and his sons from Crawford Appliance and Hardware. The word must have gotten around town that folks were supposed to show up at tonight's meeting, because a group of people I'd certainly not spoken to were in attendance—Gerald, owner of the Kwik-E-Mart; Sheila from the Kit Kat Lounge; Ella from Ella's Boutique and about twenty other residents of Potter Lake were loading in and finding seats.

And, of course Earline, who was none too pleased with me. She'd come in to get her hair done earlier that day, more surly and mean than I'd ever seen her. Tamera did her hair and her brows. Earline paid and walked right out, but not before poking a bony finger in my arm and telling me that I ought to be ashamed of myself.

"Your mama and Grandy didn't raise you to go against city leaders. I hope you know what you're doing and what you're putting at risk."

Then she huffed and, her freshly coiffured head held high, marched right out of my salon. Somebody told me that Earline was thinking about moving her standing appointment over to Guys N' Dolls. I laughed and laughed. I really wanted them to mess up her hair and jack up her eyebrows. Really wanted that.

"Let's get started," Jack Cable, head of the city council announced, taking a seat at the table. "We have a full house and we've allocated time on the agenda to discuss a matter put before us by a member of our community. I want to remind everyone that this is an official proceeding. Minutes are being taken and this meeting is being recorded. We will remain civil and discuss our issues peacefully."

He paused, taking a breath to look down at his notes, it seemed. Looked more to me like he was bracing himself.

"Let us begin with opening prayer, followed by the reading of the minutes from the last meeting and the agenda for tonight's meeting."

I bowed my head, as did the rest of the room, while Mr. Cable zipped through the same prayer he always prayed whenever he was asked to. The Lord was probably tired of hearing that same old prayer.

After the formalities, Mr. Cable opened the floor to the first guest on the agenda: Kade Cavanaugh, Owner, Guys N' Dolls Salon.

A low murmur wove through the crowd as KC stood. His shoes made a squeaking sound on the gymnasium floor as he made his way up the aisle to the front, then stood at the podium. He had to bend so far over the microphone that the janitor came to adjust it, raising the stand as high as it could go. KC laid a folio on the podium and opened it, pulling out a page of notes. When he spoke, his voice boomed across the room.

"Good evening, ladies and gentlemen of the Potter Lake City Council. Some of you may know who I am. For those of you that don't, please allow me to introduce myself. My name is Kade Cavanaugh. I attended Healy University. I was drafted to the NBA from Healy and played on several NBA teams before retiring a few years ago."

He paused, clearing his throat and letting the murmurs die down again.

"I've come before you tonight with an issue that I want to make you aware of, if you aren't already. That issue involves the Mayor of Potter Lake. I can't imagine that you don't know what's been going on with my business, with the businesses that have chosen to break ground and build here, but also with the existing businesses in this town."

Mayor Adams sat in his seat, staring at the surface of the table with a scowl on his face. He didn't even have the decency, it seemed, to act contrite or embarrassed. He just looked mad.

KC began to tell the story of how he, and others like him, sat in on a presentation that the Mayor gave about investing in the City of Potter Lake. KC produced the signed contract, the one he'd been told was worthless, for the council to view. He handed it to Mr. Cable and it made its way down one end of the eight person council, and ended up at the other end of the table. A few members, upon viewing the Mayor's chicken scratch signature, had raised eyebrows and questioning glances.

"So, what is it that you're hoping to resolve this evening, Mr. Cavanaugh? The Mayor informed you that the contract was null and void. It was drawn up in fraudulent circumstances and would have never been enforced."

"I was made aware of that, yes. But you have a man in office that swindled more than half of this room—"

"And he's killing the other half," said Pops, struggling to his feet. "May I speak, young man?"

"Please, sir," said KC. "Go ahead."

"I operate Hill Automotive with my son in law. We've been around a good while, been doing good business, towing and repair for the town. All-a-sudden, we not gettin' no more business. Come to find out, the Mayor set up some kinda deal for some Jiffy Lube or Midas or big tow company to come out here and open up shop. I heard tell he's spreading rumors that there ain't nothin' over on the old side of Potter Lake and that just ain't true."

"Yeah," said Daddy, standing. As did Joe Jessup and Frank Crawford.

"I mean, that's the rub. Fine, if you want to expand the town and bring people here. Welcome. More people should mean more business. But don't lie and say there aren't services across the lake. We've got land to build houses on, too. We got grocery stores and ice cream shops and bowling alleys. More than that, we've got people that depend on being able to open up shop, have a good day of business and go home to their families. Frank, back there, he's looking at maybe having to look for work in Healy since the Landry's opened up on the other side of the lake."

"Well, maybe if Frank Crawford wasn't still selling appliances from 1967," shouted a woman from across the aisle. I ventured a guess that she worked at Landry's Hardware.

"Woman, I don't sell nothing from no sixty-seven," Frank shot back. "But most people in this town have older model washers and dryers. You take that thing to Landry's, they'll tell you to drop it off at the dump and wanna sell you a set that cost almost a grand. Don't make no sense. I can repair a washer, dishwasher or dryer, basically any household appliance from 1980 and forward. Fine if you want something shiny and new, but Crawford and Sons is still open and I still want to do business."

I stood, raising my hand and looking directly at Mr. Cable. He'd given up control of this section of the meeting a long time ago. He shrugged his shoulders and waved me forward. I worked my way through the row and up the aisle to stand next to KC, but now the microphone was too tall. He lowered it for me, catching my eye.

"Ladies, gentlemen, business owners and employees. The point of coming to this meeting is not to fight amongst each other. We all have a stake here. Each of us owns a piece of this town, or this town owns a piece of our hearts. We wanted to come here tonight to talk about how the old side of Potter Lake—Jessup Plumbing and Crawford & Sons and Ella's Boutique and Gerald's Kwik E Mart—can continue to thrive alongside all these new business that are popping up. In the middle of this drama, amid all this fighting is one person, telling lies to everyone he comes into contact with. That person has got to go. And if the council knew what he was up to, I'd say y'all got to go, too."

My speech drew applause and shouts of that's right! Uh huh! That's what we talkin' about from the back of the room to the front. People were on their feet, either yelling at the

Mayor about the money they weren't getting or yelling at the Mayor about trying to kill their businesses.

I guess he'd finally had enough. Mayor Adams stood, pulled at his suit jacket, straightened his tie and moved toward the podium.

"The council yields the floor to Mayor Quincy Adams," Mr. Cable announced.

KC and I stepped aside and the Mayor gripped the microphone, pulling it from its stand.

"Now look here," he started, beginning to pace from one side of the room to the other. "Most of ya, I've known a long time. Some of ya are new to Potter Lake. All of ya should know that I don't have any intention, whatsoever, of swindling anyone out of money. Now, I spoke to Mr. Cavanaugh and I apologized for my misunderstanding, for offering him money that wasn't available to be offered. When the city council told me about a fund where we had been setting aside money, I didn't realize that those funds were already earmarked for another project—"

"So why wasn't there a meeting set up where you could tell us all that there wasn't any money?" That was asked by a middle aged gentleman in the second row. His t-shirt had the logo of one of the smoothie shops in the same strip mall as KC's shop. "If we had known that, some of us might not have put so much money into our projects."

"Well, that would have been a problem, wouldn't it? Look, the salon—Guys N' Dolls... y'all are doing good business. I mean, I'm not asking, I've seen the annual business tax reports. Sweet Smoothies is turning a profit. Landry Hardware, Rita's Pita's... all of ya are making money hand over fist, what with new people moving out here every day."

"And that's all well and good for your pet project across the lake," shouted Pops. "Meanwhile, ain't nothing happening over on our side of town. What you got to say about that?"

"Well, the plan was to wait until the new side filled up and people were thirsty for land. And then we could get y'all top dollar for the land you're sitting on. Somebody would come and buy Hill Automotive or Jessup Plumbing—the land and the business. It's worth good money. Just got to be patient enough for it to come to fruition."

KC stepped to the podium, then. "With all due respect, sir, it's obvious these businesses are starving to death. When were you going to present the idea to offer their land up for purchase? I know for a fact that my shop directly affects The Curl & Dye. You were going to let me kill Leslie's shop before you offered her money for her land?"

"Uh... I... I mean, I... didn't have an exact plan," he sputtered. "It... it was an idea-"

"That was never presented to city council," said Eugene, my client Angela's husband. I cringed when I looked at his hair. That Guys N' Dolls cut did nothing for the shape of his head. "You've been freewheeling for a long time, Mayor. Running roughshod over this town and it looks like people are sick of it."

"Well, here is the thing," said Mayor Adams, drawing himself up taller, yelling to be heard above the growing din in the room. "Thing is, I'm the Mayor. Thing is, I'm an elected official. Thing is, none of ya can run this town like I can, like I have for the last good while. On the whole, Potter Lake is pretty good. Thing is, what's past is past. I'm done talking about this issue, now. What we need to talk about right now, is how to move on."

He replaced the microphone in the stand and waddled back to his chair, dropped into it and resumed scowling at the table.

"Uh, let's take a recess," suggested Mr. Cable. "And then we will continue with the agenda and the discussion of street lamps and traffic signals. Reconvene in twenty minutes."

He slapped the surface of the table and stood, then walked straight out of the room. I didn't blame him.

"I guess that's it for our piece," said KC. He picked up his folio from the podium and inserted his notes, then closed it and tucked it under one arm.

"Yep. And the Mayor basically gave us the one finger salute and said we could kiss his ass."

"That he did," said KC, nodding deeply. "So. What's the plan, now?"

KC viewed the crowd that was already dispersing and thinning out. People from both sides of the lake were mingling and talking, shaking hands and exchanging business cards. He returned his gaze to me, the gold flecks in his eyes glowing.

"I'll be damned if I kiss that man's ass. How about you?"

"Wouldn't dream of it."

"I hoped you'd say that. Can we talk?"

twelve

. . .

KC

A small crowd of people milled around the front of the recreation center building, random conversations falling on my ears in snippets. I'd told Kendrick and TC that I had plans after the meeting, so they had already headed out. I watched Leslie walk Tamera to her car, no doubt breaking the news that she and I were going somewhere together.

I saw Tam's head pop up, then she shook her head, then seemed to sigh in resignation and got into her car. After Tamera drove away, I led Leslie to the truck and let her in on the passenger side. Once she was settled, I jogged around the front of the truck and got in. I backed out of the space, weaving around cars and people, making my way to the street.

The recreation center was an older building on the other side of Potter Lake, so I headed towards the bridge.

"Where are we going?" Leslie asked.

"This place that I like over near me. It's called Thai Bistro. Have you ever been there?"

"You know good and well I haven't."

I laughed. "Now how do I know that? You think I stalk you? You think I've been paying attention to where you go?"

She propped an elbow up on the windowsill and fixed her gaze to the scene outside the window. "Just drive, KC."

It didn't take long for us to pull into Thai Bistro. The place wasn't busy at all, which was why I liked hanging out there so much. I didn't want to sit in a loud lounge trying to talk over music.

The hostess led us to a booth at the back of the restaurant. We each ordered a Coke, lots of ice. Leslie pulled the dessert menu out of its holder at the end of the table.

"You must come here a lot. The waitress acted like she knew you."

I chuckled, tilting my head. I was trying to figure out if Leslie was being funny or not. "When your face was all over ESPN for ten years, everyone thinks they know you. But yeah, I come here a lot with Kendrick and Monica and some-times my sister."

"Monica is Kendrick's wife?"

I nodded. "They met at Healy, after I left. Been going strong ever since."

Leslie got quiet... melancholy. Her gaze dropped to the surface of the table and she had stopped fiddling with the dessert menu.

"We should clear the air, I think. I feel like we have a lot to talk about."

Finally. "Nothing would make me happier. What do you want to talk about?"

"Well, first off, I had to find out about your mother's MS diagnosis in some Sports Illustrated interview. You said you found out when you were in college. So when we knew each other. Why didn't you tell me?"

"It just... hit me pretty hard. I couldn't really talk about it, and we didn't disclose family business outside of the family.

MS symptoms are flighty... it comes and goes, hides under a lot of different ailments. But when they said, for sure, it was MS, it just felt like... like they put an end date on her life. You know what I'm saying?"

She nodded, slowly, her lips in a downturn. I knew her grandmother was laid up at a nursing home due to a stroke, so maybe she got where I was coming from. It never really occurred to me that it would hurt her that I'd never told her, but her eyes told me differently. I should have told her.

"My parents hadn't been saying anything but they were in debt, just from years of trying to find out what was wrong with her. And then the diagnosis came and her doctors were talking about treatment programs and medications and MRI's. It about broke my dad. I just saw the dollars adding up. It was stressful."

"But you and me were close, KC. Were we really friends at all if you couldn't tell me that's what you'd been dealing with? That's why you were so distant and cold to me?"

The waitress arrived, bringing our drinks and napkins. She was chipper and cheerful as people tend to be around me. I gave her about ten minutes before she asked for an autograph and a selfie.

And then about one minute before the photo showed up on Facebook and Instagram and my notifications went nuts. Some days, nobody knew who I was. I could move around town easily and not get any attention. And then some days it was hard to just leave the house and go to the grocery store without being approached for a signature, for a picture or some kind of story.

"I didn't really know what was up, you know? Not enough to get my feelings together to talk about it. I went for the draft on the chance that I would get picked up. I got lucky with a couple of really good offers and I went with the team that offered the most money. I sent that money home to pay off bills."

"Don't you regret leaving college to go play basketball? I mean, now you're out here in your 30's and you don't even have a degree. You own a barbershop and a truck."

I chuckled. "You have a degree and you're not doing much better. But if you just have to know, I do alright. I paid off my parent's house. They're selling it and building a new one. Cavanaugh General Contracting is debt free. My mom is comfortable and her treatments are taken care of. TC lives in a house that I bought her. She's debt free, student loans been paid off. I own the unit next door. I don't ever have to worry about money if I don't want to. And yeah, I own a salon that's making money hand over fist. Regrets?" I shook my head, a sardonic grin on my lips. "Like I said, I do alright."

I watched a blush creep up Leslie's chest to her neck and take over her face. I'd pissed her off and I knew it, but she tried to jab me, like that piece of paper made her better than me.

"Sorry," I threw out, before she could snap at me about it. "I know the salon is a sore subject, but you brought it up."

"I did," she said quietly. "I shouldn't have."

"I tried to reach out to you, to tell you about my mom. I wanted to keep in touch with you. Everything was returned to me. You never called, you never wrote."

"I was mad."

"In one of my letters I said that I wanted to talk to you about something and asked if you would call me. That's when I was going to tell you about my mom. We knew more and had more information and I was ready to share. That was right before I did that Sports Illustrated spread." I shrugged my shoulders. "But you never called."

"I know, KC. I was wrong for that. And if it means anything all these years later, I'm sorry. I wish I could have been there for you."

I held my tongue for a few moments. I was trying to stop

snipping and starting arguments, so I waited until I was sure a smart ass remark wasn't on the tip of my tongue.

"It actually means a lot to me. Thank you."

"So, you running off halfway through our sophomore year had nothing to do with us sleeping together?"

"I didn't run off, first of all. That decision was calculated. I put a lot of thought into it. And second, me leaving Healy had nothing to do with you and everything to do with me needing to contribute to my family's financial situation. I had a chance to make a huge dent in those bills before they bankrupted my dad."

"Okay," Leslie said, a hint of something... sympathy maybe, at the edge of her voice. "I get it. I just wanted to get that off of my chest. Have wanted to get that off of my chest for a long time."

"Well, now you have. How do you feel?"

She shrugged her shoulder and started playing with the dessert menu again. She wanted to smile, I could tell. "Fine, I guess."

I unwrapped my straw and dunked it into my glass, sucked it down about half of it and then pushed it away, stifling a belch behind a fist. Leslie unwrapped her straw and dunked it into her glass, sucking slowly and deliberately. I think she was doing that shit on purpose.

"I don't know why you're acting like you have manners," she said, between sips. "The KC I know would drink that down and then burp in my face."

"I'm trying to get you used to being around me again before I let my true gross nature hang out."

"I know it's lurking, right on the edge. Might as well be yourself."

A beat of silence passed, then she asked the question I knew was coming. "So, how do you feel about tonight's meeting?"

"Half and half, good and... so-so. I achieved what I set out to do, which was to expose the Mayor to the city council. Something tells me they all know he's a crook but he's the only person that has signed up for the job for the last 20 years and clearly no one feels fit to run against him."

"Are you serious about throwing your name into the ring?"

"I might be. I don't see anyone else stepping up to the plate. What's going to stop Mayor Adams from doing something else in the next couple of years that affects the business owners of this town? He's thinking about money. He's thinking about himself and not about the people that live here."

"It's nice that you have realized that there are real people that live here."

"I always knew that real people live here. I'm real and I live here. Kendrick is real, Monica is real, TC is real. I see customers that come in and out of my shop everyday that are real. Folks I run into at the grocery store and the hardware store and when I'm just hanging out at the recreation center trying to get in a game of basketball. They're all real." I paused, catching Leslie's eye. "You're real."

"I am. I live here and have a livelihood."

"And I'm not trying to take that away from you, for the millionth time. If what I have to do to secure my future and yours and everyone else's is to step up to the plate and make sure that Mayor Adams doesn't have a controlling hand anymore, I'm going to have to get up the nerve to do that. But I don't think I can do that without your help."

"Me?" She reared back in faux shock. "You're the one that's going to be running for office."

"You are my connection to the town of Potter Lake. The heart of this place. Everybody knows you, everybody loves you. If you support me, I feel like people will listen to you and follow your lead. We could join forces, go at this together. Me from my side, you from yours."

But Leslie's head was already shaking. "KC, I'm not sure that I have it in me to bang the drum for you. I'm supposed to tell people to take a chance on you? To remove their support from a man they have known for so many years and put the future of the Potter Lake in the hands of someone who has zero political experience and no history with this town?"

"I have history with this town."

"You have history with Healy. If there's one thing you need to learn about Potter Lake, it's that we don't want to become Healy."

"But see, that's why I need you on my team. I need someone that knows this place, that has some kind of influence. Somebody that can speak to my intentions. You know in your heart, Leslie, that I'm not trying to kill any part of this town. Mayor Adams is like a wild dog off leash. Things will get worse if we don't at least try to remove him from office."

"Unfortunately, you're right. I think tonight's meeting opened a lot of eyes. Especially since the Mayor basically said I did it, and y'all ain't gonna do nothing about it."

I grabbed my glass, which was so cold that it had sweated a puddle of condensation around it. I used the napkin to sop up the puddle.

"I really can't stand to sit back and do nothing about it. If there's someone more qualified that wants to run against him, I'll throw all my support behind them. But if there's nobody else, I'm going to do it."

Leslie wore her heart on her sleeve, always had. I could always tell what she was thinking by just looking at her. I watched her expression turn from peaceful to nervous, anxious twitching. She sucked in her bottom lip and her eyes became shifty, focusing on everything but me. I reached across the table and looped my finger around one of hers, wanting to touch her but not freak her out.

"I'll give you some time to think about it. All the time in

the world if you need it. But if I do this, I could really use your help. I'm not demanding an answer right now—"

"I'll do it." Leslie began nodding. And kept nodding as if she was trying to convince herself that this was the right thing to do. "I'll do it. I'll help."

Leslie

People are going to think I'm crazy. That exact thought rolled through my head on an endless loop as I sat in the passenger seat of KC's truck. I just kept thinking, over and over. People are going to think I'm crazy. And by people, I meant... everyone I knew.

I hadn't been paying attention to where we were going. I assumed KC was taking me home, but he pulled into the driveway of a beautiful two-story brick duplex. The garage door slowly yawned open and an overhead light popped on. The place was neat and organized, I noticed, as he pulled inside.

"Where are we?" I gripped the handles of my small purse and shoved my hand inside for my cell phone.

KC opened his door, causing the dome light in the truck to glow. He glanced over at me, then rolled his eyes. "What, you think I brought you somewhere to hurt you?"

"Never know. You NBA types sometimes get to acting entitled."

"Oh, now I'm an NBA type?"

"Aren't you, former Point Guard for the Baltimore Herons?"

He huffed out a laugh. "This is my place, Leslie. I wanted to show you where I live, since you have ideas about what I own, what I'm into. TC lives right next door. I can call her and have her come over if you're uncomfortable."

I shook my head, feeling dumb. Sort of. I knew KC and I knew he'd never hurt me. But it also never hurt to be cautious.

"So you coming in or what?"

"I guess," I grumbled, popping open the door latch on my side and hopping down from the truck. I walked around to the interior entrance and waited for KC to open the door and turn off the alarm. We stepped into a modern, spacious kitchen. Not understated in the least, but not gaudy either. Granite countertops, dark wood, stainless steel appliances, a large 12 person table with stately white fabric covered chairs.

I followed slate grey hardwood floors past the kitchen and dining room toward the front door, which split the house right and left. To the right, a formal living room with expensive looking furniture and an enormous saltwater fish tank that gave the room an ethereal blue-green glow. Floor-to-ceiling windows were covered by shades and curtain sheers.

KC swiped his thumb across a screen built into the wall and it lit up. He pressed a button and the shades started to roll up, showing off a great view of the growing but still sparse subdivision.

"It's called Smart House technology. I invested in it after they showed me what it can do. The whole place can be controlled by these panels. Got 'em all around the house. That's my favorite part. My dad's too."

"Oh, I bet. Y'all probably stood around grunting and pressing buttons, as men do."

KC laughed. "Should have seen him when it was being installed. I know he's bid it out on a couple of jobs since then and they're putting it in the new house they're building. Mom needs something on one floor, with wide hallways and doorways, because of her wheelchair. He's having the panels installed, but at wheelchair height and also voice responsive, so she can control things herself and she doesn't have to lift a finger if she doesn't want to. Or can't."

He was so... casual and matter of fact, talking about his mother and her illness. His words were stabbing me right in the heart.

"So... your mom is..."

"Declining," he answered plainly. "Not, you know, dying or anything. It's just... she's been living with MS for a long time so we've been expecting it, you know? We're trying to make things as easy for her as we can."

I never met KC's parents. They came to Healy once, but I was off campus and they had left by the time I made it back. I had heard a lot about them, though. Enough to love Gladys and Kelvin Cavanaugh, sight unseen.

"This is the room I hang out in the most," KC said, forcing a little lift and light to his voice.

I followed him to the right, into a much more lived in space. A plush grey couch with multi colored throw pillows and matching ottomans took up more than half the room, across from the biggest flat-screen TV I'd ever seen in my life. The thing looked like he'd stolen it from a theater.

"Well, that is not a tiny ass TV," I joked.

"It sure isn't."

On the walls were framed, blown up images of KC mid-play on all of his teams. I recognized the Lakewood Wildcats and Baltimore Herons uniforms. Not that I'd been paying attention.

"You want something to drink?" KC headed to a corner of the room, where there was a cooler stuffed with beverages. "TC keeps me stocked over here. I got Vitamin Water, Smart water, soda... you like iced coffee?"

"What kind?"

He shrugged. "That Starbucks stuff in the glass bottle. TC keeps it here for her and Monica when they come watch movies."

"Uh... can I just... pick something?"

He stepped aside, letting me peer into the cooler and grab a Starbucks caramel latte. "She won't be mad if I take this?"

"Nah. She'll take money from me and buy more."

I popped open the bottle and took a long, cool swallow. "Ahhh... that's good."

KC had been staring, I realized as I lowered the bottle. I blushed a little when he said, "Yeah. Looked it. So anyway... come have a seat."

I trailed him to the couch and sat down, sinking into the softness of the furniture. It was springy but firm, comfortable and enveloping but I didn't feel like I was about to be swallowed up in it.

"Wow, KC. This couch. Wow."

He grinned, sitting next to me, toeing off his sneakers and bringing his feet up to the ottoman. He stretched one arm behind me and lifted a bottle of Vitamin Water to his mouth with the other. I drank my iced coffee, looking around the room that was like a shrine to his old life.

"You probably get asked this a hundred times a day, but do you miss the court?"

He started to nod, then grimaced. "That right there makes a hundred times today that I've been asked that. Nah, I mostly miss being on a team, traveling, playing for TV cameras, whatever. I was kind of a ham."

"Yes, you were," fell out of my mouth before I could stop myself from saying it. But he was. KC knew where the cameras were at all times and managed to get his face in one at every open opportunity. The headline wasn't usually by how much whatever team he was on won or lost; it was about whatever gesture or expression KC showed the crowd that night.

"See, I knew you followed my career. You're not as cold and uncaring as you want to seem."

"It's not like I could help it. Those first two years, everyone at Healy went crazy. You're all anyone talked about."

"But you didn't have to keep watching."

"I sort of did. My ex was a fan, since you both went to Healy and all. You were on all his Fantasy teams."

"Oh yeah?" He nodded, halfway smiling. "That's wassup. Did he know that you knew me?"

"Yeah. That's why he wanted to date me at first. He was always trying to see if he could get tickets to a game if your team was playing in Chicago. I told him I didn't know you like that. I couldn't just ask you for tickets."

"You could have just asked me for tickets. You did know me like that."

"I know," I said, lifting the bottle to my lips, trying to hide a smile. "He didn't have to know that."

"So what happened with him? Y'all broke up and you moved back here. Just showed up is what I heard."

"Is that what you heard?" I rolled my eyes and shook my head. "Try having a private life in this town. That's one thing you'll have to remember if you're planning on running for office. These people already know everything about you, from what percent of milk you drink to what size jockeys you wear."

"Jockeys?"

"Hanes. Fruit of the Loom. Whatever kinda undies you got on, they already know what color they are."

"Do they know what color undies you have on?"

I choked on my coffee, trying not to laugh. "I mean...they might."

"Well then, I'm jealous. 'Cause then everybody knows but me."

I didn't know what to say to that. So I didn't say anything. I drank my coffee and stared straight ahead at the flashes of light moving across the muted TV.

"So you're not going to tell me what happened to old dude?"

"Why do you want to know, KC?"

"Call it morbid curiosity. I want to know what he did wrong. I want to know how two men let your fine ass get away from them."

I snorted. "Flattery will get you everywhere, Kade Cavanaugh."

"Everywhere?" he asked, eyebrows high on his forehead. "Like... everywhere?"

"Except there. Stop flirting, Mr. NBA. You must miss the groupies."

"Aw, here we go. Why does every woman bring up the groupies? Y'all jealous or something? At least they're bold, they step up, they shoot their shot."

My eyes rolled as I snickered. "Been there, tapped that. Remember?"

"How could I forget? You've brought it up twice."

"Whatever," I said, but mentally chastised myself. I did bring it up both times. Maybe I wanted to see if he remembered. Why, though? I needed to change the subject. In a hurry. "So the KC I know always has candy. You brand new now, or what?"

KC grinned. "Look at you, thinking you still know me. Check it out, though. That ottoman right there in front of you? The top flips open."

I flipped up the lid to the ottoman and almost cried at the sight. The hollowed-out space was full of candy—and not that new, modern stuff. The candy we used to eat back in the day when we'd hang out... Red Vines, Mike & Ikes, Jujubes, and the like.

"TC must stock this up too."

"She knows I like to lay here and watch movies and eat candy."

Wistful and lost in nostalgia, I grabbed a package of Red Vines and ripped them open, then pulled out a long twist and bit off the end.

"I know," I said, my teeth blissfully stuck together. "Me too."

KC turned on a movie but we were ignoring it. I had made myself comfortable on the couch, kicked off my sandals, tucked my feet up under me and angled toward him. KC had one leg tucked under him and one leg stretched out on the ottoman.

"Does your knee hurt?"

"A little," he answered, rubbing it with his palm. "Might be about to rain."

"Oh, you're one of those people, now."

"Maybe my knee could get me a job at the local news station."

"Maybe you should run for weatherman. Clyde ain't been right about the weather in twenty years."

"So you're really not going to tell me about what's his name, huh? You're just going to keep changing the subject, thinking I forgot about it?"

I bit off another Red Vine and chewed. "I was kind of hoping you would."

"Nope. What was his name?"

"Dexter."

"Dexter," he repeated, adding a certain...air to the name. "Dexter sounds like a guy that wears suspenders and glasses and high-water pants."

"So... Steve Urkel?"

"Yeah. In my mind he looks exactly like that. So was he?"

"No," I answered, laughing hard. "I'm not the kind of girl that would go for that. He was actually very cool, for a Finance and Business major."

"Hold up. I was a business major."

"I know. And I know you saw the upperclassmen in those majors. They all look like Urkel."

"I wouldn't have looked like Urkel. I would have been...Urquelle," he finished, referencing the nerdy Steve Urkel's suave and debonair alter ego.

I knew he was going to say that, so I was already laughing.

"So anyway. Urkel. Dexter. What he do? I don't mean for a living. I mean how did he get sent to the pokey?"

"Dexter..." I began. "Let's say he didn't start out that way but it turned out that he was... shady."

"Okay, let's say that. But then let's say more."

"I didn't know the depth of his involvement. I tried not to know a lot. There was some kind of fraud scheme with their investment firm. He definitely turned a blind eye to it, profited from it."

Everyone had finally stopped asking about what happened in Chicago, what happened to my job and my boyfriend and my relationship. Tamera knew, because she flew up to Chicago to pack me up and drive me back. The last thing I wanted was my past flying around Potter Lake.

"Dexter's partner was running a scam, taking money from certain investors and not investing it, but using it to pay off someone else. Or pocketing it. Or spending it. And then creating dummy records for money that wasn't even invested. How he thought he could get away with it, I don't know. Too smart for his own good."

"Well, he didn't get away with it, did he?"

"Well, he's in prison, so no. Dexter took bonuses, knowing the firm wasn't performing at a rate that would merit that kind of payout above his salary. Then the SEC showed up, asking questions. They told Dex he was culpable, and that he could go to prison for longer if he didn't cooperate and testify against his partner. I was terrified, and I confided in Tamera. She got on the next flight, rolled into our apartment, started packing stuff into suitcases and boxes. She was like... what's that character that's like a tornado?"

"Taz? Tasmanian Devil?"

"Yeah. That. She came in on a Thursday. By Sunday, we had shipped most of my stuff back to Potter Lake and she and I were in the car headed back here. She thought I could be implicated and it was better that I left before things even really got started. Some of the stuff Dexter bought me, I had to leave in the apartment. I didn't want to take anything that they could hunt me down and ask questions about."

"Wow. Have you ever heard from anyone?"

My mind rolled back to the day I opened the front door to find a man in a dark suit, wing tips and mirror shades standing on the front porch. My first thought, I remember, was am I gonna have to do hair in prison? But it was just Dex's slick ass attorney trying to sweet talk me into coming back to Chicago.

"His attorney wanted me to come up and speak on his behalf at the sentencing. I declined. Never heard from them again."

"So he's gone. How long is he gone for?"

"Mmmhmmm," I hummed, nodding while I finished off the strand of licorice. "Six years."

"Damn, girl. Getting involved with criminals. Running from the law. You're different, Leslie. You're wild."

"I'm not wild! And I'm not different. I'm the same Leslie you knew back at Healy."

"Nah..." He shook his head, a more serious expression clouding his face. "You're different. But good different. Older. More mature. More...grown and sexy..."

I watched his eyes roam my body, even curled up as it was on the couch.

"KC...stop it."

"What I do?"

"Just... don't go there."

"Why not? Huh? Why not, Les?"

It wasn't that I was uncomfortable. It was that.... I was... uncomfortable. The look in his eyes made me believe he wanted me. I got in trouble with that line of thinking before and I wasn't going down that road again.

"I should be heading home," I said, uncurling myself from the confines of a really comfortable couch and using a toe to pull my sandals closer to me. "You have a staff to open your shop, but I don't, so..."

"I'm not gonna put up with too many more snide comments about my shop, Les."

I laughed, sliding my foot into one sandal and then the other and tightening the straps around my ankles. "Them's the breaks, KC. You made your bed, you get to lie in it."

I pushed myself up from the couch, then watched him slowly get up, taking care to not over-exert his knee.

"So what's up with the knee?"

"It hurts," he quipped, bending over to shove his feet into a pair of giant black sneakers. "It hurt when I met you. Remember?"

"Yeah. But I also remember you've had surgery. Multiple surgeries. How does it still hurt?"

"Surgery doesn't make pain go away. I mean, in theory it should, but it's still injured, just not the same as before. Every injury forces me to change how I play to compensate. Those concessions make me susceptible to further injury. I hurt it, had surgery, went through rehab. Then I reinjured and..." He blew out a long, loud breath, shaking his head. His keys jingled in his hand as he led me out of the house and back to the garage.

"KC?" I heard a female voice call from outside. He stepped to a door that, I guessed, led to the back of the house.

"That you?"

He pushed the door open and poked his head out of the small opening he'd made. "Who else would it be? What are you doing out here?"

"Having a drink, talking to Monica on the phone. The baby is giving her heartburn. Where are you about to go?"

"I'm about to run Leslie home. I brought her over to show her the place. I'll be back."

"You brought who? To show what?"

"I'll be back," he said, pulling the door shut again. "So that small town thing you talked about? She is my small town. I can't do nothin' without her, Monica and Kendrick knowing about it. Then I get a call from my parents wanting details." He opened the passenger side door and helped me up into the truck, then shut it and came around the driver's side. "When I was about to switch teams, I damn near had to call them first, otherwise I'd hear all about how they had to find out on ESPN."

"At least they care. They're concerned and interested."

"Yeah. I guess." The garage door slowly rose, revealing the half built house across the street. KC backed out of the garage, then pulled forward, heading for the subdivision exit. "But if that's how a person shows they care, you didn't give a half a shit, Leslie."

"I already apologized for that, KC."

"I'm still mad about it."

"Well, you're going to have to get over it."

"I think not. Somebody just told me that I made my bed and now I get to lay in it. I think you get to just deal with me mentioning, all the time, how you did me dirty until I'm done complaining about it."

I chuckled. "Fine. If that's how you want to play it. Though I should remind you that you need my help, Mr. Trying to Run for Mayor."

"And you need mine, Ms. You're Taking my Business."

Potter Lake didn't have a lot of street lamps. That had been on the agenda for discussion at the city council meeting that evening, along with stop signs and traffic lights. That meant the late night drive was quiet and dark, with few headlights accompanying us on the road. And lots of time to think.

We had each other over a barrel... the same barrel. My business needed him to back off and send my customers back to me. He needed me to help him win the favor of half the town. I needed to forgive him for dropping us at the first opportunity. And he needed to forgive me for being hurt about that.

We had a lot of work to do.

thirteen

. . .

KC

"So for regular cuts, or a wash and trim, it's cool for the ladies to get their hair done here. Chemicals, color, anything real fancy, anything you'd have done at a spa like nails, brows, wax, stuff like that? Let's send them over to the Curl & Dye. Any questions?"

"Yeah, I got a question." Tracey piped up with her hand raised high in the air. Her hair was platinum blonde, which was striking against her honey-brown skin tone. Her cupid's bow lips pursed in a scowl and her arched brows were knit together. I knew she'd have something to say. She always had something to say.

"Let me head you off at the pass," I offered, both hands raised to quiet the murmurs. Tracey lowered her hand and assumed her previous pose, arms tightly folded across her ample chest. "The owner over at Curl & Dye is going to be working with me on a project. You'll find out more in the coming weeks, but she's doing me a favor. I'm doing her one back. The Dolls side of the shop isn't the earner I want it to be.

I don't have enough stylists that can work with chemicals to confidently staff that side of the shop. So for now, keep it simple."

I paused to direct the next comment directly at Tracey. "I know you can do a mean military cut and a nice fade, so feel free to grab a customer from the Guys side if your chair is getting slow. It's not like it's pink and frilly over there. It's the same setup, just the other side of the shop."

Tracey seemed pleased with the compromise that she could cut on whichever side she chose. At least, she didn't argue when I made the suggestion. I scanned the room, trying to catch the eyes of the staff I'd gathered for a quick pre-opening meeting. Most of them looked bored, which I expected. The announcement didn't affect them, really. I only had a few female stylists and it looked like they were relieved to not have to work with chemicals. Only Tracey, who liked to show off her skills, seemed upset.

"Any other questions? Problems? Issues or concerns?"

Erik's hand appeared in the air. I propped my hands on my hips and cut my eyes at him. That boy was foolish as anything and I didn't have time for his jokes today.

"What, man? Is it a real question or are you wasting our time?"

"It's a real question! Dang. So..." Erik rubbed his dry palms together and shot me a look that told me he was about to ask a stupid question. "I heard you been knowing that Leslie chick. Is that true? And y'all been hanging out a lot lately. So, we're like... doing favors for your girlfriend?"

"Heard that, did you? Well, unhear it, because it's none of your business. Next question."

I rolled my eyes at Erik's hand in the air again. "What, man?"

"Okay for real, for real. I heard you're running against old man Adams in the fall. What's up with that?"

I dipped my head, glancing at the toes of my sneakers.

When I lifted my head, I had a shop full of very interested staff members, all paying rapt attention.

"That's something I'm looking into and that's what Leslie is helping me out with. That's why us sending business over there is good for us both. That's all I'm willing to say, until things are official. Alright?"

I clapped my hands together, ending the meeting. "Let's cut some hair."

Hours later, the sound of a basketball on the rec center court was music to my ears. The echo of the rubber bouncing against the hardwoods resonated with me, down to the soles of my ball shoes. I'd gotten a new pair from Aris, the sportswear brand that I still repped—not just shoes but activewear as well. I wanted to test them out, so I asked Kendrick to play me.

Kendrick was a good player, as good as I was back at Healy, but decided to forego the draft for his degree, figuring he could try again after graduation. Then he met Monica and a life on the road playing ball wasn't his dream anymore. I'd told him to keep his skills up, though, because when I came off the court, I was coming for him. We played at least once a week, and then on a basketball league with a very loose game schedule.

When I asked Kendrick to "run me", he knew exactly what I meant. I wanted to be dripping sweat and breathing hard when we were done playing.

Kendrick was playing light tonight. And it was getting on my nerves. He began a lazy lay-up but I jumped and grabbed the ball mid-air and held it, wedged between my arm and my body.

"You got something on your mind? Is it Monica? The baby? The shop? What?"

Kendrick pulled up the hem of his shirt and wiped the nearly non-existent sheen of sweat from his face. "Play the ball, man."

"You're not even sweating hard and we've been out here for an hour. What's up, K?"

"Nothin' man. You want me to play harder? You got it. Send me the fuckin' ball."

"Man..." I slammed the ball to the ground hard, sending it flying toward the other side of the gym. "Fuck this ball. You got something to say. Just say it."

Kendrick paced for a few seconds, then stopped, hands at his waist. "Aight. so...Guys N' Dolls is our shop. You know? It's you and me in business together. It's how I feed my family, man. I guess I don't feel comfortable with how close you seem to Leslie, seeing as how we compete with her for business and the Dolls side of the shop isn't doing the numbers we want it to do. I know y'all go way back. But I also know you feel guilty about how this has gone down."

He moved a few paces away, then stopped. "And uh. I knew you liked her, back at Healy. You tried to keep in touch with her and it didn't work out, and you feel like this is some kind of second chance at her but—" He used his t-shirt to wipe sweat from his forehead again and rolled it back down.

Stalling. "Just... don't jeopardize the shop for some nostalgic pussy. That's all I'm saying."

My head tilted toward him, just slightly. I wanted to make sure I heard every syllable from his slick mouth. "Did you just call Leslie nostalgic pussy? Did I hear that right?"

"I mean, I don't mean any disrespect to her..."

"You called her nostalgic pussy. I think that's plenty disrespectful."

Kendrick shrugged, staring at the floor.

"Is there an apology coming, or do I have to step to you? Because I will."

"Alright, alright," he said, his hands raised in surrender. "I'm sorry. That was over the line. But I mean, that right there proves it. You're pissed I said that. Because you do care about her."

"So what?"

"So... it's a conflict of interest."

"No, it isn't. It's one friend helping out another."

"I believe that's what you want it to be. But KC, man...if that shop was owned by anyone but Leslie you wouldn't give a rat's ass about what happens to it."

"You're right. But it's not owned by anyone else. It's owned by someone I care about. Someone who's going to help me change the future of this town, so if I have to send her the business she can do better than me, then okay. I can do her that favor. Is this going to be a problem?"

He shook his head, but the taut line of his lips said otherwise. "Not if it means my job. I'm just there to cut hair."

"Wrong. You're my head barber. You teach, supervise, and lead. You support the vision. The shop isn't going anywhere, Kendrick. This isn't going to kill us. We're doing great, to be honest. You're not going to cut fewer heads. You know this, right?"

"Yeah. I know. I just—"

"You're concerned. I appreciate and welcome that. But I also need you to trust that I know what I'm doing. I would never put your livelihood at stake, man. Not with my niece coming soon."

That got the smile I was hoping for. Kendrick was out of his mind with anticipation of his daughter's arrival.

"So. Trust you. Follow your lead. Send our business out the door." He turned to rescue the ball from where it had wedged itself between the wall and the bleachers. He jogged back, dribbling across the court. "If my clientele drops by even one person, I'm taking it outta your ass on this court. So be ready."

"Bet," I said, in crouch position, ready for him to deliver one of his patented lazy lay ups so I could block it, steal the ball and run the court to make my shot.

fourteen

. . .

LESLIE

"How long you gonna be mad at me, Tamera?"

"Until you wake up," she snapped, popping her gum and slamming haircare products around in the cabinet we used for extra stock.

"You mind not throwing my shit around while you have your temper tantrum?"

She huffed, then slammed the metal doors shut. "I have an appointment."

I followed her to her chair, which she knew I would do. Tam was prone to getting hot under the collar. She and I needed to talk things out so she could get her attitude out and her mood in check. If I didn't force the conversation, there would be nothing but sniping and side commentary from her. She and I were too close for that.

"What are you mad about, exactly? Do you even know?"

Halfway to her chair, Tam whirled around. "Oh, I know exactly what I'm mad about. And I told your ass. I told you not to let some dust and cobwebs get you in trouble. That man is nice to you for fourteen seconds, eats your mama's meatloaf sandwich and all of a sudden you two are working together." Her espresso brown eyes rolled nearly all the way back in her head. She turned to walk to her chair, but stopped and whipped around to face me again.

"Do you remember, after you let him hit and he ran off, that you came crying to me? You sobbed on my shoulder. Now you're standing here telling me that you two are friendly and you're going to help him run for Mayor!"

She turned again and this time, made it to her chair, opened a drawer and pulled out a cape with a fading Curl & Dye logo. She laid it on the chair and pulled her apron from its hook on the wall, looping the top over her head and tying the strings behind her.

"Seriously, Leslie. Are you out of your damn mind? I feel like you don't learn from past mistakes. Didn't I just rescue you from some other fool? Is this going to be my job from now on? Pulling you out of situations you should have never damn been in?"

"Whoa, wait. Hold on. What do you mean, should have never been in?"

"You knew KC was doing that sorority girl. You were jealous as hell and wouldn't admit it. You went to his room hoping to trump her like your pussy was sweeter—"

"Nope, see that's where you're wrong. They broke up long before I slept with KC. He was available, fair and square."

"She said they were still sleeping together, right up until he left Healy. And Dexter..." She sighed, shaking her head. "You wanted the opposite of KC and you got him. And it still didn't work out, did it?"

I scratched my temple, trying hard to keep my temper in check. We needed to have this conversation. This conversation needed to stay a conversation and not turn into an argument. But Tamera was pushing buttons like only she knew how.

"So, you're mad about some rumors from my college years and a relationship that went sideways, through no fault of my own? What does that have to do with right now and why you're cutting eyes at me and slamming shit around this shop?"

"Because I'm sick of rescuing you from stupid leaps of faith, Leslie. I hope I'm wrong, but KC fucked you and left you on the side of the road like the original groupie. I know you think you're different. But you're not, not to guys like him."

"I'm not—and never was a Kade Cavanaugh groupie. Get that through that thick head of yours, first of all."

"Whatever, Leslie. You slept with him—"

"He wasn't anything but a Healy University basketball player back then. I cared about him. We cared about each other."

"He had a funny way of showing it. Look, all I know is he'd better watch his step, because if he so much as looks at you the wrong way, I'm going. to go. off."

I had wandered over to my chair and, much more calmly, began to prep for Mrs. Isaac's appointment. She wouldn't be getting a color refresh, just a wash and roller set. At Tamera's threat, I stopped arranging things and turned around.

"This attitude is because you're protective of me and you think KC is going to fuck me over like he did in college. Like Dexter did a few years ago. And you're going to be on the 'Put Leslie Back Together' Team. Is that it?"

Tamera, folding towels at her station, didn't answer for a few seconds. But then, quietly, she said, "I can't stand for you to be hurt again, not when you can help it. There's no reason to invite heartache, Leslie."

I moved a few feet away to her chair and pulled the towel she'd been folding out of her hands. I wrapped my arms around her shoulders and waited for her to relent and hug me back. I laughed when I finally felt her spindly arms around me, then shrieked when she poked her pointy nail talons in my side. I backed away, laughing. Tam was trying hard not to, but the corners of her mouth were creeping up.

"Go on, now. Making me all soft. Our apprentices have graduation stuff today, so we're down two people. It's going to be a busy day and I actually have appointments, so I got shit to do."

"Fine, Miss 'I Have Shit to Do'. I love you too. But if I don't do this and get Quincy Adams out of office, this place goes down in flames. And besides..." I stopped to laugh, nervously playing with the small hoops in my ears. "I'm helping him run for Mayor, not screwing him."

"Mmhmm," she hummed, stocking the freshly folded towels in the cabinet behind her chair. "You forget that you wear your emotions. You are falling for him again. I don't even want to argue about it, Leslie. I've seen that look on your face before. Just be careful."

"Tamera, I promise—"

"Nah uh," she protested, a hand up to block my words. "I don't want to hear promises you know your dusty, hard-up ass can't keep. Do me a favor and get some dick or a vibrator or something to fight off those KC vibes because... girl. You are a sucker if I ever saw one."

It was so lucky for Tam that Mrs. Isaacs walked in at that very minute, because I was wearing some feelings on my face, alright.

fifteen

· · ·

KC

The first meeting of The Committee to Elect Kade Cavanaugh to Potter Lake City Council—which, at the moment was just me and Leslie—happened on a Thursday night. I had asked her to meet me at Thai Bistro and, by the time she walked in, had commandeered the booth at the back of the restaurant. It wasn't that I was hiding, but I didn't want to be in sight of the extra friendly waitress.

I'd officially filed papers a few days before, making me a candidate for the October Mayoral election. If I was being honest, I'd admit to being out of my mind with nerves and anxiety. Not so much fear, but so much was riding on this election. I couldn't screw it up. That's where Leslie came in and why I was relieved she had agreed to help me run.

A few minutes after 6 o'clock, Leslie walked in, wearing an army green, button down belted dress that just hit her knees and a pair of low-heeled sandals. Her locs were twisted up in a bun so the gold hoops in her ears caught the summer evening light. Her skin was golden, like she'd spent her day in the sun.

I stood so she could see me and waved her over. Her vibrant lips bent into a smile at the hostess and then, surprisingly, smiled at me as she approached the table.

"Sorry I'm a few minutes late," she said, sliding into the other side of the booth and dumping her keys into the small bag she'd sat next to her. She flipped her shades up so they were perched on top of her head. "I only had two appointments today so I spent the afternoon with Grandy."

"Oh yeah? How's she doing?"

"She's always the same," she answered. "We take turns going, so she always has someone around. She likes sitting outside, so after lunch we sat on the porch and I read her newspapers and magazines aloud. She seemed to like that."

"That's nice. My dad said he's putting a swing out on the back porch for my mom. She'll really like that."

"I bet she will. I'd love to see pictures of this house your parents are building. It sounds amazing."

"It really does. I mean, this is the last..." I paused, glancing across the table at her. She gave me a small smile. She got it. "It's going to be their dream home. Everything she wants, she's getting."

"I'm a little surprised you're not out there helping."

I laughed, relaxing against the fabric of the booth. "You know I'm not about that life. I spent my off seasons at home, helping here and there. I brought him along when I built houses for Habitat for Humanity. But..." I let out a grunt, shaking my head. "That's as far as that goes. We clash, big time. Can you work with your mom?"

She tipped her head side to side and hummed. "I guess we did okay, when I first moved back. There was a lot about hair care that she had taught me over the years that I had to unlearn and then teach her. She wasn't very receptive at first but she came around. And then she turned the shop over to me, so... I guess she trusted me."

"My folks can't believe I did this. You know, moved back here, opened up a salon—"

"Well they must think you're crazy now. Do they know you're running for Mayor?"

I nodded, trying to hold in my laughter. "They're like you. Skeptical."

"I'm not skeptical! I just...." She paused, her lips moving but no sound coming from them. Then she laughed. "Okay, I'm skeptical. But this is our shot to take this town back. We have to take it, right?"

"Yeah," I nodded, reaching for my bag where I'd stashed my notes and folders. I pulled out a few stacks and started spreading them across the table. "Speaking of all that, I'm registered as an official candidate. That was the easy part. Now I need to put together my campaign. I've been doing some research, and I like how Obama came up. I think I can take some tactics from his Senate run and maybe his Presidential run as well. Focus on the people, focus on the issues, make people feel like they're part of the process."

I slid my folder of printouts over to her, which included the standard wikipedia page, plus a few articles from the era where we actually had a black President. "Like, I'm watching what's going on nationally and I don't want to look like an idiot. I've never been a Mayor before but that doesn't mean I can walk into the job with no knowledge."

Leslie was flipping through the folder, nodding and humming. "Well, if you want to come up like Obama, you're going to have to get in people's faces. There was no one too low in position for him to speak to. He would bump fists with the janitor."

"Okay... so. You're saying I need to spend some time with the people out here."

"Exactly. And you need to concentrate on the old side of

town. Those people are diehard Adams supporters. Put your energy into winning them over."

"Okay. How should I do that? Just... stand on Main Street and wave? Shake hands as people walk by? Hand out money?"

Leslie chuckled. "Spend real time with them. Patronize their businesses. Spend money. Ask questions about current city government and really listen. We go to Mayor Adams with a lot of suggestions, but if it doesn't make him money, it never gets implemented."

"I can do that. But I mean... where do I start?"

"Honestly... at the Curl & Dye. Aside from the Kit Kat, it's the place people gather to talk about goings-on around town. You'll meet people. Get some invites to dinner, probably." She paused to wink. "Might get asked out on a few dates."

"Aw, man. I definitely don't know how to handle that."

"It won't be as bad as you think. It'll mostly be middle aged women flirting and their husbands standing behind them grumbling."

"So I should start at the Curl & Dye, huh?"

"Yeah. You might pick up some techniques for when you're sick of offering that tired generic cut."

"That cut gives me a good profit margin."

"But does the cut make your shop a place people want to hang out? People should feel taken care of, at a salon. It's more than an item on a to-do list. A haircut, a manicure or pedicure is self care, especially for those who don't have much to spend. People shouldn't feel like cattle at a salon, KC."

"Okay. I hear you."

She smirked as she waved down a waitress. "I'm going to get a drink. You?"

"I got you. What are you drinking? And they don't serve Trashcan Punch here."

Leslie glowed red, then tossed her head back and laughed. "I hate that you reminded me of that, KC. I really, really do."

She ordered some fancy craft beer. I tacked onto her order and waited for the waitress to leave the table.

"So, won't people see right through me hanging out on that side of town? Won't it look like I'm pandering for votes?"

"Yes, they'll see through it. And yeah, it'll look like you're pandering for votes. That doesn't mean it won't work. And it's better than doing nothing and hoping people will see your name on the ballot and suddenly change their minds about who to vote for. You have to get your face out there. Speaking of your face..."

She stopped talking long enough to accept a bottle wrapped in a napkin and a tall, empty glass. I watched her empty half of the bottle into the glass and sip some foam off the top, then lick her lips. I stifled a groan... how did she not know how sexy that was?

The waitress set a Sweetwater Ale in front of me and left a menu on the table, which I grabbed and started to leaf through, even though I knew it front to back by heart.

"You need some publicity. Billboards, fliers, posters, mailers. Maybe some newspaper articles, some news interviews."

"I still have my headshots from my last team photoshoot—"

But Leslie was shaking her head. "You need people to think you're a hometown guy, not a rich baller. You need at least one current, casual shot. A photo taken here, in Potter Lake. Maybe..."

I saw the wheels turning in her head and my eyes narrowed. Whatever was running through her mind caused her to draw her bottom lip between her teeth and chew on it for a few moments.

"Right before the city council meeting, I saw that the basketball association was looking for a coach. You could—"

"Oh, no. Nope." I shook my head and pursed my lips in defiance. "Nah."

"Why no, nope, nah? You know how to play ball and those kids will look up to you."

"You know what they say about those who can't play basketball."

"What?" She giggled, making her brown eyes glow. "They coach? That's a bad thing?"

"Coaching is for people who are done, who are washed up, who can't play anymore," I spat.

Leslie reared back at my outburst, her eyes wide.

"Okay. I mean, whatever, KC. I thought it was a good photo opportunity and a chance for you to get involved in something. Parents and grandparents—families need to know that you're trustworthy."

I propped an elbow on the table and pinched the bridge of my nose with two fingers. "I'm sorry for snapping at you, but that's not me. My knee might give me shit, but I still run the court."

"Like I said, whatever. Sorry to bruise your ego by suggesting some area kids might love to be coached by you. Not to mention a photo of you playing basketball with our city's youth would go a long way toward helping your image. But yeah, keep thinking it's about you and running the court," she finished, using air quotes in the most sarcastic way imaginable.

"Okay, I'll think about it. I'm listening to your suggestion. Anything else?"

"No. Yes. Well... you're not going to like this suggestion. And frankly, neither is she—"

"She, who?" I asked, afraid of what the answer would turn out to be.

"It's just that... Tamera is a really good photographer. And if you offer to pay her for her time, she could do some nice shots for you."

I was already cackling in laughter the moment her name fell out of Leslie's mouth. "You know that girl doesn't like me. I'm supposed to trust her to take nice pictures of me?"

"I'll talk to her, KC. Like I said, if you pay her like a professional and treat her like one, and let me be there to sort of... buffer between the two of you, it'll go fine. You'll get a nice set of shots to use for advertisement."

"I don't know if I trust Tamera. But you do, so..." I bumped my shoulders a few times as I sucked down half of my beer. "You know, it's not that she doesn't like you. It's that we have mutually hated you since you left Healy. I'm over it but Tam..." She sighed, dropping her gaze to the table for a few moments before bringing them back up to meet mine. "I was hurt. My hurt made her angry."

"I'm sorry about that. That wasn't what I was going for. But if you're over it, why isn't she?"

Leslie smiled. I noticed that even though she'd chewed on her lip, licked her lips and drank her beer that her lipstick hadn't budged an inch. That meant that it would probably last through a wild, passionate kiss. Some part of me wanted to test that out.

"Girlfriend code. She's trying to protect me. Even now, she thinks you're going to do the same thing you did back at Healy."

"Which was what? I didn't do anything to you. I mean... nothing you didn't want me to do." I lobbed a smile across the table.

"You know what I'm talking about, KC," she shot back at me.

"You and Tamera are always snapping at me about something and I swear I have no idea what your problem is."

"You were never gonna make a move, so I made one. We slept together. And it was nice, I thought."

"I did, too. I never said it wasn't."

"Except the way you treated me after... it felt like you pushed me away. And then you left."

"You... thought I didn't like being with you? And that I left because of that?"

"That's how it played out in my head. I could never tell if you liked me back or just kept me around for entertainment. When we slept together I thought I had confirmation that you did like me. But then you kept me at arm's length."

She paused, breaking eye contact. Her cheeks glowed pink and if I could blush, mine probably would have, too. I had no idea that actual, real feelings were in play.

"Les... no offense but we've gotta move past all that. What can I do? What can I say? 'Cause... I can't keep apologizing for things that happened in college. Do you know how many lifetimes it has been since college?"

"Yes, I know. And I told you, I'm over it. My best friend is not. You're going to have to get on her good side. And the best way to do that is to put some money in her pocket."

I groaned, long and loud, which made Leslie laugh. I meant it, though. We had never really gotten along, but I didn't see her regularly, back then. These days, I felt like I was wrestling a pit bull every day.

"I need her to chill a little bit. I'm happy to back off but what I'm not going to do is let her attack me and not say anything. You know how I get when I feel cornered."

"I do. And no one wants that." She grabbed the straps of her bag and started to scoot out of the booth. "Speaking of Tamera, she and I have a date. We watch The Suitor on Thursdays and since I'm over this way, I'm headed to her house."

"That corny dating show? Ya'll watch that?"

"By now we're hate watching it. We don't like any of the men and we think the female contestant is a bitch. But it's fun to pop popcorn and drink wine and guess who's getting voted off."

"I guess. I'm about to bounce, too. Kendrick and I are going to get in some time on the court in the park."

I left a few bills on the table and followed Leslie out of the restaurant, careful not to let my eyes drop to the way the dress clung to the shape of her ass. But I was far enough behind her that I didn't have to drop my eyes to see it.

"So, I'll be in touch about the photo shoot. I'm going to call Arletha King over at the news station and see if I can hook up an interview. She covers the newspaper too so she'll just do both at the same time."

She had reached her car and I'd followed, listening to her instructions.

"And KC, remember what I said, about small towns. Stay out of trouble. Keep your nose... and other things... clean."

She winked, pulled open the door to get in the car but I grabbed it before she could.

"Leslie. Hold up. Uh...I want to..." I'd paused long enough for her to cock an eyebrow and almost glare at me, urging me to finish my sentence.

"You want to..."

Maybe it was gratitude, maybe it was guilt, maybe it was just that she was beautiful standing in the sunlight, all the golden rays behind her, illuminating her skin like an angel. I don't know what it was that came over me in that moment, but whatever it was made me lean over the open door and press my lips against hers.

Right there in the parking lot outside Thai Bistro. And right after she told me to stay out of trouble and keep things clean.

I was never good at following directions. I let my lips linger on hers before tilting my head and opening my mouth, teasing the seam of her lips until they opened and the tip of my tongue met hers. She tasted like hops. And mint.

Before we could get in too deep, I pulled away, slowly

ending the kiss. I took a small step back, in case she felt like hurling her purse at my head.

"What...what...what..." Leslie stammered, blinking those pretty doe eyes at me. "What was that? What was that for, I mean?"

"An apology. For making you think I didn't like being with you. I really liked it, actually. I would have told you so, if you would have talked to me. I wouldn't mind being with you again, to be honest."

I let go of the car door and stepped back, then turned around and walked to my truck, feeling the grin spread across my face the further I got away from her. I hadn't been planning to do that. But I was glad I did. The game she and I were playing just took a dramatic turn.

sixteen

. . .

LESLIE

"And I hope she throws him off a roof in next week's episode."

My attention had been weaving in and out all evening. One minute I was wrapped up in this week's episode of The Suitor. Neither of us wanted Anthony, the Boris Kodjoe look alike—he thought—to be a contender but it looked like he might make the final two. The next minute, my mind had wandered off to a place where I replayed the moment that KC's lips touched mine in the parking lot at Thai Bistro.

I didn't see it coming and it didn't last more than a few seconds, but it took up a ton of real estate in my mind. Well that, and it happening again because Tamera was right—I was hard up as hell.

Dating in Potter Lake was non-existent. Smart people left and never came back. I thought I was being smart. I just didn't realize my ex boyfriend was a crook and I would end up fleeing our home in the dead of night. Or the dead of a Sunday afternoon.

"You hope she does what?" I asked Tamera, pulling myself, yet again, out of my daydream replay of that kiss. I reached for the bowl of popcorn on the coffee table in front of us, but she grabbed it and held it off to the side, out of my reach.

"Where is your head tonight? I'm over here talking away and you haven't said three words all night. If you didn't want to hang out, you could have said so."

"Oh, Tam…" I shook my head, looping an arm around her neck and bringing her close… then grabbing the bowl of popcorn from her. I giggled and dug in for a handful. "My brain is full today; I'm sorry. I'll try to be in the moment. What did you say about a roof?"

"Anthony! I want her to throw him off a rooftop. I see why he's single. He's so insufferable."

I chewed a mouthful of popcorn and hummed my agreement. From trying to serenade the contestant, Michelle, with a ukulele that he couldn't play to telling terribly unfunny jokes to acting like he was the world's gift to women, Anthony was inarguably the worst contestant the show had ever had. Whatever the network was doing, it was infuriating. And it was working, because we were watching every week.

"If he ends up being in the top two I don't think I can watch the finale."

Tamera leaned forward and picked up a stemless wine goblet. "I keep saying I'm going to stop watching but it's a train wreck. I can't look away."

"Mmmhmmm," I hummed again, my mind uncontrollably rolling in the direction I'd been trying to keep it from going all night.

"There you go again. Leslie, what's up with you?"

"Nothing. I just had a long day, that's all."

The TV popped off with a snap of Tamera's wrist. She set the remote down on the table and twisted her body toward mine, tucking her feet up under her. She fortified herself with another sip of wine and said, "Tell me about it. You left the shop before I even came in today."

"I had two early appointments. Then I had lunch with Pops and Grandy and spent the day with her."

I filled her in on my afternoon, which was pretty much just talking to myself. No matter how optimistic we tried to be about her condition, the simple truth was that she was no better today than the day we had admitted her, after her stroke. Some days she was just... there. Every day was just talking into the air, hoping she was somewhere in there.

"Honey, I'm sure she knows you're there. My mama says stroke patients can definitely hear and understand. She might not be able to communicate, but keep up the visits. It's good for her."

"I know. But I miss my Grandy. We always had really good talks about everything. And she was funny. Earline wasn't always the center of attention in this town. I feel like when we lose her, we'll lose so much."

"It's about time for a new generation to come up. Me and you better pop out some babies or we're going to end up being the Potter Lake Golden Girls."

Babies. Why did the thought of babies bring KC to mind? I had never imagined having babies with that man and now... itty bitty chocolate replicas were dancing through my head. I gulped down a huge swallow of wine, trying to rid myself of that vision. Now was not the time for my biological clock to start ticking.

"So, there's something I need to ask you, Tam. A favor. And I don't want to hear your arguments about it, because I need you to do it."

"Why do I have the feeling this involves KC? And if it does, I'm not doing it. Just on general principle."

"You don't even know what it is. And he'll pay you. And I'll be there. I promise."

One eyebrow rose, accompanied by a suspicious twist in

her lips. "We're not talking about anything hinky between y'all are we? I don't go there. At least not for cheap."

"I need you to do some publicity shots for KC's campaign."

"Publicity shots. Where I have to hold a camera and point it at him and look at him through the lens and make him look good?" She shook her head. "I said I would help, but I don't know about all that, Leslie."

"You act like looking at him is a burden. Anger and whatever aside, that man is fine."

"Hella fine," she agreed, surprisingly. "Don't mean I want to spend my time taking pictures of him."

"Did I mention he would pay you? Weren't you just talking about needing to book some serious projects to get your photography business off the ground?"

Like me, doing hair at the Curl & Dye was never Tamera's dream. It had just taken her a little longer to realize her life's desire revolved around capturing captivating images. She'd done a few family shoots, a couple of local weddings, but had been dragging her feet on getting her side business off the ground. Part of it, I felt, was that she didn't want to abandon me at the salon.

"Leslie, why do you have to use my actual words against me? I'm so tired of you making sense."

"Because you like to be obstinate and hot headed. I can send him to Healy, or I can get Arletha to shoot some photos. But I told him you were good. And you are. And that he needed to get on your good side by putting money in your pocket."

"On second thought, don't you dare send that very rich man over to Healy so they can do some boring, vapid, pro basketball-esque photo shoot. You've convinced me with money in my pocket. So when are we doing this?"

"I'm talking him into a couple of good opportunities. Keep your camera with you; you never know when the perfect shot will pop up. And if you need anything before hand, let me know. KC will pay for it."

"Oh I have a list of things I need beforehand."

I snorted. "Don't get greedy."

"Ugh, you and your scruples. It's muggy in here," she whined, fanning herself. "Let's take our wine outside to the patio."

A few minutes later we had relocated to the back porch patio with the rest of the bottle of wine, a sleeve of crackers and sausage and cheese slices that Tamera grabbed from the fridge. It was beautiful night—warm, peaceful, nothing but the sounds of cicadas and the bright arcs of light from the fireflies. And you could actually see the stars across the sky. That was one thing I'd missed in Chicago, being able to see the stars.

"Did I tell you I'm doing a session for Monica? A couple of them." She angled her head to nod toward the house next door. We hadn't been over there since the day she had invited us over and we'd confronted KC about the salon closing.

"You didn't! What kind of sessions?"

"A pregnancy shoot, before the baby comes. She wants it to be kind of sexy, like a boudoir set, so that'll be fun to design. And then some newborn shots. Not... fresh newborn. I don't think I can handle that. But a couple of weeks after the baby is born and it stops looking like a little old man."

"Tamera, you are so mean!"

"I can't help it! Babies look like little old men for like... a month."

"You are not taking pictures of any of my babies."

"Like I won't be in the room anyway."

"Nope. I'll take them to Healy, to a real photographer."

"A real—fuck you, Leslie."

"Back atcha, Tamera."

We glanced at each other and burst into giggles, then turned up our wine glasses.

"You think you'll marry someone from Potter Lake, Les?"

"Oh, I don't know. I don't really think about it. I'm just talking."

Really, seriously. Just talking. And just when I didn't need his big head to show up, I heard KC's voice, faint but getting louder as he approached. He and Kendrick were joking with each other on their way back from the park. They couldn't see us, but I felt like we were eavesdropping. I stayed quiet, practically holding my breath so he couldn't hear me breathing, until they stomped up the front porch steps and went into the house.

I heaved a sigh, and tossed back the last swallow of wine. "Hit me," I ordered, holding out my glass. She poured, giving me about half a glass more. I needed it for this confession I was about to dump on her.

I licked my lips and inhaled a deep, fortifying breath before I blurted, "So...KC kissed me."

Tamera's blank stare lasted for a few beats. "Uh....when did this happen?"

"Today. Tonight. Before I came over here."

"Like... a kiss, kiss? Or just a kiss?"

"Uhm... a kiss, kiss. There was tongue."

"Oh." She blinked, seeming confused. "And... that's why your head is in the clouds and you're acting dickmatized?"

"Yeah. Probably. Kinda."

"Okay, then. And you kissed him back?"

"Of course. Who just stands there while they're being kissed?"

"I mean..." Tamera reached for her wine glass and took a few sips, then asked, "So how, exactly, did his lips end up on you? Did he trip and fall into your face?"

My glass hit the tabletop with a thunk and pushed my chair back from the table. "Okay. You don't want to talk about it. I'm gonna go."

"Leslie—okay, I'm sorry." Tamera grabbed my arm and

dug one of her talons into my skin. "Please, please stay. Talk to me."

"Are you done being a sarcastic bitch?"

She had the nerve to pause before answering, "Mostly. Yes. Talk to me. Why did he kiss you? And how do you feel about it?"

"Well, we were talking. I brought up when we slept together. I said I thought we had a good time together and I thought he did, too. But then he treated me like it was the worst thing to ever happen to him."

"Okay. And then he said..."

"Do you remember KC talking about his mom's illness in Sports Illustrated right after he went pro?"

Tamera shrugged and shook her head. She'd never followed him all that closely. I had to hide that I knew his every move.

"She was diagnosed with Multiple Sclerosis right when we started our sophomore year. The bills were already piling up by the time he found out. Going pro helped pay her medical bills. Still helps pay her medical bills."

Her lips formed a perfect 'O' as she began to understand. He didn't withdraw from Healy over sweaty, awkward sex with his good friend Leslie. It really had nothing to do with me.

"When I was leaving, he stopped me and... he kissed me. He said it was an apology for making me think he didn't like being with me, because he did. And..."

"And? There's more? Did ya'll screw in the parking lot?"

I glared at Tamera, nervously rubbing the back of my neck because her question threw my imagination into overdrive and...I really needed to take the edge off.

"He said he wouldn't mind being with me again."

Tamera was so quiet, practically speechless for so long that I looked up, just to see if I could tell by her expression where her thought train was running. She was staring at some spot above me, her head tilted to the right. I recognized that head tilt and sighed.

"He...." She began, a finger already in the air. "Kade Cavanaugh, that is, said he wouldn't mind being with you again. And you're all twisted up about this?"

"I'm not twisted up. It was just was the last thing I expected to hear from him. I'm... I'm a little out of sorts, is all."

"So... you know I just have to be honest, right?"

I nodded, accepting my fate and halfway regretting even telling her about the kiss.

"You need to think with your brain and not your inner hot in the ass, I have a crush on KC college girl, mkay? He's a tall, handsome, rich, sexy as fuck, tattooed muhfuckah. Y'all have history and that means it's so much easier for you to fall for him again. You realize this, right?"

Slowly, I bobbed my head. I did not want to know this, but I did.

"But Leslie, don't let any part of your brain accept that mediocre bullshit. You are a gorgeous, smart, resourceful, successful entrepreneur who happens to be lit as hell. Many, many men wouldn't mind having sex with you. Do you care what the hell random men want?"

I shook my head.

"If you're gonna give him the pussy, make sure it's because he can't get the pussy off his mind. Not just because an ex-NBA baller, as fine as that muhfuckah is, wouldn't mind sleeping with you. You just told me last week that you ain't no damn Kade Cavanaugh groupie. Don't act like one."

I started to argue but I knew she was right. KC was probably delivering the same old lines he was used to delivering, because he was used to them working. And they weren't going to work on me. Anymore. I threw myself at him fifteen years ago. He could work for it, this time.

I reached across the table and squeezed her hand and

smiled. "Thanks for the pep talk. I can always count on you to remind me how fine I am."

"My chief job is reminding you how fine you are. You're welcome." She squeezed me back, then pulled back to stifle a yawn. "I'm thinking about getting in bed and watching last night's Power again. Mama talked through the whole episode."

"Yeah, I'm going to go. We have a long day of appointments tomorrow. Getting in the bed sounds like a great idea."

Tamera sniggled and I rolled my eyes. "Alone. Good night, Tam. I'll walk myself around to the front."

I walked around the side of the house and stopped when I got to the gate that led to the front yard. I had to lift the latch and walk past the house next door to get to my car, but I heard voices coming from next door. From the porch next door. Shit. I couldn't get out of the yard without them seeing or hearing me.

"This is the stuff I was talking about, KC," I heard Kendrick say. "No disrespect to Leslie at all, but you're acting real wild about her right now—"

"How am I acting wild?"

"You kissed her. What part of the business plan—or the campaign plan, for that matter—is sucking face with her?"

"It wasn't like that, man. I didn't let it get that far."

"But why, is the question, when it's going to throw everything off?"

"Couldn't help it. You've seen her mouth, right?"

I blushed, lifting my fingertips to my lips. Hearing him rave about the kiss made them swell with the memory of his lips on mine.

"Man, I am married and my wife is like... eleventy hundred months pregnant. I technically don't see lips, tits, asses—none of that, if I want to live or not sleep on the couch."

KC laughed. "Okay, okay. But off the record?"

"Off the record? I mean... she's aight. If you like girls with thick hips and a pretty mouth."

"I don't know, man. We just... we were having a conversation about some things back in the past. About me and her, together, you know? Maybe I got caught up or whatever. But it wasn't like she didn't like it. She didn't push me back or anything."

"KC... a large percentage of women want you to kiss them. Your busted knee doesn't make groupies disappear."

"She's not a groupie, Kendrick."

"You know what I mean. Just don't get to thinking that it means anything that she didn't push you away and spray you with Mace. I mean, if you're lonely we can find you someone. Tracey would love to—"

"Nah, man." KC laughed. "I can pick up my own women. I'm not trying to make things harder on myself, but there's something there. I liked her back then. I like her now. I think she's actually coming around to me, lately. If there's another chance with her, I definitely don't want to miss out."

"You also definitely need to focus. If you lose this election, you get to cut Mayor Adams' hair from now on."

I heard KC scoff and both men laugh. "I don't have a license to cut hair."

"He doesn't really have hair. Couple swipes with some scissors and some oil to shine up that dome—"

They collapsed in loud laughter. Even I giggled a little, under my breath. Before Guys N' Dolls opened, it used to be my job to clip those little wayward hairs growing from the Mayor's severely receded hairline. That was one client I was happy to turn over.

I leaned against the side of the townhouse, listening to two men talk. About women. About me in particular, and my thick hips and pretty mouth. I didn't want to be flattered, but I was. I ran my hands down my body, self-evaluating. So my hips were thick? And thick hips were a good thing?

I needed to get away from the conversation before I heard something I didn't want to hear, but I was trapped at the fence. They wouldn't miss me walking past the house.

Saved by the bell. A ringtone blared into the night. I heard KC answer, then say goodnight to Kendrick. His voice carried as he walked toward his truck parked in front of the house.

I peeked through the bushes and saw Kendrick open the screen door and step into the house. As soon as I heard KC's truck start up, I breathed a sigh of relief and flipped up the lock on the gate and slipped past the house. I'd just made it to my car when I heard a voice call my name. Shit!

"Leslie! Hey, I thought that was your car over there."

KC was hanging out of the window of his truck as it sat at the curb, huffing quietly. I smiled and gave a little wave, then ducked into my car and started it up before he got any ideas about getting out of his truck to come talk to me. Or kiss me. Because after eavesdropping that conversation, I was sure I would let him.

seventeen

. . .

KC

"So then in '76... or was it '77?"

A stout, dark skinned woman with a freshly shampooed, blow dried and flat ironed shoulder length bob had planted herself next to me in what Leslie called the "lobby" of her shop, a short row of chairs along the window across from the desk.

I couldn't figure out if she had been warned that I would be at the shop that day, or if she just walked around with photo albums in her purse, but I had been looking at pictures of Dolores Robinson and her family for over twenty minutes and there seemed to be no end in sight. She'd started with telling me about meeting her husband at Howard University, and now I was listening to her life story.

"I think it was '77 when me and Walter moved down here from Maryland." Except she pronounced it *Muhrlun*. "He got a job with the railroad and I started working over at Augusta Manufacturing. That was the textile mill that closed up shop a while ago now. A lot of us worked out there, mmmhmm." She nodded, her lips drawn in and the edges of her mouth turned down.

"So when the mill closed, what happened? Where did everybody go for work?"

She closed up the photo albums and tucked them into the large bag she'd brought with her. "We tried to find jobs in Potter Lake, but we was always real small out here. Not enough jobs in this little town to employ everybody from the mill. Some of us went to Healy, cause it's bigger. We worked so hard, you know, to have our own, so when it came to workin', wasn't no room or use for pride. We took jobs doing anything to pay the mortgage, to keep food in the refrigerator. My husband, Walter, ended up going away to find work. He's been driving back and forth to Alabama for a long time now."

"Ms. Dolores, he's still with the bank out in Birmingham?" Leslie butted into our conversation from behind her salon chair, where she was twisting strands of her client's hair together and arranging them into an attractive style. I hadn't even thought of being able to provide more complicated hairdos like twists and locs, styles that required skill and technique. It made me tired to think about how much I'd have to expand to care for my female clientele.

"Unh huh," she confirmed, adjusting her wide rimmed glasses. "He just celebrated fifteen years there. He leaves out early Monday morning and he's back late Thursday night. It's actually been nice. Right about the time I start to miss him, it's time for him to come home. And then when I'm about tired of his mouth, off he go."

I chuckled, as did Leslie. "Well, why not just move to Birmingham?"

"By then we had children in school and friends. We built up a whole life here in Potter Lake. And you know, that means something. This town means something to us—we didn't want to leave. Then the Mayor says he wanna bring some businesses over to Potter Lake, so maybe Walter wouldn't have to drive three hours to work and keep a place in another state, I was all for it. But...."

She grunted, wagging her head, pursing her lips. "He ain't built much that anybody cares for. Nothing Walter could retire from; some restaurants and gas stations and what not. We already had them here. And he's steady inviting big box companies to build out here. We don't want no Walmarts or KMarts. We're just fine with Kwik-E-Mart."

"Okay, so... say I win this election. On day one, I invite you out to city hall and ask you what's one thing I could do today to make your life easier. What's your answer?"

"Well..." She propped a hand on a hip as her gaze lowered to the dull linoleum. "I think a nice thing would be a little shuttle to go from place to place. We don't have public transportation. Mayor said it takes too much money, but I'd rather pay toward that than a new convenience store. If you're askin', that's what I'm sayin'."

Leslie hummed her agreement. I added another item to my growing list of town needs—street lights, neighborhood watch, road repair, paved sidewalks. And public transportation. I had to agree with Leslie—sitting in the shop was a great way to meet the real people that lived here, not just the recent transplants or those that still lived in Healy but commuted out here to work.

I'd already heard so many stories and picked up so much history about the town. Mayor Adams had an advantage in that he'd lived in this town for most of his life. But he obviously didn't care about the people... so even if I was new, if I cared more, I could win over his most loyal supporters.

"Thank you, Ms. Dolores. I appreciate you being honest with me. And I hope it continues."

"It's no bother, young man." She paused to beam a bright white smile at me. "Now, if you win, you let me know when I can come down to your office and give you an earful about what this town needs."

I smiled, tucking my pen back behind my ear and sliding the small moleskin notebook I'd been using into my back pocket. "I'm sure you won't be the only one. Does Mayor Adams have regular town hall meetings, anything like that?"

"He sure doesn't," snapped Tamera. "He barely goes to city council meetings and when he does, it's the same story as it was a couple of weeks ago. He's very much into the power he wields as Mayor and dares anyone to come up against him."

She untied her client's cape and removed it, then hung it on a hook near her chair. A middle aged woman with a short salt and pepper afro stood and handed Tamera a few bills, telling her to keep the change.

"Thank you, Ms. Jackie. See you next week?"

The woman nodded and walked out of the shop, smiling as she passed me. Tamera used a towel to wipe down her chair, then tapped the back of it.

"KC, come on over here. I've been staring at your hairline all day and I can't take it anymore."

I stared at Tamera from across the room. Even Leslie stopped twisting to bounce her gaze between me and Tamera and back.

"Uh... me? Come over there?"

"Yeah, you. Come over here. I've been wanting to snap some candid shots of you, but you need a lineup and your fade is sloppy. Let me fix you up so you look good."

I glanced at Leslie but still didn't move. I didn't trust Tamera to not jack my hair up. As if she could read my mind, she laughed.

"If I was gonna mess you up, I'd break into your house with some clippers. I'm not going to make you look bad. I promise." She tapped the chair again, swiveling it around toward me. It was just... there. Welcoming me to sit.

I groaned, then got up and slowly loped across the shop to Tamera's station. I lowered myself into the chair and sat still while the cape floated over me, then draped around my shoulders.

"I promise, I'm not gonna mess your hair up, KC. You want to look good in these pictures, so you can win this election, right?" She lowered her head next to mine and got close, so close I could feel her breath on my neck. "But since I have you here... I'm being nice to you because Leslie asked me to. I assume she asked you to do the same. I'll play this game, but let's get real clear on something: no one loves Leslie like I do. No one. And so help me, if you fuck with her... if you give her any reason to even think about shedding a tear over you, you will regret it. Not all my crazy is on display. There's plenty in stock in the back. You get me?"

I swallowed. And nodded.

"Glad we're on the same page. Hate to see you limping around here with two bad knees. We just have to act like the adults we are and get you into office. I can do that. Can you?

Again, I nodded. "That's good. Real good," she responded, straightening. I heard a click and then the low buzz of the clippers near my ear. I closed my eyes and braced.

A half hour later, I was grinning ear to ear. Tamera had done a great job with my cut and I was impressed. I would go so far as to say it was one of the best cuts I'd ever received, which was a problem because I ran a barbershop and my best friend had been taking care of my haircuts.

"If you weren't so mean, you'd be my new barber," I teased her, holding the mirror up so I could see the crisp, razor sharp line and classic low fade.

"I don't know why you sound so surprised." She poked the broom around the chair, sweeping up tufts of hair and gathering them into a pile. "I can do hair. There has never been a doubt about that—man or woman, I'll fix you up."

"She's right," Leslie agreed, putting the finishing touches on the twists she'd been installing. "But I can't wait until doing hair becomes your side gig and you start doing your photography thing. You can snap a picture too."

"In time, in time. Maybe doing this campaign will get me some business. Speaking of..." Tamera opened a cabinet and pulled a bulky black bag from inside. A quick zip around the perimeter revealed two cameras and a set of lenses. A side pocket held a portable tripod.

"Hey, yeah. You wanted to take some pictures today?" I slid her hand held mirror onto the cart she used to store her materials and untied the cape, pulling it from around my neck. I'd made it a point to look presentable, in a blue and white plaid shirt and pressed khakis, just in case I'd need proof that I did, in fact, venture over to the other side of Potter Lake.

"Why don't we take one by the front door, so everyone is working behind you. Leslie, can you manage to look busy for a second?"

She smirked. "Doing what?"

"Sit at the desk and pretend to make a phone call. I need good background action."

Leslie sighed and walked to the front desk, dragging her feet as she did so. As she passed me, she winked, then pulled out the chair at the desk and took a seat. By a stroke of fate, the phone actually rang and Leslie had to pick it up.

"Okay, great!" She lifted the camera and brought it to her face. "Let's get a shot real quick while she's on the phone."

I stood in several poses and smiled so hard my teeth hurt before Tamera felt she got a good angle. We took that photo— and many others—several hundred times. By the time she put the camera down, I needed a break.

"Can I stop pretending to still be on the phone?" I heard Leslie ask as I stepped outside, dragging one of the lobby chairs with me.

"Yes, you whiner," Tamera replied. "God forbid I ask you to do one thing for me—"

"I got you this job, heifer."

"Who you callin' a heifer?"

"You, heifer!"

Just when I was about to head back inside to break up a potential girl fight, I heard snorts and giggles. I shook my head. Women were a trip.

"I'll be outside. By the way, that was Ms. Paulette on the phone. She said she's coming in for you to do her pedicure."

"Unh uh, Leslie. If you catch it, you take it!"

"Uhm, if you own the shop, you assign it to someone else. She'll be here in a few minutes, so fix your face."

"I—"

"Nope. I can't hear you. Bye."

Leslie came out of the shop through the door that was propped open with a box fan. She was cute in jeans and a blouse that had cut outs where the sleeves should be. I'd seen the style on a lot of women lately but I liked it best on Leslie. Her gold sandals showed off painted toes and a toe ring and her locs hung down her back in a low ponytail. Simple. But beautiful.

"Hey. You want to sit?" I moved to get up from the chair, but she raised a hand to stop me. "No, don't get up. My spot is right here, on the curb. You want some water?" She handed me a bottle and sat down with hers.

I felt stupid sitting in a chair while she was sitting on the sidewalk, so I got up and sat next to her. She didn't say much once I sat down, just sipped her water until about half the bottle was gone. I sucked mine down in record time and, as was my habit, crushed the plastic bottle in my hand.

Leslie laughed... just a chuckle at first, and then a long stream of giggles that sounded pretty. I just didn't know what caused them.

"You okay? I mean... the heat isn't baking your brain, is it?"

She shook her head, an errant strand swinging in front of her face. She grabbed it and tucked it into the ponytail. "It's just... every once in a while, something reminds me of you. I remember you doing that all the time with water bottles. It was... a memory."

"Oh." I looked at the mess of crushed plastic in my hand. "Just a habit, I guess."

"Yeah. I guess." She smiled and took another sip from her water bottle. "Sitting down here can't be good for your knee, KC."

"Let me worry about my knee, alright? Everyone's always worried about the knee. The knee is fine."

"Okay, damn!" She sucked her teeth and flung her head to the side with attitude. "Didn't look fine when you limped in here this morning. I don't remember you being so sensitive. I just didn't want you to sit down here if you didn't want to."

"I'm right where I want to be."

That made her blush. Kinda made me blush, too. I hadn't intended to show that much of my hand... but now it was out there. She hadn't brought up the kiss, and I had no plans to but that didn't mean I hadn't been thinking about her, about how cool her mouth was, about how she smelled like brown sugar and vanilla, about how her skin looked like it had been kissed by a ray of sun. Leslie had worked her way into a large majority of my thoughts since that night.

I had promised Kendrick that I would cool it with her, and I had every intention of doing so when I agreed. But now I was sitting next to her, listening to her laugh. I'd spent the day with her at this little rundown beauty shop that she loved so much that she was willing to cross the line and work with a mortal enemy to save it.

I wasn't sure I'd go through all of that for Guys N' Dolls if it came down to it. There was no hometown connection, no history. We were just another shop and if something came along to threaten that, I'd like to think I would fight for us, but I'd probably just close up and do something else. I guessed that was the difference between me and her.

"My knee is real stiff in the morning, until I get moving. Usually I work out, loosen it up, but I wanted to be here on time, not tired and sweaty, so..." I shrugged a shoulder. "That's why I was limping this morning."

"Mmhmm." Leslie hummed, giving me the suspicious side-eye. "KC you are always limping. I don't know if you realize it, but—"

"You know what? I do need to get out of here though. I have some things to take care of at the shop." I pushed myself up from the sidewalk, suppressing a groan as I shifted my weight off of my bad knee. Eventually, I would have to make it back to the doctor, because the pain was getting worse. And yeah, I had noticed that I was always limping. That could mean a lot of things—re-injury, inflammation, or another, new injury. None of which I was in the mood to deal with.

I offered Leslie a hand to help her stand, and she took it. While I had her hand in mine, I held it and pulled her close to me.

"You want to come to the Kit Kat Lounge with me tonight?"

Leslie chuckled. "You're going to the Kat? The crowd is... I mean, those are real ass black people up in there. Not just old ladies coming to get their hair done. Not Thai Bistro kind of black people. You're about to meet the real workers in this town. You feel that brave?"

"I can handle it, so long as I have a beautiful tour guide beside me."

"Uhm..." Her eyes fluttered closed and for a second I thought she was going to say no. But they flicked open again and she said, "Sure. I'll go. But... I think we should all go. Like, as a group. I can call ahead and get a table."

"Okay. Cool. So do they do bottle service or whatever?"

She snickered. "No one at the Kit Kat knows what bottle service is. And you wouldn't want it from them anyway. We get the table and that's it."

"Alright. I guess I can deal. You want to meet me around 8 o'clock?"

"Better make it 9. Most people don't get over there until then."

I nodded. "See, you're invaluable to me already."

"Un huh." She slipped her hand out of mine and stepped back. "Don't look like you're going to a club in New York. Slacks, collared shirt, nothing designer if you can help it. Remember you're trying to look trustworthy, not like you're ballin' out of control."

"When do I look like I'm ballin' out of control?"

She laughed. "Your shirt is Gucci, KC. Just tone it down. Bring cash, small bills. No Amex Black, no Blue, no VISA gold. Don't flash your money, but do spend it. Get me?"

I bobbed my head. Money spends, but don't act like I own a money tree. "I got you."

"Good. I'm gonna..." She thumbed at the door before heading in that direction. "Get back on the clock. I'm actually doing Ms. Paulette's feet. I just like to give Tam a hard time. I need to prep my station."

"See you around nine, then?"

"Sure. Yeah. Nine," she said, before turning on her heel and re-entering the shop.

eighteen

· · ·

IT TOOK every ounce of skill and cunning to convince Tamera to come out to the Kit Kat Lounge. I had to practically get on my knees before, begrudgingly, she agreed to come.

"I don't know why you even suggested that place to KC." Tamera untied her apron and hung it on a hook. It was the end of a great business day and we were all heading home to have some dinner, change and meet at the lounge later.

Word must have traveled around town that KC was at the Curl & Dye. We saw faces that we hadn't seen in a long while, some people we hadn't seen in nearly a year. Even a few men came in for a cut and a hot towel shave, a ritual involving pressing hot towels to the face and neck to soften up the hairs, then using a straight razor for a clean shave or trimmers to even out an unruly beard or goatee. The practice had been a staple at the shop many years ago, but most men these days didn't—or wouldn't—take time to indulge.

"Because it's the perfect place to shill for votes," I said. I locked the desk drawer and grabbed my bag and the bank deposit. Evonne and Tamera left the shop first. I followed behind and turned the two locks on the front door. "The people that frequent the Kat are going to be labor workers—

construction, railroad personnel, mechanics. KC needs all of those votes and he needs to get in those faces personally because they're not likely to pay attention to billboards and feel-good news stories."

I pointed the keyfob at my car. Clicks and beeps welcomed me as I approached. "Besides, they're more likely to have followed his NBA career. He has a built-in reason for people to want to talk to him."

"Oh yeah," Tamera mused. "I forgot about that small town hero thing he has going for him. Should be a fun night, sitting around listening to KC wax nostalgic about his basketball days."

Evonne, who I didn't have to work very hard to convince, practically squealed. "I can't wait! I can't even believe I live in the same town as Kade Cavanaugh. And he came and hung out in my place of work all morning. And I get to hang out with him tonight?" She jingled her keys and added a dance to her step as she walked to her car. "See ya'll tonight. I'm going home to get fine!"

Tamera and I laughed, watching her lithe body cross the parking lot.

"She's fun," I commented, nodding in Evonne's direction. "What do you think about bringing her on? As a stylist?"

Tamera pressed her lips together and twisted them to one side. "I'm not sure we have the clientele to sustain her full time. But if she can pay her chair rent and sell her share of product..." She shrugged. "She could make it work. That is, if we manage to stay open."

"Let me worry about that, Tam. People are starting to come back over here, for some reason. Not just today but the last week has been crazy with folks coming in. I don't know what changed, but—"

"Really, Les?" Her eyes rolled and she shifted her weight to one foot, planting a hand on her hip. "You really don't know what changed?"

"No. I really don't. What?"

"I heard someone say yesterday that Guys N' Dolls didn't have anyone over in the Dolls section so the manager said to come over here. Isn't his sister the manager?"

"I... I mean, I noticed an uptick but... you really think KC is sending business over here?"

"That girl you did the twists for? Have you ever seen her before in your life? Where did she come from? How did she even find us?"

"I guess I see it. But... why?"

"Who cares why? Let's make this money."

"Well, okay but what if... what if he loses? Won't he want his business back?"

"You know it pains me to say it, but this is why we have to work extra hard on this campaign. I'm not KC's biggest fan, but him being Mayor means he'll be too busy to put us out of business." She hopped into her car and pressed a button that folded down the canvas hood. "And not that I wish ill on his salon, because he has employees and whatever, but... that's just fine with me. See you at the Kat later."

I lifted a hand to Tamera and watched her back out of her parking space and roll through the parking lot, out onto the street. I had been so preoccupied that I hadn't even noticed what she pointed out; the increase in clientele, from people we didn't know and hadn't seen before. And, curiously, it had begun right after I agreed to help KC with his campaign.

Maybe he was trying to make up for the past. Maybe he was just being nice. Either way, I didn't want to be in his debt. Nor did I want to be at his mercy. Tamera was right about another thing—we had to get KC into office. Otherwise everything would fall apart.

I had a few errands to run before I could go home and get fine, as Evonne put it. I swung into the parking lot at Potter Lake Community Bank and stood in the short line to deposit the day's receipts. My favorite manager, Jamilah, was working, so we chopped it up for a few seconds while her fingers flew over the keyboard to enter my deposit.

"I heard that fine Kade Cavanaugh was at Curl & Dye today. I wish I had the day off, I would have come to get my locs tightened. Or my brows done. Or... something. I just wanted to be in the same room."

"Don't let Dwayne hear you talking like that. He's liable to break something if there is a chance you're looking at someone else." Her fiancé, a former NFL fullback, was now running sports education programs for Potter Lake School District.

In addition to a full, illustrious career in professional football, he earned a degree in Sports Management and had recently graduated from Healy with a Masters in Education. He was approximately the size of a monster truck and was serious about Jamilah; so serious that men didn't even chance looking at her if he was around.

"Ain't nobody thinking about Dwayne and his mean self. He's settled down some since we got engaged. I told that boy I'm not going anywhere. I just like to look." She slid the receipt from the deposit across the counter to me. I grabbed it and slipped it into my wallet until I could get back to the shop to file it away. "Okay, I like to touch, too. A little. Don't tell D."

I laughed, turning to go. I was the last patron before the bank closed. Jamilah almost always worked on Saturdays and tried to stay open late so I could make my deposit.

"I'm introducing KC to the Kat tonight if you two feel like coming out."

"The Kat? We haven't been over there in ages. I'll talk to Dwayne, see if he wants to come hang out."

"Good. I want Dwayne to help me talk KC into coaching for the rec center. And I'm hoping they can talk about KC finishing his degree."

Jamilah nodded deeply. "Dwayne says he doesn't regret

going back at all. It was hard work, but he saw so much value, he went on to get his Master's. The School Board offered him a position."

"Really? That's great."

"Sure is. I'll be able to quit this job in time for uhm..." Though she was dark skinned, I swore I saw Jamilah's cheeks flush red. She smiled as her gaze swept down to her belly, which she was gently cradling.

"Shut up!" I squealed. "Are you serious?"

"Yeah," she said, beaming. "We will be married before I start to show, thank goodness. As much money as my mama spent on my wedding gown, I had to peel her off the ceiling when I told her we were pregnant."

"That's amazing, J. I'm so happy for you two! But are you sure you should come out tonight? You'll probably be tired and the atmosphere is—"

She waved me off with a flick of a wrist. "I'll be good. We haven't been out in a while and won't stay long. We have church in the morning. I'm going home to eat some dinner and power nap. We'll see y'all down there."

I left the bank with a bounce in my step and joy in my heart. I truly loved to hear about couples coming together and falling in love and starting families, despite my failure to make it happen for myself. I thought Dexter would be the one for me. I'd moved away from Potter Lake and set up house with him, threw all my eggs in one basket on that hope and prayer.

And even when it was obvious that wasn't going to happen, I had to be dragged back to Potter Lake to face my reality.

I thought about all of the older, single women I knew around town and groaned. Was I going to end up like them? Not that remaining single would be a bad thing. I could rock it like I'd rocked everything else in my life, but those visions of KC and Leslie replicas that danced through my head days ago were so tempting to wish for.

I pulled into the driveway at home and parked next to Mama's car. I'd stopped to pick up Pops' insulin and grabbed a few things for her at Kwik-E-Mart, so instead of going up to my apartment, I went into the house through the kitchen door.

Mama was in the kitchen, as usual. It was where she loved to be. Cooking was her love language and I loved that about her.

"Hey, Les," she called over her shoulder. Her fingers were wrapped around grandy's wooden rolling pin and she was applying pressure to a ball of dough to flatten it out. The kitchen smelled like roast chicken and vegetables and the crock pot was bubbling. My stomach rumbled in anticipation of her special pot pie recipe. She'd ladle big chunks of chicken, broth and vegetables into ramekins and cover them with dough, then bake them until the buttery crust was so flaky, it broke apart in the soup.

"Hi, Mama." I slid up next to her and leaned in, dropping a kiss on her cheek. "I'm putting Pops' insulin in the refrigerator. And I picked up the stuff you wanted for Grandy. It's on the table."

"Okay, thank you. How was the day at the beauty shop?"

"It was good. Real good." I sat at the kitchen table and pulled out my phone so I could scroll through it while we talked. "We had a lot of clients today, more than we've had in a long time."

"Heard you had a handsome guest today. Folks probably dropping in just to lay eyes on him."

"It's not like he hasn't lived here over a year. People can go to his shop and lay eyes on him."

"You know how folks over here are about the shops on the other side of town." Mama huffed, rolling the pin back and forth, making the dough flatter and flatter. "They don't step foot or rubber tire on that bridge unless they're going to Healy. I guess it was your idea to bring him across the way. Part of his campaign." She spit out the word like it was a curse word. Lee Baker did not believe in coarse language.

"It was my idea. I told him there was no way folks over here would vote for him without meeting him first."

"And how did it go?"

"I guess it went pretty well. He met a few people, learned a lot about Potter Lake today. If nothing, he understands a little more about why this place means so much to us. And why we need to keep it afloat."

"I wish you young folk put as much faith in the people that set this town up and got it running as you do in a man that can make a basket from the... whatever line that is, they call it."

I giggled. "Mama, you didn't go to that meeting. The Mayor was adamant that he's gonna do whatever he wants, so long as he's in office. I know you support him now, but wait until he threatens something that actually means a lot to you." Not that the near-closing of the Curl & Dye had been enough to turn her away from Quincy Adams.

"Just make sure to pick up my ballot ahead of time so I can fill in that circle next to Quincy Adams. That boy KC is nice and nice looking, but I need a leader who has more going for him than a flashy salon and some basketball money." With a loud humph, she reached for her cutter and started making the round forms that would be the tops of the pot pies.

Some people, like my mama, were opposed to change and loved things the way they were. They would support the Mayor no matter what. Little did they know, the die had been cast and change was already coming. Nothing would ever be the same again.

———

Tamera and Evonne were already at the Kit Kat when I pulled up, each of them with their faces in a compact mirror while they added final touches to their looks for the evening. Tamera's long legs were on full display in leather shorts, fishnet stockings and stiletto heels. Her oversized, off-the-shoulder blouse was a weave of mesh and lace and showed off a black bra underneath. She finished off the look with huge hoops that picked up glints of light from the illuminated sign that flashed Kit Kat Lounge.

Evonne wore a mini skirt and over-the-knee boots, paired with a midriff baring, sleeveless sheer blouse. Long, dangly, sparkling earrings hung from her ears and a matching choker circled her slender neck.

I had to dig way into the back of the closet for something to wear. I wanted something that accentuated my curves and thick hips but also made me feel like I looked good. I grabbed a white slashed sleeve bodycon dress that I'd only worn once, on the last New Year's Eve I'd spent with Dexter. It was a hot little number that hit me mid thigh and clung to all the right curves. I braided and twisted my locs into an updo and accented my look with big jewelry—white leather teardrop earrings and leather cuffs and strappy sandals I wore with the ties wrapped up my legs for extra drama. I dropped my keys, phone and a tube of lip gloss into a small clutch.

"You'd think we never went anywhere, with how we went all out tonight."

"We really don't go out much," Tamera said, then pressed a tissue against her lips to blot extra lipgloss. "We should change that. We do too much sitting at home yelling at the TV about some dumb dating show."

"You know I'm game," said Evonne, tucking away her compact and smoothing down her short bob, a lace front wig she was evaluating for a new black hair care company. Her side-gig, a youtube channel called Hair by E, reviewed black hair care products and showcased hair styles. She was still small time, but quickly gaining popularity. Adding her to the staff at Curl & Dye would benefit us both—she'd been bringing a younger crowd to the salon and it gave her a place to practice and show off her skills. Only her favorite hair creations made her website.

"Have y'all seen KC or his crew yet?"

Tamera opened her mouth to answer, but the glare from bright headlights and the thump of bass from a high quality sound system interrupted. KC maneuvered his jet black Escalade into a spot next to mine. A line of cars followed and pulled into spots next to him. The rumble coming from KC's truck stopped, the lights went dark and the driver's side door opened, then slammed shut.

For a tall, well muscled man, KC had a light gait as he came around the front of the truck and stopped to wait for his friends to get out of their cars. KC looked... amazing. Well put together in a button down shirt, dark jeans, sneakers and a blazer. Tamera's cut looked even better hours later, as did the great edge she'd given to his goatee. The matte black studs he wore in his ears were understated and perfect with the rest of his look. He was close enough to send a rugged, sharp, masculine scent in my direction. It washed over me in waves, driving my attraction higher with each hit.

My breath caught in my throat, which made me cough a little. Tamera must have sensed what I was feeling, because she appeared next to me to pat me on the back and mumble in my ear.

"Steady, girl. You alright?"

I nodded and gave her a small smile of thanks.

"Ho. Lee. Shiiit," Evonne muttered, appearing on my other side. "Why is he so fine? Damn!"

"Evonne, honey," Tamera warned. "Breathe. You're going to explode."

In response, she gave us a guttural grunt and smoothed

her hair down again. "If I don't get a drink, like right now, I'ma jump somebody."

"In a second," I told her, then approached KC, who had propped an elbow on the hood of his truck and was watching me watch him.

"Leslie," he said, giving me a nod that was more like a lift of his head. "You're looking..." He paused and licked his lips, then laughed. "I was going to say something that I really shouldn't. Suffice it to say, I'm really into this side of you."

"What side is that?"

"The grown and sexy, you don't even know what kinda ruckus you causin' side."

I laughed, almost choking again. "I wasn't aware I even had that side, but thank you. I think. It sounds like a compliment."

"It is," he said softly. "All day, every day, Les." He stood up straight and made a turn for me, so I could see his entire outfit. "So how did I do with not ballin' outta control?"

"Very good. Very... very good. You look nice, KC. So does your crew." I nodded to the small group that had gathered near us. TC and Monica had already enveloped Tamera and Evonne into their crowd and were chatting amongst each other.

"We clean up nice. Are we ready to go in?"

"We are. I called ahead and reserved the best table in the house. I guess we should lead the way, since this was our idea." KC held out his arm and I tucked my hand into the bend of his elbow. We stepped around the group and KC called over his shoulder, "Let's go have some fun, ya'll!"

The Kit Kat Lounge was Potter Lake's oldest drinking establishment, a holdover from Prohibition, which was repealed in 1935, but the county stayed dry and the lounge didn't serve alcohol (at least openly) for many years after that. It wasn't until nearly thirty years later that lawmakers lifted the ordinance that kept Conrad Chase, owner of the Kit Kat, from serving alcohol.

Though other bars and lounges existed in Potter Lake, the Kat was definitely the most iconic with its brick walls, leather furniture, wood floors and long bar with vintage beer taps and cash registers that were still in use. On one end of the lounge were tables for two or twenty. In the center of the lounge were groupings of leather couches, chairs, low tables surrounded a fireplace that was usually lit in the winter.

The walls were decked, from one end to the other, with African paintings and artifacts as well as prints and paintings depicting black history and culture. The other end of the lounge held a large, empty space that served as a dance floor.

Normally, the playlist was pre-arranged but on Saturday nights, a DJ from a Healy radio station would come and play music. I'd been to the Kat a time or two for a Saturday night Old School Party, but it was disappointing to see the music mix coming from a laptop and not a turntable.

The entrance to the lounge was bathed in a red glow from the overhead lights installed in the high ceilings. Sheila, the assistant manager and Conrad's daughter, waved from behind the bar, where she was switching out drawers in the cash registers.

"Hey, Les! Good to see you. How's your mama n' them?"

"Everybody's good, Ms. Sheila," I called to her. "Nice of you to have us this evening."

She laughed, her voice raspy and ragged from years of having to yell above music and the sounds of a lively bar. "Anytime you wanna bring some folks in here to spend money, these doors are open. You know what section y'all are in, in the middle? The grey couches."

I led our small crowd past the bar and through the restaurant full of people enjoying plates of the cook's specialties: fried catfish, barbecue ribs, smothered chicken and all the sides, with an enormous square of buttery cornbread. I detected a dull roar as we wove a path through the tables. KC was hard to miss and not many people were missing him.

Our section was at the center of the lounge, with the fireplace giving us a little bit of cover from the rest of the place. Music from the dance floor was piped in through speakers that hung in each corner of the room, turned low so that conversation was possible. A grouping of large furniture took up most of the space—two long couches on either side of a low table, love seats and chairs intermingled, a few chairs and tables on the perimeter.

"This is a nice spot. I was expecting something a little more... rough."

I laughed. "Well, it's Saturday night. They try to behave."

"Wait until after eleven," said Tamera, "when the restaurant closes and the liquor is pouring heavy. It gets live in here."

Sheila happened to walk by and turned into our section. "Everything okay? Can I start y'all off with anything?"

"Uh, I guess a round for everyone but preggo over there." KC laughed and nodded in Monica's direction, which earned him a show of her middle finger. "What do we want? Vodka? Patron?"

"We got something we call the Absolut Bitch—it's got vodka, Bailey's, Kahlua, some brandy..."

"That!" Tamera decided. "Absolut Bitches all around. And uh... something virgin for mama-to-be over there."

Sheila said she'd be right back with our shots and disappeared around the corner again.

"Les, I know you know Kendrick and Monica, but you haven't met Erik—he's one of my barbers. He's been volunteered to help me with this campaign. He's got a lot of energy so I want you to work him hard." KC pointed to a handsome young man with smooth skin the shade of a pecan hull. His eyes were dark but lively and his smile was easy as he nodded in my direction.

"Hey. Good to meet you. Looking forward to this campaign, man. I've never been this close to politics before."

"It'll be good to have you on board."

"Hey, Leslie," said Kendrick, leaning forward and around KC. "Uh... I'ma need to steal Tamera from you. KC's line-up and fade are tight. I need that kind of skill."

"Man, you know how long it took her to do this cut? Like, a half hour."

"Yeah, but... it looks good."

"Yeah, but... I'm not paying Eric to take thirty minutes on a head. In the chair, out of the chair."

I groaned, rolling my eyes. "This is exactly what I was saying the other night, KC. You can't roll people in and out of a shop like cattle—"

"Yes, I can. Men are used to it. We don't need much more than a couple of swipes with the clippers and clean up the line."

"I can see that for a maintenance cut," said Tamera. "But it's not enough for a special occasion. Y'all aren't taking your time, doing good hair and it shows."

KC laughed. "No one at a barber shop is concerned about doing good hair, Tamera."

Sheila and one of her bartenders arrived to our section with trays of shots and began setting them out on the table.

"That's why the Curl & Dye matters, KC. We care about doing good hair."

"We care about you not walking around town looking like someone ran over your head with a lawnmower," Evonne added, to which everyone laughed.

"My cut wasn't that bad." KC paused, glancing around the room. "Was it?"

Tamera cleared her throat loudly and reached for her shot. "Uh. Let's toast, shall we? To Kade Cavanaugh for Mayor?"

"Wait, wait, wait! We can't miss the first shot!" Dwayne and Jamilah stepped into our section, both looking crisp as new hundred dollar bills. Erik yelped as he leapt off of the couch.

"What the... you're Dwayne Newsome! I heard you was here, man. I just...wow! I'm a huge fan. I can't believe my life right now..."

I thought Erik might cry but Dwayne laughed and clapped him on the shoulder with a huge hand. "Relax, young man. What's your name?"

Erik stuck out his hand and, voice shaking with excitement, introduced himself. Sheila arrived with another tray and this time, the entire room, except for the two who couldn't drink, downed shots in honor of KC's campaign.

"Whew!" KC fanned himself as he set his glass down on the table. "I haven't had anything stronger than a beer in a while."

"I know the feeling. I try to pace myself."

"Good call. I remember how you get around alcohol." My eyes rolled, but I laughed. KC was predictable. I knew that would come up. I also knew he would keep poking at it until I reacted.

"Would you like to meet my friends Jamilah and Dwayne?"

An hour later, we were all cozy, comfortable and warm, spread out around our section. TC, Monica and Evonne were deep in conversation about Monica's maternity and newborn shoots.

"Do ya'll do makeup? I want my face beat when I take those pictures with this baby. This is our last, so I want to do everything I ever wanted to do with this one."

"I do makeup," Evonne said, sipping on a cocktail. "And I can do your hair, too."

The guys were all standing near the unlit fireplace, their hands wrapped around bottles of cold beer.

"I mean, yeah. It's work," Dwayne was saying. "But at that age, there's a lot of hero worship. Those kids will just be excited that you're there and they'll do whatever you say. Plus, it's what, one night a week? Especially since you're running for Mayor, I'd definitely consider coaching the basketball team. Good PR...and to go further than that, the district would love to have you come speak at some of the schools."

KC shrugged. "I did plenty of that when I was in the league, so that's no big deal. But kids don't vote—how does that help me?"

"Kids coming home talking about how Kade Cavanaugh came to their school and gave them a word of encouragement and hope, talking about how they can make it out of here, that they could be somebody?" Dwayne elbowed KC, who appeared to be deep in thought. "That goes a long way, man. I mean, no pressure, but think about it."

"I told KC it would be a good idea, but he said—"

"Hey, Leslie," KC interrupted. "Let's uh... why don't you introduce me around the place? I should be meeting people, right?" He set down his beer and rubbed his palms together.

I set down my glass of wine, giving him a hard stare. Lately he was cutting me off and interrupting me, especially if I was about to talk about his knee. I wanted to know what the big deal was, but I didn't want to start something with him tonight. Later, though? It was on.

"Okay. Fine. Yeah, let's meet some people." I led him out of the section and immediately ran into the bar manager, who introduced KC to the head cook and most of the kitchen staff and the wait staff. We made our way into the dining room, where dinner was wrapping up, so people were basically hanging out at the tables. After ten, the kitchen stopped serving except for small plates of easy to cook, finger food.

It didn't take long for a small crowd to gather around KC. He shook hands, signed a few napkins and took more than a few pictures.

"So you all know that I'm running for Mayor of Potter

Lake, right?" Heads nodded all around and a few murmurs filled the air. "I know Mayor Adams has been leading this city for a long time. He's done a lot to prop the town up after the closing of the mill..." KC glanced back at me, to make sure he was delivering the spiel correctly. I nodded, gesturing at him to continue.

"But there are some things, I'm sure you've noticed, that need attention. The town is growing and that's great. But if the changes don't benefit us all, then they hurt us all. I believe Mayor Adams' time leading this town has come to an end and in the absence of anyone else that wants to take on the job, I'm asking for your trust, for your vote for Mayor in October."

"Well, what kind of things are you talking about changing around here?" asked a person from the back of the room.

"Uhm..." KC nervously stroked his goatee while he pondered the question. Then he grabbed a chair and took a seat, resting his ankle on the opposite knee. "I'm not so much looking to change things, as keep things that are working... working. And to stop things that are killing us, like big box and chain stores."

Someone snorted and hummed, "Mmmhmmm..."

"A wise person told me that Potter Lake doesn't want to be Healy, and I understand that. I'd like to be involved in keeping the charm of this town intact, while bringing improvements that we actually need, that the Mayor is stalling on—like street lamps. Maybe some kind of bus or trolley system."

"What's to say we elect you and things don't change? What if things get worse? Shouldn't we stick with the devil we know?"

KC lifted both shoulders and held up his hands, palms up. "I'm not going to trash talk the Mayor, and I'm not trying to persuade anyone. If your vote is for Mayor Adams because that's who you're comfortable with, so be it. But if you're looking for someone with a positive vision for this town, who's looking to protect you as a homeowner, as a business owner, as a resident here and not looking to fill my pockets, my name will be on that ballot. The choice will be yours."

KC stood and thanked everyone for their time.

"How'd I do?" he asked, as we walked back to our section.

"Really good. You were down to earth, you got them thinking about what matters. Now that there's a choice and they have to think about who they want as Mayor?" I nodded, glancing up at him. "You've given them a good alternative to a crook who doesn't have their best interest at heart."

"Okay. Good. So uh... come with me a second." KC gripped my arm, pulling me down a hallway that was dark, since the kitchen had closed down. He stepped closer, gently edging my back against the wall. And then stepped closer until our bodies were almost in contact. And then stepped closer.

My body reacted to his mere proximity like his hormones were calling out to mine.

"What about you? Have I given you a good alternative to a crook? And I'm not talking about the Mayor right now."

I swallowed hard, looking everywhere but at KC, until he tucked his finger under my chin and tipped my head up. In the shadows I could only see his silhouette, but I had memorized that face. I knew his expression was intense.

"Leslie?"

"What? What do you want me to say right now? We've had two, maybe three civil conversations and you felt like that meant everything was good and you could kiss me—"

"Did I offend you by kissing you? If I overstepped, I'll apologize."

"That's not what I'm saying. I'm just, I don't know. Confused."

"About what? Me and you had a thing back in the day. There was a huge misunderstanding... on your part, I might add."

"Okay, that's what this is about? I'm not going to stand in a dark hallway and argue about how us falling apart was my fault. I'm going back to our group." I tried to sidestep KC, but he slipped an arm around my waist and pulled me firmly up against him.

"Alright, alright. I might have played into it, a little, by keeping things from you. But let's stay on task. The point is, here we are. All this time later, in the same place. With... feelings for each other. I'm not just being cocky, right? There's something there. I kissed you and you liked it. Or did I misread that?"

I was tempted to lie and say I didn't, but I couldn't. I shook my head. "No. You didn't misread that. But it doesn't mean that—"

My argument was cut off by the dip of his head and the brush of his lips against mine... feather soft, the kind of soft that was almost a tease, that was there, but just barely. The sensation sent tingles down my spine and a flush of heat through my body. And then it was a full on kiss—his tongue slowly, languidly exploring my mouth. He tasted faintly of the beer he'd been drinking and the sweetness of the shots he had bought for our section.

He cupped my chin, his thumb stroking my cheek and his fingers threatening to undo my updo. I pulled back, not because it wasn't amazing but because I knew that if we kept kissing, some things were going to happen in that hallway. And if I got caught in a dark hallway at The Kat, my mother would hear about it before 8am.

"KC, we can't do this here." I placed my palms on his chest and pushed him back so I could maneuver out of his arms, but KC still had those lightning fast reflexes that had served him well on the court. His other arm shot out and caught me, bringing me back to him.

"Then let's go somewhere where we can do this. Because I like doing this and I want to do more than this. Don't you?"

"Yes," fell out of my mouth before I could stop it. "But we shouldn't—"

"Why? Because we're not grown people that like each other? Or because our friends say we shouldn't? Or because you're helping me run for Mayor?"

"At least two of those reasons sound really good."

"I know. Common sense and all that. But this thing between you and me, it throws common sense out the window. Let's just... let's just go talk."

Both he and I knew we weren't going anywhere to "talk". But I didn't feel like calling it out... because I wanted to do everything but talk. My bottom lip crept between my teeth as a whirlwind of thoughts chased themselves around in my head. I didn't know what to do. Or what I wanted. Well, that was a lie.

For almost a year before he showed up in Potter Lake, there were rumors that he was moving back. And the whole town made sure I knew the second he had arrived. I made myself stay away from him, or at least I made sure I never came into contact with him; not when I stalked his salon, and not when I figured out where he was living.

I knew I was weak, and I had baggage when it came to him and he probably wouldn't even care that I was still here. And that I still cared about him. When he never sought me out, not even to say hello, I had my answer. I was determined not to be the old girlfriend that still pined for him like a lovesick teenager. He'd see that from a mile away, and take advantage.

But this... was different, I thought. I felt. We were both older. And wiser. Had lived and learned. To have an oppor-tunity to reconnect with him as an adult was a gift. Besides... yeah, we were grown adults that made our own decisions.

"There you two are!" I audibly sighed at the sound of Tamera behind me, butting her nose in as usual. "The dj tonight is really good. He's spinning records—like actual records, not computer keys. Come dance with us!"

"Give us a minute," said KC, his gaze fixed on mine.

"Ya'll should really—"

"Give. us. a minute. We're talking."

"Les—"

"Tamera," I snapped, over my shoulder. "Go away."

I heard her scoff an angry, haughty breath, and then the clack of her heels on the wood floor as she walked away. KC chuckled.

"You told Tamera to go away. Am I going to have to pay for that?"

"No. I will, though. So I think we should probably rejoin our party but later... what were you saying about going somewhere where we could... talk?"

nineteen

. . .

KC

Becoming the next Mayor of Potter Lake was the very last thing on my mind.

My potential constituents, our friends, the Kit Kat Lounge, the semi-private section Leslie arranged for us, our drinks, the dance floor, the music... the DJ. Not a single one of those things mattered more than knowing that in a very short time —though Leslie was not aware how short—I would steal her away and take her home with me. Where we would... talk. There would probably be very little talking happening, at least not for a while. But I was willing to keep up the pretense for her comfort.

We made a deal. We would return to the party and live it up with our friends, try to meet more people, make sure folks around town saw me actually hanging out around town, spending money and tipping well. And just when everyone was deep into having a good time, we would make our escape.

I couldn't wait to get her alone, to taste her tongue in my

mouth, to feel her skin under my fingertips, to hear those sounds she made when she was getting it good. So we went back to our party and had a good time drinking cocktails from mason jars, eating cajun catfish bites, fried macaroni and cheese balls and cornbread, talking to people—talking to lots and lots of people and grinding and swaying to the hard, heavy beat thumping from the speakers overhead.

The opening beats of "Feelin' Myself" poured out of the speakers and the crowd went wild. Leslie and I were already dancing, her body pressed tight up against mine. I gripped her waist and bent my head so she could hear me.

"I think we should go. Everyone's so into this song, no one will see us leave."

"Now?" She asked, her eyes wide.

"Yeah, now. You're not backing out, are you?"

"N-no. I just... okay. Let's make it quick, before they notice."

I grabbed her hand and made a beeline for the edge of the dance floor, then I pulled her through the lounge and the restaurant and out the front door. Total time... about 39 seconds.

"Okay, I said make it quick. I didn't say drag me through the place."

I chuckled, leading the way to my truck. "That's the only thing I'm going to do quick, Les. Don't get used to it." I pressed the keyfob button to unlock the doors, then opened the door for Leslie to help her up into the truck.

"Wait, what about my car?"

I leaned in to press my lips against hers. "I'll bring you back to get your car tomorrow. Or the next day." I laughed and shut the door, then jogged around to my side and got in. I started up the truck and pulled out of the parking space, careful to not tap Leslie's car in the process.

"That's a nice ride," I said, eying her Infiniti G37. "Did ole boy buy that for you?"

"Ole boy? You mean Dexter?"

"Yeah. Inmate 67343—"

"Do you really want to go there, KC? We aren't even out of the parking lot. I can easily jump out and head back inside."

"Okay, okay." I turned out of the parking lot and onto the street, before she really did jump out. "I thought it was funny."

"Obviously," she said, her tone dry and unamused.

"I really am sorry. I'll shut up."

"Thank you," she snapped, folding her arms and staring out the window.

Shit, I cursed at myself. I thought we'd talk and joke and flirt on the way to my house, building up the tension until we couldn't keep our hands off of each other once we got out of the truck. But the way things were going...if I could rewind the past five minutes and not make that sorry ass joke about her ex, I would have.

"I bought that car," she said quietly. "About five years ago, I got a check in the mail from a financial institution. It was a disbursement from a trust account. My Grandy had been saving money my whole life, sending off a little here and there. When I turned twenty-five, the account paid out. I had no idea she'd done that. I was so excited, I ran right out and used some of it to buy my dream car."

She sighed, unfolding her arms and stretching them out, then rested her hands in her lap. "The next year, she had a stroke. Then I found out about the charges against Dexter. Sometimes I wonder if I'm being punished for being materialistic."

"I've never known you to be materialistic. And I know if you bought that car, you sought out a good deal. You didn't just buy something right off the sales floor."

When I glanced over at her, she was gazing out of the front window and smiling. "Look at you, thinking you still know me."

"You used to compare Ramen prices, Les."

She giggled. "We're not going to argue about this fifteen years later. The store brand was cheaper."

"The packaging was smaller. The ten for a dollar deal was better. I'll go to my grave arguing that."

"We're gonna argue about that until we die, then?"

"I hope so. I hope you're around to bug me about it when we're in our eighties."

"You do, huh?" She glanced over at me, just as I looked over to see if she was looking at me.

"Yeah. I do." I reached across the center console to lay a hand on her thigh. I squeezed, not hard but enough that she knew it wasn't an accident. She didn't brush my hand away or suck her teeth or anything, so I left it there. And I didn't want to screw things up anymore—or again, so I used my thumb to turn up the volume on the satellite radio station that had been playing in the background.

After a few minutes, she dropped a hand on top of mine, tucking her fingers under my palm. She said something I didn't hear, so I turned the music back down.

"What's that?"

"I said... I'm sorry I snapped at you. Dex was important to me, once upon a time. I'm not over here making jokes about Lauren."

The mention of Lauren Hastings made my gut twist into knots. She was a starfucker, a money-hungry fame whore that preyed on ballers of all kinds, the type of woman that considered a restraining order to be a suggestion and thought nothing of taking a baseball bat to property that wasn't hers. To be honest, she scared the shit out of me. It wasn't a good idea to make her angry. I tried very, very hard not to do that.

I only got away from her by introducing her to a bigger, richer player on my team. I hated his ass anyway. Served him right. Crazy thing was, those two apparently deserved each other because they were still together.

"Yeah, let's definitely not bring her up. Let's just talk about us tonight. Me and you. And every thing me is gonna do to you."

"Oh, Lord," she muttered. But I saw her smile out of the corner of my eye.

A few minutes later, the garage door was slowly rising, revealing the space I was obsessed about keeping neat. I hated a messy garage—it indicated a messy life, to me. If nothing else, my tools and toys were always put away. I pulled into my spot and pressed the overhead button for the door to close, then popped the locks on the truck.

"Hold up a second," I told her, before I got out. I stepped around to her side and opened the door, then offered her a hand climbing down from the cab. Once she stepped onto the running board, I wrapped my hands around her waist and lifted her up, then set her down. She'd laughed when I picked her up, but the chuckles died in her throat when I bent toward her to claim her lips. It had been nearly two hours since I kissed her in the hallway at the Kat, and my mouth missed hers.

I felt the whimper and deep exhale that rose from her throat. I walked her backward, pressing her against the body of the Escalade. Considering she was wearing a white dress, I'm glad I'd had the foresight to run it through the carwash earlier. She didn't seem to mind, though—she wrapped her arms around my neck and opened her mouth. We might have stood there all night, kissing and grinding our bodies together, had the overhead light not popped off. The sudden darkness reminded me that we were standing in the garage.

"Guess we should go in," I muttered, against her lips.

"Yes, please," she mumbled back. "These shoes got my dogs barkin'."

I laughed at that, then pulled away, running my palms down her silky soft arms until I was holding her hands in mine, then walked us to the door. I keyed in a code and the electronic locks and the alarm disengaged. As soon as we entered the kitchen, the alarm and locks re-engaged.

"So, are you locking me in here?" She moved closer to the control panel built into the wall.

"I'm not holding you hostage or anything. The alarm is on, so you have to press this..." I pressed a key on the touchscreen and the alarm indicator turned green. "Now it's off and you can leave without alerting the police, the fire department and everyone within a six block radius."

She reached up and pressed the key to turn the alarm back on, making the icon glow red. "I'm not going anywhere," she said, turning to face me. "For a while."

"Happy to hear that. Come here." I led her to the island counter, grabbed her by the waist and lifted her off of her feet again. Now we were face to face, which made it easier to lean forward and resume the kiss that had been interrupted in the garage. She leaned in and slid her arms around me. I got as close as I could without climbing up there with her.

When our lips parted, she snickered. "You like throwing me around, I've noticed."

"I do like that." I couldn't keep my hands off of her, indulging in the softness of her skin, from her waist to those hips I'd been thinking about, down her thighs to her shapely calves. I untied the strap of one shoe, and then the other, letting them fall off of her feet. "You're easy to throw around."

She tossed her head back and laughed. "Oh, you do flatter me, Kade Cavanaugh."

"You told me a couple of weeks ago that flattery would get me everywhere. Remember what I asked you?"

She rolled her eyes to the ceiling like she couldn't remember me asking, but I knew she was faking. "Uhhh... you asked if I meant everywhere."

"Uh huh. And you said, except there. And I'm just wondering where there is right now, Les?" I ran my hands back up her calves, over her thighs, between her legs that were spread to accommodate my body between them. I slid my fingers beneath the hem of her dress and gripped her, my thumbs stroking her inner thighs and traveling higher.

When my fingers reached thin wisps of lace, I made long, slow strokes that brought squirms and deep sighs. Her head tipped forward, about to land on my shoulder but I caught her with a kiss, swirling my tongue around hers, sucking and teasing, pulling back and going deep again.

I found the magic button that made her scoot her body forward and wrap her legs around me. I pulled my lips from hers long enough to mumble, "Am I there yet, Leslie?"

I got my answer in a whimper and the tightening of her limbs around me. I kept stroking, pressing, rubbing, teasing until I detected her hips matching my rhythm. She pulled back from the kiss and sucked in a loud, sharp breath, then leaned back on her hands and opened her legs wide.

"Holy shit, don't stop," she moaned, her head tossed back.

I didn't stop. I tucked my fingers under the band of her panties so I could really feel her, skin to skin. I was rock hard, watching her chest heave and her hips roll against my thumb. When I slid one, then two fingers inside her, she let out a guttural grunt and her back arched. She rocked faster, drawing my fingers in deeper, soaking them.

"Ooh shit, I'm com—" That was all she got out before she yelped and her body did an epic jerk-convulse-shake combo. I didn't pull out until she stopped pulsing around my fingers, until her hips stopped pumping, until she was reduced to heavy breaths and whimpers. Her locs were starting to come out of the pins she'd used to hold them in place, so random strands of her hair were spread out around her head like rays of sun. She was beautiful, glowing and glistening with a light sheen of sweat, laid out on my kitchen island.

"There... you made it there."

I bent over her to drop a kiss on her lips. I wanted to let her recover, but Leslie had plans. Moments ago, her limbs were limp but she found the strength to loop her arms around my neck and lock her thighs around my waist. She hunched her hips, grinding against rigid muscle.

"I need you," I heard in my ear. "Please KC, don't tease me. I need—"

I chuckled, capturing a bit of her skin in my teeth, just enough to tease her. "Babygirl, you're not going anywhere until I'm done with you, so relax."

She writhed beneath me, sending up a sultry smile. "I'm trying, but I feel you."

"I feel you too, baby." I dipped my head to kiss the rise of her breasts where they were popping out of the top of her dress. I felt Leslie move, then realized she was pulling the zipper that ran up the side of her dress. I helped, pushing the dress up over her waist. The sight of her barely there lace thong made me light headed. I hardly knew where to start, but I couldn't resist tasting all the golden brown skin on display.

I braced my hands on her hips and licked a long, slow strip from her belly to her soft mound. Leslie sighed what sounded like a pleasured breath. Her hands moved to my head and her legs spread wider so she could guide me where she wanted me to be. She was warm, her scent a sexual, sensual musk that drove me higher. I looped a finger under the band of her panties and pulled, sliding them down her legs until they hung off of one foot, where they fell to the kitchen floor.

"Guess we gotta find those later, huh?" She hummed in response, moving to prop herself up on an elbow. Her eyes were at half mast, her lips parted. She palmed the back of my head and gently pushed me toward her.

"Please," she whispered. "I want to feel your mouth on me."

I was more than happy to oblige, nipping at her inner thighs for a few moments before capturing her clit in my mouth. I ran the tip of my tongue top to bottom, using my fingers again to tease her pussy lips before pushing into her.

"Oooohhh... fuck, you're driving me crazy." Leslie rolled her hips, falling into a rhythm between my tongue flicking and sucking her clit and a finger pumping in and out of her. I was ready for the next step but I had to stop what I was doing to reach back into my pocket for my wallet, which got me a disappointed, strangled moan.

"Hang on a second, baby. I told you, you're not going anywhere until I'm done." I flipped open my wallet to pull a condom out of the slot where I'd slid it earlier in the day, then tossed the wallet onto the table behind me. Leslie sat up and reached for my waistband, unbuckling my belt and then undoing the button on my pants.

"Fuck this relax shit," she said, a sexy cackle coming from her throat. "Let's go, Cavanaugh." She ripped the zipper down with so much force that my pants sagged, falling down my thighs to my knees. I smiled when she gripped my length through the boxer briefs and gave an appreciative moan. Her hands climbed higher, unbuttoning my dress shirt and pulling it open, then smoothing her hands down my chest.

"Your body is... umph. I thought you were hot in college, but damn, boy." She shook her head, licking her lips. "The last fifteen years have been really... really good to you."

"Thank you, sexy. That and more back at you, with your thick snack self." I ripped open the condom package and pulled out the latex ring. I was unceremonious about pulling down my boxer briefs so I could put it on. My dick bobbed, the head damp with evidence of just how much Leslie turned me on. Her hands were warm, thankfully, as she wrapped a hand around me.

"I remember you," she cooed, stroking.

"You talking to my dick, babe?"

"I am. Is he gonna talk back?"

"Yeah." I rolled the condom on and waived her hand away,

then hooked my hands around her thighs to scoot her to the edge of the island. "He's got a couple of things he wants to say to you."

I heard her squeal, then toss her head back and groan when the tip pressed against her opening. She rolled her hips and I planted my feet, thrusting in short strokes, working my way inside her.

"Shit shit shit shit," she was chanting, getting louder the deeper I sank into her. After a few moments I lengthened my strokes, withdrawing until I had almost pulled out, then sliding back in. I loved feeling her, every inch of her, tight and wet around me, clenching and then releasing.

"Mmmmph, girl. Whatever it is you're doing, keep doing it."

"Does he like that? Are we talking, now?"

"Yeah, we're talking. Had some things to say."

"Like?"

"Like..." I grabbed her hips and pushed deep into her, so deep the sweat of our bodies intermingled. "Like I missed you. Like I thought about you all the time. Like I hated hearing about you moving away, being happy with some other guy. I wanted that guy to be me, Leslie."

"I—"

"No... just....let me finish. I'm sorry for what I did wrong, the things I didn't say, what I didn't share with you. For pushing you away. Seeing you again and you being willing to help me with this election showed me what I gave up and I regret that. But right now we're two grown ass people that like each other and I want us to be together."

"Me too, KC. Me too."

"That's good, baby. That's what I wanted to hear." I bent to kiss her, stroking again. I moved a hand between us and my thumb found her clit, engorged and slick with her juices. Her hips jerked and she whimpered in my mouth before she pulled away to tip her head back and hurl a grunt into the air.

My mouth dropped to her neck and shoulder, where I ran my tongue across the spot I'd been thinking about since that day at her shop.

"You close, Leslie? I don't want to come before you."

"Yes," she panted, laying back on the counter and locking her thighs around me again, pulling me close to her. "Fuck me. Make me come."

I kept my thumb on her clit, applying gentle pressure to her while I worked my hips against her body. I moved faster, harder, egged on by her moans. Her pussy clenched tight around me in quick pulses, milking me. I rolled my head to find her lips and clamped my mouth onto hers. I kept moving, pumping into her, feeling her entire body crash into orgasm. I wasn't far behind her, spilling my load into the condom, giving everything I had to give.

Eventually, there was only the sounds of heavy breaths in the air, the two of us trying to come back to Earth.

"That was amazing... you were amazing... I feel amazing..."

I laughed quietly, knowing Leslie could feel me.

"Don't laugh at me. I feel... I feel high, kinda."

"Do you even know what being high feels like, Les?"

"I do now," she said, sighing dreamily.

"You good?"

"I'm real good, baby. Real good." I kissed her, then pushed myself up and pulled out, holding the condom so it didn't slip off. "Let me take care of this real quick. And then I have a surprise for you."

twenty

. . .

LESLIE

I really did feel high. A little drunk and kind of sleepy. At the same time, I felt vibrantly awake and alive, as if every nerve ending in my body was standing straight upright. I loved the feeling, this mix of awareness and bliss, and wasn't in a hurry for it to go away.

KC disappeared into a powder room. I heard the toilet flush and then he came back down the hall, shedding clothes as he approached me. I liked that idea, so I pulled my dress off.

"Damn. You look sexy sitting in my kitchen butt ass naked."

"I have a feeling you think I'd look sexy sitting anywhere butt ass naked."

"I have a feeling you'd be right about that." He stepped between my legs, which brought him close enough to reach for his dick bobbing between us.

"Did you enjoy your conversation with him?"

"Mmm...I did. We had a good, good talk."

"That's nice. I enjoyed my talk too. You ready for your surprise?"

He wrapped his arms around me and lifted me off of the counter to my feet. I almost slumped to the floor, but KC caught me, scooping me up against him and walking me toward the stairs.

"You think you can make it up there by yourself? I have a couple of things I need to grab from down here."

I bobbed my head, still feeling a little drunk and light on my feet.

"Hang a left at the top of the stairs. You'll walk right into the bedroom."

The high pile carpet was soft under my feet as I climbed the stairs. I followed his directions and walked into a spacious, airy room that was more like a room and a half. Enormous king sized bed, oversized furniture, huge windows and a set of french doors that led out to a patio overlooking the backyard and a pool.

A couple of doors, which I assumed were the closet and bathroom were closed. A gas fireplace and large flat screen TV hung directly across from the bed, which must have been raised a half foot off of the ground. I stood next to it, trying to figure out how to climb up into it.

KC came up behind me and set a tray with two glasses on the nightstand.

"Want me to throw you up there, or something? I like throwing you around."

"How... how do girls get into this bed? Or do you not have girls up here, just on the kitchen counters?"

"Why are you hinting about other women? No girls have been here, Les. Just you. Seriously, do you need a hand?"

"I can do it," I insisted, hiking a leg up and pulling myself up onto the bed. I crawled to the middle and sat. "See?"

"I see you, sexy. Here." He tossed two thin DVD cases at me. I picked them up and flipped them over. Then laughed.

"Hitch and Man on Fire! Wow, I haven't seen either of these in forever."

"Me either. And..." He opened a drawer in the nightstand and started pulling out packages and tossing them to me. I squealed as soon as I saw Mike & Ikes, Jujubees and Red Vines land in my lap.

"You went all out. Is this a nod to the first night we hung out?"

"Sort of." He closed the drawer, then picked up one of the glasses of bright red juice and handed it to me.

"You made Kool-Aid?" And then it hit me. The scent. "Kade Cavanaugh. You did not."

He grinned and dropped onto the bed next to me. "I did. Good old Trashcan Punch. Bring back some memories?"

"I don't know if memories is the right word. I definitely remember some feelings. Like, heaving stomach and raging headache."

"So, you know what this is, right? Our first date—" He paused, pointing to the DVD cases. "And our last date."

"But... those weren't dates, KC."

"Sure they were. We were both too chickenshit to call them dates, but—"

"Nah, what you had with that sorority girl were dates. I had to watch you go around campus with that airhead—"

"She wasn't an airhead, Leslie. You just didn't like her."

"Whatever. I had to watch her hang off of your arm when I wanted to be there."

"She's a chemist for Dow, now. I ran into her at a game a few years ago."

My eyes rolled as I brought the glass to my lips for a tentative sip. It actually tasted good, more fruit juice than alcoholic kick, but I remembered that it tasted good to me back then, too. And then the alcohol punched me in the face and before I knew it, I was offering to have KC's babies. And hurling into a trashcan.

"So you're trying to get me drunk so I'll sleep with you?"

"Too late for that," he answered, reaching for the movies. "I just thought we could chill. Relax. Do stuff we both like doing, like we used to. Are you in a hurry to go home?"

I shook my head and smiled. "No. I have all night."

"Good. That's exactly how long I plan to take." He picked up a remote and navigated to a menu, then gestured to the DVD's. "Which one first?"

"Hitch. Because if it sucks—"

"We can fall back on Man on Fire," he finished, grabbing the DVD and crossing the room to slide the disc into the player mounted below the TV.

I looked up, noticing the surround sound speakers installed in the corners of the room. We pulled down the covers and crawled into bed, just like we did the night we slept together, and started the first movie. And argued over the first box of Jujubes.

"Why do you always eat all the Jujubes? You know I like those, too."

He shrugged a shoulder. "Same reason you got a death grip on those Red Vines. How do you know I don't want some?"

I grunted a humph and handed him the package of red licorice. "Here. Have your Red Vines then. Give me those Jujubes."

"Nah," he said, dumping out another handful of candy and pouring them into his mouth. "I'ma keep this box."

"Ugh, you're a rude ass."

He leaned over and kissed my cheek, then my temple, then rolled over on top of me, working himself between my thighs. He was warm and firm, cocooned between our bodies. He lowered his head to whisper into my ear, low and husky.

"You like my rude ass, though."

"I do." I murmured, the movie already forgotten. I wriggled into position, looping my arms around his neck. "I really do."

———

I glanced at the alarm clock on the side table and my eyebrows shot up at the realization that it was nearly noon. KC was spooned around me, one arm under my pillow, the other across my hip and his chest at my back. I was comfortable and warm and worn out. And my inner thighs were deliciously sore. But I needed to pee.

Slowly, I edged out from under KC and scooted to the edge of the bed, then almost fell out of it. As soon as my feet hit the rug, I made a beeline for the ensuite bathroom and eased the door shut. If my bladder wasn't making such a fuss, I would have had time to admire the time and care that had gone into the design of the room.

It wasn't until I had achieved relief and was washing my hands that I noticed the double vessel sinks mounted on a teak grey cabinet, under a mirror that basically took up the whole wall. I found a soft terra cotta colored towel hanging from a stainless steel rack and dried my hands while I checked out the rest of the room—large, glass encased shower with four rainfall shower heads; the massive garden tub with jacuzzi jets and so much unused shelf space, I was already imagining all my bath salts and bubble concoctions lined up along the edge; and the toilet, which I noticed had been tucked away where it was almost inconspicuous. There was nothing relaxing about staring at the toilet while you were sitting in a jacuzzi tub.

The room was painted in a soothing, muted blue grey that I probably wouldn't like if it was described to me, but seeing it in action with the understated but classy decor, it had grown on me.

I had intended to be quiet since KC was still asleep, but I yelped so loudly, I swore I heard an echo when I opened the door. He was leaning one arm against the doorjamb, his wide, bare chest in my face.

"You made that sound a couple of times last night. Done checking out my bathroom, nosy?"

I chuckled and stepped aside so he could come in. "Do you blame me? I don't get to use the word pretty for bathrooms much."

"Yeah, it's nice. My mom helped me put it together, the colors and the fixtures and everything. You should see what TC has going on next door." He moved toward the toilet, then looked over his shoulder. "You staying in here? I mean, you've already seen all of me."

"While you pee? No thanks."

I left him alone in the bathroom and tried not to hear the sounds of him doing his morning routine. I walked into his closet, which was about the size of my apartment. Easily a hundred pairs of shoes, most of them Aris sneakers, were lined up on shelves on the wall, angled with toes pointing north so they were easy to grab. Long sleeved dress shirts and short sleeved polo shirts, casual slacks, jeans, belts, caps were all neatly hung in their respective sections.

Along the wall were a couple of tall bureaus. I pulled one open and found t-shirts upon t-shirts. KC must have saved every shirt he'd ever been given. Playoff tees, championship tees, charity game tees, gifts from schools and universities and companies... every drawer was stuffed with them. I pulled out a random shirt from a 2012 charity basketball game and slipped it over my head. Then laughed because it nearly fell to my knees.

I padded out of the closet and pulled the door closed. KC was out of the bathroom and was lounging on the bed. He frowned at me.

"What?" I asked stopping at the edge of the bed.

"I don't know why you went through my drawers to find a shirt to put on. I'm just gonna take it back off."

I grinned, my body already coming to attention at the

thought of morning... err afternoon sex. "I need to find my phone. I'm sure Tamera blew me up last night."

"Might be in the truck." KC grunted as he sat up and threw the covers off of his body. He'd pulled on a pair of black boxer briefs that didn't do much to conceal or control his erection. "I don't remember you bringing your purse in."

"Don't get up, I'll go get it."

"You'll get in that bed and be ready for me when I come back," he said, dropping a kiss on my forehead as he passed me, then nudged me toward the bed. "That's what you'll do."

I huffed, but I wasn't arguing all that hard. I climbed back up into the bed while I yelled, "Bossy!" at his retreating back. I picked up a remote and pointed it up at the TV mounted across the room. A morning news program popped on and the room was full of the sound of political pundits loudly arguing their points.

I heard bare feet and looked up to find KC coming back into the room, my clutch in his hands. He tossed it to me and slid into the bed again. I zipped it open and pulled out the phone, which I had set on silent the evening before. I had just enough battery to check my messages.

Just as I thought, I had several texts from Tamera, who at first wondered where I had disappeared to. Then she told me not to bother calling, because she already knew where I was. And called me a brazen hussy. I laughed to myself.

I also had a text from Mama, who wondered if I was attending church with the family this morning. I felt a twinge of guilt at the thought that I was in bed with a man and they were at Solid Rock Church of Christ listening to Pastor Glen preach down the house. I promised myself that I would pray about it later. Much later, because KC wrapped an arm around me and slid me across the bed and up against the warmth of his body.

I snuggled in close to him and finished scrolling my

messages, checked my email for any changed appointments, then tossed the phone a few inches away.

"Am I in trouble?" KC asked.

"Oh, for sure. So am I. Mama texted."

"Uh oh. Ima get it from Ms. Lee. Were you supposed to be at church, sangin' about the Lord's goodness and whatnot?"

"Kinda. Instead, I'm in this bed, about to sang about KC's goodness and whatnot."

"Hallelujah! Amen!"

I nuzzled his neck, dropping kisses along his jawline from his ear to the edge of his mouth. He turned his head in time to catch a long, sweet smooch.

"I like you in my bed, you know that?"

"To be honest, I like me in your bed, too."

"I don't just like you in my bed, though. I like you around. Like... in my life. I was serious about us being together. You think you could handle it if we spent more time together?"

"I think I can handle that. If you can."

"What do you mean, if I can? I'm not the one that's been stomping around this town, mad about my shop."

"You act like I had no reason to be mad, KC."

"You had plenty reason to be mad. But if I was anyone else, it wouldn't be so personal. That was about more than my shop."

"It was, was it?"

"Yeah. It was all this... unresolved sexual tension—"

"Oh, that's what it was?"

"—between you and me. I get it, though. It can drive people crazy, make them scary—"

"Scary? Are you scared of me?"

"Girl, I'm terrified of you."

I laughed, moving around to sit on his lap. His hands fell to the roundest parts of my ass and squeezed.

"So... what's uhm..." I reached up to lay my hands on his shoulders and smoothed them down his inked arms, then back up, concentrating on the images embedded in his skin. "They're beautiful, so... intricate. What are they about?"

He glanced down at each arm and rolled his shoulders, as if he hadn't looked at his own artwork in a long time.

"I was on TV all the time and I wanted to be loud about things that were important to me. So, I decided to tie every- thing together with my mom. This is for MS." He brushed his finger across a vivid orange ribbon. I realized, then, that all of the colors and images coordinated with that single tattoo.

"There's some symbols that mean hope, love, family. She likes hummingbirds, so there's a couple of them. Her favorite color is blue-green, like that jewel tone. Had to get a couple with that color in them."

"Does she like the tatts?"

He smiled. "Not really. She's touched that I did all this and she'll never say it, but she's not a big fan of tatts. So, I stopped updating the sleeves. And... well, I ran out of room. And because it didn't do what I wanted it to do."

"Which was?"

"Make me feel like I could do something for her. Give me some hope that there would be a cure for MS and my mom would be with us longer."

I made a throaty, sympathetic sound that produced a half smile. I cupped his chin with one hand, my thumb grazing the stiff hairs that had grown into his goatee overnight. He turned his head to kiss my palm, then leaned forward and kissed my mouth. We both moaned softly when our lips met. Between us, he stirred under the fabric of his boxer briefs.

I dug for the always-present hole in men's underwear and pulled him out, rubbing the tips of my fingers along his length.

"Well, good morning."

"Y'all gotta have a conversation?"

"We might need one." I scooted back far enough to be eye

level and took him in my hands. "Let's see if he has anything to say to me."

KC squirmed in anticipation. I caught the faint scent of cologne lingering on his skin. The mental image of him rubbing his palms together and stroking himself with the hope—or assumption that I would eventually make my way down here made me throb.

I blew a warm breath across the head and felt him pulse in response. I stuck out my tongue and took a long, wet, wide swath across and then around his head, then down one side and up the other and around again, using my hands and my vocal chords—humming like a vibrator, squeezing, rubbing, twisting.

KC was obviously enjoying it, grunting and thrusting himself into my mouth. Once he started rolling his hips and twisting the sheets bunched in his fists, I knew he was close. And so did he. He reached down and cupped my chin, pulling me off of him, then bringing me to him for a wild, intense kiss. When our lips parted, he pointed toward the strip of condoms he'd left on the nightstand.

I reached over and grabbed one, ripped it open and rolled it on.

"I wanted to finish inside you," he said, resuming our kiss while pushing me until I was laying back on the bed. He hooked an arm behind each of my knees and positioned himself above me. "And I got some more that I want to say to you."

———

I ended up smack in the middle of the bed, with most of a 240 pound man resting on top of me. With my thighs locked around him, he didn't have an option to move, but he also wasn't arguing about being held there.

"Am I too heavy?" KC mumbled, his lips brushing against the breast he was laying on. "You want me to move?"

"Not necessarily. But uhmmm... aren't you hungry?"

"Starving," He answered, lifting his head. I was rapidly learning that the way to KC's heart was with food. "You cookin'?"

I laughed, then laughed again at his incredulous expression. "Oh, I don't cook. I know how to... I just don't."

KC groaned. "So you wait until I've had a taste of the good-good to drop in stuff like you don't cook. How do you eat?"

"My mama! And before that, my Grandy. She'd whoop my tail if I tried to take over her kitchen. You know that."

"Yeah, I don't know that life, Les. My mother had no trouble giving up control of her kitchen. You're saying I might starve to death?"

"Fool, have you seen these thighs?" I tightened them around him. He groaned again, smoothing a palm down one, to my calf and back up again.

"I eat. You're gonna eat."

"So you're saying you're gonna fix me something?"

"No, I'm saying I'm taking you to Helen's Kitchen. It's Potter Lake's best soul food restaurant."

KC's eyes lit up. "Soul food?"

"Yes," I said, giggling. "So back in Potter Lake's humble beginnings, Helen used to sell plates out of her kitchen on Friday nights. She got so popular, her husband found her a building. She recruited some ladies to help her cook and Helen's Kitchen was born. It's pretty much where Potter Lake eats after church. You could meet a ton more people, including Helen. Getting her on your side would go a long way in turning the tide in your direction."

"Old black ladies cookin' sounds like a good meal. I guess I should get back to thinking about this job I'm trying to get." KC sat up, stretching his long limbs and emitting a lion's roar of a yawn. "Why don't you hop in the shower and get dressed, then you can take me home?"

"Who said I was taking you home? We're not done talking."

"Am I supposed to go to lunch in your t-shirt and no underwear?"

KC chuckled, leaning in for a kiss. "I think you look good in my shirt. Throw a belt on and some slides and you're good."

I laughed and pushed him back before we got caught up again and I passed out from hunger. "Shower! I'm hungry."

twenty-one

. . .

LESLIE

KC let me borrow a pair of shorts and some flip flops so I could get home and change. I crossed my fingers that my family would observe their usual Sunday habits—church, then lunch and then a visit with Grandy. As the Escalade rounded the corner, I breathed a sigh of relief to see the empty spot where Mama's car usually sat. I directed him to park in my spot and unhooked my seatbelt.

"I'm just going to grab a super quick shower and change. I promise I'll be fast and be right back down."

KC leaned back in his seat and turned the music down and the air up. "I'm leaving in twenty minutes. You better be in this truck."

"If you leave without me you better sleep with one eye open and grow eyes in the back of your head. Don't forget Tamera is crazy and I'm right behind her."

"Yeah, yeah. Ya'll some big talkers, always have been. Just hurry up, aight?"

I laughed, hopped out and bounded up the stairs as fast as

I could bound in flip flops and shorts that were many sizes too big. I unlocked my apartment and dropped the bag that I'd stuffed with last night's outfit on the couch, then rushed through my bedroom to the bathroom to start the shower. The pipes were old and the water heater needed to kick in, so I liked to let the shower run for a few minutes.

I went back to my bedroom to sift through my closet for something to wear. I'd settled on a pair of skinny jeans and a peasant blouse with long, flowing sleeves when my cell phone rang out with Tamera's ringtone. I glanced at it, then glanced at the shower, and then glanced at the phone again. Then I sighed, knowing she would keep calling until I answered.

"T, I don't have time to talk. I'm trying to get in the shower so we can go to lunch."

"Well, good afternoon to you too, Leslie. How you feeling? A little uhm... sore?"

I chuckled, a sly smile on my lips. "I'm okay. But I seriously don't have time to talk. Can I call you later?"

"No need. I was making sure the man hadn't sexed you to death. I'm only going to ask you this once—are you sure this is what you want?"

I dropped onto the bed, cradling the phone between my shoulder and my ear. "I don't even know how to answer that, Tam. But last night was fun. And tonight is going to be fun. And tomorrow might be fun. And frankly, I'm sick of sitting up under my mama and daddy—and my best friend, watching a dumb dating game show. I want to actually date."

"Okay, hon. I just... you know..."

"You care. And you'll be the first to know if I change my mind. He asked for a chance and I want to give that chance to him. I need to do this. I also need to go. I just have a couple of minutes to change and I'm taking him to lunch."

"Aight, I won't keep you. Where y'all going?"

"Helen's," I said, my voice muffled by trying to pull the t-shirt over my head. "I figured it would be a good place for him to meet more people. And get some good food."

"Oh yeah, half of Potter Lake will be out there this time of day. Well, when you come out from under KC, you have my number. I'll tell you where I ended up last night."

"What do you mean, where you ended up?"

"Naw, you in a hurry to go have lunch with your man. We'll talk later."

"Tamer—"

She hung up on me. I rolled my eyes and grabbed my kit, covered my head with a cap and headed for the shower. Fifteen minutes later, I was back downstairs—fresh faced, my locs pulled into a low ponytail and my feet in a pair of sandals. I climbed back into the truck to find KC staring at his phone, a deep "V" between his brows.

"Everything okay?"

"Yeah," he muttered, but didn't sound convincing.

"KC... really. Is everything okay?"

He set his phone into one of the cup holders in the center console and reached for the gear shift. "That was Kendrick. He said something popped off at the Kat after we left, but that everything was under control."

"Uh oh... something bad?"

"Not really... bad. Erik bumped into a guy on the dance floor. Spilled his drink, messed up his shoes. Erik apologized but the guy was already lit up. Guy threw a punch, got Erik right above the eye. Skin split open, blood everywhere. Kendrick and Dwayne stepped in, pulled Erik out. Then security took over."

"Shit..." Now my face bore the same concerned squint. "Is he okay?"

"Yeah. He's hard headed, so..." KC chuckled, then pulled out of the driveway. "I guess the guy was wearing a ring, because Erik had a gash, was bleeding real bad. Kendrick offered to take him to the hospital, but he said he was okay.

Called to check on him this morning and it turns out someone persuaded him to go to Urgent Care and uh... was still hanging out at his place." KC paused to glance at me. "Guess who?"

My jaw dropped. And I laughed. "Tamera Louise. When I was upstairs, she called me. She was eager to brag about her evening."

"Guess we didn't have an original idea, last night."

"Nah, spin that. We weren't the only ones with a good idea last night."

"See, that's why we make a good team." KC held out his fist and I bumped it. "I like the way you think, babe."

Helen and Orlando LeBlanc purposely picked a building at the center of town, equidistant from the multiple houses of worship, not far from the Recreation Center and a few blocks from city hall. Ms. Helen was playing hostess at the counter, talking to the two customers that had come in before us. When she saw me, her lips spread into a smile and her eyes grew wide as saucers.

"Leslie Baker, as I live and breathe! Where have you been, little girl? I just told Lee that I ain't seen you here in a long time."

"I've just been busy. Evenings are about the only free time I have and you're not open for dinner anymore."

"Well, Doc Moore said I had to get off my feet, can't be working these eighteen hour days anymore." She waved a hand in the air like it wasn't a concern at all. "I like serving breakfast and me and Orlando are awake anyway. Lunch is my biggest crowd, and there's plenty of places open for dinner, so..." She shrugged her shoulders, lifting her hands in surrender. "Quiet as it's kept, though? I do a special dinner every now and then, an invite only thing, just to do it. Make sure you get on my email list, so you get the invites."

As if she hadn't noticed KC standing there, she took a step back and cranked her head so she could see him. "Young man, you are a tall drank of water and I'm right thirsty. He with you, Leslie?"

"Yes, ma'am. This is Kade Cavanaugh. I don't know if you heard, but Kade is going to be running against the Mayor in October's election—"

"Oh, uh uh. Yeah. I heard about that meetin' over at the center. Heard the Mayor got a little bit ugly and a lot indignant." She shook her head, clicking her teeth. "Quincy was always a hot head—I ain't never known him to have much sense. Been getting worse as he's getting older. My granny used to say, I wanna buy him for what he's worth and sell him for what he thinks he's worth." She chuckled and tucked a fist in her hip. "So young man, you think you got the cajones to run this town? You ain't been here but a year or so, I hear."

"Almost two years," KC corrected. "And I admit to not knowing enough about Potter Lake, but I care enough about this community to be the person who steps up to make sure Helen's gets to stay open. And, with Leslie's help, I'm hoping to meet with some of the more influential people in Potter Lake. We consider you one of those people, and we hope that you'll decide to give me your vote on election day."

"Well, now that was some real pretty talk, young man. Kade, you said your name is? What kinda name is that? You got some black Irish in you?"

KC opened his mouth to answer, but she barreled forward.

"I confess I'd planned on voting for Quincy out of habit, because I didn't know his opponent. I hadn't even seen his face and he wanted my vote? Tuh." Her hard expression softened into a smile, from her eyes to the laugh lines around her mouth. "But now this tall, handsome young thing come in here with Leslie, who knows this town like the back of her hand, talking about caring about the community and being everything Quincy ain't. I say, anybody that Leslie trusts can earn my vote."

"I appreciate that, Ms. Helen. I'd also appreciate a plate or two of whatever is smelling so good in your kitchen 'cause I'm starving and my body is ready."

I'd never seen Ms. Helen so delighted to serve someone. She set us up at a small table with the usual plastic gingham table cloth near a window.

"I'll be right back with a couple of plates for ya'll," she said, as soon as we'd been seated and waddled between the tables back to the kitchen.

"We don't get a menu?" KC asked, his gaze bouncing around at the other tables. His knees brushed mine under the table, but I didn't really mind.

"Helen's is the kind of place where you eat whatever she cooked," I explained. "There's no menu, except what she puts on that board up there." I pointed toward the chalkboard that hung above the front counter. "Today she's serving buttermilk fried chicken, collard and turnip greens—if you want them with turkey, just ask—candied yams, macaroni and cheese, black eyed peas, and cornbread and biscuits with butter and honey. That's pretty much the Sunday menu."

I leaned in, almost whispering. "Now, if you want something special, you call her the Friday before and place your order. She'll have a meal ready for you to pick up. Her family is Cajun, so she can do jambalaya, gumbo, shrimp creole, boudin... and her red beans and rice will make you cry."

As we talked, food started appearing, starting with fluffy biscuits and thick squares of cornbread with cute little stoneware cups of butter and honey. I caught KC practically drooling as the towel covered basket hit the table.

"Does Sunday dinner come with a gym membership?"

I laughed. "We haven't even started talking about dessert. She serves the best pecan pie I've ever tasted, and that's saying something cause my Grandy could throw down. Now you see why I haven't been in here in a while."

"Well, that stops now, because I'm about to get fat up in

here today." He plucked a slice of cornbread from the basket and took an enormous bite, followed by a gut level groan and his eyes rolling back in his head.

I picked out a biscuit the size of my fist and reached for the butter. "I'm glad you like it here. It's one of my favorites. So now that you've been in here and talked to her, she'll expect to see you again."

"That won't be a problem," he said, his mouth full of cornbread. "And she'll sing your praises to everyone that comes in here. I suggest you get a picture with her. How is Kendrick coming with your campaign website?"

He swallowed, but his cornbread was primed for the next bite. "I'm supposed to look at it in the morning, give my final okay."

"I'll take a shot with my phone and send it to Tamera so she can work her magic. You should add the photo to a prominent place on your home page. She'll look for herself there. Same with the pictures we took last night."

"I'll make sure they get on there," he said, around the last bite of cornbread. "We need some shots blown up, big enough to hang in the window at the Curl & Dye. And Guys N' Dolls. Do you have a campaign headquarters yet?"

"Not yet. But I'm thinking..." He cleared his throat and straightened up, folding his arms and leaning forward. "I'm thinking about shutting down the Dolls side of the shop and using that as my headquarters. I don't need much room and I don't want to rent a place for what will amount to a few weeks. I can fit a few more chairs on the Guys side and move the rest of the chairs..." His brows lifted. "Do you want some salon chairs? I bought them used but they're in good shape."

I blinked, confused. In the last few seconds, KC had said something about shutting down half his shop and in the next breath offered me chairs. "What... wait. Why would you close down half of your shop? And I can't afford to buy those chairs. You know that."

"I'm not talking about you buying them. You'd be... storing them for me, if you want to call it that. I can put them in storage or you can use them. Look..." KC reached for a napkin and wiped the buttery residue off of his fingers, then reached for the tall glass of water the waitress set in front of him. "The Dolls side of the salon is a challenge. My heart is not in meeting that challenge. Women's hair is..." He whistled, shaking his head. "I'm not into all that doing good hair stuff Tamera was going on about; that's all Curl & Dye. If a head takes more than ten minutes, I'm all for sending them over to you. Especially now that I know Tamera can cut her ass off. We get a ton of business just on maintenance cuts and even without the Dolls side, I'm making profit."

"So you are sending business over to my shop. I've noticed a lot more traffic lately."

"Les, I have one stylist and she's better as a barber. I don't want to mess up somebody's head because I'm trying to be the hottest thing going. So maybe, until this election is over, I don't have a Doll's side of the shop. That gives me space to run my campaign."

The hair on my arms stood up straight. KC didn't even understand the importance of what was happening—he was so damn nonchalant, like it was so easy for him to just toss my business back over to me.

"I really want to argue with you about this..." I started, my voice shaking with emotion. I swiped at a tear. "I mean, I shouldn't let you shut down half your shop."

"But?"

"But I'm not going to. If you're willing to send the business, I'll take it. But after the election—"

He reached across the table and grabbed my hand, curling his pinkie finger around mine. "I'm not competing with you anymore, Leslie. Me and you, we're partners. It's the only way we can move forward. And once this election settles out, we figure out how we make this work long term. Deal?"

I sniffled and sat up straight, got myself together. "Deal. Thank you."

A waitress arrived and began to fill the table with plates of food. KC rubbed his hands together, his eyes virtually dancing with glee. "Don't thank me. You're helping me. Let's eat. And let's talk about when I can get rid of those chairs. We have headquarters to set up."

twenty-two

. . .

LESLIE

I pressed 'End' on a call just in time to see the way KC and Erik had to practically drag themselves through the front door at Guys N' Dolls.

"There's gotta be a way to bottle and sell all that energy kids have."

"There is, but it's illegal." I grinned, a hand on my hip. "Look at you two. Don't tell me some ten year olds ran two grown men ragged."

"Two old grown men." KC had finally heeded my pointed and relentless advice to coach the youth basketball program. His team was comprised of 9 to 12 year olds and was co-ed. That many boys would be a challenge, but refereeing boys and girls—girls who could play serious ball—was a full time job. The boys thought the girls had no place on the team but KC was determined to find and mentor the next WNBA legend Sheryl Swoops.

KC wasn't the only recruit to the coaching roster. He felt like more people should feel his pain, so he made Erik his assistant coach. Kendrick helped as much as he could, but since baby Amerie made her debut, he'd been preoccupied.

KC's campaign, dubbed "It's Time for Change," was underway. He'd finished clearing out the Dolls side of the shop and set up his makeshift campaign headquarters. The Guys side ran like clockwork as usual, but on the other side of the wall were long tables and chairs, mobile phones plugged in and charging, a desk with a laptop and printer connected to it, and stacks on stacks of campaign paraphernalia—posters, yard signs, flyers, brochures, postcards, all bearing KC's likeness.

The Curl & Dye took the chairs that KC intended to "store" and swapped out my re-engineered laundry sink, which KC made fun of nonstop, for an actual shampoo bowl. We also took a few cabinets to store extra product that TC had ordered but never used.

We'd coated both sides of Potter Lake with flyers and postcards, gone to every business to drop off brochures, shake hands, say hello. There were yard signs and banners and almost life-sized posters hanging in most of the storefronts. We'd caught Mayor Adams by surprise, it seemed. He'd never campaigned because, aside from the first election, he'd never had to.

"Rough night?" I asked, lifting my face to KC for a kiss. He dropped his lips to mine and gave me the usual loud smooch that made everyone groan.

"Babe, these kids. Like... I'm pretty sure their parents are Adams voters and they're feeding them sugar before practice, so I'll be too tired to run this campaign." He dropped heavily into a chair and stretched out his legs. He was wearing his brace, but mindlessly massaging his knee.

I hadn't wanted to bring it up, but I'd told him weeks before that he was always limping and his knee was always hurting. Advil wasn't cutting it anymore—he was taking so many pills for pain relief and didn't seem to be getting any.

The Advil would burn a hole in his stomach before it would relieve any real pain. He needed to go to a doctor, but every time I brought up the subject, he'd change it to something inane. And then limp away.

I got it. He didn't want to talk about the reason he had to leave the NBA, but his quality of life was slowly declining. We hadn't been together but a few weeks, but I was hoping for a good, long future with him, one where he could run after his children, play basketball with his sons—or daughters, and not let pain or injury change the course of his life again.

KC saw me eyeing him, and then his knee. He stopped rubbing and brightened, wrapping an arm around my waist to pull me toward him. I stepped between his legs and gingerly sat on his lap, on the leg that wasn't giving him fits of pain.

"It's late. Why are you still here?"

"I was on the phone with Arletha at the news station about those pictures."

"Did she say she was planning on using them?"

"She had to do the 8 o'clock newscast, then get ready for the 11, so we didn't have a long talk, but I got the idea that she wasn't really interested in them. I think people are about sick of Quincy Adams."

Mayor Adams had started playing dirty, bringing up innocuous issues and creating drama. Some of the photos we'd taken at the Kit Kat a month before were posted to a private Facebook page. Somehow, they ended up in Mayor Adams' hands and he'd had a field day with them, insinuating that KC was a "rich party boy" who didn't have the town's best interest at heart.

I yawned and propped an elbow up on his shoulder, then leaned my head in my palm. "I am tired, though. It's been a long day. Are you ready?"

"In a minute. I want to see if TC left today's receipts on my desk. I can drop off the deposit in the morning."

I kissed his cheek and got up from his lap. "Okay. I'll shut down here and meet you at the front door in a few."

I watched him get up, only using one leg, and limp around the corner to the Guys side of the shop.

"It's getting worse," I heard behind me. Erik had been sitting across the room the entire time, his Nike clad feet crossed at the ankle. His arms were folded across his chest and his gaze was on the partition that divided the two sides of the shop. "He never used to limp like that."

"Did something happen tonight? Why is it so bad?"

Erik nodded once, a dip of his head. He sucked in a breath and sat up. "Trying to show the kids proper form for a lay-up. I told him, you know, that's why I'm here. Let me show them. I've done a lay-up or two in my life." Erik shook his head. "Stubborn as hell. Determined to do it his way, on his own. He runs down the court, comes in for the shot. He made it, but when he landed, he like... something must have happened, because he fell out. He was trying to be strong for the kids, but I think he hurt something."

Just as I had figured, he was injured and it wasn't going to heal itself. "Thanks for telling me, Erik. I'll talk to him."

"Yep." He kicked his feet out, then and stood, stretching his arms and barreling his chest before relaxing. He looked like he was ready to pass out. "Ya'll about to bounce?"

I nodded. "You headed over to Tamera's?"

He nodded and tried to hide a smile but the turned up corners of his mouth were a dead giveaway. "Her mom is working overnight. I told her I'd come by, eat up her food, keep her company."

"Good. I'm glad she has someone to... keep her company. You know how to get along with Ms. Gina, right?"

"Oh, yeah." He dug his keys out of his pocket and shuffled toward the door. "We have an understanding. As long as I eat everything she cooks and treat her daughter right, I'm welcome in her house. Either of those start to falter, and we're gonna have a problem."

I laughed. "Sounds like it ain't gonna be a problem."

"Not at all. See ya'll." He pushed his way out of the front door.

We weren't too far behind him. KC followed me out, shut off the lights except the emergency lamps, and locked the doors behind him. We hopped into the truck and KC started it up.

For the past few weeks, I'd been staying with KC. If I went home, it was to pick up more clothes, shoes or something I needed from the house. It was grating on my mother's last nerve, I just knew it. I could sense Lee Baker's moods from across the lake. At the same time, I was an adult and I still contributed to the household—gave her grocery money, picked up Pops' meds, visited with Grandy, just like I had been doing since I moved back to Potter Lake.

There wasn't too much she could say, though she did ask me to "bring that man around" so the family could get to know him.

KC only got a home cooked meal if I took him to the house for dinner, so he'd spent a good bit of time with my family and they loved him. Well, Mama tolerated him, since he was looking to take over for Mayor Adams. We agreed to leave campaign talk on the porch and that was keeping the peace, for now.

KC must have sensed that I wanted to talk. He filled every quiet moment with babble about the team, the campaign, his shop, my shop, the next four weeks before election day. I didn't offer much in the way of conversation, the occasional mmhmm in response to a question.

I propped an elbow on the window ledge and stared out the window at the dotted landscape of Potter Lake. The sun was beginning to set earlier. There was a crisp feel to the air and a fresh and delicious scent I had always loved. The beautiful landscape of changing colors and the shimmering lake between the two sides of town made us seem idyllic. No one from the outside would know it was being torn in half.

KC was back to his favorite topic, lately. He'd been good about brushing off the Mayor's tactics in public, but in private he was seething, itching to lash out. "I wish I could say something, you know? Put him in his place. I said I was going to run a clean campaign and I meant that but—"

I glanced over at him, his skin glowing golden in the evening sun. He punched the steering wheel with the heel of his hand and heaved a frustrated sigh.

"He's just digging in," I soothed, reaching across the console to squeeze his arm. "If this is all he has, we're in good shape. The people that would choose him over you because of some pictures would choose him anyway. Don't get caught up in that. Focus on the positives. Focus on all the support you already have."

He dropped a hand from the steering wheel and intertwined his fingers with mine. "I know, babe. I hear you, and I'm grateful." He brought our jumble of fingers to his lips and kissed the back of my hand. "But I'm frustrated. There's so much I could say about him and haven't. If I lose because I decided not to fight on his level..."

"Listen, if you lose, you lose fair and square. You go down fighting. But we are not talking about losing right now. We have a few weeks left and we are going to give it everything." I squeezed his fingers wrapped around mine. "Right?"

KC nodded, rolling his lips in. He was still consumed with it, mentally and emotionally. And he would be, I realized, until the election was over. Time to change the subject.

"Did you talk to your folks about coming for the election?"

"I ran it past my dad the other day," he said, turning onto his street and approaching the duplex townhomes at the end of the block. "He said he would talk to Mom and see how she felt about it. Last time she was here, she wasn't in a wheel-chair. It's just extra logistics we have to play with."

"Can they stay at the house with her chair?"

"They'd probably stay over at TC's. She has a bedroom downstairs. The chair is more for comfort but I don't want her going up and down the stairs."

"Okay. So, I guess we'll plan to see your parents in a few weeks." I shot a soft smile over to him. He pulled into the garage and put the truck in park. "What are you over there smiling at?"

"I get to meet your parents, finally. I mean... I do get to meet your parents don't I?"

KC chuckled and popped the latch, climbing out of the truck and leaving me inside. He keyed in the code to unlock the door. I opened my door and hopped out.

"KC? Be serious. I do get to meet them right?"

He laughed again as he opened the kitchen door. "Come on, here. The alarm is about to reset."

I walked into the house and he closed the door behind me. Locks and beeps automatically sounded, letting us know the house was secure.

"I'm just going to assume yes, because you can't hide them from me. But are you introducing me as... your friend? Your... campaign manager?" I stepped close to him and slid my arms around his waist, tipping my face up so he could kiss me. "As... the love of your life?"

"Mmmmmm," he hummed, his lips opening and head tilting to deepen the kiss. After a few moments, we came up for air. "They already know who you are, Leslie."

"I know they know who I am—you know what? Never-mind." I pulled away, heading down the hall. "I'm going to hunt them down and tell them I'm the love of your life. How about that?"

KC grabbed me by the arm and pulled me close again, up against his molded chest and taut belly. Sometimes I wondered what planets aligned that let me be with this beautiful, sexy man every day. I probably did some real good deed, or something.

"That's what I'm saying, baby. I talk about you nonstop. They already know how I feel about you, that you're special to me. I don't have to introduce you as anything but Leslie. They know who Leslie is."

"Oh." My breath hitched in my throat and I couldn't say much else for a few seconds. But then I found my voice. "Well, how come I don't know all that?"

KC rolled his eyes and smirked. "You serious? Where are you standing right now? In my arms, right? Who brings you lunch when I know you have back to back appointments and you didn't schedule yourself a break? Who got that new leak at the salon fixed without you asking me to? Who's trusting you with his future, right now? Who... who's standing right in front of you, hoping you that you'll be my future?"

I blinked, waited half a second, then asked, "That was a lot of questions. Can I get a clue?"

KC snorted, then bent to drop a peck on my lips, turned me around and pushed me toward the stairs. "I don't know why I like you, Leslie. You don't have any sense. Get up there and get ready for me."

"Where will you be, while I prepare myself?"

"Gotta check on TC. I promised my parents I'd lay eyes on her at least once a day."

"You're such a good brother."

"*Unh*," he grunted, limping toward the kitchen door. Seeing him in pain twisted up my insides. I climbed the steps, a little heavy hearted but hopeful that I could convince him to see a doctor.

twenty-three

· · ·

KC

I knocked a quick tap-tap on the metal door before I tried the knob. If TC was home and awake, the door was unlocked. She was way too used to small town living and her bold attitude made me nervous. When the subdivision was empty and it was just our places, I tried to come over and check on her if I knew she was home. Now that more houses had been built and people had started moving in, I was even more wary.

"T!" I called out, stepping inside her house and closing the door behind me. I would sneak and lock it on my way out. "Where you at?"

"TV room!"

I weaved through the entryway toward the den, where she spent most of her time. Her floor plan was similar to mine, but not exact. The differences amounted to a few hundred extra square feet. TC was spread out on her sectional in her usual lounging clothes, a t-shirt and some leggings, her head covered in a colorful scarf. A bowl of popcorn sat in her lap and she held the remote aloft, muting the oversize TV she'd been watching.

"Am I interrupting?"

"Not at all. Have a seat." She made room for me on her section, despite the fact that there was a whole room full of couch I could sit on. We were used to being close, sitting together.

"How are you doing? How were the kids? How's Leslie?"

"I'm good, the kids were holy terrors and Leslie is amazing."

She tossed a few pieces of popcorn into her mouth and chewed. "So why are you over here bothering me and not over there with Miss Amazing?"

I swiveled my head from the TV to my sister. "Excuse me?"

"No shade, absolutely none to Leslie. She's great, I like her a lot. Better than Lauren." We both shuddered. Then laughed. "But uh... you're here and she's there and it's after 9 o'clock. These are sexin' hours."

"I mean... I know you're one of the guys and everything but I don't want to talk to my sister about sex with my girlfriend."

"Why aren't you over there doing it?"

"I can't come check on my little sister?"

"You're only older by three minutes, KC. Settle down. Besides, phones don't exist? You saw my lights on, you knew I was home." She dug into the bowl again and pulled out a handful of popcorn before offering it to me. I took it and had a couple of pieces. "She wants to talk about the knee. She's been wanting to talk about the knee. I had a rough night and I already know I'm going home to a bunch of questions. I don't think I'm going to be able to get away from it this time."

"So, don't try to get away from it. Answer the questions. You can do that."

I stared at the bowl in my lap, trying not to meet her

gaze. TC had this way of looking at me that confirmed she knew what I was thinking and was already inventing arguments against it. I hated that look. She got it from our mother.

"It's in my past. Can't I just leave it there?"

TC laughed, louder and longer than I cared for. I lifted my head to glare at her and she quieted down. "Uhm, it's not in your past, KC. It's here and now. It's less and less weight that you can put on that knee. It's wearing your brace every day, lately. It's the almost empty industrial size bottle of Advil on your desk at the shop."

"Alright, alright. I get it. I was hoping you could tell me how to get around this."

"Why would I do that? Of course I'm going to side with your girlfriend. And your parents, by the way. If you think they're not talking about you, think again."

I already knew TC was running her mouth to them. A few days after Leslie and I got together, my mom called me, her voice so gushy and happy, hinting and prying for information. Like I said, TC was my small town. I couldn't keep a thing from her and didn't try. She knew all of my secrets.

"Yeah. I figured that, big mouth."

"Look, I know y'all are fresh and everything, but I see how you look at her. She's not the kind of woman you want to let get away. Again." She made it a point to widen her eyes and lift her brows on that last word. "You have to come clean. It won't be as bad as you think it will. If you keep hiding, it's going to drive a wedge between you. And if she finds out from someone else... boy..."

She stretched her leg out to kick me, though luckily in my thigh and not my knee. "Don't let that happen. Go home. Talk to your woman. She's the real thing, KC. Don't let something else come between y'all." She kicked me again. "I want to finish this movie before I go to bed. Go."

I pushed up from the couch, then pointedly set the bowl

back in her lap. "It's Boogie Nights; you've seen it twenty times."

"So? Get out."

"I'm locking your door and setting the alarm."

"Whatever."

I let myself out of TC's place, but not before I glanced at the top of the line security system that she barely used and shook my head. I engaged the locks, then turned it on and pulled the door shut. Maybe I should have called our mom about that.

When I got back into the house, I headed straight for the stairs. At the second floor landing, I followed the beam of light spilling from the bedroom. Leslie liked the overhead lights off and the side table lamps on, dimmed low. She was partial to soft lighting before we went to sleep. She said it calmed her. I said whatever kept her comfortable in my bed was okay with me.

The TV was on ESPN, with SportsCenter droning in the background. Leslie was sitting on the bed, flipping through an issue of Cosmetology Today, in one of my t-shirts and a pair of boy shorts. A growl rose from my throat. She looked up from the magazine and smiled, appreciating the implied compliment.

She could dress in the sexiest clothes in her closet and I would love the look, no doubt, but my favorite way to see her was dressed down, at her most comfortable. And I loved her in my shirts and a sexy pair of underwear.

I walked through the bedroom, reaching behind my neck to pull the collar of my shirt up and over my head. I balled it up in one hand while the other worked the button and zipper of my shorts.

They fell to the floor and I kicked them toward the laundry hamper in the closet. I approached the side of the bed that had become hers; not that it mattered because I always dragged her to the middle of the bed and pulled her body close to mine. At some point every night, she worked her way out of my clutches, but for a few minutes, her soft skin was pressed against mine, chest to feet.

I climbed up on the bed and crawled toward her until I was close enough to nuzzle my favorite spot on her neck. I worked my way up to nibble on her ear, then around to lay soft kisses on her lips. I leaned into her, nudging her to lay back on the bed, but she hummed "hmm-mmm" and placed her hands on either side of my face, breaking the kiss.

"I know you know I want to talk. And I know you know what I want to talk about."

"So you're saying I can't seduce you into not having this conversation?"

"I'm saying you can seduce me after this conversation. Come over here." She gave the space next to her a couple of quick pats. "Relax. I'm not trying to stress you out or come at you some kinda way. I'm just trying to understand."

I puffed my cheeks out with a heavy breath, and hung my head. Then, slowly I crawled over her to the spot she'd designated for me to sit, scooting up so my back was against the headboard. Leslie backed up so she was up against me. I looped an arm over her shoulder.

"So..." she began, gesturing toward my right knee, the troublemaker. "When we met, you had knee problems, but you could still play. What was that about?"

I huffed a sarcastic breath. "Me being stubborn. Basketball was better than running the streets, so as long as I kept my grades up, my parents let me play as much as I wanted. Summer leagues, city intramural teams, school teams. It was all basketball, all the time." I smiled a little, feeling nostalgic about that point in my life when all I had to worry about was an algebra test and making a game winning free-throw. Sure, I thought I was under pressure, had a lot on my plate, like any kid would.

"All those years of jumping and running, plus all my

weight on my frame took its toll. My knee started giving me problems in high school. I ignored it because I was on three teams that year and I didn't want to drop any, but my dad caught me icing. Doc said the cartilage was degenerating, and if I didn't take it easy, I'd be working with bone on bone. It was something they wanted to keep an eye on before they looked at surgery. I wanted to hold off on that, as much as I could and so did my dad. He made me drop two teams and I took the summer off, just to give my knee a break."

"Hmmmm," she mused. "That must have sucked, after playing nonstop for so long."

"Sort of, but my senior year, I was focused on trying to get some attention from a college scout. It was the only chance I'd really get to leave Austin, but I needed a scholarship to go. I played the best I'd ever played, our first game that season. The coach from Healy University was in the crowd. Came to the house, met my parents and everything. Between my dad and I, we decided not to say anything about the knee. I felt like the rest had done me some good and I didn't want to be penalized over it. What's funny is, coach talked to me about the draft, too. He asked me did I want to wait a year and see how I did in the NBA draft. My dad said hell no."

I laughed, remembering that tense conversation, then me trying to convince my father that it could be good. "He was worried, you know, with the condition my knee was in, it'd get worse sooner than later. And he didn't want me to be under that kind of pressure at eighteen. So I went to Healy and shit was sweet for a long time. It's cool being the big fish in a little pond. Then I got that call, my sophomore year..."

I hardly ever talked about this stuff, about my mother's illness and our family issues. I'd only done that Sports Illustrated interview because a reporter called me asking about her and if something was going to hit the airwaves, I wanted to spin it. I felt forced to do that interview, and after I gave it, I clammed up again. Hell if I was going to let this come between me and Leslie, but baring my soul was harder than I thought it would be, and I hadn't even got to the real reason I never talked about the knee.

I knew I wasn't about to be met with judgment or harsh tones or pity, but I was the person other people talked to. I didn't lay my problems on people. I inhaled deeply and tried hard to push forward, trying to remember that the more Leslie knew, the better she would understand where I was coming from.

"We had a long talk about mom's MS. About how the doctors had been misdiagnosing her for so many years, fighting the symptoms and not the disease. About what they wanted her to do, all these tests—MRI's and scans and clinic visits. Dad let it slip that the bills were just barely manageable. Cavanaugh GC does good business, but the health care plan didn't cover what mom needed. They were coming out of pocket on a lot of expenses, plus sending money to me and TC. I just... I just felt..."

I shook my head, suddenly at a loss for words. The emotion of that call swelled in my chest like it had just happened yesterday.

"Helpless," Leslie said, laying her head on my shoulder. "I felt some of that when I learned about Grandy's stroke. I was thousands of miles away. There was nothing I could do."

"Exactly. But I knew a thing I could do. I went and talked to the Coach at Healy a couple times. He's a good guy; he let me dump on him about the situation and I asked him, you know... what if I went for the draft? Just to see what would happen."

"You'd lose your scholarship, though."

A short laugh caught in my throat as I revealed yet another secret. "I was about to lose it anyway. I was flunking out that semester, just barely eligible to play. The idea that I was causing a burden to my folks, that I could be of more use at home?" I tipped my head back against the headboard, my eyes on the muted SportsCenter broadcast but my mind back at Healy, 2006.

"It messed with my head, you know? I couldn't concentrate. Half my mind was on my mom and the other half was on the draft. I wanted to be home. And you and I were in that class together. I wanted you to have that internship—"

"That I didn't even get, because I was so busy crying over you leaving Healy." Leslie smirked. "So we all know what happened, next."

"Yeah. I got a couple of offers and I picked the one that served my best interests. I wanted to play for the NBA. Of course, I had my dream teams, but most of all I wanted to be able to help my family out."

"What did your parents say when you came home, talking about entering the NBA draft?"

I laughed. "Dad was hot. For a minute, he was hot. I was all kinds of irresponsible, ungrateful, stupid. But I did a lot of work for him, basically managed his company while he was doing stuff with my mom. By the time the draft came around, they were hopeful. I walked away from a lot, to help them out. I got lucky." I nodded, realizing again just how lucky.

"So your knee wasn't an issue?"

"Nah, cause I took six months off. Worked out, kept it loose, didn't stress it. I was a rookie, so I wasn't getting a whole lot of play. But the better I played when I did play, the more I played in subsequent games and then the knee started to bother me again. But I didn't want to be benched so early out of the gate. My rookie contract was only two years and I was coming up for trade, so I played like my life depended on it.

"Got on the Warriors and everything was good, except now I got a lot of play time. I did a lot of pivoting on the knee. I was used to moving a certain way, to protect the knee, but I got bumped one night, landing a jump shot."

"I watched that game. And all the ESPN replays. You tore

your ACL. Dexter was upset. He had you on his Fantasy team that year."

I nodded. "You know the deal, after that. Surgery, rehab, kid gloves for five weeks. That's rough on a young player when the season is only six months."

I grimaced, reaching up to rub the knots of tension from my neck. "So... for pain, the docs were giving me these pills. Oxycontin. I took them and they worked. I'd keep asking for them and they'd keep giving them to me. I was playing hard, but I was on the pills so I didn't feel it. Got traded again to the Baltimore Herons. Played okay through most of my career with them, but this one game... I was like Jordan, you know? Shot after shot after shot. Until the same thing happened... landed on the wrong knee in the wrong way.

"The second ACL tear was the worst time to have an injury. My contract with the Herons was coming up. I tried to convince the league that I could be back up to 100% in no time, just give me the off-season to rest. The Herons offered to waive me, forgoing the last year of my contract, if another team wanted to take me. But at that point, I couldn't even play. My knee wasn't healing like it was supposed to, probably because I wasn't rehabbing right. And... things were getting weird, with the pills."

"Weird," repeated Leslie, her forehead creased. "Weird how, with the pills?"

I couldn't swallow the hard lump in my throat. I couldn't even look at Leslie, but she reached up and cupped my chin and turned my face toward her. I didn't want to be this man, in front of her. I wanted to have been stronger, better, healthy. But I wasn't. I was just Kade Cavanaugh. And that was going to have to be okay for Leslie Baker.

"When I came back to Healy, I didn't go home because I couldn't go home. I didn't want my folks to see me. If it wasn't for Kendrick I don't even know where I'd be right now..." My voice trailed off and I broke eye contact.

"Were you... addicted to the pills?"

"Nah," I said, chewing on my bottom lip. "I mean... maybe. I was dependent. I hated every minute of needing pills to function. I'd seen people lose everything behind an addiction and I didn't want that shit to get worse. I came to Healy to shake the pills. And then I needed something to do because I had too much money and free time. I had too many people reaching out to me. Hey, Kade. How you doin'? You need anything?' Like, legit doctors calling me, offering to write a script. You know how many players go out on that floor, high on something their doctors gave them? Or buying shit on the street? I've seen guys go from Oxy to heroin because it's cheaper. That's hard core."

"Shit," she whispered, incredulous. "So you take enough Advil to kill a horse."

"Babe, I would rather limp around the rest of my life than have to be on those pills again."

Leslie shifted so she was on her knees next to me. "Okay, I get that. But... from what Erik said about tonight's practice, I think you tore something. That's not going to magically heal—"

"I told him not to say anything," I grumbled, rolling my eyes.

"He didn't have a choice. Don't be mad at him, Mister Limping Around, Pretending Nothing's Wrong."

"My leg's not gonna fall off or nothin'."

"Babe—"

"Look, Les—I'm not going under the knife again if it means I need narcotics for the pain. Not during the campaign, anyway."

"Kade, what campaign? You can't even walk!" Leslie's nose flared, her eyes widened. Frustration vibrated from every cell, making the air between us thick with contention.

I wasn't trying to be stubborn—really, I wasn't. But I wanted her to understand where I was coming from and to what lengths I'd be willing to go. I was not going past the stopping point I'd decided on in my head. Surgery wasn't happening. Narcotic pain pills were not happening.

Leslie closed her eyes, her chest barreling with the breaths she inhaled—in, out. In, out. When she opened her eyes again, she appeared much calmer—for which I was grateful, unless it was the calm before another storm. But it wasn't. She sat up, wrapping her arms around me, bending to press her lips against mine.

"I'm gonna stop. And say thank you for sharing that with me. I know it was a big deal for you to do that and I'm so glad I know. I'm so glad you trust me enough to tell me. And I'm not judging you. Not now, not then, not ever. Okay?"

"Okay," I said, sensing the but or however that was coming.

"Now... if you want Kendrick or Erik even Dwayne to go to the doctor with you, fine. If you want me to go to the doctor with you, I absolutely will; but with or without me, KC...you're going."

I frowned.

"No one is saying we let the doc cut you up that day. But we at least find out what's wrong, what's torn, what can be treated without surgery. We find out if we can wait until the election is over to make a decision. And we get you something not quite a narcotic but stronger than Advil because I swear if you get an ulcer from that stuff..."

I chuckled, smiling at all her we statements. And her demands. It had been a long time since a woman other than TC had had the right to boss me around. To be honest, Leslie had been the only woman I'd ever given the privilege. Resolute, I tilted my head up for a kiss. I could deal with the compromise and even if I couldn't, I'd been defeated.

"So I can't seduce you into not making me go to the doc, huh?"

She giggled, settling on my lap and scooting up so she and

I were chest to chest. My hands settled in their normal position, around the perfectly round orbs of ass cheeks. She cradled my face in her hands and brought my lips to hers, kissing me again.

"You can seduce me whenever you like, but you're not going to change my mind on this. I can't stand to see you in pain anymore, KC. And if it turns out that you have to have surgery, I'm here to help you. I'm not going anywhere."

"Yeah?" I grinned. "I was thinking I would stick around, too."

"Oh? Not running off to follow some other dream?"

"My dream is right here, sitting in my lap."

I knew that would make her cry. She sucked in her bottom lip, trying to stave it off, but I saw the shine in her eyes and the red glow in her skin. I'd make it up to her. For the rest of my life, if I had to.

"Matter of fact, I'm so here, I'm trying to get a job as the Mayor of this town. I'm not going anywhere. Not without you."

twenty-four

. . .

KC

Two days later, I was in the backseat of the Escalade, my right leg stretched out and knee brace on, headed to Healy. Potter Lake didn't have an orthopedic specialist, which is what I would need. Leslie had called Dwayne and got a referral and a recommendation for Dr. Irons with Belaire Orthopedic and Sports Medicine Clinic. He was, Dwayne said, the best in the Southeast and would be responsive to my requests for treatment that didn't involve medication.

"Besides," Leslie quipped, "Doc Moore would probably tell you to just put a bag of frozen peas on it."

TC and Leslie sat up front, chatting like they'd always been life long friends. Kendrick was next to me, flipping through screens on his phone.

"What are you doing over there, man? You're real quiet."

"My other job—checking on our social media campaigns. Getting good interaction on SnapChat with the Top Five Cuts feature," he muttered. "Instagram is looking good, too. Still getting hits on that cut Tamera did for you."

I perked at that. "Yeah? Let's see."

Kendrick showed me his screen. He brought up the

picture that he'd taken that night at the Kit Kat and posted under the Guys N' Dolls account. Kendrick began to scroll through thousands of comments. Most were nice, some fans that had watched me during my NBA days.

"That's cool," I said, relaxing against the leather seats again.

"So, Kendrick," Leslie called from the front of the truck. "That snap thing? Does that get you foot traffic? Like people walk in and say they saw a cut on... whatever... gram and they want it?"

Kendrick laughed. "First of all, you're too young to not know what you're talking about, Leslie. You need to let me give you a tutorial. Secondly...yeah. That's why we do it, and stay on it. Your girl Evonne has a page on here. You should get her to run one for the shop."

"Hunh, really? I think I will."

"See, when I tell her stuff like that, she says I'm being bossy. When you say it, she listens and decides to take your advice."

Leslie turned in her seat and shot a playful glare back at me. "That's because you usually are being bossy about it, KC. Kendrick is more likely to give me advice that doesn't sound like an order."

"Ain't he?" TC had to add. "Just bossy!"

"Whatever," I grumbled, mindlessly rubbing my knee. It was swollen and didn't easily bend. It also didn't hold much weight, so I'd been using a cane. I'd fought the appointment, but deep down I was looking forward to getting some relief.

TC pulled into a parking lot in front of a tall glass and aluminum building. The curved design of the architecture caught the sun just right, reflecting into my eyes. I squinted, climbing out of the truck, leaning heavily on the cane on one side and Leslie on the other.

We inched our way through the sliding glass doors and into

an entryway that looked more like a hotel lobby than a medical center. Instead of tile or linoleum, the floors were carpeted, the chairs were comfortable microfiber in muted colors.

Leslie pressed the call button for the elevator and helped me shuffle in when the doors opened. I leaned against the stainless steel wall and pushed out a heavy breath. I hadn't taken any anti-inflammatories since the day before and the thump of pain radiating up my thigh and down my calf was overwhelming.

"Must be bad, huh?"

"Yeah," I bit out in a harsh whisper. "It's like... tight. And hot."

"Hang in there," she soothed, rubbing my back through the thin jacket I'd pulled on. After weeks of over ninety degree temps, there was a slight chill in the air, which gave Leslie an excuse to light up the gas fireplace. The trees were already bright hues of red, yellow and orange and suddenly, everything was pumpkin or apple or squash flavored.

The elevator stopped on the ninth floor and slid open and I was relieved to see a comfortable waiting room. I limped my way to a chair and lowered into it, heaving a loud gust of relief. Leslie went right to the front counter to check us in. I heard low murmurs from across the room.

"Babe, you have your insurance card?"

I nodded, leaning over to pull my wallet from my pocket, then the glossy card from its slot. I had played in the league just long enough to qualify for the upper tier of coverage for retirees. The plan would cover me and my spouse, however potential she may be, until I was eligible for Medicare. Little things like that were starting to matter to me, the closer Leslie and I became. I was serious when I said I wanted her to be my future...those were words I'd never said before in my life, but I meant them.

Leslie finished with the nurse, and took the seat next to

me. "It'll be just a few minutes. Dr. Irons is finishing up with a patient. How are you doing?"

"Okay, now that I'm sitting." I looked up to see Kendrick and TC walk in. They took seats near us. "I just want to get this over with. I shouldn't have been messing around with those kids. I knew better."

"I'm sure you'll remember all this pain and regret."

"And if you have problems remembering," TC said, "I'll remind you."

A door swung open and a nurse came out into the waiting room. "Mr. Cavanaugh?"

I raised my hand, then braced myself to stand. Leslie grabbed my arm on one side and I leaned on the cane as I followed her through the door to Dr. Iron's office.

"You'll sit and chat for a few minutes, then the doctor will probably send you down to the scanning suite for an MRI, so I'll come back to get you."

"Oh... he'll do an MRI today? Like... not weeks from now?" Leslie asked.

I hid the amusement in my voice when I answered. "Welcome to dating an NBA type, Leslie."

―――――

"Well, young man. It seems as if you've been through quite a bit, as far as your knee is concerned."

I nodded and swallowed, adjusting in the chair. Earlier, we'd met with Dr Irons, who looked like he'd been a former ball player himself, though he swore he hadn't been. Tall, muscular, angular face framed by a trim beard. His accent was light, but the lilt in his voice told me he was from, or had spent significant time on an island. After our conversation and my description of what had happened at practice he'd sent me three floors down for an MRI and CAT scan of my knee. Now we were back upstairs in his office and he was poring over the films.

"Yessir," I responded. "I've put my knees through a lot, ever since I was young."

"Yes," he mumbled, viewing a set of x-rays behind a light box. "I see that. Although the situation, for the moment, isn't as bad as you've probably thought it to be."

I glanced at Leslie and she glanced at me. There was a possibility that there was good news, here.

"I see a great deal of scarring and inflammation. Your cartilage is seriously degraded. We will want to talk about an implant quite soon." He glanced at me over the rimless glasses he wore. I was expecting to hear that, since I'd been putting it off since high school. He continued, "There may be be a re-injury to the ACL. I'd like to check out the meniscus as well but for now it seems intact. I need to treat the swelling, as it is severe. That's why you can't bend your knee. The pressure is causing the pain and I can't see much until we get that taken care of."

"What do you recommend, Dr. Irons?" asked Leslie. Her brows were knit together and her face had that look she got when she was highly concerned. I was touched that she as so invested.

"Kade is running for office out in Potter Lake. The election is in a few weeks. He doesn't really have time for bed rest."

"That's what Dwayne told me. Good luck on your efforts, young man. However, the knee doesn't have a concern for our schedules. If it needs rest, then that's what we must give it, no?" His voice was so soothing and grandfatherly, I don't think Leslie took the reprimand like she would have normally taken it. I sure didn't. I wanted to be able to stand, to walk again. Short of downing some pills, I'd do what I had to.

He turned off the box and pulled his glasses from his face, folding them and tucking them into a pocket in his pristine white lab coat. "I'm going to prescribe a treatment that won't require full bedrest, but I do want you to take it easy on the knee. No standing for long periods of time, no walking long distances. Certainly no running or jumping. And you could stand to drop about twenty pounds. There's no need to be so bulky—you haven't seen a court in years."

Did this dude just call me fat? I opened my mouth to react, but Leslie's grip on my forearm stopped me. I paused, breathed, and swallowed my response. Besides...he was right. I'd been eating like crazy, especially the last few weeks, and I had put on some pounds.

"Tell me, have you heard of cryotherapy?"

I nodded. The machines were like putting your arm or leg in a freezer. When I left the league, the machines were being added to a lot of team therapy rooms.

The doctor reached for a pad from his desk and began scratching out some notes. "The idea is that the forced, cool air and the compression lowers or eliminates swelling and encourages healing. You can rent or buy one—I'd suggest you buy one, with your history, and begin a course of forty-five minutes to one hour therapy in the morning and at night."

He handed the notes to Leslie, who squinted to read them. "You should feel improvement within a few sessions and daily therapy will limp you along until the election is over and until I can see you again. I'll be going on vacation at the end of next week, so I'll need you to keep it together on your own until then. Alright?"

He nodded and so did I, but I was more interested in long term treatment. "But after that—"

"After that, I'd like to do another MRI to check out the ACL. My diagnosis, though not official, is that the repair was poorly done and has torn. I treat a great many professional athletes and I'm good at what I do. With my techniques, I don't see reinjury. I'd also like to remove some of the scar tissue so that you can have full movement. With physical therapy, you should be like new in a matter of months."

My chest swelled with the huge breath of relief I sucked in. It looked like things were going to be okay...not immediately, but soon. Soon, I could handle.

"I'm well aware of your request for a treatment that doesn't require narcotic pain pills. I respect this request greatly. While you're here, you'll receive IV pain meds. Once discharged, you will be prescribed Tylenol 3 and cryotherapy."

"So, what about now, Dr. Irons?" Leslie asked. "He can't stand or bend his leg."

"R.I.C.E.," he spelled out, poking out his fingers with each letter. "I'm sure you've heard this from team doctors. Rest, Ice, Compression, Elevation—"

"You're not going to tell me to put a bag of peas on my knee, are you?"

He chuckled. "No, but it wouldn't be a bad idea. Get yourself a good, big ice pack that straps to your leg, a compression garment and rest with the knee elevated. You should get your cryotherapy machine as soon as—" He paused, then perked. "One moment."

He slid his chair out from under his desk, then stood and rushed out of the room. Puzzled, Leslie and I glanced at each other. Then he rushed back through the door with a box under his arm.

"You're in luck. I ordered one of these for a patient, but he'd already purchased one and it's been sitting in a closet for months. Until you get your own, you can use this one. It's top of the line." He handed me the box, which was surprisingly small and light. "As soon as you get home, set up a treatment. Remember, at least forty-five minutes. Then put on the compression garment and leave the knee elevated as long as you can. Understand?"

His dark brown eyes moved from me to Leslie and back again. Once he was sure we'd understood his orders, he clapped his hands together and stood. "It was a pleasure meeting you Mr. Cavanaugh. I cannot conclude this meeting without saying that I was a big fan. I have already expressed my thanks to Mr. Newsome for his recommendation. I look forward to treating you."

Leslie stood and took the box from my lap so I could maneuver myself out of the chair. We inched out of the door and back to the waiting room, where TC and Kendrick were still sitting.

"Sorry, ya'll. I was expecting him to drag out scheduling the MRI and CAT scans. Didn't know he had all that stuff on site, but at least I don't have to come back."

"You don't have to come back?" TC repeated. "So no surgery?"

We walked out of the clinic together, Kendrick and Leslie in front, TC and I falling behind.

"Not right now. We're going to try cryotherapy, rest and elevation. That should get me through the election and then we'll take it from there."

"Did you like him? Was he nice? Did he seem knowledgeable?"

I laughed, looping my free arm around my sister, my caretaker, the person who knew more of my business than anyone. "He was great, T. Really. Leslie came through the good recommend from Dwayne. He said he was a fan."

From her expression, TC didn't seem impressed, but that didn't mean anything. She was built to see through bullshit. After so many years of handling my affairs, she could spot a doctor trying to scam free tickets and NBA gear from a mile away.

TC and Kendrick left to get the car. Leslie was trying to read the directions that came with the cryotherapy machine. I dipped my head to drop a kiss on her cheek. Her head popped up, turning toward me, so I grabbed a taste of her lips before she could open them to say something.

"Uh..." She blinked a couple of times, and then smiled. "What was that for? I mean...thank you. But...are you okay?"

I gave her a deep, resolute nod. "I'm more than okay. I wanted to say thanks for being here with me today. I'm glad you came. I'm glad you made me make this appointment, and did all the legwork with getting the recommend and everything. And taking the day off, considering your salon is poppin' lately."

Leslie rose up onto her toes so her lips could capture mine. The kiss was interrupted by a loud honk from the Escalade. Kendrick was driving, and pulled it up close to the curb.

"Ya'll two get in back with all that cakin'," he called out.

I was happy to climb in the backseat, prop up my knee and lean against Leslie for the ride back to Potter Lake.

————

"KC, I'll bring your wings to you, if you want to relax in the living room. You don't have to sit there with your leg propped up and the machine running."

Monica smirked from the kitchen, apron tied around her body, elbow deep in wings coated in Thai Curry Lime sauce. I hadn't had her wings in months. The girls wanted to get together to watch the finale of some silly dating show, but Leslie didn't want to leave me to fend for myself. Somehow she talked me into inviting everyone to watch the show— which I would only allow if wings were on the menu.

So I was posted up at the dining room table with Erik and Kendrick and we had a good poker game going while the tempting scent of wings filled the air. Leslie arranged a stack of pillows on a chair so my leg could still be elevated and the cryosleeve was running, sending a current of freezing cold, compressed air around my knee.

It was unnerving at first, but after the first few treatments, it felt good, to the point where I craved it and couldn't wait for my next treatment. I wished I'd had the option back when I was playing, because it was working. I could stand and bend my knee a little...enough to function, but still not full strength.

"Nah," I said, arranging the poker cards I held in my hand. "I want to be close to the greatness. Besides, I don't want to get sauce all over my couch."

"And he wouldn't dare leave his poker hand, considering he's hot tonight."

"Yeah, I'm hot." I tossed a poker chip into the center of the table. "I raise y'all sorry asses five."

Erik grimaced, staring at his hand, but tossed a chip in. "Ay, just keep in mind that my bank account doesn't look like yours."

"We're not playing for real money, dumbass." Kendrick tossed in a chip and rearranged his cards. He glanced down at the slumbering baby in the Bjorn he was wearing before asking, "Right? KC?"

I laughed, not answering, and plunked down a card. "Depends. How lucky are you feeling tonight?"

Tamera came from the living room and stood behind Erik, bent over his shoulder. She plopped a noisy wet kiss on his cheek, then stole a look at his cards. "Ooh, I hope you're not playing for real money. Erik ain't got shit."

"Damn!" He threw his cards down onto the table in front of him. Kendrick and I burst into laughter. "I was trying to bluff, Tam!"

"Well, you suck at it." She bent to give him another kiss and walked past him to the kitchen. She opened the refrigerator and pulled out a bottle of water, uncapped it and look a long sip. "The Suitor is about to start, Monica. You still slaving away in here for these men?"

"Hey, Tamera, Leslie didn't tell you? There's a water tax, now. Five dollars for a bottle. Pay up."

I thought she'd ignore me like usual, but she didn't. She

stared right at me as she brought the bottle to her lips and drank a few more gulps. Then belched.

I shook my head. "You kiss your boyfriend with that mouth?"

"Yup," she answered, sauntering past the table again, stopping to cup Erik's chin. "And he loves it."

"I do, actually," Erik muttered.

"You know Erik is a little touched in the head, right?" She moved a few steps over and stopped right in front of me. "Stop being mean to me, KC. Or I'm going to tell Leslie, and you don't want that. Or do you?"

"I ain't scared of—"

"Les, come get your man and his big mouth!"

"I didn't even say anything to you!"

"If I have to come in there I am kicking asses!" I heard from the living room. I snickered.

"Tamera! Monica! The show is starting. Get in here!"

Monica untied her apron and laid it on the counter, shouting orders as she rushed through the room. "When the timer goes off, pull the wings out of the oven. Paper plates and napkins are on the counter."

Erik and Kendrick grunted their agreement. Erik had picked up his cards again.

"Yo, I thought you folded."

He angled his head, and screwed his lips to the side. "If I look at my hand with my good eye...I might can make something of it. Let's play."

After a few more rounds, I'd eaten a plate of wings and taken all of their chips. Though we really weren't playing for money, it was still a blow to the ego. The cryotherapy had long since finished. I needed to switch to the cold pack ice sleeve but Leslie was still watching her show. Erik, who actually watched The Suitor, had escaped to the living room after the last brutal beating.

I ripped the velcro ties off of the leg-length sleeve and

disconnected the tubing, wrapping it up neatly in the machine. "You mind grabbing my other sleeve out of the freezer? Getting around is a pain in the ass."

"No problem," Kendrick offered. "I'll clean up some of this mess Monica made, too."

Kendrick started to get up, but Amerie, who had been peacefully sleeping all night, started to stir. Without even thinking, I reached for her. I'd never reached for a baby in my life, but my arms automatically opened.

Kendrick looked at me...then looked again. "Do you even know what to do with a baby? You know you don't bounce her around like a basketball, right?"

"Yeah, yeah. I won't break her, I promise."

He unhooked the Bjorn and pulled the baby out of the contraption that had held her close to him all night. She was a tiny little Hershey's Kiss with dark curly hair and an itty bitty nose and huge brown eyes...so fragile but amazingly one whole complete human being. I held her in the crook of my arm and stared at her. She stared back like she expected me to say something to her.

So I said, "Hi, Amerie."

She cooed and squirmed and balled up her fists, but didn't cry. I considered that a victory.

"You want me to put this on?" Kendrick asked, holding my portable sleeve.

"Yeah, man, if you could. I'm busy choppin' it up with your baby girl."

"I knew it. I knew it!" Erik came storming into the kitchen. "I knew that Boris Kodjoe look alike asshole was gonna win. With his corny ass—"

I punched him in the arm as he walked by me, then pointed at the baby. "You mind? Young ears."

"She can't understand me, man. She's a baby."

"Delicate ears, then. Shut up."

Erik sucked his teeth and tiptoed to the refrigerator.

"Didn't I say I didn't want to watch the finale if he made it —heyyyy."

Leslie had come from the living room and stopped cold when she saw me. Her left eyebrow cocked up and she asked, "How did you end up with the baby?"

"I needed my ice pack. Kendrick got it so I said I'd hold the baby. I promised not to break her."

Leslie bent over me to peer at Amerie, who was getting sleepy again. "She's beautiful. And so little."

"Yeah. She's lighter than a basketball."

Leslie giggled, then kissed my cheek, then whispered in my ear, "I kind of like you with a baby in your arms."

I knew for sure that she wasn't expecting me to say it, but when I opened my mouth and, "we better get busy making one," fell out, she jumped back, eyes wide. Then her lips twisted to the side and she smiled.

"In time, Mr. Cavanaugh. Mayorship first. Then...other stuff."

Tamera took a seat at the table next to Erik. Both had helped themselves to a beer.

"Beer is even more expensive than water. Like $10 a bottle. I hope ya'll are planning to pay up before you leave."

"Stop it, KC," Leslie called from the kitchen. "You know good and well beer is only $7."

Later that night, after we'd ushered everyone out and, for real, hassled Erik for $7 for the beer he drank, Leslie helped me hobble up the stairs.

"Its funny how I was so worried about my mom getting around in this house and I need you to get up the stairs."

Leslie laughed, both of her arms around my waist so I could lean on her as we made our way down the hallway and then into the bedroom.

"We made it," she said, heaving a breath and falling out across the bed. Much more slowly, I maneuvered myself to the bed and laid next to her.

"Hey Les... earlier...I mean..."

Leslie rolled over, looping a leg over mine and grabbed my face, turning my head toward hers. She moved in for a long, slow kiss that I really, really enjoyed.

"I'm not holding you to the babies comment," she said softly. "So relax. It was a moment and it was cute. But we should really talk about stuff before we make big decisions."

"I was serious, though. I know things between us are so different, so fast. And I'm not trying to rush or anything. Just...if you want that—"

"I know," she whispered, laying a finger over my lips. "But like I said...first things first. Let's not get caught up. Let's make wise decisions. When it's time to make them."

"Les...do you doubt that this is good? That this is real?"

She shook her head. "I don't doubt a thing. Really. I just want to be ready."

"And you're not. Okay. I got it." I sat up and busied myself with pulling off my t-shirt.

"Are you really having a temper tantrum because I'm not acting like all your groupie girlfriends, practicing using your last name and poking holes in your condoms so I can have your baby and be set for life? I didn't say I wouldn't ever be ready. And I'm not saying I'm not wildly happy right now, because I am."

She sat up and scooted next to me, then looped her arm around mine and leaned her head on my shoulder. "I'm just saying..." Her soft lips played on my skin as she spoke. "We have a big fish to fry. The biggest ever. Let's get through that. And then let's make all the plans and decisions we want. I want you to be focused on this election, KC. It's important."

I hung my head, knowing she was right. But I'd spent a long time thinking about her, wondering about her, wishing I could talk to her. Now I had her in my arms and didn't want to lose her. But she was already in my bed every night and had pretty much moved into my house. She had a key and a spot in the garage and a security code. She was getting mail already, somehow and the neighbors greeted her like she had always lived here. She probably...likely...possibly wasn't going anywhere.

"Aight, then. We stick a pin in it for now. But win or lose...we win. Right?"

Leslie offered her pinky for our patented pinky swear. "Right. Now let's get you ready for bed. You have an interview tomorrow and I don't want bags under your eyes."

twenty-five

. . .

LESLIE

"That girl was dumb as a sack of hair. Everybody knew all of her business, and if they didn't know, they were as dumb as she was."

One of my favorite customers, Sylvia, sat in my chair, angled so that she could regale the place with a hilarious story about one of her former coworkers at the textile mill. Every chair was occupied and there were a few people waiting for a spot to open up.

The chairs KC had "lent" us had kicked off a small facelift for the shop. Erik, Tamera and I had spent a weekend priming and painting the interior of the shop, giving it a fresh coat of brilliant white paint. I'd ordered posters and frames online and hung them, interspersing them with a few vintage photographs of some of Potter Lake's oldest residents, including Grandy and Earline.

Nothing kept her from her weekly hair appointments and she was less salty as time went by, especially when she learned that KC wasn't planning to hire a new secretary. If she wanted to work for the new Mayor, she was welcome to stay.

We had business coming out of our eyeballs and I couldn't be happier about it. Tamera and I had both been coming in early and staying late, just to serve the additional clients. We hired Patrice, the girl whose hair we had rescued from a dye job gone disastrous, as a part time shampoo girl. Her grandmother figured it would keep her busy, and working at a salon would teach her about how to better care for her hair.

Evonne was an official full-time stylist and she was busy, too. Gisele, thank goodness, decided to look for a job in Healy. Last I heard, she was working a chair at a Dominican salon and the grapevine told me that she wasn't doing well. I rejoiced that she wasn't my problem anymore, and once I got rid of the space she occupied, I had more room for spa services. I was on the hunt for a masseuse to come in a few days a week and I had my eye on a couple of spa pedicure chairs.

And then Frank Crawford walked in with an air conditioning unit under his arm. It was one of those that had to be installed in the window, but I was a beggar that was not choosing. The fall season was well under way but some days with people, hair dryers, plus the hot utensils and the machines in the back, the temperature still rose above a comfortable level.

"You and that young man been doing so much for this side of the lake, lately," said Frank, "I thought it would be nice to repay you with a little something."

I was moved beyond words, and though I suspected KC was involved, he swore on everything that he had nothing to do with the generous gift. So on days like today, when I'd been on my feet serving customers since early that morning, at least I was cool and comfortable, which I appreciated as I ran a hot flat iron through sections of Sylvia's shoulder-length hair.

"When that baby came, and it didn't look like the shift supervisor, who was real dark skinned, but instead looked like the security officer, who was real light?" Her devilish chuckle rattled around in her throat until she could hold it in no longer. "Well, first of all, the supervisor was done with her, because she'd cheated on him, even though he was cheating on his wife—"

"Who worked for the owner in the front office, right?" Another customer offered. "My mama was good friends with her."

"Unh huh, that's the one," Sylvia confirmed. "Her husband was sleeping with this gal who didn't have the sense God gave a chicken."

"So she must have been hoping like hell the baby wasn't the light skin dude's."

"Like hell! But girl, when that baby came, there was no doubt. Baby just as bright as anything, and got his eyes too? Shift supervisor was out of a marriage, a girlfriend, a baby and a job, when the mill owner got wind of everything. So, the security officer wasn't interested in being with this gal, seeing as how she was dumb as a stump, but he ended up taking care of the baby. The scandal caused a huge uproar in the mill. He ended up moving all of them somewhere near Valdosta."

The shop tittered in laughter and town gossip as usual. I tipped my head to catch Tamera's eye, but her gaze was focused on activity outside. A few moments later, I figured out what caught her attention. KC swept through the salon door, his hands full of bags, followed by Erik with more bags. They dropped them on the front desk, filling the salon with the scent of what could only be containers from Helen's Kitchen.

I opened my mouth to scold KC since he wasn't supposed to be on his knee, but he limped across the room to my chair and dipped his head to drop his lips onto mine.

"I know you want to yell at me, but I had to move around a little. I wanted to talk to Helen about the menu for the election night dinner. And... I have news."

"What kind of news?"

"According to Arletha, the news station is doing an informal poll and your boy is leading. Just over half of Potter Lake residents say they're voting Mayor Adams out."

I forgot that I wanted to yell at him and rose up onto my toes, throwing my arms around his neck. "That's great, baby! You're doing it!"

"We're doing it, Les," he said, cupping my face in his hands and kissing me again. "We are doing it. So..." He pulled back, leaving an arm around me. "Erik and I figured you and Tamera wouldn't take a lunch break and you'd have a spot full of hungry people..."

A cheer sounded throughout the salon. KC nodded and Erik started emptying the bags.

"I got a little bit of everything. Helen is probably mad at me."

"Probably not, if you bought her out of lunch."

I finished bumping Sylvia's ends and fluffed her now silky, shiny hair around her face, then turned her toward the mirror so she could take a look and make corrections like normal. Today, she took a quick glance, tossed a few bills at me, muttered at me to keep the change and headed toward the desk to pick up something for lunch. The line of people in black capes, hair half done, picking out pieces of fried chicken wings, squares of cornbread and dishes of macaroni and cheese and green beans made me smile.

"Hey, you." I nudged KC, who was watching the scene with bright eyes, too. I could tell from his smile that he loved doing this kind of thing. I tapped the back of my chair. "Get off that knee. Let's not undo all of your good progress. You want me to grab you something to eat?"

KC had just settled into the chair when the front door flew

open, so hard that it banged against the brick wall behind it. My mother burst into the shop, eyes wild and wide, loudly panting. My mind went right to Grandy, especially since Gina ran in behind her.

"Mama! What's wrong? Is it Grandy?"

But she bypassed me, headed straight for KC. "You!" She pointed at him, getting so close that the tip of her nail poked into his chest. KC tried to stand, but she was too close, bent over him, in his face. KC reared back, probably terrified of my mother.

"What I do, Ms. Lee?"

"It's what you got to do. You got to do something!"

"About what? What's going on?"

"Mama... come here." I grabbed her by the shoulders and pulled her back, then directed her toward an empty chair. "What has you so upset? Is it Grandy?"

She used a handkerchief she'd pulled from her purse to dab sweat from her forehead. "Everybody over at Primrose is walking around with worried looks and sad eyes. I asked what was going on, and the nurses told me I had to speak to the director. So, I go on up to Edward's office and ask what everybody's wringing their hands and looking so upset about."

She stopped to breathe, then wiped more sweat from her brow. "Edward says that that Mayor Adams has been hinting at selling the land that the home is on. You know he owns that piece of property, there."

I folded my arms across my chest, my mouth already set in a frown. "Yeah, that's how he built that facility so cheap; he already owned the land."

"Well, he's been talking about how the center owes him more money on the lease and if they don't pay, he's going to sell it. Whoever buys it, there's no guarantee they'll leave the place open. He's liable to sell it to a company that intends to tear it down and build a big box store or something stupid like that."

She sighed, dropping a hand to her lap. Her shoulders sagged with stress and her voice cracked with the tears she was holding at bay. "He says they can't pay more on the lease, that they're strapped as it is, with what they get from the state and the private beds, like what we pay for. And if that home closes, everybody there got to find a place to go, including Grandy. I can't care for her at the house and I don't know about moving her to Healy..."

"That's why we came to find you, KC," said Gina. "Your sister said you'd probably be headed over here. I know you're not the Mayor yet, but..."

"I'll vote for you," Mama said suddenly, jumping up from her seat. "I'll tell everybody from here to Healy and back to vote for you if you'll help us. Please, Kade. This is my... this is my mother—"

She finally broke down, her cheeks damp with tears. I couldn't remember the last time I saw my mother cry. The sight broke my heart and after a few moments, I was tearing up too.

KC had managed to stand. He lifted both hands, showing his palms, then placed them both around Mama's shoulders. The feeling of those big, warm hands on her seemed to calm her almost instantly.

"I'm not going to use this as a lure to get votes, Ms. Lee. I want to see what I can do because it's the right thing. Let's get that straight, okay?" Mama bobbed her head in agreement. "Now... let's find out the real deal. It's not like he can sell the land and close the facility tomorrow—"

"Oh, Mayor Adams says he has a couple of bids in already. That's why he's demanding payment, or he's gon' accept one of them, and then there's no telling—"

"Okay... okay." KC squeezed her shoulders, then brought her in for a brief hug. "I'm going to see what I can find out.

I'm not promising anything, but if Grandy has to move I'll do whatever I can to make her comfortable. You have my word on that. Alright?"

KC turned to me. "I'm going over there to talk to the Director. I need to get to the bottom of this demand for more money. Doesn't make any sense."

"I'm going with you." I turned off my irons and grabbed my purse from a drawer in my cubby.

"Les, it's the middle of your workday—"

"It's my grandmother, KC. I want to know what's going on as much as you do, plus we'll need to talk strategy for dealing with this so close to the election. Besides, you've never met her. You should know who you're working for."

I grabbed my purse and walked out of the shop, determined to go over to Primrose myself if I had to. I heard the salon door open behind me, then, "Leslie! Wait for me, please."

I turned around to see KC slowly limping and trying to catch up.

"This is why you shouldn't be on your knee. Where's your cane?"

He nodded toward the Escalade. "In the truck, actually. I needed both hands."

"You'd better grab it if you're coming with me."

I turned and headed toward my car, pointing at it with the remote to unlock the door. On the passenger side, I opened the door and slid the seat all the way back so KC would have room, then walked around and got in on the driver's side. Impatient, I watched KC slowly maneuver himself into my car, and as soon as he'd shut himself inside, I put the car in gear and shot out of my parking space.

"Okay, Les...Leslie!" KC reached for the seat belt and snapped himself in. "Don't get pissed, but calm down! It's not like he's selling the land right this second, okay?"

KC laid a hand on my thigh and squeezed. I dropped a

hand from the steering wheel and laid it on top of his. He was right... I was a little out of control. My shoulders lowered from around my ears. I dropped my speed and tried to relax.

"I guess we don't need to screech into the parking lot of Primrose Gardens like Bo and Luke Duke driving the General Lee."

"Nah, probably not. And I can't climb out of this window anyway." He tapped the pane of glass with his thumb. It made me laugh, which I guess was his goal.

"So... what is the Mayor's end game, here? We're so close to the election. Why would he do this now? Is he trying to throw it? Is he playing to some... committee or group?" I struggled for words to even try to explain his actions. It didn't make much sense at all to alienate those in town who had relatives at Primrose. The moment they heard about this rumor, the support for him would drop further than it already had. At the moment, it looked like KC could win by a land-slide—something I never would have predicted.

"Maybe he knows he's losing and he's trying to suck as much money as he can out of these deals before he leaves office? Or... maybe he's cocky enough to really think he can do whatever he wants with no consequence."

"I want to find out what's going on, and then to hell with my clean campaign. I have to call this guy out."

I made a slight turn onto the road that led to Primrose, catching a glimpse at KC while I did so. "I'd hate to see you sink to his level. He's digging his own hole. All you have to do is throw the dirt on top."

"I hear you. But the people that are going to vote for him need to know what kind of man they're dealing with. Even if he loses, he's still threatening to shut down the home. Maybe I could call Arletha and talk to her about doing a story on tonight's broadcast."

I pulled into a space up front at Primrose. The facility was still relatively new and in beautiful condition, with walking paths and a garden, right on Potter Lake. The three story building featured a patio outside every room, a great room for activities and programs and a caring, dedicated staff. As soon as I stepped out of the car, the director, Edward, came out of the front door. Casually dressed in a polo shirt and a pair of jeans, he politely waited to approach us until KC had climbed out of the car.

"Edward Mabry," he said, offering his hand to KC.

"Kade Cavanaugh. I guess you heard we were coming."

"Yes. Mrs. Baker was here earlier and left very upset. She said that you might stop by, once you heard about what's going on here. Come on inside."

KC and I followed him through the double doors into the facility. The foyer was grand, with high ceilings and shiny, glossy floors and windows everywhere. We hung a right toward the Director's office. He offered us the two chairs in front of his desk.

Edward, a Healy transplant, had taken the job as Director after a lot of arm twisting. It seemed to be as stressful as he feared it would be, but after the first year, he came to love the work and the residents. Still, the near nonstop work for median pay, keeping up with code, complying with regulations and making Primrose an enjoyable place to live was a juggling act.

"I appreciate you taking the time to meet with us. Ms. Lee said there was an issue with the lease and since the Mayor owns the land, he's threatening to sell if he doesn't get what he wants."

Edward grimaced, fist clenched like he wanted to pound something—likely Mayor Adams in the face. "The lease is up for extension at the end of the year. We've been working with the Mayor for a few months on concessions and provisions. He promised that after the first three years, certain improvements would be made. Now he says he never agreed to that."

"But... isn't that in the lease?" I asked. "How can he say he never agreed to it, if he signed it?"

"We weren't specific when we drew up the documents. We said we would identify those issues that needed to be addressed at the time of renewal. The new lease calls for a five percent increase in rent. Primrose can't afford that. And Mayor Adams disagrees that the parking lot needs to be repaved, that he needs to put a streetlight out on the corner, that the land over on the banks of the lake has degraded and needs attention. If nothing, the city needs to build a fence—I can't have a resident fall into the lake. I requested a compromise; let's keep the lease rate where it is, even lower it a bit and we'll make these repairs ourselves."

Edward frowned, shaking his head. "No dice on the lower rent and he has no plans to address the safety issues. And if we continue to make these demands..." he paused using air quotes around the word demands. "He'll sell the land to the highest bidding developer, and he's already got a few to choose from."

"Could he be bluffing? Seems awfully convenient to suddenly have multiple bids on a property."

"Every once in a while, he brings someone through here, under the guise of showing us off. I wouldn't put it past him, to be honest. I've heard about the money he promised to the new business owners over at the strip mall. How he's basically swindled everyone. This seems par for the course."

I shuddered. What evil, ugly little man.

Edward poked his bottom lip out and tipped his head. "I have until the end of the month to agree to the new lease terms, or the Mayor will assume we plan to move the facility. Which, of course, we can't do. We can't afford the increase, but we could make it work if we didn't also have to make improvements he says he won't make. That would be a significant investment."

KC sat back in his seat, his lips rolled inward, eyes glazed over. "Unbelievable," he whispered, his head beginning to wag.

"I regret that some of my staff heard me arguing with the Mayor when he was here. It's affected the atmosphere. Everyone thinks we're closing and they're being fired. And people like Mrs. Baker, who depend on us are going to start panicking."

Edward reached up to nervously scratch at his temple, then clasped his hands together as he leaned forward onto the desk. "I'd planned to vote for you. Not trying to bribe you or anything but no matter what, I want this guy out of office. If there's anything you can do to assist, I'd sure appreciate it. I'm sort of a loss. This is my first job in this capacity, you know, and I... I guess I need a little help."

KC pushed himself up from the chair and grabbed his cane with one hand. The other he extended to Edward. "Hang tight, man. Let me see what I can work out. Do you have a business card?"

As soon as we left Edward's office, a stream of quiet profanities rolled off of KC's tongue. Enraged, he paced as best he could with a cane and a bum knee.

"Babe. Baby..." I stepped in front of him and pressed my palms to his chest. "Kade. Relax. Breathe."

"That motherfucker is going down. You hear me, Les? How did he get elected? How did he stay elected? I'm just—" His jaw clenched so hard I thought he was going to break a tooth.

"I know, KC. I know. That's why, when you said you wanted to run, despite all of our issues, I was willing to work with you. He hasn't always been this bad, but it's been progressively worse lately. And now? He just really thinks he can do what he wants to do."

"Well, he's wrong. What he can't do is fuck over this town anymore."

I smiled, then grabbed his face and kissed him. I felt him

sink against me as soon as my lips touched his. His free arm slid around my waist and pulled me close.

"You know what?" I mumbled against his lips.

"Mmm..." He growled. His hand slipped from my waist to the curve of my behind.

"If we were at home we'd be nekkid and horizontal, because you are sexy as fuck right now. But we're not, and I want you to meet my Grandy, so I need you to curb your filthy, nasty mouth... until later. Can you do that?"

I felt him smile against my cheek, then take a nip at my ear before he inhaled a deep breath and blew it out. "I guess I can put on my post game interview face. But his ass better hope I don't catch him in a dark alley."

"That's my NBA type." I chuckled, sneaking another kiss from him before grabbing his hand and leading him to the wing where Grandy lived.

"I've seen this place a couple of times, driving by. How many people are in here?"

"About seventy five. There's capacity for twice that, but they don't have the resources to staff more than the main building and this one."

We strolled the sidewalk toward a pink stone building and entered a set of double doors that led to a quiet, carpeted, dormitory like floor.

"Hey, Leslie girl!" One of the nurses paused throw her arm around me and give me a squeeze. "Grandy just got in from a few minutes outside but I'm sure she wouldn't mind going back out."

"I'm not staying long. I wanted to introduce her to KC. Have you met him? He's running for—"

"Mayor, yeah." She smiled, nice and big, switching the thick stack of folders from one arm to the other. "I was at the Kit Kat last month when you stopped in and talked with everybody. That was nice of you."

KC nodded humbly. "Great to see you again."

"If I wasn't voting for you before, I sure am, now. I can't believe what that egomaniac is trying to pull. Nobody wants to move these residents and none of us can afford to lose our jobs. Are you going to help Mr. Mabry stop him?"

"I'm going to do my best. I'll—" He bit off the rest of his sentence and gave a single nod. "I'm going to do what I can to see that Primrose stays open. Not only that, but this place should be able to run at full capacity. I want to work with Edward to figure out how to make that happen."

"I hear the words. I'll back you with my vote, but I'm going to hold you to those words."

KC extended a hand and gently clasped hers. "I want to be held accountable, so I really hope you do."

She beamed up at him and I could tell she wasn't ready for KC to let go of her hand. But I was. She was single and more than ready to mingle.

"Yeah, so... we'd better check on Grandy and...uhm..." I thumbed toward her room two doors down. "Yeah. Yeah."

KC finally dropped her hand and nodded to the nurse. "It was great running into you again. Hope we see you on election day."

"For sure, Mr. Cavanaugh," she said, dropping her voice a whole octave and decibel.

I tucked my hand into the crook of KC's elbow and gently pulled him in the direction of my grandmother's room. When we were out of eyesight and ear shot, I rolled my eyes up at him, making sure he saw my death glare.

"What I do? I was making sure she was planning to vote."

"You didn't see her flirting with you? Thought she was going to break something, she was working it so hard."

"I was using it to my advantage, until you pulled me off. What if she gets offended and decides not to vote for me now? It'll be all your fault, with your jealous ass."

"I know her. You don't. I have a reason to be jealous."

I stopped at Grandy's door and pulled on the handle. It

swung open and we stepped into a bright, sunny, spacious single bed unit. Grandy was awake, her brilliant silver hair cropped close to her scalp. Mama liked to keep it short, so that it was easier to take care of. She was dressed in a pretty pink gown and sitting in a lounger, angled toward the TV. Her long, thin fingers were curled around the remote, which she usually held in her lap. She couldn't actually change the channel, but she was comforted by holding it. The staff kept cable news running at our request.

"Hi, Grandy! It's Leslie." I called to her like I usually did when I came to see her. Her gaze didn't stray from the TV, but her fingers twitched. I took that as a sign that she knew I was in the room. I bent to kiss her cheek, and she blinked.

KC was still standing in the door, leaning against the doorjamb and watching me greet her. I motioned him in and directed him to sit on the bed near her chair. I pulled a low ottoman around and sat between them, reaching for one of Grandy's hands.

"Her name is Edith but she's Grandy to everyone in Potter Lake. She's one of the most vibrant women in this town. Aren't you, Grandy?"

She blinked, still staring at the TV.

"Before the stroke, Grandy always had a good story to tell, which she'd share with you over whatever she'd just pulled out of the oven. She was a master at desserts—I told you she could thrown down on some pecan pie. Pound cake, cheese-cake, sweet potato pie, all of it. Back when the Curl & Dye was just a chair on her front porch, she'd sell her pies for extra money."

"So... how long has she..." KC swallowed, his gaze on Grandy. For a moment, I worried that maybe meeting Grandy was too much for him, that maybe the scene was giving him foreshadowing thoughts of his mother's future.

"Three years. I didn't come home because of her stroke, but I arrived pretty very soon after it happened. It was heart-breaking. To know the woman that she was and to see her now... there's such a huge difference."

The scene played out in my head like it had just happened the day before and not years in the past. My mother had come home from a half day shift at the salon to find Grandy slumped over and unresponsive. High blood pressure had already taken her out of the salon—she couldn't work those long hours anymore. Add diabetes and the chances of a stroke or heart attack occurring were almost guaranteed. She was flown to Healy, where they couldn't do much for her since no one knew how long she had been unconscious.

The last time anyone had seen her functioning normally was earlier that day, well outside the four hour window used to gauge if a person could receive the life saving TPA shot, which dissolves the clots that causes a stroke and restores blood flow.

"Grandy loves all her children and her grandchildren fiercely. There's never a doubt how she feels about me. And I love her back just as hard." I squeezed her hand as I spoke. She blinked. And then blinked again. That kind of thing happened a lot when I spent time with her, and I didn't care what anyone thought... I knew she heard me and she was communicating with me.

"Grandy, I want you to meet somebody," I told her. KC pushed himself up off of the bed and walked around to the other side of the lounger. I got up and pushed the ottoman over and let him sit, so he was eye level with her. He'd caught her attention. Instead of staring at the TV, she was staring right into KC's golden browns.

"You know Mayor Adams isn't doing a good job lately, right? This young man here is Kade Cavanaugh. He's a real good friend of mine and he's trying to replace Mayor Adams in the election coming up. He's also trying to help Edward with this place, so they can take better care of you."

He reached for her hand and gently curled his fingers

around hers. "It's a pleasure to meet you. May I call you Grandy?"

She stared and stared and stared at him, her eyebrows nearly tied together.

"Your granddaughter has done a great job as Potter Lake's Ambassador, introducing me to the people of this town and teaching me what it is to love this place." He stopped for a second and flicked his eyes over at me, then continued talking to her like they were having a full blown conversation. "I care about your granddaughter. I care about her a lot and I want to make her happy. Do you trust me with her, Grandy?"

She didn't move, nothing changed. But KC looked at me and said, "I feel like she's trying to tell me something. Like... I'm supposed to pick up the brainwaves."

We both laughed, though quietly. Grandy's eyes moved back to the TV, and then she turned her head toward me and gave me the same stare she'd given KC. She blinked, once. Nice and slow. And then turned back to the TV. One of her favorite news anchors was on the screen and suddenly, it was like we didn't exist.

"Well. I think we've been dismissed."

We left her in her room, sitting in her chair, watching her favorite news program.

"You really think she was trying to say something to us?"

"A lot of people don't, especially some of the staff here. They tell me it's reflexes. The way she looked at you though? She's in there. So it's important that she knows we're still here for her. We love her the same and we're going to take care of her. That's why, if something happens to this place, we have to secure something for Grandy. We're not going to dump her in some rehab center full of patients sitting in the hallway or in one room while no one talks to them or interacts with them."

KC was pensive as we walked. I helped him into the car and got in on the driver's side.

"So, everybody here... they're all like Grandy? Stroke patients?"

I pressed the ignition button and the car roared to life. I put it in gear and backed out of the spot as I talked. "A few stroke patients, a lot of age related dementia, some Alzheimer's. This is Assisted Living—patients that require intensive, round the clock care are usually transferred to Healy. The idea was to keep them in Potter Lake, near their families, but there just isn't money to fully use the place as it was designed."

I was frustrated with how helpless I felt. "The Mayor was so proud to build Primrose. I'm just... it's crazy that he's threatening to shut it down over money and filling in some potholes and putting up a light pole."

"I guess I need to think about what I can do to help."

"We could talk to Mr. Cable on the city council. And we could talk to Arletha, like you suggested. I really hate to blast it on the news, though. I don't want people in a panic."

"We can go public if we have to but let's keep it in our back pocket."

I made the drive back to the Curl & Dye in a few short minutes and pulled in next to KC's Escalade. I turned the engine off, but before I could reach for the door latch, KC dropped his hand on my thigh.

"Hang on a second. Let's just... can I have a couple of minutes with you?"

I relaxed in my seat and leaned my body toward the center console. He did the same, letting me brush my lips against his cheek. He reciprocated with a soft peck on my lips.

"Thanks for introducing me to Grandy. I thought about asking to meet her but I know she's important to you. I figured you would let me in when you were ready."

"You're welcome. I'm happy you finally got to meet her. And, I should add that I'm touched by how involved you've become in how this town runs. My mama running in here to find you is really, really huge. She's... was Quincy Adams' biggest fan."

"I sense that, you know? That people are starting to count on me. I hope it translates to votes, but if it doesn't, maybe I should think about city council, something like that."

He chuckled, his eyes flitting to the front doors of the Curl & Dye. "You said something to me awhile back. Remember, we were standing right out here. You said the this salon was your bread and butter. Your life line. And Guys N' Dolls was a get rich quick scheme, that I could lose a customer and it wouldn't matter, but it would be death knells for you."

"I remember." My voice was husky with both the memory and the embarrassment of saying such a thing. I didn't know that his motivation behind his co-ed salon was to keep his mind off of his personal issues. "And KC... I wanted to apologize for that. I was upset and desperate—"

"No, no. That wasn't what I meant, by bringing that up. I mean, you were right. I shut down half of my shop and I'm doing better business than I was before. All the people that we can send over here, we do and your business is growing." He looked at me and I nodded to confirm.

"It's just that... I get it now. I get what you were saying about this town, about how everyone is here for each other. Helen was telling me about the old days, when her husband had lost his job when the mill shut down. She was making plates, selling them out of her kitchen and people wanted to support her so much, they'd drop by to get a plate, even if they'd already eaten."

He paused to let a small bubble of laughter rise from his throat, but kept going. "And like Frank bringing that air conditioner over here and installing it. Jessup finally replacing that pipe that keeps springing leaks, I mean—" He shook his head. "This town is the embodiment of We All We Got."

"Exactly. And in a couple of weeks, you become part of

that." I leaned over and kissed him, lingering a little on his lips. "Hey, you know what?"

"Mmm," he hummed, dipping toward me for another taste. "What?"

"I was thinking that I might actually cook for you tonight."

One second he was there, all warm and sexy and smelling good and the next minute he'd pulled away, leaning back against the door. "Who are you, and what did you do with my girlfriend? Because the Leslie Baker I know doesn't cook."

I laughed. And laughed and laughed. "Shut up, fool. I told you, I know how to cook. I just never did because my mama is a control freak about her kitchen. Fell out of the habit, but..." I reached for him and pulled him close to me again, looping an arm around his neck. "You've earned a home cooked dinner. At your own house. By me."

"You don't have to do that, Les."

"Actually, I do. Because Dr. Irons told you to lose twenty pounds and I need to start taking care of my man. Pretty sure that's what Grandy was trying to tell me today and I always take her advice."

KC grinned at that. "Your man, huh? You're really getting into dating an NBA type."

"It's growing on me." I sighed, my gaze drifting to the customers coming out of the front door of the shop. "Guess I should get back to work. What are you about to do?"

"I need to get a couple of things done at the shop. Might see if I can meet with Mr. Cable. Get to thinking about how we're gonna solve this Primrose problem."

"Keep me posted, okay?"

"I will. And uh... I know I say this a lot but it's true. We make a really good team. I think you should start thinking about... you know... after this election. What you and I look like, how we run our businesses together, how we..." He moved his hand in the air between he and I, indicating the both of us. "How we keep this town great. I haven't been able to do any of this without you. I don't think that's going to change if I'm elected. I need you."

"I'm here," I choked out. "And whatever you have in mind, after the election, I'm here for that, too."

"Good to hear." He leaned over and dropped a kiss near my ear, then popped the door latch to climb out of the car, and got right into the Escalade.

I sat in my car for a few minutes. Marinating. Things were good. So, so good with KC. But we'd moved quickly, scary fast. Months ago we were at each other's throats. Yesterday, Mama was hassling me about moving the rest of my things to KC's so that she could rent my apartment out to someone at the church. I'd been putting it off because... what if?

What if things were real good... until they weren't?

What if something else popped up?

What if... his mom got sick and he decided it would be good to move home to be closer to her?

What if... he got a job offer to be a commentator on ESPN and had to move to LA or New York?

I could pull what if situations out of the air all day. None of them ever ended up with me next to him.

The front door to the salon opened and Tamera stepped out. She tilted her head and raised an eyebrow. Her way of asking if I was okay. I smiled, climbing out of the car. In three steps she was in front of me, her spindly arms around me.

"Hey, girl. Sorry for running out earlier."

"It's all good. Grandy's okay?"

"Yeah, she's fine. I introduced KC to her. How was the day?"

"Handled," she answered with a shrug and a smirk. "E has a customer but my chair is empty. Why don't you let me hit those locs and brows while you tell me what happened?"

twenty-six

. . .

KC

I hopped in the truck and pulled away from Leslie's shop, my mind spinning with thoughts I'd never imagined myself having, a year ago. In two weeks, I would stand in front the town of Potter Lake and ask them to elect me as Mayor. How could I guarantee a win and start putting good things in motion for the people that lived here?

Primrose Gardens was a new addition to the town but it was sorely needed—all of it. What could I do to keep it open, to keep the Mayor's money hungry hands off of it?

And then there was Leslie. Talk about someone I'd never even imagine knowing again, a year ago, let alone dating her. And falling for her, rock hard. I'd loved her, in some way, since college I realized. Righting things between us was the best thing I could have ever done. All I knew was, I was ready. For... whatever. Whatever life wanted to throw at me, whatever happened in two weeks, whatever happened in this lifetime, I knew I wanted Leslie to be a part of that. I had plans for us. And not a lot of time to put things into place.

With my thumb, I brought up bluetooth. "Call dad."

After a few moments, the line began to ring.

"Hey, son." My dad's rich, warm baritone rang through the interior of the truck. "Everything okay?"

"Yeah, dad. I'm good. How are you? How's mom?"

"Real good, son. Mom went in for a nap. She wore herself out, directing the annual garden planting."

"Oh yeah? I know she throws herself into that, doing maps and stuff."

"Yep, she had her diagrams out and everything. But the garden at the new house is bigger, so it took a lot more this year. She's talking about fish ponds and things like that." I heard him laughing, but also sensed his eyes rolling. My mother could be a bit... much when it came to her garden. But it was always worth it when vegetable harvest came around. "We had planned on calling you later on."

"Oh. Well, should I call back?"

"No, no. We thought we'd come out for the election. It won't be but a day or so, but we'd definitely love to be there to watch you win."

"That'll be great, dad. I'm looking forward to seeing you guys. Win or lose, I hope I make you proud."

"I have every confidence in you, son. Did you need to talk to us about something?"

"Yeah, actually. I wanted to run something by you real quick, foundation wise. You got a minute?"

I'd pulled into the parking lot at the strip mall and sat in my spot in front of Guys N' Dolls talking with my dad, who was the controlling manager of my charitable foundation. The Cavanaugh Fund granted annual donations to benefit children's charities and sports programs for lower income communities.

On an individual basis, an organization or family could apply for a grant to cover a one time monetary need. Dad and I went through the applications on a quarterly basis. Between he and my accountant, recipients were awarded and notified.

I spent a few minutes detailing the situations that I'd been dealing with during the campaign, ending with the dilemma of trying to keep Primrose open.

"Well, what do you want to do, son?"

"I mean, let's be real. A bag of money would make this go away. I hate to suggest it, though; I don't want to insult anyone, or for anyone to think I'm trying to buy votes. But that place has to stay open and money is the only way that's going to happen."

"Unh hunh..." In my mind, I could see my dad pacing the deck outside the house, his thumb and forefinger stroking his chin. "You're right. A self sufficient town like Potter Lake might not take too kindly to a rich basketball star just dumping some money on them. But uh... what about the city?"

"I'm supposed to talk to the city council president later today. What do you have in mind?"

"A facility like that shouldn't sit on privately owned land, because exactly what's happening could happen. The city should own that land. If there is a way for the city to buy the land from Mr. Adams, then lease the property. Now, from there if you want to use your foundation to establish a grant to go toward Primrose, that would be appropriate."

"Okay. Yeah, okay." The light at the end of the tunnel was blinding. That's how close I felt to resolving this issue. "I'll want to set up that grant pretty quickly. We need to move on this."

"Sure. There's a process, but we can move fast. Let me know."

"Man, dad... between you and Leslie, I'm pretty sure I wouldn't get anything done in my life. I appreciate your insight."

"Anytime, son," he said, laughing. "Speaking of Leslie, we get to meet her, right? TC said she was absolutely beautiful and she was doing so much for you."

"For sure, for sure, dad. She's really looking forward to it. I gotta run, let's talk soon. There's another thing—about Leslie —that I want to bend your ear about. Give my love to mom."

I ended the call and killed the engine in the truck, then hopped out, making sure to land on my good leg. I grabbed my cane from the backseat and hobbled into Guys N' Dolls. Instead of going back to my office to hide, though, I checked in with TC up front, got some dap from some of the barbers and talked college and pro football with a few clients who were mid-cut. I was already on too many Fantasy Football teams but talked myself into a couple more.

When I eventually made it back to my office, I went through the mail. The Leaning tower of Late Notices had been demolished, but that was to be expected when I put TC in charge of that, too. When I filed for candidacy for Mayor, I knew I wouldn't have time for things like keeping track of the bills. Besides, giving TC more power primed her for the job I wanted her to take, if everything worked out right.

"I heard it was an eventful day."

Speaking of TC, she'd snuck into my office behind me, just as I'd settled into my chair. She took her usual seat in front of me and propped her feet up on the desk. I didn't say anything, but I scowled at her. Surprisingly, she dropped them.

"Yeah, man. It's crazy, the stuff that goes on in this town. Even crazier that people come to me to help resolve it."

"Well, that might be what your life will be like for at least the next four years. You sure you're ready for that? You know you like to hide back here, let me be the face of the shop. You're going to be the face of Potter Lake in a couple of weeks."

"If I win..." I reminded TC.

She snorted. "What's this *if I win* bullshit? I mean, cockiness aside, seems like the Mayor knows he's on the way out. He's just trying to get all of his goods before he leaves. That's what that whole Primrose thing is about. He's hoping the facility can't come up with more money so he can sell it and get the hell out of town. I bet he wants you to win."

"Heh," I chuckled. "His evil plan is working. I talk to more and more people every day that plan to vote for me instead of Adams. Just a couple of weeks to go. How are you coming on that list I gave you?"

"It's coming together," TC assured me. I'd put her on a committee with Tamera, Evonne, Monica, Kendrick and Erik —basically everyone but Leslie. What was supposed to be my post election celebration would turn into something that, I hoped, was memorable for the both of us, really, but especially for Leslie.

"I'll let you know if we run into any problems, but don't worry about it. Things are looking good."

"Remember, if Leslie asks...."

"I know how to handle her, KC. We got this. You worry about becoming Mayor Cavanaugh, aight?"

TC stood, stretching her limbs. "Heading back out. We always get a little rush around 5 o'clock. See you later?"

TC walked out of my office. I needed to talk to Larry Cable, city council president. I had no idea how to reach him —I didn't have anyone's phone number. I pulled out my phone to call Leslie, but my eye landed on a Potter Lake phone book. More like phone pamphlet. This was a tiny town. Surely Mr. Cable's phone number would be listed.

————

The moment I pulled into the garage, the scent of an actual hot meal being cooked in my house seeped through the walls. I heard music, John Legend, to be exact. I picked up the bouquet of wildflowers from the passenger seat and headed inside.

Leslie was standing at the island, looking like the snack she was in a crop top and leggings, drinking wine out of a bulbous goblet, swaying to the sounds of You & I coming from the speakers mounted on the wall and chopping spears of asparagus, which she laid out on a pan.

"Hey, hey, sweet thing. Smells real good in here." I sidled up next to her and gave her ear a little nibble. She liked that move, evidenced by the giggle and squeal. "Look at you, chopping stuff. You really can cook."

"I can at least chop stuff. Careful, babe. Chopped fingers are not delicious."

"You're trying to say you lose all control when I'm around, huh? I know, I know. I have that effect." I brought the flowers out from behind my back. "These are for you."

The smile that popped up on her lips and lit up her whole face made the trip back over the lake so worth it.

"And you got them from Potter Lake Petals! I love that shop! Thank you babe, they're beautiful. Do you have a vase to put them in? Set them on the table so I can look at them."

I dug out a vase, rinsed it out, trimmed the stems and arranged them in the thick crystal as a centerpiece on the table while Leslie put the finishing touches on dinner.

"Look good?"

"Looks great," she swooned, loading up two plates with roast chicken, riced cauliflower and roasted asparagus. "Do you want me to set up your machine so you can rehab your knee while we eat?"

"Nah." I grabbed the plates from her and set them at the table, then nodded for her to sit. "Let's just eat. How was the rest of your day?"

We talked through first and second helpings before we got around to my conversation with Larry Cable.

"Turns out the build for that big box department store isn't going well. The developer has stalled. They bid the project too low and he's asking for more money; the city is saying no. Things are at a standstill."

"Hmmm..." Leslie took a sip from her wineglass. "The

things you learn when you have an inside track. How does that tie to Primrose?"

"Well, I told you I talked to my dad earlier. He runs my foundation for me—"

"Wait. Foundation? You have a foundation?"

I shrugged, like it wasn't a big deal to have a multi million dollar charitable foundation in my name. Because, for the most part, it wasn't. Until it mattered that I had one. "A lot of players set one up. It's a way to give back to communities. And to be able to write off a few million on your taxes."

"Okay, so... you're just going to cut a big check? That's how you're going to fix this problem, KC? You're not going to always be able to do that, you know."

"As a matter of fact, that's the first thing I said to my dad. I can't just throw a bag of money at this. But between Larry and I, we think we have a solution."

"Okay." Leslie folded her arms across her chest and sat back in her chair. "I'm listening."

"Larry proposes that the council takes the money they had earmarked for the department store build and buy the land that the Mayor is trying to sell. Then—"

Leslie sat up, her eyes wide. "Then the city owns the land and controls the lease."

"Exactly. The council is going to hold a special session to discuss the issue and vote on it. If the Mayor agrees to sell the land to the city, I talked to my dad about establishing a grant through my foundation. Primrose can apply for a one time disbursement to address those safety issues Mabry was talking about. I wouldn't be involved in awarding the funds at all. It happens by committee and the Foundation has its own accountant. It's as hands-off as I can get, but still providing a way to help Primrose stay open and operate."

I stopped talking, more to take a breath but also to gauge Leslie's reaction to my idea. If she hated it, felt like I was just dumping money to solve the problem, I'd have to go back to the drawing board.

"I love it," she said, relief washing over her features. "I love the idea, especially about that department store going away. But also about the city buying the land and leasing it to Primrose. So they stay open—"

"And your Grandy gets to stay right where she is, close to you, where you want her to be."

Leslie was a mess, but trying hard to keep it together. Red eyes, red nose, flushed face, swallowing and swallowing and swallowing. I laughed a little, trying to lighten the mood, but it had the opposite effect. She burst into tears, almost wailing behind the hand she'd clamped over her mouth.

"Babe..." I pulled her up from her seat and planted her on my lap. I wrapped my arms around her and let her drop her head to my shoulder and cry until she had soaked the collar of my shirt. When she'd stopped sobbing and it was just hiccups and sniffling in my ear, I landed a gentle pat on her thigh. "You okay?"

She nodded, wiping away tears with the heels of both hands. "I just... I was just really worried about having to move Grandy, about Primrose closing. I know things aren't set yet, but I'm just so... relieved that you're working on it."

"Of course I am. It's important to you. This town is important to you, so I'm all over it. But you know, TC reminded me that this is probably how life is going to go, if I win this election. Hearing problems all day, solving them all night. Sometimes by myself, sometimes with help from other people. Like you. I need you to be ready for that, baby girl. I mean it, like full time."

"I hear you. I said I was here for whatever you had in mind. I won't fall into an emotional heap every day."

"Good. Cause I want to be here for you, but you can't be dripping mascara and snottin' all over my good shirts."

She giggled and play punched my arm. "Shut up, fool, or

you don't get any of these cupcakes mama dropped off for you."

"Cupcakes?" My eyebrows involuntarily rose. "Those big ones she makes? Carrot cake? With cream cheese frosting?"

"Yup. She knows you love them. Spoiled brat. She didn't bring me any red velvet cupcakes and she knows those are my favorite—"

"Wait a minute. I thought the deal was that you were actually cooking me dinner."

"And I did." She snorted, then got up from my lap. "I didn't say anything about dessert. You want to set up your machine and have dessert in the living room?"

"Sounds good, baby." I smacked her ass as she walked away. My mind raced ahead two weeks in the future, when I would ask the owner of that ass to be my wife. Scary thing was, I wasn't actually sure of what her answer would be.

twenty-seven

. . .

LESLIE

"Erik, Dwayne… that banner is crooked. It's higher on the left. Can you guys grab the ladder and fix it?"

I pointed to the cattywampus banner and watched as the two men grabbed the ladder and raised and lowered it until it was even. Satisfied, I smiled and pulled the clipboard from where I'd been storing it under my arm. I'd stuck a pen in my messy bun and pulled it out to mark the next item on my list.

I walked through the Kit Kat lounge, which seemed expansive and bright when it was empty, during the day. This evening it would be jam packed with people who would, we hoped, be celebrating KC's win. We'd invited people to stop by beginning at 8 o'clock to watch the election coverage and await the final vote count.

Not that we were really worried about the results. KC still held a majority vote, according to the news station informal poll. Unless Mayor Adams pulled something out of his ass at the last minute, Potter Lake would usher in a new era tonight. And I was so ready.

In anticipation of KC's win, he'd already been meeting with the City Council, getting briefs on how the town runs, what his job would actually entail, should he win, and what the town would expect from him. To say he was excited and energized every night when he came home would be an understatement. Seeing him throw himself into Potter Lake politics, caring about the people, the community— *our* community— made me love him more every day.

We'd been doing a funny, sexy little dance around the L word. Around our future. We both knew there was no going forward unless we were together, but with so much going on, we hadn't really dedicated time to saying the words and making the plans. But we would. As soon as we got this election out of the way.

I turned the corner into the hallway that ran past the bar, the hallway where KC had cornered me and told me he wanted to be with me. Where he made me admit that I wanted to be with him, too. I pushed through the double doors into the kitchen, where Helen was busy directing an army of cooks.

"Ms. Helen, how are you doing? You need anything? I have a couple of people doing nothing but running errands."

"Need a scotch on the rocks, to be honest," she joked, pulling an apron over her head. "Naw, missy. We good. Just prepping everything for tonight. Orlando and I will be ready to serve going on about 7:30 you think?"

I nodded, checking her off my list. She had been so happy to plan KC's election night menu. Her staff and the cooks at the Kit Kat were working together to produce honey drizzled nuggets of chicken inside mini waffles, roast beef sliders, mini beef pot pies and an endless buffet of other treats. KC bought out the lounge, so our guests would enjoy soft drinks, wine, beer and liquor while we waited on results. No matter what happened with the election, at 10 o'clock the desserts would come out— apple cream cheese monkey bread, pecan and sweet potato pie tartlets and Mama had decided to bring a few sheets of carrot cake, just for KC.

Spoiled brat. She still hadn't baked me any red velvet cupcakes.

"Okay, well let me know if you need anything, alright? I've got more things to check on." Helen nodded and got back to work, organizing her army. Everything was being made from scratch, so fruit had to be peeled and sliced, crusts had to be made, chocolate had to be melted. I walked out and left her to her task.

"Okay," I muttered to myself, studying my list of to-do items. "Next is..."

"A kiss for your man. Is that on the list?" I whirled around to find KC behind me, smiling down at me. He hadn't done anything to his hair, and he was wearing an old wrinkled Baltimore Herons t-shirt and a pair of shorts, but the sight of him lately just made me happy. I angled my cheek so he could drop a kiss there.

"Nah uh. I said a kiss. Come here, girl." He slid an arm around my waist and drew me close to him, then dipped his head to press his lips against mine. My mouth opened by instinct; I groaned as his tongue swirled around mine, tasting the coffee he must have been drinking before arriving at the Kit Kat.

"Damn, y'all always in each other's mouths." KC started to laugh, which broke the kiss. He reached out to tap Kendrick as he passed us, still shaking his head.

"Good morning, almost Mayor-Elect Cavanaugh. You sleep okay?" I'd left the house well before KC woke up to meet the team and get started setting things up. KC surveyed the room, hands on his hips. People were scurrying left and right, arranging tables and hanging banners and cleaning surfaces. Sheila stacked glasses at the bar; Reginald ran a dust mop past us, bobbing his head to the beat of whatever he was listening to.

"Looks like things are coming together. You're doing a great job, babe."

"Thanks. We'll have all of the TV's tuned into election programming. And in here—" I walked him through the lounge, toward the dance floor, where a makeshift stage was being built. "Landry's is lending us a 75 inch TV to broadcast the results. They should be here in about an hour to set up and get connected. I figure we'll pack this room out to watch the results. Arletha will be here around seven, right as the polling locations close, and her camera crew will capture it live. She'll also get your acceptance speech live. You wrote a speech right?"

KC shrugged, nonplussed. "Kade Cavanaugh. Did you write a damn speech?" He chuckled, sliding his hands into his pockets and walking away. God, he liked to fuck with me.

"Fine. Whatever. I just want to remind you that your parents will be in the room." He laughed and kept walking, aiming for Kendrick. I rolled my eyes and consulted my list again.

KC's parents had arrived the day before. Gladys and Kelvin were delightful and funny, full of stories about their twins and the trouble they always got into. My parents met us for dinner at Southern Star, a newly built restaurant on the other side of Potter Lake, which was a miracle in itself, because my parents rarely crossed the bridge. The bond between our families was instant, like we'd all known each other forever. After dinner, we'd taken his parents to TC's and got them set up in her ground floor bedroom. When Kelvin stepped out of the room, Gladys started to pull herself from her chair.

"Wait… oh… can I help you, Mrs. Cavanaugh?" I felt awkward, not knowing if I should insist on helping her or let her do it herself.

"Oh, honey," she said, waving me off. She stood, then moved a few inches away. "I'm old hat at this. I'm just fine.

And call me Gladys." She perched on the side of the comfortable king sized bed and patted the spot next to her. I sat and let her draw her arms around me. I figured I was due for the don't hurt my son or else conversation and braced for it. But she surprised me.

"I'm not going to get into your relationship. And I'm not going to issue any threats. I can see that he loves you and that you love him back. Take care of him, honey. And let him take care of you. Let him love you as hard as he needs to, and you return that. And that is what keeps things going past ten years, twenty years, thirty years. Love is hard, relationships are hard, but the work is worth it. Start today and every day, and keep loving through everything. You hear me?"

I nodded, hearing her. And planning to follow every word of that advice.

"Hey, girl. You look like you need this." Tamera appeared next to me, holding a large latte from Rooster's coffee. I took it from her with a grateful sigh, sipping a little off the top.

"How's everything coming?"

"Good. Really good. Kind of waiting for something to go wrong, actually, things are going so well."

"Don't be negative," she said, cupping my chin. "I came to check things out, give my boyfriend a smooch and then steal your man. I want to take my time with his cut today. Are you coming by later? Whatever you're doing with your locs right now isn't working."

I scowled, pretending to be offended. "I can handle myself. You just take care of KC."

"I was being honest, as your best friend. Call me if you need me." She flounced away, bellowing at KC. "Hey you, with the mess on your head! Did you sleep in the arms of a bear? How does your hair look like that right now? I guess I have to clean up your goatee, too? I'm charging extra."

"Tamera, don't start with me. I'm about to be very powerful in this town."

"Okay, you're not going to be King, just Mayor. Let's go; I've been ordered to make you pretty and we have a long way to go."

I snorted, and consulted my list. So many items checked off. So many to go. But everything was turning out great.

———

A few hours later, I sat next to KC, fresh from the salon with his stylish cut and trimmed goatee, while he watched intermittent election coverage and local news and ran therapy on his knee. He'd skipped his morning treatment and felt it, so I made him come home and relax with his leg elevated. It would be a long night of standing and walking around. KC's parents were on the other side of the sectional, murmuring to each other during the broadcast.

"What time are you planning to get dressed, son?" Kelvin squinted at the face of his watch, then tapped it a few times.

"Soon as I finish my therapy, dad. Can't rush it."

"I'm sure Leslie has him running on time. Don't you, dear?"

"You would think so," I said, elbowing KC. "But he likes to mess with me. Everything's all set, though, when he's ready."

"Now that sounds familiar. I'd wake him up in plenty of time to get dressed for school. This one was always running for the bus, buttoning his shirt." Gladys clicked her tongue and sipped from a glass of water.

"Speaking of getting dressed, though, I'm going to head upstairs and start getting ready." I pushed myself up from the couch and stretched. I wished I would have taken a nap, but there was no way I could have fallen asleep. "TC will drive you over to the Kit Kat for the election results."

"Alright, dear. We'll see you both later on."

I headed upstairs and went straight to the bathroom to turn on the shower. Our clothes for the evening were already hanging on the back of the closet door. KC had so many suits in his closet that he felt funny buying something new, but Kendrick said he looked like he was about to turn into the Incredible Hulk in all of his old suits. Ella's Boutique came to the rescue.

She ordered him a simple black suit and tailored it so well that it fit like it was cut just for him. He paired it with a crisp white shirt and he'd wear it with the collar open, no tie. Mayor Adams never went anywhere without a tie. Mayor Cavanaugh planned to be a little more laid back.

I picked up a black cocktail dress from Ella's that just brushed my knees. I couldn't wait to put it on and strut around Potter Lake with a handsome man on my arm. The bathroom mirror was beginning to cloud with steam, my sign that the shower was hot and ready. I pulled my t-shirt over my head and unhooked my bra, tossing them both in a corner of the bathroom.

I was just thinking that I'd grab them later when KC appeared in the bathroom door, his eyes on my breasts. My nipples responded to his lusty gaze, but I had to corral my longing for him to run the tip of his tongue across them right quick. I unzipped my jeans and pushed them down my hips, kicking them to the same corner. KC sauntered into the bathroom and stood behind me, dipping his head to brush his lips across my shoulders. Like we had nowhere to be tonight.

"Babe...we do not have time."

"Sure we do. The party can start without us." He slipped his arms around my waist and he stepped close, close enough to feel him pressed into me. His hands smoothed up my belly to my breasts and grabbed a healthy squeeze before his thumbs found my nipples.

I moaned, leaning my head back against his chest, putting my neck on display so he could nibble my ear and land a line of kisses across my skin. Some part of my brain was still functioning, reminding me that we had to keep things moving if we were going to make his party.

"Can't you...shit... seduce me after you win this election?"

"Sure could. But I want to seduce you right now." One of his hands traveled south to my mound. Two fingers dipped to part my lips and massage my clit.

"Ba—umph.....your parents are downstairs."

"So you probably want to be quiet, then huh?"

"Ugh, that's not fair."

"What's not fair is how sexy you are right now. You have no idea how much I want to skip tonight and crawl into bed and do nasty things with you."

"I think I have an idea of how much you want that." I turned in his arms, sad to feel his fingers leave my body, but I needed to get my bearings again and I couldn't make sense with him touching me. "Okay, let's get in the shower, take care of..." My eyes flicked down to the obvious tenting in the crotch of his shorts. "Your situation. Then we wash up and get dressed and celebrate your election. Can we do that?"

KC answered by dropping his lips to mine, then grabbing my hands and placing them on the band of his shorts. Nimble fingers twisted the buttons and pulled at the zipper. I looped my thumbs in the band of his boxer briefs and pulled everything down, then stepped back and rolled up the hem of his tee shirt. He pulled it over his head and stood back.

For a quick half second I admired his molded chest and taut belly, bulging biceps wide, strong shoulders, and despite the knee injury, muscular legs and calves. He had filled out a lot, no longer in starting lineup physique, but to me, Kade Cavanaugh was perfect. I sighed, also wishing we could get into bed and make love all night. But we couldn't, so I stepped into the shower. KC got in behind me, pulling me back against his chest.

"You want me to put a condom on?"

I shook my head. Though it had been a long while since

his last casual encounter, I didn't know what kind of life KC lived while traveling city to city with women at his fingertips.

I'd been on birth control since before Dexter, but I wanted to be protected in case he was carrying something he didn't know about. Over time we'd been using them less and less and after his checkup came back clean, I preferred that we didn't use them, but he always asked if I wanted one.

His fingers returned to the spot they'd been moments before, between my pussy lips and stroking my clit, but KC's movements were more calculated. He knew exactly what to do to get me where I needed to be, and quickly. I leaned back and let the expert work. It was hard enough to concentrate on keeping my moans low enough that only he could hear them.

My body responded to the sensation of a hand cupping my breast, his fingers circling and stroking and rubbing my clit and his tongue in my mouth, sucking and swirling, driving me so high I had to grab his wrist. I tore my mouth from his and moved forward, warm water cascading down my back. I reached for the towel rack for leverage and waited for KC to make his move.

He gripped my hips, pulling me up against him and in the next moment, he was thrusting, little by little, until every inch of him was inside me. I bit down on my lip but I was finding it hard to keep my voice low. The sounds of his wet body smacking against mine helped to mask the growing volume of my yelps and gasps of yes yes yes.

"You ready, babe?" He leaned forward to murmur in my ear, his chest against my back, his hips hunching against me fast and hard. It was delicious and I didn't want him to stop. "You bout to come for me?"

I nodded, not trusting myself not to scream. KC slid one hand around to the front of my body and found my clit. It didn't take but a couple of strokes before I yelped out, "fuck... oh my God, I'm coming!" and my entire body started to convulse. My pussy clenched and pulsed around him so violently, I saw stars.

"Oooh…." He cooed in my ear, not missing a single stroke. "That was a good one. Taking me over the edge right now."

"Do it," I whispered over my shoulder. "I want to feel you come for me."

"I wanna tell you something first though."

"Like... right now?"

His movements slowed to less of a frenzied thrust and more of a sultry, languid motion. Dragging it out was killing me.

"Like right now, while we're joined together, skin to skin. While I feel so close to you."

"Okay… what… what did you want to say?"

"You already know, Les. You know what I'm going to say because I can't hide how I feel about you. I know you feel it and I know you know it, but I never want you to go a day without hearing how much I love you. How much I care for you, how sexy you are to me. How I never want to be without you again."

I'd started sobbing halfway through his speech, both from the height of orgasm and the beautiful words that came from this man I was so in love with, had been in love with. I had tried to deny how I felt about him for so long, but he was unwilling to accept my rejection and kept pushing his way into my life. I felt him pulse, then a long loud groan rolled from his throat as he moved against me.

"I love you, Kade," I whispered as I felt him release inside me. "I love you so much. I'm going to love you forever. You'll never, ever be without me. I'm always going to be right here."

"*Yessss*," he hissed. He panted, his hands already roaming my body again. "That's what I needed to hear."

An hour later we had finally pulled ourselves together. We were so, so late. But at the moment, I didn't care. I'd twisted my hair into an updo and added a few light touches of makeup. KC was buttoning his shirt and staring into his sock drawer.

"Just pick a pair, babe. They're all mostly black anyway."

"Yeah, I guess." He grabbed a pair and sat on the bed to pull them on. "Hey you know what I forgot to tell you?"

"Hmm?" I grabbed his cufflinks from his jewelry box on his dresser and reached for one of his arms so I could help him put them on. "Are you wearing earrings tonight?" He shook his head.

"Uh… my parents went over to TC's right after you went upstairs. Mom wanted to change and dad wanted to lay down for a few minutes."

I paused, cufflink in hand while I glared at him. "So we didn't have to be quiet? So I almost drowned trying not to scream and they weren't even here?" He laughed, not answering. As usual. I tried to scowl at him but it wouldn't stick. I finished adjusting his sleeves and his collar, then leaned down to kiss him.

"Have I basically agreed to a lifetime of you fucking with me?"

"Yep. It's in the fine print."

"Good thing I love you, then huh? It's the only way I can deal with it."

"Good thing." He puckered his lips for one last kiss. "Love you too. We ready?"

"We are, Mr. Cavanaugh."

"Mr. Cavanaugh is next door, Les. I'm just Kade." He slid his arms into his jacket and buttoned it closed. A more handsome man, I had never seen. He slid his keys and wallet off of the dresser. I grabbed my clutch and tucked my hand into the crook of his arm.

"Let's go win this election."

If we hadn't had a spot reserved at the Kit Kat Lounge, we wouldn't have been able to find a place to park. The lot was jam packed already, with cars spilling over onto the street and parked along the shoulder of the two lane highway.

"Good turnout," KC mumbled, hopping out of the truck. I agreed, meeting him at the front door and stepping inside. The building was teeming with people indulging in drinks and hors d'oeuvres. Faces were angled up at the TVs, trying to catch the latest coverage.

Bright lights popped on, nearly blinding us. Arletha stepped in front of KC, followed by a camera man. She shoved a microphone in his face.

"Kade, how are you feeling about the election so far?"

"I'm feeling pretty good," he answered, his post game interview voice coming through strong. "I ran a great campaign, I learned a lot about this town, I fell in love with this town. I'm hoping that Potter Lake agrees that Kade Cavanaugh would be the best choice for Mayor."

"Have you seen any of the exit polls today? And have you spoken with Mayor... Mr. Adams?"

KC smiled at the slip and the nod to his imminent win. "We watched the coverage here and there, but my parents are in town and we had so much to do to get set for tonight; I just haven't had time to obsess about the results. I've not spoken to Mr. Adams, but you know, I wish him the best."

"A few residents have said this wasn't a fair fight, that you came in from nowhere and bought the town with your money and fame, most notably the arrangement that you worked out to keep Primrose Gardens open. What do you have to say to that?"

KC smiled again, his eyes dancing. He was utterly amused by that rumor. He slipped his hands into his pockets and planted his stance, feet wide apart.

"I mean, what can I say to that? If that's how people feel, that's how they feel. Primrose needed help and I was in a position to offer that help. If people feel like I used my famous face, my name and my money to help their loved ones remain in a facility where they're well-cared for?"

He shrugged, playing to the camera. "They'll just have to be mad about that. I'm always going to do what's best for this town, despite what people think of me."

Arletha smiled and started to move away to take over the broadcast, but KC grabbed the microphone again.

"By the way, that's whether I win or lose. I'm a resident, now. I love this town. I love this woman. Y'all know Leslie, right?" He dropped an arm around my shoulder and pulled me close. "So get used to seeing me. I'm not going anywhere."

That made Arletha laugh. KC stepped away from her and her cameraman to let them continue the broadcast. We pushed through the crowd, stopping at the buffet to pick up some of Helen's beautiful creations.

By the time we made it to the open area, a crowd had swelled in anticipation of post election results. KC grabbed my hand, intending to help me climb the steps onto the stage. Distracted, I raised a hand to wave at my mom and dad in the crowd and completely missed a step. When my foot caught nothing but air, I screeched, my arms flailing.

With the same cat-like reflexes that had served him on the court, KC caught me by the waist and twisted me around. We fell together, but he wanted me to fall into him. The quick motion and tight space meant that his leg twisted unnaturally and when KC landed and let out a loud, pained cry, I knew.

KC laid on his side, in his nice new suit, gripping his knee with both hands, writhing in what looked to be the worst pain in his life. His teeth were clenched, his face beet red, and he was trying hard to hold in deep grunts.

"Oh my God! I'm sorry! I'm so sorry!" I turned to the crowd, who were nothing but a sea of faces to me. "I need a doctor! Somebody get a doctor!"

"I'm here," I heard, through the crowd. Dr. Irons' familiar

figure stepped through the opening made for him. "Thank God. He fell—"

"I saw," he said, reaching for KC's knee. He was still writhing and groaning, and wasn't about to let the Dr. touch him. "Good thing I came out to watch the election. Mr. Cavanaugh, you'll need to hold still."

"Hurts," he seethed. Tears rolled down his face, into his hairline. "Hurts so fuckin' bad. I tore the ACL again, Doc. I'm sure of it."

Dr. Irons turned to me and placed a heavy hand on my shoulder. "Take him to Healy General. I'll meet you both there."

I looked around for someone— anyone to help. Tamera pushed through and kneeled next to me. "I called an ambulance when he didn't get back up. They're on the way."

"He was trying to help me. It's my fault. It's my—"

"Honey, it was an accident. Don't torture yourself. He needs you to be strong right now."

"Ambulance is here!" Someone behind us yelled. The crowd began to part to make room for the stretcher to come through. KC was glistening with sweat, still groaning as they loaded him on the gurney and began wheeling him out.

"Find TC and their parents and tell them we're going to Healy General." Tamera gave me a nod, then pulled me into her arms before pushing me after the paramedics.

"And call me with the results!" I yelled to her as I followed. The medics had given him something for the pain, so KC's groans grew quieter as we sped toward Healy. I leaned over him, trying to talk to him.

"Baby? You're going to be okay. Dr. Irons is going to meet us at the hospital."

"You okay?" he whispered, his eyes opening enough for them to roll up so he could see me.

"I'm fine, sweetheart. I'm so sorry, KC—"

"N-no." He shook his head, closing his eyes. "You're okay. All I care about."

The ambulance swerved into a bay outside of the emergency room and the medics got out, then swung the doors open to pull the gurney out. Dr Irons came out of the ER entrance, wearing a pair of surgical scrubs and a cap. He was followed by a few nurses, who took over pulling the gurney. And then KC disappeared through the doors.

"He's going to be fine," said Dr. Irons. "Come inside. I'll show you where you can wait."

"Can I see him before he goes into surgery?"

"Of course, my dear." He wrapped an arm around my shoulder and ushered me inside the hospital. Dr. Irons went to scrub in, so it was his nurse that came to get me to see KC.

He was prepped for surgery, his nice suit, shirt, socks and shoes in a pile on a chair. I clicked my tongue at the sight, then looked over at KC. I expected him to already be under, but his eyes were open. I rushed to his side and grabbed his hand. He held onto mine and squeezed.

"Doc says I'll be fine. Maybe I'll get a bionic knee. Awesome, hunh?"

"Yes, baby. Awesome." I chuckled, realizing he was probably pretty high and almost ready to pass out. "I'll be here when you get out. Your parents are on the way."

"Before…" He paused, swallowing. "Before I go. Tell me. One more time."

"I love you, KC. You're going to be fine and I'm going to tell you that every day."

"Look… jacket." He motioned toward the pile of his clothing in the chair. I moved a few feet away and picked up his jacket.

"Am I looking for something?"

"Pocket," he whispered. I dipped my fingers into the inside pocket and brushed against something soft but solid. I pulled out a box. A velvet ring box.

"Oh… baby…" He shook his head, and in my mind I could hear him tell me we didn't have time for me to have an emotional breakdown.

"Love you," he mumbled. "Marry me, Les."

"Yes!" I wanted to scream it, cry it, shout it for the world to hear. "Yes, KC. Yes, I will marry you!"

His eyes fluttered closed, but he forced them back open. "Put... it on."

I pulled the ring from the box and slid it onto my hand, then I grabbed his hand and put it on top of mine so he could feel it. "It's on. It's on, baby...KC?"

"I think he's out," I heard Dr. Irons say behind me. "Time for me to fix him up and give him back to you." He tipped his head to the nurse, who began to wheel him out of the room. A nurse slipped an arm around mine to gently escort me to the waiting room. A small crowd was waiting for me there— TC and the Cavanaugh's, my parents and Pops, plus our usual crowd.

"First things first." Tamera stood, handing me her phone. It was a replay of the live broadcast from The Kit Kat, where they'd let KC's dad stand in his place while they announced that he'd won the Mayoral election by a landslide. Kelvin looked incredibly proud, on camera. Through rapid blinking and nodding, clasping his hands together he gave a brief speech, thanking the crowd on KC's behalf and inviting them to celebrate for the next few hours. The clip ended with a shot of him pushing Gladys' wheelchair out the door, TC bringing up the rear.

"I mean… I thought he would win. But this election is over and I'm so happy about that."

"You ain't even lied," grumbled Erik, slouching in his seat. His tie had been loosened and his shirt unbuttoned. "Listen to him, like he did any work. You did a great job on his campaign, Leslie."

Kendrick gave me a hug, then pulled back and grabbed

my hands. "Uh... somebody got some new hardware. Did he..."

I couldn't even try to hide my grin, but I started crying before I could say yes, so I just bobbed my head while everyone gathered around to gawk at the full carat cushion cut engagement ring that sat snugly on my finger.

"Yep," said Kelvin. "Told him that would be a good investment."

"I told him that cut would look great on her hand," said Gladys, looking pleased.

"I told his ass to propose a long time ago," said my dad, leaning against a window sill at the back of the room. "But he had to wait till he broke his damn knee. Shit."

"He said he's gonna be bionic, Daddy. Better than before. You wanted a bionic son in law, right?"

"I guess," he grumbled. "We'll have a lot of time to watch football games on that big TV ya'll got."

"Now you're seeing the bright side." My dad came forward and folded me into a hug. "You tell that young man to take care of himself alright? He's got a piece of me, now. Can't have him falling apart on my baby girl."

"I'll tell him. Thanks dad."

Tamera pulled me toward a chair and I sat, heaving a sigh of relief.

"Hope you don't mind," TC said, pulling a bag off of her shoulder. "I figured KC would need some clothes to come home in and you would want to change. Grabbed some stuff for y'all."

The relief must have been evident on my face. I had been so worried about KC, I hadn't even realized that my feet were killing me and my dress was too tight. All I wanted was to put on one of KC's t-shirts and a pair of leggings. I looked inside the bag and almost cried, pulling out the exact outfit I'd just wished for.

"Excuse me. I gotta get out of this getup."

A few hours later, Dr Irons came through the doors, pulling off a pair of gloves and removing his mask. We all stood and crowded around him.

"Everything went just fine," he began. "There was a tear to the anterior cruciate ligament. There was also severe degeneration of cartilage. I repaired the ligament and replaced the cartilage in his knee with tissue from a cadaver. Recovery will take some time, but he should recover, nonetheless if he follows my instruction and continues cryotherapy."

He paused, hands clasped and looked directly at me. "Leslie, Mr. Cavanaugh is awake and asking for you."

I opened the door to KC's room slowly, peeking my head in. The overhead light was off. Only the light above the bed was lit. His leg was propped up and wrapped tightly. He had a cannula under his nose for oxygen but for the most part he looked like my handsome KC.

"I had them do that low light thing you love," he said. His voice was raspy, as if his throat was dry. I stepped closer, reaching for the pitcher of water and the disposable cups that had been placed near his bed.

"You sound like you need this." He took it and gulped it down. Then crushed the cup in his hand, which made me laugh. I lowered myself to the edge of the bed and lifted my feet up, careful not to bump his knee.

"Why are you like this, Kade Cavanaugh?"

"No idea. I'm just Kade. That okay with you?"

I smiled, tipping my head up. His lips brushed against mine a few times before his head dropped back against the pillow.

"I'm sleepy," he mumbled. "But I wanted to see you. Are you wearing it?"

I pulled my hand out from where it was wedged between us and showed him. The diamonds glittered in the low light.

"My mom was right. It looks great." He yawned and closed his eyes. "Can I tell you something?"

"Depends. Are you gonna fuck with me?"

He chuckled, just once. "I had big plans for proposing to you during my speech tonight. Flowers and music and champagne toast with everybody there. The best laid plans, right?"

"And I had to go and ruin it."

"Don't blame yourself, babe. Was an accident. But the other thing is… surgery scares the shit out of me. I'm scared I won't wake up. So in case… just in case, I wanted to make sure you had the ring. That you knew I wanted to marry you."

"I have the ring. And I know you want to marry me. I want to marry you, too."

"And you'll help me with this Mayor thing? And you'll be my business partner? We could be Guys and...Curls. Or Curl and… something. TC is ready to take over operations for both shops."

I giggled. "KC, are you still high from anesthesia?"

He opened his eyes, though only half way. "I'm saying, I want us to run everything together, Les. We combine businesses and run them as a joint unit. No competition, just me and you. You in?"

I nodded and bent to kiss him before he passed out again. "I'm in, baby. I'm so in."

epilogue

. . .

KC

"Alright. Give me the baby."

Leslie stood next to me where I had stretched out on the bed, her arms open and waiting for me to just hand my son over to her. I wasn't ready, though. I stroked the fine hairs on his tiny head and kissed his crown.

"Why?"

"Because you're just staring at him while he sleeps."

"So?"

"So you have an exam in your business class, a meeting with the city planner that I bet you haven't prepared any notes for and a council meeting tomorrow night."

Leslie plucked Kade Junior, or KJ from my arms like a ninja and cradled him to her chest. He was such a little bitty thing; I liked laying him on my chest while he slept.

"I'm going to lay him down. Did you do your therapy yet?"

I shook my head, getting back to my Business Strategy textbook. After my first six months as Mayor of Potter Lake, I had to agree with Leslie that having a degree would be a benefit in my position. Running a city was nothing like running a business, but the people I was working would approach everything from a business perspective. It would be my job to fold in the concerns of the people of Potter Lake.

Kendrick was enjoying his new job as Director of Media and Publicity and he'd been on me about finishing up my degree, too. So I re-enrolled at Healy, except I was taking courses online and very, very slowly. It was like riding a bike. Sort of. I was doing well and the material was actually interesting to me; just not more interesting than my wife and our newborn son.

My wife didn't want a fancy wedding and that was fine with me. She wanted everyone she loved in the same room, so we got married on New Year's Eve, at the stroke of midnight at the Kit Kat Lounge. We figured we'd never forget our anniversary, and we were overdue for a celebration since I'd injured my knee the last time we were there.

But about a month before our wedding, KJ stole our thunder by showing up on a sonogram. He was… unexpected. But happily and highly anticipated.

After a few minutes, she came back from the baby's room and disappeared into the bathroom. I tried to dig into my text book, reviewing my notes from the last few weeks. Unless the professor threw a curveball, this exam was going to be a piece of cake.

When she emerged from the bathroom, which normally wouldn't be an event, she caught my attention by wearing my favorite thing to see her in— one of my t-shirts and boy shorts. She pulled my machine from under the bed and was bent over, setting it up next to me.

"So I'm supposed to study for this exam while you're looking all thick snackish over there? Is that... is that the deal?"

She laughed, looking back at me. "Looking what?"

"Monica said women's hips spread when they have babies. And baby..." I licked my lips and moaned. "Yours have spread thick snackishly."

Leslie smirked, handing me the sleeve to wrap around my leg, then left to grab ice and water to fill the reservoirs in the machine. When she came back, I was ready for her to plug it in and turn it on. I credited cryotherapy and Dr. Irons strict rehab to my knee feeling the best it had felt in a long time. I could walk with no cane and my limp was barely noticeable.

"So come talk to me, pretty girl." I gave a pat-pat to the bed next to me. "I might have some stuff to say to you."

Leslie climbed up onto the bed next to me with the latest issue of Cosmetology Today, smelling like she'd just stepped out of a cocoa butter rainforest. Her breasts bounced freely under the t-shirt, reminding me that we'd been "active" but hadn't had sex since the baby was born.

"You're not studying tonight, is what you're trying to say."

"Not if you're gonna be teasing me, all thick snackishly, with your legs out and your titties bouncing around over there."

"I'm not teasing you, babe. I'm right here; you can seduce me whenever you want."

"So you're trying to tell me that you're ready for some... conversation?"

"Maybe," she said, rolling her eyes up to mine. "I thought you might wanna watch movies and make me mad by eating all the Jujubes."

I slammed my textbook closed and tossed it onto the nightstand next to me. Leslie leaned over to open the drawer next to her, pulling out our stash of favorites and dumping them in my lap, then settled back against the pillows and snuggled up close to me. I dropped my arm around her and kissed her temple. She hummed, smiling as she tipped her head up to press her lips to my chin.

"Love you, Kade."

That right there… I'd been hearing it every day for the last year. I never got tired of it. I never got tired of saying it back.

"Love you too, baby. But don't be slick; I know what you're doing. Hand over those Jujubes and start the movie."

———

Want to be the first to find out what's happening in Potter Lake? **Join my newsletter** and get a free short story.

about the author

For as long as I can remember, I would much rather be in my bedroom reading and writing than doing anything else, but I began seriously pursuing a writing career in 2011.

I love coffee and Sunday Brunch, especially on a patio, but my true obsession is water— lakes, rivers, oceans, waterfalls! And sand... dig your toes in, soft! On the weekend, you'll probably find me near water and if I'm lucky, on an ocean beach.

By day I am an Executive Administrative Assistant at a world renowned beverage company. By night, when I'm not writing books, I'm devouring them. I blog my reviews and thoughts on writing at BooksbyDLWhite.com.

Find me online at:

booksbydlwhite.com

authordl@booksbydlwhite.com

acknowledgments

First to my readers, new and seasoned, thank you as always for riding with me. Being an author wouldn't be nearly as fun without people who like your work and rep you in the streetz. Especially my black indie romance readers— y'all rock hard.

Thanks for putting your faith in me and your dollars behind me.

To my author #frans- I love y'all. Thanks for keeping me sane and focused on what matters— gettin' #deez words out!

To my Betas- Bless you for being willing to read my scribbles and help me turn a mess into something people actually want to read. You're a gift and much MUCH appreciated.

To my little bro Big Mike, HNIC at HeadHunters Barbershop in Spokane, Wa, thanks for the inside information and expertise. Heavy is the head that wears the crown… and you wear it well.

To everyone I envy and idolize… you keep me going, keep me pushing, let me know that it's always possible to level up. Keep doing what you do.

books by dl white

Find Books and Merch at Booksbydlwhite.com/shop

Brunch at Ruby's, a Ruby's novel

Dinner at Sam's, a Ruby's novel

Beach Thing, a Black Diamond Romance

Elysium, a Black Diamond Vacation Romance

The Pearl at Black Diamond, a Black Diamond Romance

Leslie's Curl & Dye, a Potter Lake Small Town Romance

Second Time Around, a Potter Lake Holiday Short

The Guy Next Door, a Potter Lake Small Town Romance

Home for the Holidays, A Potter Lake Holiday Novella

The Kwanzaa Brunch, a Holiday Short

A Thin Line

The Never List

Hey, Lover, a Second Chance Romance

Unexpected, a holiday short

The Festival at Evergreen Falls

Grumpy Valentine

Calculated Risk *(Coming Spring 2025)*

next potter in lake small town romance

Meet Bennett & Sage in Second Time Around

Two souls are drawn together in a quaint town and discover that their meeting is not so accidental but fated.

Meet Taj & Evonne in The Guy Next Door

Evonne, a stylist who's just getting good at adulting meets Taj, a musician and reserved cancer survivor turned RN and turns his life sideways in the sexiest, happiest way possible.

Meet. Reid & Sabrina in Home for the Holidays

Reid Gallagher hasn't returned to Potter Lake because he misses his family, or because he wonders how his hometown has fared since he left. After many years away, this visit is strictly business....until he meets Sabrina.

Sabrina Ward has escaped a crumbling marriage to her Aunt Cara's comfortable home in a slow, southern town. Her stay was always going to be temporary... but for Reid, she might consider a permanent change.

And get ready for Kingston and Renda in *Still I Rise*, Coming fall 2025!